Excavating Fate

A Novel

Also by This Author

Pawn of the Gods

978-1982934248

The New Role of Parenting in Leadership

978-3639420197

X: @andreainpages

Instagram: @andreafrancocook

Website: www.andreafrancocookauthor.com

Excavating Fate

A Novel

Andrea Franco-Cook

London, UK
Washington, DC, USA

First published by Lodestone Books, 2025
Lodestone Books is an imprint of Collective Ink Ltd.,Unit 11,
Shepperton House, 89 Shepperton Road, London, N1 3DF
office@collectiveinkbooks.com
www.collectiveinkbooks.com

For distributor details and how to order please visit the 'Ordering' section on our website.

ISBN: 978 1 80341 896 4
978 1 80341 929 9 (ebook)
Library of Congress Control Number: 2024942601

A CIP catalogue record for this book is available from the British Library.

Design: Lapiz Digital Services

UK: Printed and bound by CPI Group (UK) Ltd, Croydon, CR0 4YY
Printed in North America by CPI GPS partners

Contents

Acknowledgements	viii
Note to Reader	ix
Pronunciation Guide	xi
Chapter One	1
Chapter Two	13
Chapter Three	20
Chapter Four	28
Chapter Five	32
Chapter Six	44
Chapter Seven	63
Chapter Eight	72
Chapter Nine	82
Chapter Ten	93
Chapter Eleven	107
Chapter Twelve	119
Chapter Thirteen	123
Chapter Fourteen	130
Chapter Fifteen	136
Chapter Sixteen	146
Chapter Seventeen	153
Chapter Eighteen	156
Chapter Nineteen	168
Chapter Twenty	176
Chapter Twenty-One	187
Chapter Twenty-Two	200
Chapter Twenty-Three	215
Chapter Twenty-Four	224
Chapter Twenty-Five	232
Chapter Twenty-Six	237
Chapter Twenty-Seven	243

Chapter Twenty-Eight 252
Chapter Twenty-Nine 261
Chapter Thirty 268
Chapter Thirty-One 277
Chapter Thirty-Two 287
Chapter Thirty-Three 296
Chapter Thirty-Four 308
Chapter Thirty-Five 316
Chapter Thirty-Six 320

To my late mother, Patrice.
Thanks for encouraging my love of reading and writing from an early age.
I hope this book makes you proud.

Acknowledgements

After years of writing, rewriting, and writing again, I have finally accomplished my dream of becoming a traditionally published author. This could not have been possible without support and encouragement from friends and family. If I listed everyone who has helped me along the way, this acknowledgement would be longer than my novel. This said, I'd like each of you to know that I appreciate all the beta reads, and comments that helped refine my writing.

I would, however, like to single out a few special contributions. Many thanks to my publisher, Lodestone Books, for taking a chance on this eclectic story. I'd like to thank my husband, our sons, and their wives for cheering me on over the years. I'm sure that tolerating a temperamental writer like me has not been easy. Words can't express my love and appreciation for you all. Last but certainly not least, I'd like to thank God above for his loving hand in my life.

Note to Reader

The seeds of this story began with a DNA test. Although I was aware of my Spanish Basque, Ecuadorian native, and Irish roots, I was surprised to learn that my heritage also included North African descent. This piqued my interest in ancient Carthage and eventually, my fantasy novel, *EXCAVATING FATE*, was born. Upon finishing this story, I felt there were a few facts the reader should know before embarking on this time travel adventure with Amara.

Historians have long debated whether the Romans 'salted' Carthage when they burned it. However, the fact that much of this city's grand history was lost after its destruction during the third Punic War (a period 70 years after this novel is set) cannot be refuted. This lack of information left many questions about the everyday life of a Carthaginian. Since this city was known as a cultural hub, it stood to reason that their lifestyles resembled their neighboring countries of Egypt, Greece, Iberia, Rome, and the Levant. Therefore, there were times when I borrowed from these countries' histories to fill the gaps about ancient furnishings, horse saddles, military uniforms, and some clothing.

It's also important to note that Adones Barca is a fictional character created to progress the plot of this story. However, much of the information about General Hannibal Barca and Carthage was based on what I gleaned from my historical research.

Last, many of my beta readers have questioned the reason I chose to write a fantastical version of Carthage instead of a pure historical retelling. I answered, "Where's the fun in that?" I wanted to write an adventure that inspired people of all ages who were apathetic toward history to learn more. This said, I hope you enjoy reading this story as much as I enjoyed writing it.

Pronunciation Guide

CHARACTERS

Adones: Ad-o-nays
Aharim: Ah-ha-reem
Amara: Ah-mar-ah
Andras: An-draz
Aurelia: Ah-rail-ya
Ba'al: Bay-all
Bomilcar: Bum-ul-car
Elissa: El-eesa
Hannibal: Ha-nuh-bul
Imilce: Ah-mil-chay
Jasim: Juh-seem
Moqerhe: Mo-care
Shadu: Sha-do
Tanno: Tan-oh
Tinnit: Tin-it
Vicram: Vick-rum

Those who cannot remember the past are condemned to repeat it.

– George Santayana

Chapter One

The dawning sun warmed my hand as I brushed centuries of dirt away from a stone in the ground. I paused and lifted my gaze to the ruins of ancient Carthage, admiring the webs of copper and gold across the pillars of the fallen temple and rubble buildings. There was an ugliness to the city's wounds that spoke of conflict and the fall of an advanced civilization. As always, I wondered, what if? What if Carthage had won and Rome had fallen? How different would the world have been under North African rule?

Voices pulled me from my thoughts. In the adjacent valley, workers and engineers bustled in front of a newly excavated tomb, preparing for today's exploration. I planned to be on the team that entered, even if they didn't know it yet. This meant getting back to work on *my* discovery.

The thought that I had uncovered something of value still seemed surreal. My smile widened as each sweep of my brush revealed a warrior on horseback carved into a stone in the ground. His sword, eroded by time, was extended upward toward lines of ancient script.

"Wow, Amara!" Sophie set an empty bucket beside me. "Looks like you were right after all. That is an ancient grave marker."

I bit my lip, fighting the urge not to be that annoying know-it-all who corrected everyone. "Ahem, it's a stela," came out anyway.

She rolled her brown eyes and huffed. "Semantics." Wisps of curly black hair escaped from beneath Sophie's ball cap as she wiped sweat from her brow with the back of her gloved hand. "This heat's kicking my ass. It's already ninety degrees and it's only five-thirty."

"Yeah, it's brutal." I returned my attention to the stela, and swept clumps of dirt into a dustpan. Then I dumped them into the bucket to be checked for fragments of bone and pottery. "Discovering pieces like this are worth it, you know?"

"Judging by the detailed artwork on that warrior and the glyphs across the top, I wouldn't be surprised if that *stela* was associated with a noble." Sophie gestured toward the tomb ahead. "Think it will reveal who's buried there?"

I crossed my fingers and held up my hand. "Hopefully. This could also be our ticket into today's exploration."

Sophie snorted. "You're dreaming. Lowly interns like us won't get in until your dad has us logging the artifacts. Can't wait for that snore-fest."

Irritation bristled down my back and my eyes narrowed from behind my sunglasses. She wasn't wrong. Interning was a rite of passage in academia, but that didn't mean I wanted to hear it from my best friend. "Quit being so damn negative. It could happen sooner. Imagine being one of the first to lay eyes on an untouched place in history."

"True. That would be cool and all." Sophie stared at the workers in safari hats roping off the tomb entrance. "First, I need to get past my fear of cave-ins."

"No danger of that," I said. "You know Dad and the engineering team cleared the tomb."

Not like this meant much to Sophie. Last year, she almost passed out from a panic attack when the dorm lift got stuck between floors. I had to block the doors to keep her from prying them open.

"Yeah, well, I signed up to draw and photograph a Roman Circus, not enter a place of the dead."

At times like this, I wondered how we had ever clicked in the first place. We were so different. "C'mon, a tomb's more interesting than a Roman racetrack. You would have been bored."

"At least I'd be safe. Let's hope your dad didn't miss something." Sophie peered past my shoulder. "Speaking of him—"

A shadow fell over us.

"Oríste to kapélo sas." Dad held out my safari hat which was as dusty as his green tee and cargo pants.

I cut my eyes toward Sophie, who watched our exchange with her brow furrowed, like a person who was left out of the loop.

"Remember what we discussed, Dad? English in public, Greek in private." I put on my hat, thankful for the shade the rim provided.

"No worries," Sophie said. "My parents speak Spanish to me all the time."

"English it is." Dad bent down and studied the stela. He lowered his sunglasses and glowered at Sophie and me through intense brown eyes. "Why didn't you grab me after uncovering these symbols?"

Sophie shifted her weight from one leg to the next.

"Uh, we just finished," I said.

Dad shook his head and held up a finger like he was about to make a point then lowered it. He returned his attention to Sophie. "Get someone to grid this off. Also bring your camera and photograph this, please."

"Sure thing, Dr. Kalogridas." She made a beeline for the tomb workers.

Once she was out of ear shot, Dad glared at me. "What were you thinking? I told you to only brush the top layer of dirt away." His voice was low and measured.

I crossed my arms over my chest, remembering how I'd spent every summer since I was twelve following Dad around dig sites, working my ass off. Now that I'd finally discovered something other than a pottery fragment, I wanted credit for it.

"I was thinking this is my find and I should be the one to uncover it," I said finally.

"Your impetuousness will be your downfall, young lady." Dad lifted his hat and combed his fingers through his sweat-dampened salt-and-pepper hair. "Look, you're only nineteen. Two years of undergrad doesn't give you the skills of an archeologist."

"Isn't that why I'm here, to get the skills?"

"Yes, with oversight." He sighed. "Consider what could happen if you messed this up? The Credo Museum and the Tunisian government trusted me to lead this dig. If that stela were damaged, you'd return to college like nothing happened, and my career would be over."

That he felt I was incompetent hurt a little and yet this was also a battle I wouldn't win. "Sorry, it's a great find, guess I got carried away in my excitement."

"Look, I don't want to be a hard ass. You did well," Dad said. "Especially since this stela's just outside the grid of the tomb and we might have overlooked it."

I inclined my head toward my discovery. "Could those symbols be written in Punic?"

"Perhaps." He wiped sweat from his forehead. "Let's take a look before it gets any hotter." He pulled a small notebook from his pants pocket, flipped through the pages, and glanced at the horizontal symbols on the stela. Then he compared them to his notes. Without averting his gaze, he said, "They're Punic alrigh—" He paused. "Can't be!"

"What?" I asked between tense bites of my bottom lip.

"Hold on." He stuffed the notebook into his pocket and pulled out his cell. After snapping a few pictures, he looked at me. "If this is what I hope, you may have discovered something I feared was lost to the ancient world."

My heart pounded so hard, I felt the pulse of it in my ears. "Plan to share?"

He chuckled, then coughed. "Let's head to my tent so I can get a definitive answer."

I wanted to push for more and thought better of it. He might get pissed and send me to the tomb to bust some fat cells until he figured things out. Best to go with the flow.

We walked quickly and in silence. Talking while moving in the North African heat took too much energy. As we passed through the ruins of ancient Carthage, ghosts of bathhouses built from large sandstone bricks glowed beneath the early morning sun. I wondered, and not for the first time, what the structures must have been like in their former glory. A port city like Carthage with five hundred thousand people was a huge melting pot of cultures. Egyptians, Greeks, and people of the Levant, probably sat alongside the Carthaginians, sharing their adventures while soaking in the baths.

The temple of the Carthaginian god, Ba'al Hammon, was a visual feast with its hundred-foot marble pillars lining the front. How anything of the city had remained after the Romans burned it to the ground was nothing short of amazing.

We soon came to the work-tents. The Tunisian government frowned on us tracking dirt through the visitors' buildings, so we had to set up at the edge of the ruins. Dad and I stepped into his makeshift office. The air was thick and heavy. Folded coveralls and helmets with headlamps lay across the top of a long table, for today's exploration into the tomb.

I gave an approving nod. "I wish Greg would take a lesson from you in organization."

Dad passed another long table laden with a laptop and several pottery fragments sorted by shape and color. Then he stopped before a cubby in the corner. "I've tried. Your brother has his own way of doing things. You know that."

My stomach dropped as he set his hat on a shelf and took a seat before the laptop. I hadn't noticed the dark circles beneath his eyes since he always wore sunglasses.

"Getting enough sleep, Dad?"

He cocked an eyebrow. "Yeah, why?"

Worry creased my brow. "You look tired."

"I'm fine. Now stop fussing and let me get some work done." Dad's voice was nonnegotiable. With a defeated sigh, I moved to his side and watched as he printed the images from the stela that he'd sent himself. He fed them into a 3-D scanner, and all the symbols appeared on the screen.

My breath hitched. "They're so clear."

"Course they are," he said in a why are you surprised tone. "Punic is a common language found on this dig, so the translation shouldn't take long."

"Great." I fidgeted with the bottom of my T-shirt. Patience was never a strength.

Dad uploaded the scan into the linguistic software, smiling wide as the system sorted through each letter. Differing symbols flashed before us. My throat tightened. This was the first time since grade school that I'd seen him this excited about a discovery. Before Mom's death nine years ago, his cancer, and the drinking that followed, Dad had been one of the most brilliant minds in archeology.

The pride in his voice still rang clear in my mind when he told Mom about his new software that translated ancient texts within minutes – how this streamlined one of the hardest processes for archeologists, anthropologists, and linguists. His wide smile when he shared how museums all over the world had incorporated this into their systems warmed my heart. Back then, he had seemed unstoppable. Maybe this version of Dad had been resurrected today.

Several minutes later, the printer spat out a piece of paper. He plucked a sheet from the bin and read. " I was right."

Adrenaline raced through my veins, and I stepped closer. "What?"

He wrote a couple of notes on the side of the page.

I pushed my hands into my pant pockets to keep from snatching the paper and reading it. "C'mon! What did you find?"

He coughed before responding. "You've stumbled on something significant." Then he read the translation aloud.

"May the great Ba'al Hammon bestow strength upon this warrior, Adones Barca, lost to this world before the summer of his twentieth year in the battle of Cannae. Nephew and adopted son of Hannibal Barca, may he find peace as he ascends to the eternal world of the dead."

My hand flew to my heart. As the daughter of an archeologist, I knew life spans were much shorter in the ancient world, especially for a warrior like Adones. Yet being a part of the discovery made the connection to the deceased more personal.

I shook my head. "He was my age."

"Seems to be."

Adones must not have married since it wasn't mentioned. He could have been like me, more focused on career and his future than romance, thinking the rest could wait. Then again, ancient civilizations were misogynistic by today's standards, they would have mentioned Adones' horse before a wife.

"God, he was so young," I observed.

"Yup," Dad said absently as he studied the printout. "An initial scope of the tomb revealed several artifacts inside, with no hint of who was in there." Dad slapped his hand against the printout. "This, this changes everything. If Adones was killed in the battle of Cannae, that was around 218 BCE, when *Hannibal Barca* was at his best."

"Okay, what does that have to do with the stela?"

Dad paced in front of me. "After the Romans destroyed Carthage, little was known about Hannibal or his descendants, which is a tragedy since he almost single-handedly sacked Rome. Maybe, just maybe, this inscription has linked us to one of the greatest generals to have ever lived."

Crunching rocks signaled approaching footsteps from outside. The tent flap opened, and a man entered. He wasn't bad looking for a forty-something guy, about six feet tall with wavy black hair streaked in gray, and a short-cropped beard.

He surveyed Dad beneath thick lashes framing dark brown eyes. "Hello, Andras, are you ready to enter the tomb?"

The friendliness in the guy's voice didn't fit his body language. He held his chin high and looked down an aquiline nose while speaking, as though he would deign us peasants with his presence.

"Sure am," Dad said with a nod. "Per your instructions, I had the engineers clear the rubble from the corridor, and your hazmat team has already scoped the place for mold and other pathogens. Infrared cameras tell me—"

"Yes, yes," the man said with a dismissive wave. "I've examined the images you sent. Looks like we're in for an exciting day."

"Definitely. Like I was saying, engineering has assured me it's ready to go." Sweat beaded across Dad's forehead as he gestured toward me. "Dr. Jasim Hamad, I'd like you to meet my daughter, Amara. She's a second year at Harvard, studying history and archeology."

"So you've said on the phone," Dr. Hamad said with a wide grin.

Dr. Hamad was just like all the other bureaucrats Dad had dealt with over the years. Talk by phone, then show up after all the leg work was done.

Hamad's dark brown gaze swept over me, appraising, assessing. "It's good to put a face with a name."

I held his stare despite feeling like an artifact on display. "Nice to meet you."

"From what Andras has told me, you're quite an impressive woman," Dr. Hamad said in a thick Tunisian accent that lilted around his syllables.

The heat returned to my cheeks. I hated it when people stared at me. "Thanks."

"You could learn a lot from Jasim," Dad said. "He's a curator here at the Credo Museum, and he's translated texts from at least five archaic languages without the use of software."

"Wow!" That explained the guy's edge of superiority. He was an impressive person. "I can barely translate Homer's writings from ancient Greek to English."

Hamad jutted his chin toward Dad. "Sounds like you're following in your father's footsteps?"

Archeology and focusing on the past were easier than facing climate change, school shootings and looming world wars. The present was such a downer, I often worried about what would be left for me or any of us in the future. Being part of a generation consumed with dystopian novels and apocalyptic movies didn't inspire much hope either.

Still, I couldn't deny that summer digs with Dad were some of the best times of my life, and once immersed in art, adventure, and all things ancient, I was truly hooked. I gave a quick nod. "I suppose I am following in Dad's footsteps. Though as he reminded me this morning, I have a lot to learn."

"Tu tapeinoo," Dad said in ancient Greek.

Dr. Hamad chuckled. "Yes, I can see she is a humble girl."

"Speaking of that, Amara discovered a stela near the dig site." Dad extended the paper containing the translation to Hamad. "I've deciphered the text from the stela, and if I'm right, some of the artifacts photographed in the first chamber could be significant for Tunisia."

"Oh?" Dr. Hamad took the paper and read it. After a long stretch of time, his eyes glazed, and his throat bobbed. "A Barca? This. Is. Incredible." His voice cracked and he cleared his throat.

Dad and I exchanged 'what's up with Hamad' glances.

"Could Adones really be buried there?" I asked in the calmest voice I could muster, while inside, every nerve in my body fired like a live wire. Being part of such a significant discovery was a dream. Yet here I stood.

"There's a strong possibility." Dr. Hamad's hands shook as he studied the paper like it was the most interesting thing he'd ever seen. "No wonder there were no markings on the entry door. If this Carthaginian noble is indeed buried there, the family didn't want the grave looted."

"Could that be why the stela was several yards from the tomb, to throw off grave robbers?" I asked.

Dad nodded. "That's very likely."

I stepped forward. It was now or never if I wanted to take part in the exploration.

"Any chance my team could accompany you today? It'd be great to see where that translation leads."

Dr. Hamad's jaw clenched as he pulled his gaze away from the paper. "Your team?"

"I divided the nine interns we have into teams," Dad said. "My son, Gregory, and a young lady, Sophie, are on Amara's team. Sophie's a second-year undergraduate art student specializing in ancient pieces, and she's also a photographer at Harvard, and Gregory—"

"I'm aware," Dr. Hamad said. "Fencing champion turned PhD student."

"Yeah, he's a student at Georgetown," I couldn't help the edge of superiority in my voice.

My brother had always been athletic, smart, and handsome too. In contrast, I was built like a small boy with long untamable curls, and the athletic ability of a sloth. Getting into a better school than him was my one claim to fame.

"I see." Dr. Hamad glanced at me. "Is it wise to allow interns into the tomb before we get a look?"

Dad coughed again, and he drank some water before answering. "Well, as you know, it would have been just the two of us today. The interns will have to log and photograph all the artifacts before they're packed off to your museum. This way you can discuss logistics with them."

Hamad rubbed his dimpled chin as though contemplating Dad's words.

"My interns are capable," Dad continued. "Gregory's two years into his PhD in anthropology and he's specializing in ancient civilizations. His input will be quite valuable. Sophie could video our entry and photograph many of the artifacts, which could give us a jump on the analysis. She is versed in ancient art. Amara's knowledge of archeology will come in handy as well."

Hamad's grip tightened on the paper as he leveled an intense gaze on my father. "All right, Andras. I trust your judgment as the lead on this team."

"Wonderful."

It took every bit of restraint I had not to jump up and down, to school my face and voice into a mask of calmness as I spoke. "Are we in?"

"Yes," Dad said.

"May I see the stela?" Dr. Hamad still squeezed the printout like he was afraid someone would snatch it from him.

Weirdo alert.

"Absolutely." Dad returned his attention to me. "Go ahead and give Sophie and Gregory the good news and meet us at the tomb." He checked his watch. "Around six-thirty. I'll bring your gear."

"Will do." I sauntered toward the tent's exit hoping to come off as cool and collected. Realistically, I looked like a sweaty nerd in an oversized safari hat. Not that it mattered in a big picture sort of way. In forty minutes, my team and I would be the first people to enter a tomb that hadn't been touched for thousands of years. I couldn't wait to see what waited inside.

Chapter Two

Running in the heat took it out of me. By the time I stepped inside Greg's tent, I was soaked in sweat and holding the stitch in my side. He and Sophie backed away from each other and averted their gazes.

I smirked. "Again? Can't you keep your lips to yourselves for five minutes?"

Greg tucked a curl behind Sophie's ear. "Unless the camp's on fire, you'd better have a good reason for barging in."

My heart raced with excitement as I stepped forward. "Oh, I do."

"Um," Sophie swiped an errant curl away from her brow. "If it's about the stela, I already told Greg."

I felt my smile tense. It would have been nice to give the news myself. Since she couldn't have known, I shook off my irritation and stepped closer. "No, not that, something better."

Greg grabbed a beer off his desk, which was cluttered with Coke cans and water bottles, then he took a swig before speaking. "What's up?"

I frowned. Dad had nearly lost everything before getting sober. I hoped my brother wasn't on the same path. "It's only six o'clock. You need to take this job more seriously." How he made straight A's in grad school was a mystery.

Greg compressed his lips. "I do take my job seriously. You didn't stay up till one in the morning logging pottery pieces for Dad." He bent at the waist and stage whispered in Sophie's ear. "How can you be friends with someone so judgmental?"

Sophie raised her hands and backed up. "Don't bring me into this."

"Look, Beer-For-Brains, you should stop drinking now," I said.

"Name calling? That's mature."

He wasn't wrong, but alcohol was a trigger for me. Although I tried not to project this onto others, Greg was my brother and he, more than anyone else, should have known better. I inhaled deeply and counted backward from ten in Greek, *déka, enéa, októ*...

"Sorry," I said finally. "Dad is letting us tag along on the exploration. If he smells beer on your breath, we'll be persona non grata."

His jaw dropped. "Are you serious?"

"Yep," I leaned against the long computer table and slowly crossed my legs. "We're in."

Greg twisted his championship fencing ring while staring ahead contemplatively. Beneath the dim light, his short auburn hair was almost brown, just like our mother's.

"How did you?" he said finally. "Is it because of that stela?"

"Yup, it's a big deal," I said. "Dad translated the text and you'll never guess who might be in that tomb."

"Who?" Sophie asked.

I paused, fighting a smirk.

Greg huffed and plopped into a chair. "Gonna tell or should we play a game of charades?"

"Be nice," Sophie said.

"Alright, smart ass. It's Adones Barca, the nephew of General Hannibal Barca."

Greg let out a low whistle.

The line between Sophie's dark eyebrows creased. "Is that the same general we learned about on the museum tour? You know, the one who marched thirty thousand troops and a bunch of elephants over the Alps in winter."

"The one and only," I said.

Greg rubbed his chin. "While that's an awesome discovery, it's hard to imagine Dad letting us go anywhere near the tomb before he gets a look inside."

"Well, he is." I checked my watch. It was ten after six. "Dad wants us to meet at the tomb in twenty minutes. Sophie, bring your video camera, you'll be filming the expedition."

She glanced between Greg and me while biting her thumbnail.

I gave her arm a gentle pat. "Don't flake on us. We'll be with you every step of the way."

"Thanks, this means a lot." She sighed. "I know this is a career maker. I just need to wrap my mind around entering a dark tomb."

Greg kissed the top of her head before returning his attention to me. "We'll meet you there."

Watching them brought a smile to my face. Even if they'd only been together for two months, it seemed my brother, who usually deflected his emotions with jokes and sarcasm, was finally taking a relationship seriously.

Not that I had much room to judge since my longest relationship had lasted nine months, and that ended because I chose this internship over him. Someday, I'd meet a guy who got me. I set my water bottle on Greg's desk since the trash can was lipping full and gave a quick wave. "See you soon."

I had just opened the tent flap when Greg said, "Mind grabbing my rubber boots from Dad's Rover?"

I paused and turned toward them ready to protest when Greg cut his eyes toward Sophie, who was still chomping on the remains of her nails. I quickly surmised that he planned to give her a pep talk so I said, "Okay, I'll get 'em. Don't be late."

By the time I made it to Dad's tent, my mouth was dry as the neighboring Sahara. I opened the flap and entered. He was dressed in coveralls and rubber boots, stuffing a bunch of gear into a canvas backpack.

"Hey, Dad, where's the Rover key? Greg needs his boots."

Dad shook his head. *"Ta écho."*

"Good, glad you grabbed 'em. I wasn't looking forward to walking to your car," I replied in Greek.

He pulled some coveralls, and rubber boots out of the backpack and tossed them to me. "Since you're here, go ahead and gear up. It'll lighten my load."

"Okay, let me get some water first." I reached for the metal canteen on his worktable.

His eyebrows nearly disappeared into his hairline, and his hand shot up. "No, not that. Er, it has my backwash. Get your own water." He gestured toward a case in the corner.

Since when did backwash matter? A familiar heaviness weighed down my shoulders. I grabbed the canteen, twisted the cap off and sniffed. The strong scent of alcohol filled my nostrils. All the neglect, hurt, and anger I had felt as a child pulsed through my veins. Red blurred in my vision. I couldn't breathe, couldn't think above the mounting pressure in my head.

I hurled the canteen against a metal tent pole with all my strength. It hit with a loud clank. Alcohol splashed all over the tarp.

Dad sneered. "What the hell's wrong with you?"

"What's wrong with me?" I poked my chest hard, before thrusting my hand toward him. "What's wrong with *you*? You're drinking. Again!" My ribs contracted against my heart. "Your precious digs, that canteen, they've always been more important than your family."

"You know that's not true. I had to work. My job requires travel."

I stared at him in utter disbelief. After a year of family counseling and healing, I thought he had changed. He was the same selfish bastard who had left us for months at a time when he was on one of his binges.

"Seriously? You left Greg and I with Yia Yia and didn't look back after Mom died."

The creases around his brown eyes deepened. "Your mother was my life. I didn't know how to deal with losing her."

"And you think we did?" My body shook so hard, I could barely stand. "You had an eleven-year-old daughter and a fifteen-year-old son who needed you. Do you even know how many nights I sat around waiting for your calls? How disappointed I was when they never came?"

Dad sat in his chair slump shouldered. "I thought we worked through all that."

"Doesn't mean I've forgotten how you made me feel."

He sighed. "I've tried to be more presen—"

"Save it." My voice cracked. "You didn't even tell us about your cancer until you were in remission. How's that being present?"

He mopped his hands over his face. "Oh, Amara, I put you through enough with my drinking. The last thing I wanted was—"

"To hurt us. What do you think that canteen's doing? Are you even sober enough to lead the expedition?"

"Yes!" he snapped. "I bought the bottle of vodka a while back. Please, believe me, I haven't taken a drink yet."

I raised my eyebrows. "Why fill that canteen?"

"Because I'm in the contemplation stage, I suppose."

I shook my head. "I can't believe a word you say."

"Look, I'm not that irresponsible. I'd never drink and lead an exploration." He paused. "Amara, listen—"

"To more lies. No thanks." I grabbed my gear. "See you at the tomb." I stormed out of the tent.

After putting some distance between Dad and myself, I ducked behind a tent and punched the air just like Greg used to whenever Yia Yia sent him to his room for smarting off. The release of energy didn't relieve my hurt. I squeezed my eyes shut and opened them to keep from crying. Then I pulled my coveralls over my clothes and yanked on my rubber boots. The whole time, my mind reeled. Why, after beating cancer, seven years of sobriety, and a thriving archeology career, would Dad throw it all away now? Why would he do this to our family? We had mended a lot of fences. None of this made sense.

My cell dinged. When I pulled it from my coveralls, I frowned as a message from Dad appeared on the screen. "You have five minutes to get here or we're leaving without you."

I fought the urge to call him a prick and texted, "Heading Your Way," instead.

While heading to the tomb, I pushed down my emotions. There was no chance of getting answers until after the exploration. If my mind kept reeling, I'd lose it and that could pose a risk to my team. No, I'd sit down with Dad and get answers later. Until then, I needed to focus on this opportunity.

When the tomb came into my view, Greg waved at me from the entrance. He was only a couple of feet shorter than the seven- or eight-foot walls of dirt and rubble beside him.

I pasted a smile on my lips and waved back. He and Sophie were already dressed in their gear, as were Dad and Dr. Hamad.

"Glad you could join us," Dr. Hamad said, frowning.

Heat flooded my cheeks, and I had to force myself to look into his discerning brown eyes. "So-sorry, I made a pit stop."

"Get the rest of your gear on." Dad stood next to Hamad with his legs apart and arms crossed.

"Yeah, okay," I said.

Dad seemed steady enough. Maybe he told the truth, and he hadn't taken a drink. Maybe he wouldn't endanger our team that way. He'd always been such a professional. Except for the time he lost his curatorship at the Smithsonian for missing too much work, for drinking himself into oblivion.

"I grabbed your stuff." Sophie handed me a hard hat, head lamp, and N-95 mask.

While putting them on, I asked, "You okay with going in there?" Her issues were a nice distraction.

"Yeah." She pulled back the sleeve on her coveralls, revealing a gold bracelet with dangling hearts. "Greg gave me this for luck. I'll be okay with both of you by my side."

"Nice." I glanced at Greg standing beside Dad at the entrance to the tomb, while staring at Sophie. When it came to money, my brother's wallet had cobwebs. For him to pull it out and blow off the dust.... Was he in love?

"Gather round. We have a few rules to review before heading in." Dad's voice held a command. "Follow Dr. Hamad and me, and don't veer from the path we take. Understand?"

We gave a nod of confirmation.

"Good." Dad donned his mask and moved to the front of the line like everything was copasetic.

The rest of us donned our masks. Then Dr. Hamad stood behind Dad, followed by Greg. Sophie steadied her video recorder in front of her and waited behind my brother.

After flipping on my headlamp, I took up the rear, determined to focus on the present, on the untouched piece of history I was about to experience. I followed my team into the darkness, away from the land of the living and into the world of the dead.

Chapter Three

The tomb was at least twenty degrees cooler than outside, and the stale scent of dust and mold clung to the air. I rubbed goosebumps away from my arms and cautiously followed my team down rock steps, flanked by stone walls. Centuries old dust motes danced against the soft glow from our headlamps as we descended.

"This isn't creepy at all. Why couldn't they have excavated the circus first?" Sophie said.

I gave her an encouraging pat on the back. "You're doing great. Just concentrate on filming the others."

She adjusted the camera in front of her.

At the bottom landing, the silence was intense. Only the steady beat of our breaths could be heard as we navigated a long tunnel filled with rubble. I had to remind myself that trespassing on this sacred space was for the greater good, to recover parts of a past stolen from the world by the Romans.

"Watch your step." Dad's voice echoed against the silence as he traversed a wide plank placed over a deep hole in the middle of the ground.

Relief washed over me. No way he could have crossed that plank if he were drunk. Dr. Hamad and Greg made it to the other side. Sophie put her video camera into her backpack and skittered across.

When it was my turn, I forced myself not to look at the dark pit below until I stepped off the plank.

"In my experience, if the architects of this tomb set a booby trap, the artifacts from our images must be significant," Dr. Hamad observed.

"I couldn't agree more." Dad continued down the corridor with our team on his tail.

We soon came to a rough circular opening about five and a half feet high and about three feet wide.

Dr. Hamad eyed the opening. "Did the engineers consider that someone above the age of twelve will have to fit through that?"

"Preservation is key, Jasim. You know this," Dad said. "I gave explicit orders to disturb as little as possible while making it safe."

"Well, the engineers will need to expand it once the artifacts are logged as we'll have to carry them out."

Dan nodded. "Of course."

"Let's see what's on the other side, shall we?" Dr. Hamad said.

He and Dad pulled large flashlights out of their backpacks and turned them on. "After you, Jasim."

Dr. Hamad crouched and crab-walked into the unknown, followed by Dad.

Sophie's eyes were wide as an owl. "I can't believe I'm actually entering a freaking tomb. This has vampire den written all over it."

I chuckled. "You're so dramatic."

"You can do this. I'm right behind you." Greg took Sophie's hand and helped her into the opening. She barely had to duck to get through.

Conversely, Greg had to enter on his hands and knees.

Several gasps, and a "whoa" came from the other side.

My heart somersaulted in my chest as I crab-walked forward with my arms close to my ribs. When I made it to the chamber, I gasped.

The rectangular room was about twelve-by-twelve and loaded with artifacts. Wooden couches with elephants carved into the sides were stacked to our front. Baskets with brass breastplates — furniture and weapons like lances, swords, and bows — wooden chests, statues, and pottery filled the space.

I sniffed. "Cedar?"

Sophie nodded. "Yeah, I thought it was just me."

"Nope, I smell it too. Those trees are all over Tunis," Dad said.

Dr. Hamad flashed a wide smile. "How magnificent. The very air we're breathing has remained unchanged through time."

Greg stepped forward. "Where's the sarcophagus?"

Dad waved a hand toward the artifacts. "We're in an antechamber."

In this shadowed space, Dad's face looked deathly pale. It could have been a trick of the light.

"Hmm, everything I've read is true. The Carthaginians buried their dead like the ancient Egyptians," Greg said.

Sophie scanned the room with her video camera. "It adds up. I suppose the countries adopted each other's customs since they shared the same trade routes."

"Only the nobles and royalty received this type of burial." Dr. Hamad made a beeline toward the weapons in the corner. He studied lances with bronze arrowheads, leather shields, and boomerangs. When his eye caught the bronze sword with a blade that had greened over time, he knelt before it. "Incredible."

"That handle is made from elephant tusks," Sophie studied it with an artist's eye.

"I'm aware," Hamad didn't avert his gaze from the weapon.

"See anything about Adones Barca?" I asked.

"Not yet." Dad set his backpack by the opening. "Those are the weapons of a warrior so there's a strong possibility he's here."

Greg slowly moved among the artifacts, touching nothing, just marveling at the workmanship. "These are pristine, and there's so much here. You know, the Phoenicians believed the deceased remained in their grave for a while before entering the world of the dead."

"Indeed, young man," Dr. Hamad said. "Thus, the reason their belongings were buried with them."

Dad walked to a rectangular chest in the corner. It reminded me of those in pirate movies, made from wood with a flat top. Except this one was more ornate with engraved images of warriors holding lances.

He wiped dust away from the top, revealing an elephant engraving, and coughed before speaking. "Beautiful."

That nagging voice of dread crept into my mind. The dark circles beneath Dad's eyes, his paleness and coughing, caused me to think the worst. Had the brain tumor returned? This explained his temptation to drink. If I was right, he was holding it together better than I would have. I shrugged the tension from my shoulders, hating how I had worked myself up without knowing for sure. Yet, I couldn't stop the bad thoughts from racing through my mind. Crap parent or not, he was the only one I had.

"Careful, Andras," Dr. Hamad joined Dad. "The Tunisian government would be most displeased if we damage that. Not to mention what could happen to the contents of that container when the air hits them."

"No offense, I was a curator at one point, and I know my way around an artifact." Dad pulled a set of leather gloves from his pants pocket and put them on. With the gentlest of movements, he lifted the lid. It opened with a squeak.

Keep it together, Amara. I momentarily set my fear for Dad aside and bent at the waist to get a better look. Inside the chest, we were greeted by a brass breastplate with six sculpted silver discs.

"It's pristine." Greg shot me an ear-to-ear smile. "Like it was placed in there yesterday."

Dad pointed at one of the discs. The symbol of a bearded man with goat horns was sculpted into the metal. "That's—"

"Ba'al Hammon." Dr. Hamad studied it through narrowed eyes.

Sophie zoomed in with the video camera.

Dad shined the flashlight on a purple cloak beside the baldric. The neckline was trimmed with gold beading. "See that, kids. Original Tyrian purple. It's in perfect condition."

I gave a weak smile. "Yeah, I see."

Greg approached a wooden table on the opposite end of the room and pointed at a small replica of a ship sitting on top of it. "Look at this Trireme war galley."

Sophie came up behind Greg. "The workmanship, the wooden serpent's head at the front of the bow must have taken forever to carve. Not to mention the three stories of little oars there."

"Yeah, and both sets of sails. I wonder what material they're made from." Greg bent forward to get a better look.

"Don't touch anything!" Dr. Hamad scurried toward them.

"I would never!" Greg protested.

As Dad reached for the lid to the trunk, the part of me that needed answers couldn't wait a second longer. I leaned in and whispered, "Is the cancer back?"

He closed the lid with a squeak. "Yes."

A dizzy feeling washed over me. I grabbed his shoulder to brace myself. "H-how long have you known?"

"I received a Zoom call from my doctor yesterday. He confirmed it."

I wanted to scream at him for holding back, but my more rational side told me to keep it together for his sake. "Are you gonna tell Greg?"

"At some point, yes."

"What about Yia Yia?"

He sniffed beneath his mask. "Look, this isn't the time or place to have this conversation. We'll talk more after we're finished here. For now, keep this to yourself."

"Man, I wish I didn't have to head back to school at the end of the month," Greg said. "I'd love to be here when they uncover the burial chamber. This would tie into my research."

Hamad's gaze landed on Greg. "On what topic?"

"The differences between ancient Carthaginian and Egyptian cultures," Greg said. "Do you have any idea where the burial chamber is?"

Hamad shook his head. "No, once these artifacts have been cleared, I suspect there's a seal somewhere that will provide a clue to its whereabouts."

Dad cleared his throat. "I need some water."

He stood up and I grabbed his hand. "We'll beat this together."

His brown eyes softened. "Love you."

Despite all I'd just learned about Dad's illness, I couldn't bring myself to say it back. I had always struggled that way.

He walked to his backpack. Just as he unzipped it, the floor shook beneath us.

"Earthquake!" Dad yelled.

"Dad!" My voice disappeared into the roar of dropping debris. I grappled for anything to hold onto.

The walls cracked. I fell backward and crashed against the chest. My head hit with a thud. Artifacts fell to the floor around me. A bunch of rocks rained from the ceiling and blocked Dad from my view.

Sophie was shrieking, Greg was yelling, Hamad was screaming.

Then, the rumbling and shaking stopped.

The silence was deafening. I rubbed the back of my head, wincing at the growing knot. Luckily, my hand came back blood free. Lights from the others' headlamps shined on the ceiling a few feet away. Debris blocked the opening. After coughing up a lung full of dust, I turned onto all fours and crawled to the rubble by the entry. There were a few gaps I could see through. A sigh of relief whooshed from my lungs when I saw movement.

"Amara," came from the other side.

"Dad!" I yelled through the crack. "You alright?"

"Yes. How are you all?"

Greg and Sophie coughed from somewhere behind me.

"We're alive and unharmed," Hamad said.

"I'll get help. Hold tight," Dad called back.

I stood on unsteady legs, pulled my cell from my pants pocket, scrolled down from the upper left corner and activated the flashlight. This made it easier to see when combined with the glow of my headlamp. Sickened by fallen artifacts and the lost history, I stepped over them and walked to the others who were now standing and covered in dust.

"You all okay?" I coughed.

"Yeah, just a few bruises," Greg said.

Tears streamed down Sophie's face, and she was practically panting. "I knew this would happen. Just knew it." Her voice was shrill and loud. "We're buried alive. What if we can't—"

Hamad grabbed her by the shoulders and shook her. "Snap out of it."

She blinked.

"This is no time for hysterics, girl. We have water. There's enough space between the rubble for air to penetrate. We'll be fine. Until the rescue team arrives, we must conserve our air and energy."

"Yeah, you're, you're right," she replied in a shaky voice. "Hopefully they'll get us the hell out of here soon."

Her words, "We're buried alive," rushed through my mind like a runaway train, and it was all I could do not to break down as well. Hamad had also been right. This wasn't the place to lose it.

"What the?" Greg pointed at an adjacent wall.

My jaw dropped when I saw what held his attention. Not more than a foot away, a secret door that originally blended with the wall had cracked open during the earthquake.

"The burial chamber?" I asked.

"Indeed. It must be," Hamad observed.

As we all drew closer to get a better look, a soft, golden glow came from the other side.

"Sunlight, could that lead outside?" I asked.

Greg stepped closer to the opening. "Only one way to know for sure."

Hamad shook his head and compressed his lips so tightly, they almost disappeared. "Absolutely not! There's too many unkno—"

"I refuse to die in here if there's a way out." Greg stepped through the small opening. Seconds later, "What the! You gotta see this," came from the other chamber.

I swallowed past a huge lump in my throat. My curiosity for all things historical trumped the risks. I looked at Sophie and Hamad. "I have to know."

As I slid through the opening, Sophie said, "I hope we don't regret this."

Chapter Four

I gasped. The enclosed room was swallowed by darkness, broken only by threads of yellow light jutting from a space between the base and cover of a white marble sarcophagus. I tucked my cell into my cargo pants. Gingerly, I inched toward the ancient coffin, careful to keep my distance from the light.

"What the hell?" Sophie said as she entered with Hamad on her tail.

Hamad came up beside me. His face an unreadable mask while staring at the sarcophagus. This reaction seemed odd since we had just entered what could best be described as *Indiana Jones* meets *Stargate*. (Watching classic movies was me and Yia Yia's thing.) I would have expected shock or at the very least curiosity.

"What do you think that is?" Greg asked.

I shrugged. "That kind of glow, maybe it's something nuclear."

Sophie huffed. "Yeah, right. Like the ancients had those types of advancements."

Hamad finally chimed in. "Until we know what it is and how it could affect us, we should return to the other chamber."

"I'm with him. It's some kind of booby trap," Sophie said.

Greg shook his head. "No. It wouldn't be so conspicuous."

I took in the sarcophagus which was at least twelve by six. "That's awful big for a body."

"Agreed. A bull could fit in that," Sophie said.

Dr. Hamad waggled his forefinger. "Not necessarily. Normally, a smaller coffin containing the body is placed inside the sarcophagus."

"True," Greg said. "If a person is in there, he's likely an average-sized man."

Hamad stared us down. "This bears repeating. We should return to the other cham—"

"There." Greg pointed at a mural on the back wall, "That may provide some answers."

We all drew closer to the image of men engaged in battle beside a blood red river sprinkled with bodies. Greg pointed at the soldiers in armor wearing red plumed helmets and Pteruges/ pleated skirts of leather. "Definitely Romans."

"Nothing in this mural explains that glow coming from the sarcophagus," Sophie said.

"Not yet." I continued taking in the painting of warriors with long hair, wearing helmets with goat horns and leather armor.

They wielded axes with blades, dripping in crimson. At the edge of the battle scene, a man with black wavy hair sat atop an elephant holding a sword in the air. He wore a leather baldric with discs on the front, much like the one we found in the wooden chest.

Greg leaned closer. "That's definitely a Carthaginian on the elephant."

"Could that be Adones or maybe Hannibal Barca?" I asked.

Greg shrugged. "It's tough to say, but I'd lay odds that mural is dedicated to the deceased."

"Since your stela said Adones died in the battle of Cannae, this is probably a depiction of it," Hamad observed.

"What's this?" Greg stood at the other end of the mural studying a round plaster seal with a raised etching of an elephant. "That's the Barcid family's signature."

My brow shot up and I joined him. "How odd. Seems out of place with this mural, you know."

Hamad crossed his arms over his chest. "I've indulged you enough. It is likely that Andras has workers moving the rubble as we speak, which could potentially cause another cave-in and—"

"Yeah, it's probably smart to stay close to the exit, just in case," Sophie looked at me. "We should go."

I continued studying the seal.

Greg tapped my arm. "C'mon."

"Okay, one sec." I leaned closer and pressed my finger to the seal. "This looks more like a button than a—"

"No! Don't touch that!" Hamad yelled.

There was a click, followed by another rumbling sound.

The room shook.

I grabbed Greg to steady myself.

Sophie lost her footing.

Greg caught her fall. "Run!"

I scrambled toward the doorway. The ground teetered in all directions. I stumbled forward. The earth was coming to meet my face fast. Greg grabbed my arm just before I hit the ground.

"Come, hurry!" Dr. Hamad's voice thundered as he stood by the opening to the tomb, blurring in and out of my vision.

The rumbling suddenly stopped and the lid to the sarcophagus moved to the side on its own. A flat golden disc about the size of a bread plate, and surrounded by a 3-D prism, emerged from inside the marble coffin. The three of us stood there transfixed, as the disc floated into the air. Stars and moons lined the inner rim, and they glowed brighter than the sun.

A high-pitched buzzing sound droned in my ears. Pressure mounted in my head, and I dropped to my knees, paralyzed by pain.

When I looked up, the disc was spinning like a top. A massive circle of golden energy exploded from the center and morphed into a vortex. A strong tugging sensation like a vacuum at the top of my head followed.

"No!" Greg yelled.

His voice was barely audible in my fractured hearing as he flew by me. Sophie tumbled head over heels through the air behind him. A shrill scream escaped my lips as my arms stretched and thinned like they were made of rubber. Blue sparks flickered from somewhere far and close at once. And then, a flurry of light swallowed us all.

Chapter Five

What just happened?

I yanked off my mask and headlamp and tossed them aside. The scents of salt and fish wafted past my nose. Sunlight warmed my skin. Guess that meant I wasn't dead. Wind rushed in my ears. I blinked several times to clear my mind and slowly sat up. As I looked around, the only word that came to mind was, *how?* How did I wind up in the middle of a beach? The blue waters, brown sands and rocky cliffs resembled those in Tunis. Except this place lacked all the ships and industrial buildings.

My thoughts flashed to the glowing disc. No way that kind of technology could have existed in a two-thousand-year-old burial chamber. I felt the knot on the back of my head, grimacing at the tenderness. Maybe the cave-in knocked me out and I was dreaming. Grabbing a handful of sand, the gritty grains ran through my fingers. They felt real enough. If the glowing disc and the vortex weren't figments of my imagination, it was possible that Sophie and Greg were brought here too.

I stood up, shaded the sun from my eyes with the back of my hand and called to them in a hoarse voice.

Nothing. Just miles and miles of empty shoreline. Where were all the hotels, and the sun worshipers and the surfers? Where was I?

My cell. It would pick up my location. I pulled it from my cargo pocket and activated it. The time was eight a.m., and I had zero bars, which meant no freaking service. That couldn't be right. Judging by the height of the sun in the sky, it was about noon.

My panicked heart skittered across my chest as the image of Dad's pale face fluttered to the front of my mind. I prayed he didn't get stuck in the second quake. Even if he was physically unharmed, emotionally, he'd lose it when he cleared the rubble and found us gone. Hamad could explain things if he was okay. Either way, Dad would be worried sick. His coping skills weren't the best and he'd hit the bottle, for sure. I had to get back to him.

I shuffled down the vacant beach. Seagulls cawed overhead as the sun beamed down on me like a furnace. I peeled off my thick coveralls and trudged on, despite my sweat-soaked tee, sticking to my body. Such a gorgeous beach should have had some sort of activity. Even a game preserve was open to tourists.

After walking for what felt like an hour, the beach wound around a series of cliffs. I licked my cracked lips. If I didn't find fresh water soon, I'd pass out. As if the universe heard my thoughts, I spotted two men walking fast down the shoreline.

"Hey," I yelled, running toward them, waving my arms like a nut case. I froze when I got a good look at the pair.

Everything about the first guy oozed masculinity. He was about thirty, maybe older, and broad as a bear, with ripped biceps and long muscular legs. His tan wraparound pleated skirt, or fustanella, was suspended by a leather belt. The material seemed to be a cross between linen and wool, and was also more authentic than any costumes I'd seen. When combined with the leather sandals that tied up the shins, his clothes were better suited for a gladiator movie than a walk on the beach.

His sidekick was also dressed similarly, except that guy's fustanella was more ornate than Bear's with silver beading along the hem, and his white tunic was etched in purple stitching. However, their clothes weren't the most shocking part of their appearance. The second guy had a brown wheat sack over his head and his hands were tied to a lead rope, pulled by Bear.

I didn't see any cameras around, so they weren't shooting a movie. They could have been participating in a LARP. My dorm hosted Live Action Role Play parties every Halloween. Only, our costumes weren't as bad ass as those on the men before me. Since I wouldn't make it much further without help, I took my chances and approached them.

"Hey, I hate to interrupt your LARP, can you spare a little water? I'm about to—"

Bear unsheathed a dagger from his leather baldric and held the blade to my throat. His movement was lithe and laced with power as he spoke in a foreign language.

My knees quaked as I slowly raised my hands in the air and backed away, checking LARPING off my list of possibilities. "I-I'm gonna go."

The hostage spoke. His words were muffled by the sack.

Bear's dark brown eyes held a deadly edge as he gave the lead rope a tug. It was enough to knock the hostage off balance and send him tumbling to the sand. I seized the window and ran. Unfortunately, I only made it a few feet when Bear grabbed my shirt.

"Let me go!" I screamed, kicked, and punched at him.

The psycho gripped both my hands in one of his and leaned so close, his breath warmed my cheeks when he spoke. Although I didn't understand Bear's words, the warning was clear.

Don't run.

I nodded.

Bear released me and stepped away, assessing me like a predator sizing up his opponent as his gaze fixed on my boots.

I slowly raised my hand and pointed at the waterskin attached to his belt. "Water, please."

His black plaits hung around his shoulders and shined like raven's feathers as he untied the skin and handed it to me.

Without missing a beat, I loosened the leather strap at the top of the skin and gulped the contents. Something tasted off, like it had been mixed with alcohol, possibly wine. Wincing, I lifted the skin to my nose. Before I got a whiff, he snatched it away.

"I would have given it back. You only had to as—"

A faint whir came from above. I turned toward the sound and spotted something long and straight heading for us.

Bear pushed me. I tumbled forwards and ate a mouth full of sand. At the same time, his upper body landed on the back of my legs, and the hostage fell on him. I shrieked and gagged, coughing up a lung as an arrow landed inches from my head. The tip jutting out of the sand was sharp and *real*.

When I caught my breath and looked up again, a bunch of men on horseback stared down at us from the edge of a cliff. Bear scrambled to his feet, yanked the hostage up and pulled the sack off his head. Then they hauled ass down the shoreline. Since a bunch of crazies who'd forgotten which century they lived in were trying to kill me, I took my chances with Bear and his sidekick. My calves burned as I ran behind them. The air whined behind me.

Another arrow?

We quickly veered to the left and entered a cove. I jogged alongside the hostage, scanning the area. With all the rock cliffs around us, we were closed in.

A horn blew in the distance.

Bear raced to the base of a cliff ahead. He moved some bushes and vines aside, revealing a tall opening and shoved the hostage inside. Without blinking, he grabbed my arm and pulled me into the cave with them. I bit my bottom lip to keep from screaming. If I hoped to get out of this alive, I needed to keep my wits.

As my vision adjusted to the dim light streaming through the opening, I got a good look at the hostage. Judging by his smooth tanned skin and thin waist, he couldn't have been much older than me. I winced when I saw the tendrils of black hair matted against a gash on his forehead. The skin beneath his left eye was purple and dried blood surrounded his nostrils. He gave me a once-over and frowned.

I fought the urge to smooth my curls back.

Bear tugged the hostage's lead. Although the prisoner didn't say anything, his glare did the talking. He might have killed Bear if given half a chance.

I would've helped if it got us out of here. Then an idea took root. Free the hostage and turn the situation in our favor. Surely, he'd get me to civilization if I helped him escape. I just needed to wait for the right opening.

A few feet into the cave, we stopped in front of a natural stone ledge on the wall to my left. A couple of torches, a bow, and some arrows were stored there. A sick feeling welled in my stomach as I processed the possible reason such rudimentary weapons kept popping up. Bear grabbed a rope from the pile of stuff on the ledge and led us to the opposite side of the cave. He gestured for the prisoner to sit. The guy widened his stance. Bear grabbed the hostage's neck and spoke in a low and menacing tone.

"Hey," I yelled in English.

The hostage spat in Bear's face.

Bear's body shook with rage. He balled his hand into a fist and drew it back.

I leapt between the two men. "Leave him alone! Can't you see he's already hurt?" I hoped Bear didn't notice how my voice trembled.

He grabbed my forearm. I tried to pull away, and he tightened his grip and twisted. Pain cut through me like a knife. I clenched my teeth and fell to my knees, hating, absolutely hating my vulnerability.

The prisoner yelled foreign words.

Without releasing me, Bear drew his dagger with his free hand and brought it to the guy's throat, forcing him into a seated position. He withdrew the blade, whipped me around like a rag doll, and pointed at the ground, muttering something. With my chin held high, I slowly lowered myself until I was back-to-back with the prisoner. I wasn't about to let him see my fear.

After a moment of silence, Bear spoke in a foreign language and his voice was low and menacing. Since he didn't bind my hands, I assumed he was telling me to stay put. Guess I wasn't much of a threat. When I nodded that I understood, he walked a few feet to the ledge in front of us and grabbed the torch. He reached into a small leather pouch on his belt and pulled out a black stone and an odd metal piece, resembling a small horseshoe. He hit them together and a couple of sparks flew.

Flint and steel?

The hostage whispered in a foreign tongue.

I sat straighter, rubbing my arm. "Speak English?"

No response.

We both had similar features, black hair, and olive complexions. Maybe, just maybe, he knew Greek. It was worth a try. "Understand me?" I asked in that language.

"Are you Spartan or perhaps Athenian?"

It took a second to figure out that he had answered in ancient Greek. Few people knew this language. Yet, it rolled off this guy's tongue like he'd been speaking it all his life. Despite all my exchanges with Dad, this guy's vowels were off, and the verb tenses sounded different.

"Di-did you ask if I was a Spartan or Athenian?" My heart pounded harder, and my hands shook as I considered that both languages existed before Greece became a country.

"Yes," Hostage guy responded. "Are you?"

"I am not," I whispered finally. "You?"

"No, yet I know the language well, girl."

The vacant beach, ancient clothing, arrows and now the antiquated Greek, had me wondering whether the disc had transported me through time. It wasn't like I could ask the hostage what year it was without sounding like I was missing a few screws.

"What is your name," whispered the hostage.

It took a moment to translate. "Amara."

Bear struck the metal object against the stone. More sparks flew. He stood, wiped perspiration from his forehead, and took a swig of water.

As soon as metal clacked against stone again, the hostage said, "That pirate is demanding coin from my uncle in exchange for my life." He fidgeted. "I find it hard to believe you're not in league with him."

My face twisted in frustration as I translated his words. "Di-did you say pirate?"

"Yes."

"I know nothing of pirates. I was separated from my tea — uh, family and accidentally came across you and your captor on the beach."

The torch ignited. Bear slung a wooden tube filled with arrows over his shoulder, attached the bow to a hook on his baldric, and approached me.

I stared at the ground as he helped me to my feet. Not that I needed to act weak. Next to Bear, I was physically weak. Emotionally, I was strong, and intellectually, I had a chance to outwit him.

Bear retethered the hostage to the lead and headed deeper into the cave. I glanced at the opening behind me one last time. If I ran, where would I go? What if those psychos with arrows found me? Since Bear hadn't hurt me, I was better off sticking with him. At least until I found a way to free the hostage.

The ceilings of the cave soon shrunk, and the walls narrowed to the point that we were forced to walk hunched over with our arms clutched against our sides. My mind flashed back to the cave-in and my chest tightened, making breathing more labored. It would suck to be trapped in here. To ground myself, I homed in on the torch light flickering along the rock ceilings. Unseen creatures screeched from the shadows.

Where is he taking me?

The answer came sooner than expected when light seeped through an opening ahead. Bear increased his pace. He tossed the torch as soon as we emerged in another cove stretching toward a sea of aquamarine water. Warm air collided with my skin. The hostage shrugged his shoulders and shivered, glancing at the cliffs above us. In the light of day, his eyes were green as emeralds. A stark contrast against his black hair.

I walked toward him and hesitated, when I noticed a Bireme ship with square sails, a big-bellied hull, and a curled bow, bobbing on the sea. Despite all the tension in this moment, I couldn't help but marvel at the massive size. No replica or painting compared to the real thing.

Bear pulled a small, round silver piece from the purse on his belt and held it toward the sun. A beam of glowing light flickered from it. Moments later, a wooden skiff lowered off the side of the ship and hit the water with a splash. Two men immediately climbed down a side ladder and boarded the small boat.

My chest hollowed out. If Bear made me board, there would be no telling what a ship full of sailors would do to me. I needed a plan and quick. I couldn't climb the cliffs behind me or get past the surrounding rock barrier without catching an arrow to the back. The cave was my only option and without a torch...

With Bear's back to me, I crept toward the hostage, hoping to loosen his bonds before the pirates made it ashore.

He just shook his head and eyed the cliffs above us.

When I looked up, something moved.

I gave a quick nod, praying that whoever was up there, planning to rescue him, would take mercy on me. As I backed away, the hostage bent at the waist and rushed Bear headfirst, sending them tumbling to the sand.

A barrage of arrows flew toward the skiff, narrowly missing it.

I screamed and dove behind a large boulder next to the cave's entrance. My arms shook as I crawled to the edge and peeked around.

The men in the skiff changed direction and rowed fast toward the ship. A conch-like horn sounded from somewhere close, and a bunch of soldiers, with short swords drawn, charged over the surrounding barrier walls. Sunlight flashed off their yellow-plumed helmets as they ripped Bear away from the hostage.

I scrambled to my feet and ran toward the cave, ready to take my chances in the dark. A soldier grabbed my T-shirt and turned me toward him. I punched at his leather breastplate and tried to knee him in the nuts. He shook me until my teeth clacked together, barking out something I didn't understand. Defeated, I lowered my arms to my sides. I cringed as he searched my body and slipped the cell phone from my pocket.

"No, me, er, necessitate that," I said, in butchered ancient Greek. Even though my cell was useless here.

He grabbed my arm and led me back to the men. My breath hitched when I saw Bear on his knees. A soldier held a sword to his throat and the former hostage was now sneering at him. A man with short silver hair sat on a horse, wearing a paludament cape fastened over one shoulder. He observed events unfold from atop the barrier. Since these types of capes were worn by nobles and military commanders, the man must have been their leader.

I needed to find my voice and take a stand while I still had the chance. "Please, release me," I said in my best ancient Greek, which wasn't saying much. "I no taking part of this man's madness."

Bear's head snapped toward me.

I averted my gaze, ignoring the twinges of guilt for selling out the guy who saved me. I had to put myself first.

The other men roared with laughter. Heat flooded my cheeks. They were making fun of my pronunciation. It wasn't like I had time to sit and think about the translation before speaking.

Hostage-guy yelled at them and stormed toward me. He angled his head at my guard. "Did he harm you?"

I processed his words a moment before answering, "No."

The hostage helped me to my feet, and hope sputtered across my chest. That is, until my guard sauntered to the silver-haired man on horseback and handed over my cell. Silver Hair turned the device over and pressed a couple of buttons on the side. A light flickered on. He gasped, and my phone dropped from his hand like it was on fire.

Translating what I wanted to say in my mind before speaking, I said, "Who is that man?"

The hostage's full lips curled into a friendly smile. "He's the captain of my uncle's regiment." He extended the crook of his arm toward me. "Come."

I accepted the offer, and together, we walked toward the captain. "I don't want to be…" A pause followed while I thought of the right word. "A burden."

"It was a brave gesture, stepping between that pirate's fist and my face. One I won't forget. I'll explain your actions to Captain Aharim, and perhaps he'll free you."

The knots in my stomach unraveled, and tightened again when the guard who caught me picked up my phone and returned it to Aharim. After staring at it for a moment, the captain turned his attention to me and spoke in an unknown language.

The hostage said something to Aharim.

The captain nodded and spoke to me in ancient Greek. "What say you?"

I cleared my throat to buy enough time to translate his words and to consider mine. "I've been, er, separated from my father and our friends. I, er, wish to return to them."

Bear called out from behind me in a foreign tongue. A loud thud followed. He grunted. I couldn't bring myself to look. He probably caught a smack on the head or worse.

A moment later, the captain shouted a command. The sentries gathered and stood at attention as he glared down at me from his mount. "There's much you cannot account for, girl. Your strange garments, your accent and this." He held up my cell phone. "Only a sorceress or a spy for the Republic of Rome would own such a device. Until I discuss you with my commander, you'll be a ward of Carthage."

"Carthage?" I squeaked.

Captain Aharim studied me. "Yes, Carthage. You'll become our ward until your fate is determined."

My chest tightened, and a clammy sweat broke across my brow. It was one thing to suspect you'd been transported through time, and a whole other to know. How the hell would I get home? And Dad, he must have been sick with worry.

The hostage's green eyes glinted with concern as he approached me.

"Calm yourself."

Breathe dammit!

I inhaled slowly through my nose and out my mouth until the contractions in my chest eased.

Hostage guy added, "Though it may not appear that I'm on your side, trust that I— "

Captain Aharim shouted in a commanding voice, probably in Punic, the language of Carthage. All the soldiers rallied together. The guards yanked Bear to his feet and tied him to a line behind a horse. His scarred cheek showed the first signs of swelling. Long plaits fell to his shoulders. My guard shoved me towards Bear and tied me next to him. When I glanced at the former hostage, he turned his back to me and joined the rest of the troops.

I wanted to run toward the cave and keep going until they either killed me or my legs collapsed. I wasn't about to die at the hands of a bunch of asshats with swords. No, I had to believe that somehow, I'd find my way home. This meant accepting my fate. Prisoner in an ancient land had just become my new normal.

Chapter Six

Every step across the brush-covered plains was torture. Yet, I kept my head held high despite the scorching heat — being tethered to Bear — while pulled behind a troop of sentries on horseback. The animals kicked up dust. I coughed and rubbed my rope-burned wrists while stepping over the horse's fresh manure for the fiftieth time in that hour.

"Breathe, girl," Bear said in ancient Greek. "You'll be dragged if you lose consciousness."

I slowly turned my head toward him and processed his words. "You speak my language?"

Bear flashed a crooked smile, causing the long scar on his cheek to deepen. "Far better than you from what I heard at the cove."

Heat rushed up my neck. I must have sounded like a child if a pirate was judging my language skills. At least I was communicating, and that was a plus. Maybe Bear could tell me if he spotted Greg and Sophie on the beach.

I sucked up my pride and mentally translated my next words. "Before we met, did you see others clad in, er, garments like mine?"

"No." His voice was low and deep. "Are you separated from your people?"

I nodded, hating the sinking feeling in the pit of my stomach. Although I had no idea how time travel devices worked, I couldn't dismiss the possibility that Greg and Sophie had landed elsewhere.

Bear cut those deep brown eyes toward me. "I'm Tanno, if you care to know."

Licking my dry cracked lips, I said, "I'd care more had you told the soldiers that I wasn't in er, uh, league with you."

He scoffed. "My words would have fallen on deaf ears."

I glowered at him. "You could have tried."

His jaw flexed.

It was best to switch gears before I pissed off the one person I'd connected with. "What will become of us?"

Bear glared at the twenty or more soldiers in metal helmets. "I harbor no illusions. They'll torture and kill me, and if the gods are merciful, you'll receive a lesser punishment. Perhaps become a slave in one of the great houses."

I translated his words, hoping I misunderstood him. "Did you say *slave*?"

"Yes," he said flatly.

My pulse pounded wildly in my ears. Given the sentence Bear was about to face, escape must have crossed his mind. I leaned in and whispered, "You speak as though we have no options. If we work together, perhaps we'll be free by nightfall."

A wry smile played on his full lips. "You think too much of yourself. You're too slight of build to wield a sword and I can't get past the guards alone. Our fate is sealed."

I bit my cheek to fight a scream. Just because he had given up, didn't mean I would. If escape wasn't an option now, I'd try later. They couldn't watch me forever.

A few minutes later, we approached an overgrown grove. Standing at least twenty feet tall, the olive trees were the largest I'd ever seen. Even the branches were different. They twisted toward their neighbors in a willowy embrace that formed a thick and dark orchard. If that wasn't weird enough, the place was oppressively silent. No birds trilled. Nor did the branches sway. It was like the wind had held its breath.

"What is this pla—"

The sentries dismounted and drew their swords.

"Stay diligent," Bear said.

Obviously.

A tug on our lead signaled that our group was moving. The horses tossed their heads, and nickered as we entered the grove. I took in the thick canopies covered in green willowy leaves, dripping with olives, wondering how this was possible. Olive trees were only ten to twelve feet high, and I'd never seen their branches form a dome so thick they blocked out the sun.

Dry leaves crunched under foot as our group moved forward, making me more aware of the utter stillness around us. Bear must have felt it too because his head swiveled from left to right, like a warrior in enemy territory. The sentries were equally as diligent, walking with their swords readied while leading their skittish horses. I drew in a deep breath to slow my racing heart. Allowing a bunch of superstitious sentries to psyche me out would only send me into a panic. I doubted that golden boy or any of his minions would be eager to help me.

About halfway in, a strong breeze rose from nowhere, causing the canopies to sway above us.

I glanced at Bear who moved with flexed arms. "Is there something you're not telling me?"

No sooner had the words left my mouth when a shrill, high-pitched squawk echoed from above. It reminded me of a raspy old woman trying to imitate a bird. All the men scanned our surroundings. The breeze picked up. Branches creaked mysteriously. Bear yanked at his ties.

Several horses nickered.

Another squawk echoed closer now. The hairs on my arms stood on end and I knew as sure as my name was Amara Kalogridas, someone was watching us.

My stomach dipped when one of the horses reared.

A sentry at the front of the formation yelled, and the others took off with horses in tow, causing Bear and I to go all out. One of his strides was equal to two of mine. My thighs and calves burned, and I stumbled. A fluttering sound, like a bunch of birds taking flight, echoed behind us.

"Keep up!" Bear spat.

The squawks resounded from everywhere and nowhere at once.

Trees blurred in my periphery. Each breath was torture.

Golden light streamed through cracks in the branches ahead. "Keep pace, girl. We're nearly there."

When we cleared the grove, we hauled ass for at least a quarter mile more. By the time the sentries stopped the horses, I was sucking wind, ready to collapse.

I bent forward and leaned on my knees. "What..." I took a deep breath. "Were ... they ... running from?"

Bear pulled his waterskin from his belt and took a sip, then handed it to me. "Harpuia."

I almost choked on my water. A harpy? No way. Maybe I had misheard him. "Do you mean a creature with the body of a vulture and the head of a woman?"

Bear nodded. "Yes. They live in groves such as the one we just entered and often prey on the weak. I hear tell they captured two farmers from this region. One lived to tell the tale of the torture he endured in the underworld."

I couldn't deny that something was off in the grove, and the screeches were creepy. Yet, numerous predatory bird species could have existed two thousand years ago. I doubted they had anything to do with a harpy or the underworld.

"Have you met the man who was abducted by the Harpuia?" I took another swig of water and returned it to him.

"No."

"Have you seen the creature?"

He shuddered. "From a distance."

The soldiers mounted their horses and resumed the journey. As Bear and I were yanked back and forth by the horse, I considered his words. More than likely, he saw a real vulture and let his imagination run away with him. The ancients were known for superstitions, and until now, I hadn't realized how this affected me. If I didn't figure out a way to escape, my captors might consider me a witch or sorcerer. No telling what kind of torture awaited if that happened.

"Are you well, girl?" Bear said.

I glared at him. "Ask me when I'm no longer tied behind a horse."

"You make a good point." He paused. "I see the judgment in your eyes. You think I'm a criminal. I tell you I am not! I have good reason for taking the noble."

"Was it worth sacrificing me?" I spat.

He nodded. "It was the only hope of saving my brother. He was taken prisoner by the Romans." Bear pointed at the former hostage, mounted at the front of our formation, riding tall with a purple chlamys draped over his shoulders. "They forced me to capture that turd in exchange for my brother's freedom. Now that I'm a prisoner, there's no predicting what will become of him."

"Perhaps you could've asked that 'turd' for help, instead of abducting—"

"He is highborn," Bear's voice dripped with venom. "He would no more have come to my aid than he did for you."

The former hostage must have felt my gaze boring in his back because he looked over his shoulder at us. Then, he turned away all dramatic, like it hurt to see me tied to the business end of a horse. Since the ancient nobles were identified by the houses for which they were born, I thought it best to start there. "From which house is he?"

Bear's lips parted. "You don't know?"

"No, how would I?"

The soldier on the horse in front of us hissed something in his native tongue. Probably shut up.

The horse jerked us forward as we headed toward a valley of farms. The sour scent of hay and manure wafted by my face. I scrunched my nose as we passed sheep grazing in the adjacent field. In the distance, impressive two-story homes constructed from tan stone served as unique landmarks on my mental map. Not that it would help. Even if I escaped, I had no clue how to navigate this ancient world.

"Where is your homeland?"

I blinked as Bear's voice pulled me from my thoughts. It wasn't like I could tell the truth. "Er, far across the sea," was the best I could do.

We ascended a hill that required all my concentration to keep from falling. When we reached the top, I inhaled shakily as Carthage came into my view. The ruins didn't touch the expansive city beneath me. Last year, Yia Yia and I flew to DC, for vacation. While in the air, I remember thinking how the city seemed to go forever. Looking at Carthage sprawled toward an aquamarine sea, with too many whitewashed and tan stucco buildings, temples, and monuments to count, it seemed just as expansive.

The first thing that jumped out at me was the massive stone wall surrounding the city. While I had a taste of it at the ruins, this one was more like pictures I'd seen of the Great Wall of China, at least eighty feet high and stretching for miles in either direction.

I tried to guess the purpose of each of the buildings. Since the two domed structures at the top of the hill were in the epicenter, they had to be temples. The semicircular complex carved into a mountain was an amphitheater. The stone fort at the highest point in the city, surrounded by another wall, most definitely a citadel where the citizens fled during an attack.

My body stiffened as reality set in. How could I escape from such a place? By the time we reached the entrance to the city, my legs were heavy as cement. Above us, a couple of guards in metal helmets stood at the edge of two turreted towers and wound a crank about the size of their upper body.

Clink, clink, clink, clink echoed through the air as the heavy wooden gate within the wall crept upward. I concentrated on the sound of my breaths to keep me calm as our troop moved through a short tunnel illuminated by wall torches. When we stopped at an arched entrance leading outside, a bunch of kids in dirty tunics took the horses. Then, one of our guards drew a short sword. He ushered Bear and me to a grassy area between the outer wall we had just walked through and another wall we'd yet to enter.

A high-pitched animalistic trumpeting sound echoed through the air.

When I looked in the direction of the sound, I almost passed out from shock. A real live Pleistocene Epoch, a freaking mammoth stood in the small courtyard. Except this animal was hairless, and at least as tall as a two-story house with tusks so thick and long, I wondered how the beast's head supported them. How was this possible? Mammoths went into extinction at least eight to ten thousand years ago. If they existed in ancient Carthage, I would have learned about them.

Our guards huddled together while pointing at the animals now led by bearded men in conical hats.

The graveness in their voices piqued my curiosity so I turned to Bear and asked, "What are they discussing?"

"They speak of impending war with the Republic of Rome."

My lips parted. Since elephants or in this case, mammoths were involved, he might have been talking about the second

Punic War. That happened somewhere around 218 BCE. If my calculations were correct, I'd been tossed back to a city that not only existed more than two thousand years before my birth but was on the verge of a second Punic War.

Captain Aharim's commanding voice snared my attention. My guard punched his chest in a salute. Then he pressed his short sword to Bear's back. I fought to keep my face even, despite the nausea welling in my stomach as we followed the captain and the former hostage through two more walls, each about fifty feet tall.

When we exited to a landing overlooking an expansive plaza, the sun had just begun to set, spraying the square below us in shades of magenta, orange, and yellow. Cobbled streets lined with swaying palms stretched toward miles of white and tan stucco buildings with flat roofs. The center of the square bustled with people. A life-size bronze elephant spewed water from a trunk that fell into a circular stone pool around its feet. Part of me was fascinated by the scene. Dad once said the Carthaginians had running water. However, the other part that dreaded what came next was drowning in a sea of fear.

"May the gods be with us," Bear said.

It wasn't in me to respond. I just stared down at the plaza, watching citizens bustle around us like they didn't have a care in the world. Some rode in horse-drawn carts with covered cargo. Women with crowns of braids, dressed in long, sleeveless gowns, chatted away. Children with sticks squealed with laughter and chased each other between the palms, oblivious to the guard holding a sword to my back.

The guy with a short sword tugged my rope, signaling Bear and me to move. A shuddering breath escaped me as I descended the wide stone stairs. The ancients must have had long legs because the drop was that of two steps from my time. When we walked onto the plaza, a team of soldiers on horseback approached from a cobbled path between several buildings to our right. Captain Aharim and the former hostage faced a man at the head of the group, wearing a black, plumed helmet. They punched their chests in a gesture of salute. The man wasn't much older than me, maybe mid to late twenties, with a strong jaw, lined by a shadow of black facial hair.

"Who is that man?" I asked.

Bear swallowed and his Adam's apple bobbed. "General Barca."

My mouth hung open. "Hannibal Barca?"

"Yes."

Hannibal was every bit the warrior I imagined, tall and powerfully built. The sculpted brass breastplate across his broad chest was armed with a dagger that could slice a man in two, could slice me in two.

Bear gave me a once-over. "Stand straight, girl. Face these men with dignity."

Throat dry, I nodded. "In the event we don't meet again, my name is Amara."

"It's been an honor, *Amara,*" Bear said.

Fear eddied inside me like a powerful tornado, threatening to suck me into the abyss at any second. General Barca dismounted and stalked toward us in a few lithe steps. He stood eye-to-eye with Bear and barked something in his native tongue.

Bear sneered as he responded. It didn't take a detective to figure out he told the general to piss off.

Short Sword Guard hit Bear on the back of the head with the butt of his sword, and he fought back hard.

I stifled a scream. My bladder threatened to loosen at any second.

Two other guards tackled Bear to the ground and sent me tumbling after them, still tied to Bear. I hit the pavers with a thud. Sharp pain shot down my spine.

A shadow fell over my face.

Hannibal stood above me. He blurred in and out of my vision. I kicked at his knees, but he just swatted my feeble foot aside and lunged at me with his dagger.

"Please, please—" I shrieked, cowering away.

He bent down and cut my bonds. Then, the great and powerful general extended his hand toward me, barking something in Punic.

A loud breath rushed from my lungs. I accepted the general's hand; thankful I hadn't peed myself as he gently helped me to my feet.

Poor Bear wasn't so lucky. Short Sword Guard and the others dragged my friend down the cobbled path on his back, screaming and kicking.

Hostage-guy joined Hannibal and spoke under his breath. The general nodded and asked me a question in ancient Greek.

I was shaking so badly it took a moment to process his words. Best I could tell, he was saying something about me coming to his nephew's rescue during the kidnapping. His nephew! Could he be *the nephew,* Adones? I should have made the connection the second Bear told me the general's identity.

"Did you hear me, girl?" Hannibal asked in a deep, rich voice.

I rubbed my eyes to clear my vision. "Y-yes."

"Uncle, she's innocent," said Hannibal's nephew.

Aharim stepped up and handed my cell to the general.

I swallowed back the bitter bile climbing to the back of my throat. How could I explain such a device?

Hannibal pressed the buttons on the side. Since my cell didn't turn on, I took it the battery had died. After a few seconds, he held it up and spoke slowly. "What. Sorcery. Is. This?"

Think quick before you end up like Bear or worse.

"Er, it was my father's. He, er, purchased it from foreign trader," I said, fighting a wince at how I mutilated the sentence.

Yet, I took pride in the way I'd pulled the story out of my hat. "I believe it was used to er, to navigate seas."

Hannibal's curly black hair shone almost blue beneath the fading sunlight. "A navigation device, eh? Why would your father allow a woman to use it?"

I scanned the ground as I translated his sentence and thought through my answer. "My father didn't know. I borrowed the device without his permission, hoping to learn how it operated. I never had the opportunity to use it."

Captain Aharim sneered at me and said something in Punic. Hannibal's nephew shook his head like he disagreed.

The general held up his hand, gesturing their silence. His dark brown eyes gave away no emotion as they swept over me. Then, without warning, he scrunched my T-shirt and rubbed his hand over my front thigh, feeling my jeans.

I was jolted by his rough and demanding touch.

"Calm yourself, girl. I've never seen such weaving."

"It's called, er ..." There wasn't a word for denim in ancient Greek, so I substituted the modern version, *"Tzin."*

"How odd." Hannibal crossed his arms over his massive chest, still assessing me like he was about to buy a farm animal. "The oddity of your garments and the navigation device is most concerning. My captain suspects you and the Numidian are spies for the Republic of Rome. What say you?"

After translating for a few seconds, I found my voice. "I understand your suspicions," I said slowly. "Yet, I'm no spy. I just met the Numidian on the beach, and these garments are common in my homeland."

The general's cheek twitched. "Where might home be?"

What could I say? My home is more than two thousand years in the future, and I was brought here by a glowing teleportation device. Can you help me get back there? I doubted he'd take it well. If I wanted to get out of this situation with my head, I had to lie again, and that was a slippery slope. Whatever I said here, needed to hold a kernel of truth so I'd remember if they interrogated me later. I held the general's gaze and spun my web.

"I come from a land far across the sea called the Americas." It wasn't like he knew they hadn't been discovered yet. "My father is Gree — a Spartan. During our journey to visit his family, we were separated when our carriage was raided." I tried to think of the word for kidnapper in ancient Greek and said, "Bandits carried me to their ship.

"After sailing for many days below deck with other prisoners, the ship hit rock. Fortunately, a crew member freed us, and we dove overboard. I must have fallen unconscious because I awoke on the beach where I met your nephew and the Numidian." I stood straight, despite my trembling body. Nothing like the threat of being enslaved or locked in a dungeon to improve my ability to lie with the ease of a con artist.

A long and uncomfortable silence passed before Hannibal finally said, "I believe you. The Romans may be cowards, yet they are too clever to send such a conspicuous girl to spy on us." He handed the captain my cell phone and spoke Punic.

With a brief salute, Captain Aharim retreated down the steps.

I blinked to hold back my tears as one of the only items from my time headed down a cobbled path toward a row of whitewashed buildings and faded into the sunset.

Hannibal returned his attention to me. Although his face remained an unreadable mask, his voice was calmer. "Allow me to repay the kindness you extended my nephew. Please, honor me by staying as a guest in my home until we decide how to reunite you with your father."

Good luck with that.

At this point, the little things mattered. I'd just been elevated from would-be slave to houseguest. This would give me a chance to scope out the city, see if I could find any hint of Sophie, Greg, or the artifact. I searched my nervous mind for the word thank you and settled on, "I'd be honored."

The general's nephew smiled. "Now that we've settled your accommodations, allow me to introduce myself." He bowed deeply. "I am Adones of House Barcid, and this is my uncle, General Hannibal Barca."

"Pleasure," I said, still trying to wrap my mind around the fact he was a live version of the dead guy in the tomb.

Hannibal crossed his arms over his chest. "From which house are you descended?"

"Er, I'm Amara, from House Kalogridas."

Adones extended his arm toward me. "Allow me to see you to my uncle's home, Amara of House Kalogridas?"

I pushed away images of the marble tomb, the bloody mural, and tucked my hand through the crook of his arm.

"I'll be along soon." Hannibal turned his back on us and returned to his horse.

We headed down a sloped street in silence. Surreal didn't begin to describe what I felt. For the second time today, I considered whether a rock from the cave-in had hit my head and caused a coma. Maybe my brain was making random connections from a hospital bed. Yet, if this were true, would I know I was in a coma? Everything from the salt-citrus air to the warmth of Adones' arm felt real. There was nothing dreamlike about the women who passed us with large clay pots on their heads or the men pushing squeaky wooden carts filled with melons.

Adones glanced down at me. "Apologies for the treatment you received earlier. The captain is wary of strangers."

That was putting it lightly. Now that I could think straight, I considered the word for thanks and came up with, "Gratitude for coming to my defense with your uncle."

"It was the least I could do after you stood up to that primitive." His voice was low and angry. "Not many women would have shown such courage."

"I'm sure you would have done the same for me." My thoughts turned to poor Bear, who undoubtedly was undergoing ten kinds of hell. If I asked Adones about him, he might have rethought my role in the kidnapping and imprisoned me, so I kept my concerns to myself.

"Perhaps," he said with a shrug. "I'm still honored my family can aid you during this uncertain time."

His comment made me question what to expect. Would I be the only girl in a house filled with soldiers? The Roman poet Silius Italicus had identified Hannibal's wife as Imilce. The age he had married remained a mystery. Guess it couldn't hurt to ask. "Is the lady of the house expecting me?"

"Yes," Adones said with a nod. "My uncle sent Captain Aharim to notify Lady Imilce."

I fought a grin. With little known about Carthage after its destruction, I was pleased to learn that this small piece of history was correct. "I look forward to meeting her."

The corners of Adones' mouth curled upward, revealing slightly crooked front teeth. "I think you'll find her quite charming."

Usually, someone with his teeth would have been ridiculed in my time. Yet, the flaw balanced Adones' strong jaw and lashes that went for days. I opened my mouth to ask whether I'd meet his parents and closed it when I remembered how his grave marker had mentioned that he was Hannibal's adopted son.

As we continued down the cobbled path, I took in the way several small stones had been cut into pieces and cemented together to make each paver — how flowering vines crept up the three-story buildings and wrapped around crowded terraces, illuminated by bronze wall braziers.

"Carthage is beautiful," I said.

"Indeed. It is the greatest city in the world."

I smiled and nodded. Trying to translate a response was exhausting.

Still, I could see why Adones was proud. His people certainly seemed happy enough. On the terraces above us, elegant women garbed in sleeveless tunics watched us. Some held children, others held silver goblets. The men wore knee-length tunics and sandals that tied up their shins. I tugged at my ponytail and smoothed my T-shirt. Compared to the terrace people, I must have looked like the ancient version of a homeless person. When I noticed Adones watching me, I tucked my hands into my front pockets to keep from fidgeting.

"Don't fret about your appearance. Carthage is a trading city filled with people from many cultures."

We turned a curve and walked down a hill facing a lake. The water shined silver beneath the crescent moon. Although beautiful, the smell of rotten fish hit me square in the face.

I cleared my throat, which didn't get the taste out of my mouth. "What's that horrible smell?"

Adones pointed toward a square building with a flat roof at the bottom of the hill. "There, where the cistern glows, is where they crush murex shells to create the purple dye of the Tyrians."

"How interesting." I fought past the tightness in my throat as I wondered what Dad, Greg, and Sophie would think about this. God, I hoped they were okay.

"This is the only place in the world that has this dye," he said in a voice booming with pride. "Royals and nobles from far and near desire our fabrics and they're sold at the agora."

"I'm sure they're beautiful."

After seeing Adones' cloak, I already knew they were. Not to mention that Dad once told me the Phoenicians were known as the Purple People because of their dyes.

We came to a tall wooden gate protected by a guard who snapped to attention as Adones and I strode by.

"Just a bit further past the gardens," he said.

I responded with a smile, pushing down the stew of nerves bubbling in my stomach as we proceeded down a path lined with bronze braziers that opened to a stately mansion. At least three stories, the white stucco home boasted rows of arched windows. A welcoming porch with fluted columns about forty feet high were wrapped in flowering creepers. Two winged lions served as decorative braziers that illuminated the base of cascading marble steps. When we ascended to the double entrance doors at the top of the landing, Adones faced me.

"Welcome to my home."

He beamed as we stepped into a wide chamber tiled in royal blue mosaics. A gold chandelier, illuminated by candles made from beeswax, burned overhead. At least that seemed the most plausible assumption judging by the honey scent in the air. Lush plants in clay pots with white, purple, and red blooms decorated every corner.

A thin girl, who could've passed for a high school first or second year, greeted us. Her age, combined with her long, undyed cotton skirt and short-sleeved tunic, told me she wasn't Hannibal's wife. She studied me through eyes the color of walnuts. When she noticed me staring, I averted my gaze. She rambled to Adones in her language while I continued bearing all the weight from the horrors of the day, hoping I wouldn't break at any second and spiral into an abyss of tears.

Finally, Adones turned to me and said, "Elissa just informed me that Lady Imilce sends her apologies for failing to welcome you. She is unwell and has taken to her bed. Elissa will show you to your quarters." He took my hand into his and kissed the top.

I resisted the urge to pull away at my first exposure to misogynistic chivalry.

"We break-fast at sunrise tomorrow. I hope you'll join us."

"Of course." It wasn't like I could refuse without insulting him.

"Until then." With a quick bow, Adones took off down the foyer, leaving Elissa and I alone.

There was a mischievousness in her stare. "Welcome, mistress," she said in ancient Greek. Adones must have told her I spoke the language. "You're the first guest in my charge."

I bristled. At Elissa's age, I had attended school, studied ancient Greek and Latin. Disney World and Dad's digs were sprinkled into my summers. Here, this girl's only opportunity was to serve a guest on her own. This wasn't much of a life. I wanted to grab her hand and run, but how could I help her when I couldn't even help myself?

"Please, follow me, mistress."

If Elissa's situation got to her, she didn't show it. She flounced down the wide foyer like a sprite and practically glided up wide spiral stairs. We stepped onto a landing, and I followed her down a narrow hall blanketed in soft candlelight cast from two metal chandeliers.

Her smile widened as she opened a wooden door and ushered me inside. "This is our most spacious guest room."

Compared to the dungeon I could have landed in, this was heaven. A small, shuttered window bathed the room in moonlight. The twin bed was suspended on a wooden sleigh frame. Firelight in a clay oil lamp on the night table danced over red throw pillows and a matching coverlet. A dressing table with a shined brass mirror framed in wood sat along the far wall. Despite these comforts, it wasn't home.

"If it pleases you, I can bring some night robes."

I shifted my weight from one leg to the other. "No, I wish to be left alone."

Without warning, Elissa reached out and touched my T-shirt.

I flinched. Clearly, the ancients didn't believe in personal space.

She retreated a step or two. "Apologies, mistress. I meant no disrespect."

I clenched my teeth. No way I'd ever get used to that title. "Please, call me Amara."

"Yes, mistress, Amara."

I looked up at the plastered ceiling. This was hopeless.

Elissa pointed to a tray on the night table containing a wooden pitcher and cup, along with a small basket. "There's wine and food."

My stomach grumbled as it occurred to me that several hours had passed since my last meal. "Gratitude."

"Are you in need of anything more?"

I shook my head.

Her shoulders slumped. "Very well. I'll return tomorrow." With a curtsy, she slipped out and closed the door behind her.

The moment I heard Elissa pad down the hall, I made a beeline for the basket and unfolded the wrapping. Salivating like one of Pavlov's dogs, I shoved some grapes into my mouth, aware of the sweet and sour splash of juice on my tongue. The bread and olives were great too. I guzzled the wine water, wincing afterward. The ancient Carthaginians often mixed the two due to a lack of rain and it was gross. This also triggered thoughts of Dad.

A large knot clogged my throat, and I fell onto the lumpy mattress and curled into a ball. I missed Sober-Dad. Since he had gone for help, he was probably okay, at least physically. Emotionally, he was so, so alone. Knowing Dad, he had drunk himself into oblivion after thinking he'd lost two children in a cave-in. Why didn't I tell him that I loved him when I had the chance?

I hugged the pillow against my chest and curled into a tighter ball, hating the helplessness of my situation. I had no clue how to get home, or what had become of Greg and Sophie. They had to be okay, just had to. Poor Bear was probably being tortured and there was nothing I could do to help him. I was truly alone and at the mercy of strangers.

My eyelids burned as all the sorrow and pain of the day rushed to the surface, collapsing my dam of control. Tears ran down cheeks, and I pressed my face to the mattress and screamed into it until my throat burned, until I no longer had anything left. Then icy cold resolve crept in. I weakly sat up and dried my cheeks with the back of my hand. Somehow, some way, I would return home.

Chapter Seven

A light rapping sound stirred me from sleep. I bolted upright in bed, fully clothed. My heart drummed in my chest as I stared at the door. Another rap followed.

"Mistress, Amara, it's me, Elissa."

I rubbed my eyes, still puffy from last night's meltdown and said, "Enter."

Elissa stepped inside, grinning. "Good day, mistress." Even her voice was bubbly.

"Good day," I responded, still groggy.

"I've come to assist you with a bath before you break-fast with the family."

My brow creased. "Assist?"

"Yes." She gestured toward the door.

Although I wanted to protest the whole shadow while I bathed gig, I also knew that the onion smell in the room hadn't flowed in from the kitchen and was likely coming off of me. If I showed for breakfast this ripe, there was no telling what the Barcids would think.

With a reluctant nod, I followed Elissa down the stairs through a wide corridor to a chamber about the size of a college TV room. Only, this space was filled with sunlight flowing in from double doors that opened to a garden, humming with birds. Elissa gestured toward a rectangular tub in the far corner of the space.

"I hope the water is warm enough."

I sat on the flat cement lip and wiggled my fingers over the flower petals, scenting the bath with hints of jasmine or lavender. "It's perfect."

Pride glistened in Elissa's brown eyes as she plucked two glass vials and a long, flat rectangular blade from her apron pocket. "You will love the scent of these oils I've—"

I shot out of my seat, and quickly regrouped. I remembered how the ancients rubbed oil over their bodies then scraped it off with a razor before bathing. "Appreciate your help, but I can bathe myself." Anything that involved sharp objects was a no-go.

Her shoulders slumped. "Lady Barca will be most displeased if I fail my duties."

Duties. The word ignited a slow burn in the pit of my stomach. How a grown woman could use a kid like this was immoral and heartless, regardless of cultural norms. Being cordial to the *lady of the house* would take some effort.

I shot Elissa a smile that was hanging for dear life and said, "You've been accommodating, it's just that I'm very private and would prefer to bathe myself."

She stood straighter and nodded. "If it pleases you, I'll fetch your headdress while you bathe."

"Yes, that would be wonderful."

The moment she headed out the door, I peeled my clothes off and sat in the tub, groaning with delight as the warm water soothed my sore muscles. That is until guilt seeped in. It was tough to relax when Bear was probably suffering unimaginable pain at the hands of his captors. Although I didn't have many options for myself, maybe I could convince Adones to drop the charges once we became better acquainted. He might show mercy once he learned the reason that Bear had abducted him.

I had just finished my bath and dried off with a long cotton cloth when footsteps resounded behind me. I wheeled around and found Elissa in the doorway, breathing hard, wiping beads of sweat from her brow. Did she sprint here?

She set the veil next to a bunch of fabrics on a wooden bench adjacent to the tub. "I'll help you dress."

Something about wearing clothes from this century made my situation feel more permanent. Despite this, I stood straight and allowed Elissa to do her job. She was professional, holding my gaze, while providing instructions about how to don an outfit made from nothing more than a long piece of green cotton fabric.

The garment turned out to be what could best be described as an empire dress that flowed past my knees, and the sash tied just below my breasts. Not that I needed the support since I was built like a small boy. Next, she brought out a flowing wrap or robe, edged in black beads, and draped it over my shoulders, completely covering my arms.

Elissa eyed my pile of clothes on the floor. "I noticed how different your garments are to these. Is this how all women in your homeland dress?"

"Yes, but some wear gowns."

Her brow shot up. "Interesting. Where is your homeland?"

This was the one question I wanted to avoid. "Er, it's across the sea." I pointed at a thin gold headband on the bench. "Is that for me?"

Elissa's mouth curled into a wide smile. "Indeed." She slid the band over the top of my head, like a crown.

Dangly black beads tickled my forehead whenever I moved. She finished off my look with a pair of Greek-inspired sandals that laced up my calves. They weren't as comfortable as my boots. If I wanted to fit in while figuring out my surroundings, I had to dress like everyone else.

Elissa took my hand. "It's time."

My legs shook as I followed her down a corridor opposite from where we entered the bathing chamber. What if this ancient family associated my differences with witchcraft? If they asked too many questions about my past, my story might fall apart, and they'd think I was a spy. This was insane.

When we entered a high-ceilinged hall, light streamed in through arched doorways, leading to a terrace overlooking a sea of flat stucco rooftops. Hannibal, Adones, and a woman with long black hair were already seated before a wooden table. Plates of grapes, cheeses, and flat breads were displayed across the top.

Hannibal's cheek was latticed with scars as he quirked a smile. "Elissa, who is this beauty? She can't be the same girl I met last night."

My gaze gravitated to the sword sheathed on the table beside him. Although he was one of history's greatest generals, it seemed overkill to have a weapon laid across the table while dining with family.

Elissa grinned.

The woman started to rise, and a man, standing at attention against the wall, ran over and helped her to her feet.

The woman was very pregnant, like stomach the size of a yoga ball pregnant. Yet, she glided toward me with the elegance of a queen and greeted me with her arms outstretched.

"So nice to make your acquaintance, Amara. I'm Hannibal's wife, Imilce. Welcome to my home."

I didn't expect her to be so approachable. "The pleasure is all mine."

Imilce gestured toward the seat between Hannibal and Adones. "Please join us?"

Adones smiled at me when I sat beside him on a wooden chair. His white tunic was a stunning contrast against his wavy black hair and tanned skin. I still hadn't wrapped my mind around the all too real fact that I was sitting beside a dead man.

"Amara, my nephew boasted about how you risked your safety to aid him during that terrible abduction," said Imilce. The fine lines around her eyes and mouth were the only clues she was older than me.

"I'm not sure that's correct, but it's kind of him to say."

Hannibal angled his head toward Adones. "My nephew seldom gives praise to anyone. He must think highly of you."

"Few women would have put themselves at risk as she did," said Adones.

Elissa set an empty plate and a cup filled with red liquid in front of me.

"Please, eat. We have food aplenty." Imilce pointed at my wooden cup. "Our cook prepared the pomegranate juice this morning."

Imilce plucked a grape from her bowl and ate, signaling everyone else to follow suit. Starving, I stuffed a bunch of fruit and cheese in my mouth. When I looked up, Adones was watching me, so I slowed my chewing.

Imilce tilted her chin toward Hannibal. "My husband tells me you're from Sparta. Yes?"

I shook my head and finished swallowing my food. "No, I'm from the Americas. My father's family is from Sparta."

"Hannibal told me about your abduction. That must have been awful." Imilce took a bite of her cheese.

"It was. I'm worried about my fath—" I gasped, trying to hold back a sob.

"Dear girl. What you must be going through."

"It hasn't been easy," I said, trying to keep the emotion from my voice. "I hope to return to him soon."

"Tell me once more the events that led to your attack in Sparta," Hannibal said. The room was deadly quiet. Too quiet. As if noticing the change in everyone's mood, he added, "I merely seek to gather the facts, to aid me in reuniting you with your father."

I'd watched enough detective series to pick up on a subtle interrogation. He hoped to trip me up. "It is as I said, my father employed a carriage to transport us to Sparta. He had been ill and wanted to, er, be closer to family. While traveling along an isolated path, we were raided and—"

"Yes, yes, and you were abducted," Hannibal said with a flourish of the hand. "What of your father? Surely, he didn't stand idly by while those brigands stole away with his daughter."

"My father was unconscious. Even if that weren't the case, he was no match for a sword."

Hannibal crossed his arms and studied me so intently my throat went dry. I'd never make a good spy.

"And what of your father's charioteer? Did he allow bandits to steal off with his cargo?"

"Enough, Hannibal. You're treating this poor girl as if she were a criminal," said Imilce.

"I agree. She's survived much," said Adones. "Though, I do wonder how we'll locate your father. Are you certain he continued his journey?"

I didn't know how to answer. My underarms were drenched. Perspiration pebbled across my brow. I fought the urge to wipe it. No need to draw attention to my nervousness. I only had one hope of getting out of this and that meant playing the scared female card, which I hated doing. Navigating a society that viewed women as the *weaker* sex was not only infuriating, but demeaning.

My throat tightened as I spun another lie, praying my answer was convincing. "I hope my father is with family in Sparta, that he's getting the medical atten—" The truth of my words hit me hard. I turned away. "Forgive me."

Why didn't I tell him that I loved him when I had the chance?

"There's nothing to forgive. I can't imagine how difficult this is." Imilce waggled a finger at Hannibal. "You will cease with the inquiries. Amara is our guest, and we'll make her feel welcome."

Hannibal nodded like a little kid who'd just been scolded by his mom. Weird how a warrior responsible for mercilessly murdering thousands of Romans in battle could be shut down by his wife and a crying woman. He returned his attention to me.

"Apologies if I made you uncomfortable. You've been through a great ordeal. For this reason, I've decided to have you escorted to Sparta and reunited with your father. I'll ensure arrangements are made before Adones and I depart for Saguntum."

I sipped the pomegranate juice to moisten my dry throat. "When will this take place?"

"In a fortnight." Hannibal gave Imilce's hand a gentle squeeze. "After our son's birth."

"Or our daughter," she said.

Two weeks?

I nodded. "That would be wonderful."

If Hannibal's guards escorted me to Sparta, it'd be game over. Check and mate. They'd know I lied about everything when they learned I had no family there. I needed to figure out a plan between now and then.

"Let's eat our meal in peace now," said Imilce.

Just as Hannibal kissed his wife's forehead, his polished sword blade, protruding a few inches from the sheath, caught the sunlight from the terrace.

The sword in the tomb was forged from bronze and had turned a greenish color. Yet this one shined like glass and had strange markings down the blade. When I leaned closer to get a better look, Hannibal shoved his sword into the sheath. I flinched as he regarded me dubiously. Imilce stared at her plate. Adones stiffened beside me.

What was up with them? "A-apologies, I was merely admiring your blade. It — it's unique."

"Indeed, it is." Hannibal said in a deadpan voice.

I waited for an explanation. Instead, he sat forward and winced while plucking a piece of bread from the plate.

Imilce cleared her throat and shot her husband a tense smile. "Take care, my love. Your shoulder wound is still fresh."

He placed his hand over hers. "You worry too much."

"Must you return to Saguntum so soon?" Imilce asked with a slight pout. "You were nearly killed there. It's through Ba'al's mercy you were spared."

"There's no need for concern. It's but a flesh wound from a small skirmish," Hannibal said.

Adones elbowed me and I dragged my gaze away from the sheathed sword. "My uncle is too humble. He led our forces against the Roman city of Saguntum and killed many enemies." He paused long enough to pop an olive in his mouth. "This should have been enough to hail him as a hero. Yet, he didn't stop there. He shared the booty from the invasion with our citizens. Today, the city celebrates his victory and his generosity."

Adones' zeal sent chills down my body. Especially since the battle of Saguntum was the inciting incident that led Carthage to war with Rome. This, in turn, caused Hannibal to march over the Alps in winter to take the battle to his enemy on their soil, which resulted in the battle of Cannae. Poor Adones didn't have much longer to live.

Hannibal curled his calloused hand into a fist. "I don't go to war for glory or riches, nephew. I fight to defend our way of life."

Imilce's voice was filled with pride. "The reason matters not, husband. You're receiving the glory regardless."

Hannibal relaxed his fist and gazed at his wife. "Now that the healer said you can move freely about, will you attend the festivities? I need you by my side."

She reached over and caressed Hannibal's cheek. "I wouldn't miss it for all the gold in Carthage's coffers. Viewing Sophocles' greatest tragedy will be an added benefit as well."

"Indeed," Hannibal pressed his lips together.

"Will you attend the celebration with us?" Imilce asked.

"You must," Adones said. "The city spared no expense. Athenian actors are performing, and the play will rival those in their country."

Although an ancient play and a mass celebration would be awesome, this could also give me a lay of Carthage in case I needed to escape, so I nodded and said, "Of course, I'd be honored to see such a great city."

A smile played on Adones' mouth. "I have some time this morning if you'd like to see this section of Carthage. Unless you're overtired from yesterday's ordeal."

I sat straighter. "Yes, that would be ... er delightful."

A frown flickered across Imilce's face. "Should I invite Aurelia? She and Amara would get along splendidly."

Adones' smile faded. "No. Sending for her will eat into our time."

"I see." Imilce studied Adones for a long moment before turning her attention to me. "Aurelia is attending the theatre with us this evening. She is—"

Adones shoved his chair back, and the legs scraped against the mosaic tiles. "We should be on our way before the heat becomes unbearable."

I nodded and rose from my seat.

Hannibal leaned forward, surveying Adones. "Take care, nephew. Return in time to dress for the festival."

"Of course." Adones' voice was swallowed up by the sudden silence.

As he and I left the room together, the back of my neck tingled. Something told me Imilce was shooting daggers at us with her eyes.

Chapter Eight

Adones led me down a corridor covered by a domed ceiling frescoed in laurel leaves. The whole time, I fought the urge to ask about Aurelia. I didn't want to come off as nosy, even though I totally was.

The corridor soon opened to a kitchen fragrant with cinnamon, rosemary, and garlic. Although the space didn't have appliances, the layout wasn't much different than kitchens from my time. In the center of the room, a tall butcher block counter was set before cubby wall cabinets. Water trickled from a trough-like spigot in the wall and puddled in a shallow pool near the arched doorway leading to the courtyard. It was amazing that the ancients had indoor plumbing. Yet, many countries, including my own, took their time incorporating this into homes. This may have been attributed to a fear of sickness in colder climates, or they may have lacked the resources.

"Adones!" An older woman with curly white hair and leathery skin called out. She pushed some dough aside and hobbled around the counter.

He hugged her tightly, then gestured toward me. "This is our guest," Adones said in ancient Greek. "Amara of House Kalogridas, this is Melania. She's the greatest baker in all of Carthage."

Melania's paper-thin lips curled into a smile as she waggled an index finger at Adones, scolding in a thick ancient Greek accent, "You'll not flatter treats from me."

I stared at the dirt beneath her nails and fought the urge to grimace. Had I eaten food prepared by those hands?

Adones kissed the old woman on the forehead. The gesture seemed out of character for someone so formal. "What of our guest? Don't deprive her of your delicacies."

"No," I blurted, concerned about the germs. When I noticed Melania staring, I added, "Please, don't trouble yourself."

Her toothless smile widened. "No trouble."

Great, Hep-A here I come.

Melania hobbled a few feet to a counter on the adjacent wall, plucked a couple of sticky square desserts sprinkled with nuts from a platter and handed me one. She passed the other to Adones, saying, "Who can resist such a handsome face."

"Eat," she said, shooting me a hopeful stare.

I pushed back the mental image of her filthy nails and concentrated on the treat. It was like baklava, made with honey and nuts, except dates had been added and the dough was thicker than phyllo, more like a pie crust. Before I talked myself out of it, I chomped down on the pastry.

She let out a hearty laugh. "You like?"

"Mmmhmm," I said, taking another bite and concentrating on the sweet blend of honey combined with the chewy dates and crunchy nuts.

She wiped her hands on her apron and shooed us toward the doorway. "Now, off with you, before you eat the rest of this night's desserts."

Adones chuckled and escorted me to a courtyard off the kitchen bathed in sunlight and bordered by an open-air shelter supported by wooden columns. Inside, a girl shoved a bronze pan dotted with loaves of dough into a stone oven.

If I didn't figure out how to get home within the next two weeks, I'd have to go it alone rather than let Hannibal take me to Sparta. With so many servants around, my escape needed to happen at night. I scrunched my nose at the fishy smell as we headed down a sloped path overlooking the city. Seeing Carthage in all its glory sent a pang of sadness and anger through me. The ruins that remained didn't touch what had been destroyed by the Romans. Miles of flat-roofed buildings and monuments built from marble seemed endless to the eye against a backdrop of aquamarine waters.

Where would I begin to look for a way home?

"Melania likes to fuss over me," Adones said.

I pulled my gaze away from the ancient city. "Ye-yes, she was very nice." And probably worn out, having to stand on her bad leg all day cooking in that hot kitchen.

"Is something amiss?" Adones asked, studying me intensely.

Dad's warning came to mind. *"Your impetuousness will be your downfall."* I bit my bottom lip to hold back my retort and said instead, "No, I'm merely enjoying the views."

Adones pointed ahead toward a covered walkway, bustling with people. "That's the Agora. Do you have one in your homeland?"

I couldn't tell him about shopping malls. Making something up might lead to more questions. I just shook my head and said, "No, nothing like this."

And that was an understatement. We passed through a rectangular gate at least seventy feet high, with two archways and fluted columns standing on tall pedestals. Sculptures of soldiers wielding swords and others with bows and arrows were carved into the top.

Inside the market, we continued down a roofed walkway, flanked by tall columns. The aroma of smoke and spices filled the air as we passed rows of stands built from wood. Adones and I navigated several shoppers perusing a display filled with bright red and purple fabrics. Judging by the cleanliness of the people's robes — the ornate gold bracelets on the women's arms — their bejeweled fingers — this must have been the ancient version of Fifth Avenue.

We walked by musicians singing for the crowds. A cobbler bartered with a woman and her servant over a pair of leather sandals.

"This place, is..."

"Impressive?" Adones said. "Only the best goods are sold here."

"Are there other Agoras within the city?" I asked.

He nodded. "Yes. Though many frequent the market beyond the walls where vendors from all over the world sell their goods."

"That sounds interesting."

"Interesting, no. Dangerous, yes," Adones said in a clipped voice. "The place attracts barbaric people like that Numidian bastard."

"Were you abducted at the outside market?" I blurted, silently face punching myself the second the question left my mouth.

Adones stopped mid-step. "Yes."

"I — I didn't mean to pry."

He raked a hand through his dark waves and sighed. "I know. You offered hope during a dark time, and you deserve to know what happened." He had a far-off stare as he continued. "One of my uncle's soldiers reported that a Roman spy would be contacting a citizen at the market outside the walls. Caught up in the thought of glory, I went alone. The Numidian was waiting, and he ambushed me from behind. The rest, you know."

"What happened to the soldier who betrayed you?" I asked.

Adones' jaw tightened. "We're still searching for him. Ba'al Hammon himself will not prevent my uncle's retribution when he finds that traitorous turd."

The blood rushed from my face. What were his plans for Bear? Was there any hope for him? "Has the Numidian been sentenced yet?"

"No, the Sufet is otherwise engaged with the Senate. Once the business there is settled, the trial will commence. Hopefully he'll be sentenced to death."

My stomach churned. "Where is the Numidian now?"

Adones rubbed his hands over his face. "Can we discuss something more pleasant? I wish to enjoy our day."

I nodded. Pushing the subject might piss off Adones. I'd have to wait for another opportunity to speak on Bear's behalf.

I turned my attention to a weaver's shop and focused on the rich tapestries hanging throughout the structure. Some were crafted in lifelike images of mammoths. Another had a centaur with the body of a horse and the head of a man armed with a bow and arrow.

"This art is beautiful. I can't imagine the time it takes to weave just one rug?"

Adones shrugged his broad shoulders. "Carthage has a multitude of talented artists. We have prominent art districts, and one of the largest theatres in the world. These rugs and tapestries are a small taste of what my city has to offer."

A few feet away, a tailor draped in tan robes sat before a large rectangular loom weaving colorful threads through it. She stopped and stood up. A wide smile graced her face when she spotted Adones.

He turned away from the gray-haired woman and leaned in, whispering, "Come, before she tries to sell me more rugs."

His warm breaths tickled my ear, sending a pleasant shiver down my back, which was strange since he was a skeleton in my time.

"I filled her coffers when last I toured her shop with ... we should leave before she makes me a pauper."

I laced my hand through the crook of Adones' arm. "How gracious of you to support the local vendors."

"I've done my part." He led me past other stands selling marble statues of elephants and tigers. When I spotted a small jewelry dealer, I had to check it out. A man wearing a white turban stood before a table. Beaded silver necklaces and golden bracelets formed in the likeness of snakes and laurel leaves were displayed across the top.

I moved to the wooden box filled with rings and tried one with gold flower petals, admiring how the jewel in the middle shimmered to blood red.

"Beautiful choice," said the vendor.

"Indeed. It's unique as you are," Adones said with a wolfish grin.

My heart fluttered and I quickly removed the ring. Just as I returned it to the box, a silver piece caught my eye. There was something familiar about it. I bent forward to get a closer look. My knees nearly buckled when I saw the sword emblem and the graduation year etched into the side of the ring.

I yanked it from the holder. "This is Greg's ring."

Adones frowned. "Greg?"

I took a deep breath to keep from losing it. "He is my brother. I was separated from Greg and his partner, er, when the ship sank. I thought they were lost to me until now." I held the ring in front of the vendor, trying to keep the emotion out of my voice as I spoke. "This is my brother's ring. He never removed it. Where did you purchase these items?"

He shrugged his thin shoulders. "From an elderly nomadic man. He sold me the entire box of jewels, along with this." He pulled up his sleeve, revealing a gold bracelet with dangling hearts.

Clenching my teeth so hard they could have broken, I yanked the vendor's wrist toward me. "This is Sophie's bracelet."

Since this man had both their items, Greg and Sophie had to be together but *where* were they?

"Unhand me!" said the man, twisting beneath my grip.

"Amara, have you gone mad?" Adones peeled my fingers from the man's wrist.

I took back my hand. Panic and dread roiled inside me as I asked, "Where's the person who sold you these?"

The vendor backed away. "I don't know. I bought the items outside the city. The man's a nomad. It's possible he boarded a ship or is roaming the desert."

"Did the nomad say where he found these items?" My voice was shrill even in my ears. I regrouped before speaking again. "Please, I must find my brother and his partner. Any information will help."

The vendor shook his head. "I know nothing else. The man merely sold me the pieces. I asked no questions, and he gave no explanation."

Dread roiled in my chest. Did the nomad kill them and steal their jewelry?

"If you don't plan to purchase that ring, madam, kindly return it," said the man.

"How much for both pieces?" Adones asked.

I tightened my grip on the ring and clutched it to my chest. "No. I can't allow you to do this."

Adones' gaze roamed to my hand, staring at how white my knuckles were from gripping the ring. "These items hold strong meaning for you. Please, allow me this small gesture if it brings you peace."

"This is only a loan." My voice cracked and I swallowed hard. "I'll repay you, somehow."

Adones stared at me as though considering how to respond. "If you insist."

I gave a thin smile. "I do."

"Only the ring is for sale," the man said. "I'm keeping the bracelet."

"No, you'll sell both pieces, or I'll inform my uncle, General Hannibal Barca, that you're selling stolen goods in his city."

The man's mouth had fallen open. "How could I have known the items—"

"Don't act surprised," I said. "You purchased a box filled with expensive jewelry from a nomad. Surely you aren't stupid enough to think he came by the items honestly."

"I will only ask you once, the price for the bracelet and ring?" Adones voice was low and measured.

The vendor removed the bracelet and rubbed his wrist a moment before answering. "Five talents."

"You'll take two," Adones reached inside the purse on his belt and placed two silver coins on the table in front of the vendor.

The creases around the man's mouth deepened as he handed me the bracelet. "I wouldn't hold much hope for your friends. Nomads only take jewelry from dead men."

My stomach plunged. Yet, I wasn't about to let that asshole see my fear. I dipped my chin and leaned across the table. "Your deal was with Adones. This doesn't mean I can't report you to General Barca. After he impales you, the nomads will be selling *your* jewels." Before he could respond, I turned on my heel and shoved past the crowd.

Adones called after me. I just kept putting as much distance between me and the vendor as possible. At the end of the stands, I slipped Greg's ring on my shaky middle finger, then slid Sophie's bracelet over my wrist. Neither of them would have given up the pieces unless…

Adones caught up and wheeled me toward him. "Pay that man no mind. If you made it this far, there's hope for your brother and his partner. Don't give up on them. The gods have good reason for bringing you here."

I sighed. "Perhaps you're right."

Yia Yia always said that life was worthless without hope. I had to believe Greg and Sophie were okay. They were both wicked smart, and together, they made an unstoppable team. Maybe they sold the jewelry to get enough money to survive.

Adones extended the crook of his arm toward me again, and I accepted it. "I can't imagine how difficult this must be for you."

I nodded, too worried to speak.

"Would you like to return home to, er, take some time for yourself?"

"Yes, that would be best." My voice was a rasp.

When we came to a cobbled plaza, Adones pointed toward a structure with a stone façade and two stories of marble columns, one stacked on top of the other. "That library holds special meaning to my family."

I did a double take, momentarily distracted from my grief and fear. "A library?" Perhaps it contained a book that provided clues about the disc that had brought me here. "Does it have Greek texts?"

A breeze ruffled Adones' black curls and he swept them away from his face. "I see no reason why it wouldn't. Perhaps we can visit one day."

I cleared my throat. "No, no, I'd like to see your library this day."

"You don't wish to return home?"

"Not now." Then, I remembered how literacy was rare during this period, and I added, "My father is a scholar. He has taught me the written word from the time I took my first steps until we were separated. I would love to see what your library offers."

Adones mouth opened. "First you come to my rescue against that barbarian. Now, I learn you read like a scholar."

Heat flooded my cheeks. "Not like a *scholar*."

With a slight bow, Adones waved dramatically toward a three-story building across the plaza. "Shall we have a look?"

"Yes, please." Optimism spread across my chest. About halfway across the crowded square, a reedy melody rose and fell from somewhere nearby, each note swelled higher than the last. When I glanced in the direction of the sound, I nearly fell over. What I saw shouldn't have existed in ancient Carthage.

Chapter Nine

Not more than ten feet away, a lion with golden wings tucked along its back and paws with bird-like talons lay stretched out beside a man playing a flute.

I shot Adones a questioning look. "That lion must be a fake."

He chuckled. "My uncle's sheep might debate that."

"Winged lions exist?"

Adones' brow furrowed. "It's a Shadu. Have you never seen one?"

I shook my head and grabbed Adones' hand. His callouses rubbed against my palm as I navigated the crowd and led him toward the lion, Shadu, or whatever it was called.

Up close, the creature's feathered wings sparkled like gold glitter beneath the sun and its white mane of fur was bright as snow. I released Adones' hand and inched even closer to the animal, awed by its massive body and razor-sharp talons. Despite the fact it could rip a man apart, the animal had no chains. Not even a collar. It just lay there; slumbering like it didn't have a care in the world.

The chase in the orchard with the weird olive trees pushed to the front of my mind. The harpy must have been real too. Not to mention the mammoths and now the Shadu. None of these should have existed here.

"These animals are quite intelligent and difficult to tame." Adones held up a forefinger. "Though once one bonds with a man, it forever serves one master."

Something wet and rough ran across my hand. When I looked down, my blood froze. The animal was licking my fingers. I bit my cheek to keep from screaming.

"Don't make any sudden moves," Adones said under his breath.

The musician stopped playing mid-melody and spoke to the Shadu in a calm voice. The animal bowed its head and lay down, watching me through yellow eyes. I'd read somewhere that animals could smell fear. Slowly, I stepped back, hoping my racing heart and sweaty palms didn't give me away. Once I put some distance between us, the musician turned his attention to me and spoke. Adones said something in Punic. Then the man switched to ancient Greek.

"Never has my Shadu connected with another human," the musician said. "You must be unique indeed."

Murmurs rippled among the crowd. Adones stared at me. His face was unreadable.

"I — I don't know what you mean."

Without taking his gaze from me, the musician set the bronze flute on the lip of the fountain and unfurled his fingers. Twin tattoos of an eye were on each of his palms. "My name is Vicram. I come from a long line of mystics, which is the reason I was chosen by the Shadu. You, on the other hand, are a mystery."

I shrugged nonchalantly, but internally, my nerves were firing on all cylinders. I got the sense he knew more about me than he was letting on. "I — I ate a treat earlier. The Shadu could be attracted to the honey on my fingers."

Vicram rubbed his pointed beard. "That's never happe—"

A masculine voice yelled something from behind me.

"This spectacle is about to end," Adones said.

A soldier stalked toward the musician, speaking in harsh tones.

The Shadu bared long fangs as it stood on all fours and sent a mighty roar echoing through the air. The surrounding onlookers scattered toward the market. Adones gripped my arm and we slowly backed away from the animal.

The soldier unsheathed his sword.

"What's happening?"

"He wants the musician to leave," Adones said. "Wild animals aren't allowed here."

Vicram waved off the soldier. He collected his coins from a basket and climbed on the giant animal's back, still studying me. My jaw went slack as the Shadu's wings unfurled in a golden mass of feathers, spanning at least twenty feet wide, and flew toward the sky in a streak of white.

Adones took my hand into his, pulling me from my stupor. "The more I'm around you in all your beauty and intellect, the more you pique my curiosity."

I coolly inched my hand from his. "Do those charms work on all your girls?"

"You find me charming?" Adones full lips curled into a sly smirk.

I rolled my eyes. "You're impossible." On some small level, it helped to think about anything other than Greg and Sophie, harpies, and Shadus, if even for a second.

With a hearty laugh, Adones waved me toward the library. We climbed several wide marble steps leading to a set of wooden-studded doors. He opened one with a loud creak. "After you."

Inside, the place was like a museum. To the right of the entry, a wall fresco displayed a naked brunette with long curls, riding a lion. They sat beneath a palm tree with a dove perched on it.

"That's Tinnit, our goddess of fertility," Adones observed.

I smiled and took in the golden rotunda, illuminated by beams of sunlight filtering through a round window in the domed roof. "This is beautiful."

"Indeed. Our library was dedicated to my grandfather, Hamilcar." Adones gestured toward a bronze bust a few feet ahead.

I stepped closer. The high forehead and strong chin resembled Hannibal, except the face was rounder and the nose straighter. "Such an impressive background," I said.

"Indeed," Adones eyed the bust. "My grandfather was taken too soon before his time, murdered by Iberian rebels. Though my uncle swears they were Roman sympathizers."

"That must have been difficult." I fiddled with Greg's ring, anxious to find the part of the library that contained ancient Greek scrolls and codices. Not that I even knew what to look for once I found them.

Something cold and hard fell over Adones' face. "My uncles were undone by the murder. Since Uncle Hannibal was the eldest of the three brothers, he kept his vow to avenge my grandfather's death. He has since continued his campaign against Rome."

"Vow?"

Adones nodded. "My uncles were brought to the temple of Ba'al Hammon. Hannibal was nine and one-half when he bowed before our god and promised to defend Carthage against the Roman Empire."

I remembered reading something about this. Yet, the way Adones framed it was weird. "Are you saying your grandfather and uncles physically met Ba'al Hammon?"

"Yes."

He was probably some phony pushing buttons from behind a curtain in the back of a temple. A super smart one if he was cozying up to the generals of Carthage. If Ba'al was still around, he could potentially help me figure out how to find Greg and Sophie, how to get home.

"Is Ba'al Hammon here now?"

Adones shrugged. "I'm not privy to a god's comings and goings, Amara."

My shoulders slumped. I should have known this wouldn't be easy.

As if he read my reaction, Adones added, "Though, in the past, he has always watched over my family. He even entrusted his sword to us."

My brow shot up. "Do you mean the sword Hannibal had this morning?"

"Yes, it's been in our family for centuries. Passed to Ba'al Hammon by Jan-Ib-Jann," Adones said.

"Who is Jan-Ib-Jann?" I asked.

"He's the king of the djinn," Adones said.

I blinked. "Djinn?"

"Yes. They're rare now," Adones observed. "Many died during the great war between djinn and mankind. Afterward, Ba'al Hammon was so impressed with my ancestor Hasdrubal's military skills, the sword was passed to him. To prevent others from stealing the weapon, a spell was cast, ensuring the blade could only be wielded by those from the Barcid bloodline."

This was insane. Yet, I found myself pulled into Adones' story. "What happens if someone else uses the sword?"

Adones smiled. "Once the sword is activated, the blade need only touch a man's skin, and he will wither and die."

My mind was spinning. How was any of this possible? If nothing else, the threat of instant death explained why Hannibal had sheathed his sword when he saw me eyeing it. He didn't want to chance me touching the blade.

"It's a lot to take in," Adones said.

I nodded. "Yes, it is."

"Come." Adones led me to a large room dotted with long marble tables.

My gaze darted between the arched built-in shelves, overflowing with scrolls and clay tablets. Overwhelmed didn't begin to describe what I felt. Adones gestured toward the center of the room, where a man with a pointed beard and matted gray curls sat at a table. He studied an open scroll spread before him.

"The scholar should have the answers you seek. What texts interest you?"

"I—" Someone bumped into me from behind. I turned around, barely catching the cups rattling on a heavy wooden tray, balanced by a young boy.

The boy's voice cracked as he stammered in his language.

Taking a knee, Adones adjusted the cups and the clay teapot and spoke to him in a consoling voice. After a moment, the boy gave a wan smile and walked slowly toward the scholar.

"We should help him."

Adones shook his head. "It's not our place to meddle with another man's property."

"Property?" My stomach clenched. "That boy is a human being just like us."

"Truly, my heart goes out to him," Adones said. "Yet, I won't be here tomorrow or the day after. He must learn to carry out his duties unaided."

"What if you were that boy?" I snapped. "I bet you wouldn't feel this way."

Something clanked loud and high. I turned toward the sound. The scholar screamed and shot out of his chair, pointing at the spilled cup on the table and the ruined scroll.

The boy backed away stammering. A horrible sneer contorted the scholar's face, and he slapped the boy hard across his cheek. A weak cry escaped his lips as he fell to the floor, staring at his attacker in wide-eyed horror.

"Stop!" I ran over and tugged at the scholar's thick robes. He shoved me and I stumbled backward, banging into a shelf.

Adones seized the scholar by the collar and threw him to the floor, hard.

A couple of other men in flowing robes emerged from another room and rushed to the scholar's aid. They shouted at Adones in their native tongue.

Undaunted, Adones' voice echoed through the chamber with the same wrath I had heard in the Shadu's roar. The men fell silent. If I was guessing, Adones told them his name, and they didn't want to deal with Hannibal.

"We should leave," Adones said.

So much for getting the scholar's help. Not that it mattered at this moment. I needed to worry about that boy. "No, not without him."

"The boy is not mine to take." Adones eyed the scholar, now finding his feet with the help of his buddies.

A fire burned the pit of my stomach. As if my legs had a mind of their own, I stormed to the boy, grabbed his thin arm, and pulled him toward the exit.

"Amara," Adones called after me.

The cabinet filled with scrolls and the mural barely registered in my periphery as I dragged the boy through the door. He pulled against me the whole time, babbling in Punic. When we reached the plaza, sunlight blared down on us. Citizens bustled about without a care in the world.

Adones grabbed me by the shoulder and spun me toward him, causing me to release the boy's arm. He ran off and disappeared into the crowd. At least he was free of that abusive monster.

"Are you trying to get yourself arrested?" Adones' glowered at me.

"Yes! If it protects a child from abuse." My breathing was shallow, and my heart raced.

Adones' shook his head. "You are naïve. You can hardly fend for yourself, much less a young boy. And what of the others? Will you save those who build our bridges, and our temples?"

I looked him straight in those damn emerald green eyes. "You know that's not possible. Still, I won't stand idly by and allow a child to be abused like that. How can you sleep at night or is this commonplace for you?"

His jaw tightened. "Is that your opinion of me, a cruel taskmaster?"

Maybe it was all the uncertainty about Greg and Sophie, or the mounting anger over being stuck in such a close-minded society, but the words just tumbled out. "Not cruel. Melania, whom you're clearly fond of, is forced to work in a hot kitchen. Poor Elissa has no future apart from indentured servitude. Yet, no one seems to care."

"So, I *am* a taskmaster." Adones turned his back to me and stalked toward the market.

Dad's words ran through my mind. *Your impetuousness will be your downfall.* I caught up to him. If I didn't get my smart mouth under control, I'd wind up on the street. "I didn't mean to call you a taskmaster. I'm out of my depth here."

"I believe you," he quipped. "Though I don't understand your indignance. Don't you have servants in your homeland?"

I kept up with Adones, despite his long strides and hurried pace as he navigated the sea of shoppers. "No," I said. "Slavery has been banned for some time."

His head snapped toward me. "How do you maintain a flourishing economy?"

"The citizens pay taxes to sustain the cities, and everyone has a chance to advance through work and equal pay."

Adones stared contemplatively ahead. When we finally cleared the market a few minutes later, he slowed down while walking uphill toward the mansions.

"Am I to believe that you live in a Utopian society?"

I shook my head. "No, it has flaws. It's just that my country is founded on the belief that all people are created equal. I've never been exposed to slavery, and this has been overwhelming and saddening."

"I must visit the Americas and see this for myself."

Good luck with that.

He stopped and faced me. "Whether you believe me or not, I've contemplated the cruelty of slavery many times, and frankly, I find it disturbing. When that Numidian bastard abducted me, I was given a rare glimpse into the life of a servant. Having no control over my destiny seemed a fate worse than death. I'd like nothing more than to stop the practice of slavery; yet I'm one man in a world where this practice is commonplace. Slavery drives the economy of Carthage, the Republic of Rome, Egypt, Athens, and your father's homeland of Sparta. Perhaps one day, when I am elected to the Senate, I can draft laws that will advance change. Until then, I can only work to help those who serve my house."

He studied me. "Are you alright?"

"Ye-yes, uh just weighing your words. Am I to understand that Melania and Elissa aren't indentured servants?"

"It is complicated." He sighed. "Melania has been with Imilce since birth. Although my uncle offered Melania a handsome sum and a chance to begin life anew, she declined. She said working for him brought her great joy. A coffer has since been set aside for her if she has a change of heart, and he also took in her orphaned granddaughter."

I arched an eyebrow. "Elissa?"

"Yes," he said flatly. "She was living on the streets, stealing from everyone she met. My uncle saved her from losing a hand and took her in. She has since served his house faithfully."

We proceeded past the mansions at a leisurely pace.

"Elissa, the boy, they're too young to work so hard."

Adones' gaze raked over me. "Amara, your mind, quick wit, and willfulness are traits I admire most about you. Unfortunately, they will also get you hung."

I almost tripped, and for once, I had no words.

He held my gaze. "I say this with the utmost respect. If you don't learn to temper your candor and control your emotions, you may end up in an untenable situation. One I can't mitigate. I know we're from different worlds and being away from your family must be unbearable. If you hope to remain in my uncle's home without incident, you must keep your opinions to yourself. I doubt he'd be as accepting of them as I am."

I nodded and dragged my teeth over my bottom lip. Like it or not, he was right. I was a guest in his cruel, hard-hearted world and I couldn't make a difference.

We silently proceeded down a cobbled path leading to Hannibal's house. In the light of day, the property appeared much larger than the one I walked through last night, at least two to three acres. Birds trilled from tall coconut palms. The flanking bushes bloomed in an array of reds, whites, and yellows.

"Your gardens are beautiful." I hoped to lighten the mood.

"Indeed, they are. We actually *employ* a gardener." Adones stopped and looked down at me, smirking. "I have a feeling you're going to complicate my life."

I fought a smile. "Aren't you up to the task?"

I couldn't help but notice how Adones' facial hair lined his square jaw, and the differing hues of green surrounded his irises.

He stepped closer. "A task I'd willingly accept."

Pride wouldn't let me back away.

"Despite your guardedness, you truly are a remarkable woman with the knowledge of scholars, and a will to defend those you care for, and strangers alike." His gaze roamed to my lips. "You're beautiful."

I swallowed hard as he leaned so close that our lips almost touched. Almost, until a soft feminine voice called out from behind us in Punic.

Adones backed away from me like I had the plague.

I faced the voice and found a petite girl about my age with small lips and a weak chin watching us with her arms crossed. Although she put off a strong vibe, her frown hinted that her feelings were hurt.

"A-Amara of House Kalogridas," Adones sputtered in ancient Greek. "Allow me to introduce—"

"Aurelia of House Bomilcar," she responded in the same language. Whatever hurt I sensed a second ago was gone. She approached me with her head held high and took my hand. "I'm Adones' betrothed."

Chapter Ten

Betrothed? I flashed a strained smile, aware of how our little chat in the garden must have looked to her, how it looked to me. I was such a dumbass.

Aurelia's array of beaded necklaces jangled as she leaned in and kissed each of my cheeks. "Pleased to meet you."

"And you as well."

If I were really pleased, why did my body tense when her lips touched my skin, or when she shot me a sugary sweet smile?

Adones' gaze drifted from me to Aurelia. "How did you know we were in the gardens?"

"I didn't, my love," Aurelia crooned. "Lady Imilce's ready to depart for the festival. I checked the grounds on the chance I'd find you."

The way she gazed at Adones all starry-eyed, made me feel like a third wheel. An underdressed one at that. Aurelia's purple robes shimmered beneath the sun. And her tiara, encrusted with red jewels, fell high on her forehead, and contrasted brilliantly against her raven hair. Hair that would make a shampoo model jealous.

Aurelia tucked her hand into the crook of Adones' arm. I fought the urge to cringe. He had a great life ahead of him with a senate career and a wife, a family.

"Come. You must don your uniform." Her gaze roamed from my feet to my shoulders like I was an annoying gnat. "Clearly Amara needs a change of clothes as well."

I bit my tongue to keep from saying something snarky and glowered at Adones instead. He could have told me he was engaged so I wouldn't have been caught off guard. I walked in silence beside him. The whole time, Aurelia babbled about how she hoped I'd attend the wedding — how Adones was the sweetest guy ever — how he allowed her to purchase enough rugs and tapestries to fill their home. If nothing else, it explained the weaver's response to him back at the market.

By the time we reached the front of the house, I was worn out. All the stress about Greg and Sophie, the slave boy, and a magical world, combined with Aurelia's sickly sweetness, made me want to run to my room and bury my head under a pillow. Unfortunately, I didn't get a chance to do that. A girl about my age, in unbleached robes, met us at the door. After a short greeting, the girl explained that Elissa was with Imilce, and she had been sent to prepare me for the theatre. The rest was a blur.

I refused to remove Greg's ring or Sophie's bracelet as the girl stripped, oiled, clothed me, and applied make up to my face. Before I knew it, I emerged from the room, dressed in a sweeping royal blue gown laced with gold beads, and a matching wrap. The girl had held up a polished metal mirror before I left the room. However, my image was so blurry, I couldn't get an accurate picture of what I looked like. Despite this, something about the richness of my dress and the shiny gold band on my head made me feel like a princess.

The way Adones' full mouth stretched into a smile when I walked out the front door told me I was right. I schooled my face into what I hoped was a mask of calm, praying my sadness didn't show when I looked at his leather breastplate. It was embedded with the very discs I'd seen in the wooden chest back at the tomb. My gaze gravitated toward his sheathed sword with an elephant tusk handle that Dr. Hamad had admired. Flirtatious bastard or not, he didn't deserve to die so young.

"You're a vision." Imilce smiled at me from in front of a carriage carved in gold leaves. Even with the belly bump, compared to her, I was Plain Jane. Her eyes were lined in black with gold eye shadow. Gold bracelets twisted up her arms. Her hair was tucked behind her ears, revealing two circular earrings with red center stones that matched her gown.

I descended the sweeping steps to the cobbled drive and approached Imilce. "I hope I haven't delayed you."

Hannibal chuckled under his breath. "Worry not, dear girl. I'm in no hurry to view a *classic* play."

Even at his friendliest, Hannibal was an imposing figure. He stood several inches above me with powerful arms, and his broad chest was covered by a bronze breastplate, studded with six gold discs. I stared at the golden handle of his sword, protruding from a leather sheath by his side. What did a magical blade look like?

"Classic? The play is Sophocles' greatest work," Adones said.

Hannibal rolled his eyes. "Yes, two hundred years ago. I'd rather view a more modern play."

Aurelia flashed a smile. "I agree with my *betrothed*." She glanced at me before continuing. "*Oedipus Rex* is a play to be revered, and we're fortunate enough to view it in Carthage's theatre."

Hannibal let out a long breath and gestured toward the carriage door. "Ladies, shall we?"

I thought the ancients used chariots, but I supposed for longer rides, or in this case, a pregnant woman's comfort, a larger mode of transportation proved more suitable. The carriage was different than I expected, made from wood with two wheels like a chariot, except bigger with an arched roof and door, pulled by a team of horses with a soldier at the reins.

Just a few feet ahead, about ten soldiers on horseback waited. They were incredible. Some were wrapped in pelts with lion heads. Others wore headdresses made from curled goat horns with elephant tusks hanging off the side of their saddles. Captain Aharim waited at the front of the formation with two horses, likely reserved for Hannibal and Adones.

Hannibal helped his wife into the carriage first. When he turned to Aurelia, she hesitated and extended her hand toward Adones, like she expected him to kiss it.

He must not have understood what she wanted, because he bowed instead. With a glance my way, Aurelia withdrew her hand and stepped inside the carriage.

I was about to follow her when Adones grabbed my arm. "Amara of House Kalogridas, I enjoyed our day, very much."

"It was an adventure." I climbed inside the carriage and Elissa entered after me.

The wooden ceiling was low enough that I had to bend at the waist before sitting. Lemony light flowed in from a small window opposite the door, illuminating two seats covered in soft leather. Since Imilce was pregnant and needed more room, skinny little Elissa sat beside her, leaving me beside Aurelia. What a joy.

"I'll stop just before we reach the theatre so we can walk in together." Hannibal shut the carriage door.

We waited a few minutes for Hannibal and Adones to mount their horses. A slight jerk signaled that the carriage had pulled away from the house. Then, we rambled down the paved road past the gate. Wheels squeaked beneath us, and the walls groaned with every bounce of the carriage. Mansions loomed in my periphery as our team of horses trotted by them.

Elissa pulled a linen bag from inside her cloak and opened it, revealing three flat sugar cookies. "Melania sent these for your midday snack."

Imilce wrapped her arm around Elissa and pulled her against her. "You know just the thing to cheer me. Would you all care for one?"

I shook my head, noting the clear bond between Elissa and Imilce. "No, thank you."

Aurelia glowered at Elissa like she was a scorpion, and I glowered at Aurelia the same way. What would it hurt to treat a servant with kindness?

"I swear by all that is good, your obsession with Elissa is beyond me," Aurelia said. "Next, you'll betroth her to your unborn son."

Elissa's cheeks reddened, and her freckled nose crinkled like she smelled something foul.

"Or she may be a fierce friend to my daughter," Imilce corrected. "My husband's strong desire for a boy will not make it come to pass. If I have a son, he deserves to choose with whom he will marry."

Aurelia glowered at Elissa.

"Elissa's wonderful." I entwined my fingers together to keep from slapping Aurelia's stuck-up face.

"Indeed, Elissa will do great things." Imilce tugged at one of Elissa's curls. "If she has a head to listen and continue her studies at the temple."

"I am trying," Elissa said.

Imilce stared her down. "I think not. I've heard you've been shirking your studies. You won't become a priestess unless you stay the course."

This was just as Adones had said. Imilce was providing Elissa a better life. There was so much more to this culture and the people than I thought.

"Yes, Lady Imilce," Elissa said with a pout.

"Stop being so glum." Imilce gestured toward the cookies. "Have one."

Aurelia clucked her tongue and sat back in her seat.

Elissa didn't need to be asked twice. She smiled and took a huge bite.

"I don't understand this girl," Imilce said. "She's been afforded the privilege of an education. Yet, she prefers to remain by my side instead of expanding her knowledge."

Elissa fidgeted in her seat and spoke in Punic to Imilce.

"We must speak the language of our guest if we wish her to participate in the conversation," Imilce said.

Elissa glanced at me. "Apologies, Mistress Amara, I meant no disrespect."

I responded with a smile.

"This must be so difficult for you," Aurelia said. "I can't imagine the confines of only knowing one tongue. Were you raised in the country, dear?"

I blinked. "No, I wasn't. I—"

"I believe you've misread Amara." Imilce shot me a wide smile before continuing. "She speaks the language of her homeland in the Americas. Her father is a scholar, and she reads the written word."

Aurelia's grin was tense. "How interesting. Who would have guessed you came from such a noble background."

What. A. Bitch. And she has no shame in front of Imilce. Well, two can play this game. "We must be kindred spirits." I laid my hand on her forearm in feigned friendship. "I thought the very same thing about you when first we met."

Elissa sucked in her cheeks like she was trying to stifle a laugh. Imilce brought her hand to her mouth and looked out the window.

Aurelia's face was unreadable as she brought her hand over mine. "How amusing." Her voice was a purr. "Well, one cannot fault you for your ignorance, dear. Clearly, you have no idea what makes a noble."

I swallowed hard. She was good at this game. Too good.

"How long do you intend to stay in Carthage?" Aurelia asked.

"Not more than a fortnight." I held her gaze and kept my hand under hers, willing to sit like this all day rather than let her know how uncomfortable she made me.

"Amara's family is from Sparta," Imilce said.

Aurelia gingerly removed her hand from the top of mine, smirking, as if satisfied that she had asserted her dominance over me. Her gaze gravitated to my ring, "That's an interesting piece. I've never seen such engravings."

I covered the ring with my hand. "Er, this belongs to my brother. I'm holding it until we're reunited."

Curiosity glinted in Aurelia's eyes. "Oh? It sounds like there's a story—"

Our carriage bounced, nearly knocking us out of our seats. I peeked out the window and saw that we were crossing a bridge lined with unlit marble braziers. A crowd of people cheered as we passed. Many were dressed like they had just walked out of a Mardi Gras parade. Some wore wooden masks, resembling long-beaked birds and goats with curled horns. A man in a red conical hat blew a horn in front of a basket. I did a double take as a winged snake with a cobra's head slowly emerged from inside.

"We're close to the festiv—" Imilce groaned and doubled over.

Aurelia and I were out of our seats in a flash, kneeling in front of Imilce.

Elissa took her hand. "Are you in pain, my lady?"

Imilce let out a couple of long breaths before sitting upright again. "No. The babe is merely restless."

"The babe has been restless since you broke fast," Elissa said. "We should turn back."

Aurelia rubbed Imilce's arm. "Hannibal should have forced you to stay abed."

Imilce pursed her full lips. "Hannibal forces me to do nothing. We're partners and he respects my wishes. More to the point, I've had no pain, just some tightening around my belly. Cease fussing over me like I'm incapable of caring for myself, and *do not* ruin this day for my husband!"

We sat back in our seats and rode the rest of the way in silence. I could have cut the tension with a sword. Elissa chewed her cookie, eyeing Imilce with genuine concern. Aurelia stared out the window, and I tried to ignore how the constant rocking nauseated me. The whole time, Imilce sat there like I imagined a true noble would, wearing a slight smile, as if she hadn't bent over in pain minutes ago. It was easy to see why Hannibal loved her. Imilce was beautiful, compassionate, open-minded, and clearly stubborn.

Although we only rode about thirty minutes, it felt like we'd been on the road for hours. By the time the footman opened the door, it took all my restraint to wait until everyone emptied out of the carriage. When I stepped outside, my back muscles did a happy dance as I stretched them beneath the mid-afternoon sun.

Hannibal and his men handed off their mounts to a couple of soldiers and waited at the front of a long procession of people. No wonder the general's reputation as a military leader had persisted for more than two thousand years. Judging by the admiration in many of the onlookers' eyes, there was little doubt that every man in this crowd would have willingly given his life for Hannibal. However, I had the privilege of witnessing a side of this man that history failed to record. The second Hannibal gently took his wife's hand and smiled down at her, he turned from hardened warrior to tender and devoted husband.

Hannibal and Imilce led the procession with their heads held high. They smiled as though it was normal to have hundreds of women throwing them kisses and men bowing and kneeling before them — as though it was normal to hear the people chanting Hannibal's name so loud it made my ears ring. The whole time, the great general's men walked behind him. Their scarred inscrutable faces remained vigilant as they eyed the crowd.

We soon left the supporters behind and entered a rectangular plaza crawling with more people. Based on how formally we were dressed, I expected to see a bunch of stuck-up nobles. Instead, it was like a huge tailgate party for the ancients. Bearded men carrying wineskins and leather flasks staggered by us. Women and children laughed and danced to myriads of musicians playing lyres, lutes, and drums. A large crowd had gathered to our right and they were heckling something.

"No!" My chest hollowed out when I spotted Bear on a platform tied to a pole.

His arms were stretched and bound to a long board, and his head hung with his chin resting on his chest. Long plaits fell over his face. I broke rank and ran to him. Elissa called out from behind as I pushed past the onlookers' throwing vegetables at him. What was next, stones?

"Tanno," I tried to climb the platform. The guard growled and shoved me backward. I stumbled toward the crowd. Quickly recovering, I stormed to the edge of the platform again. My chest tightened as I took in Bear's beaten and bruised body. He slowly raised his head. Blood dripped from his nose and one of his eyes was swollen shut.

"What can I do to help?"

"Nothing. Go! Before you end up sharing my fate." He gazed past my shoulder.

When I looked behind me, the crowd parted as Hannibal and Adones approached. They climbed up the platform without glancing my way. Hannibal stood before Bear and spoke in a menacing tone. Whatever he said made Bear perk up. He bared his teeth at the general then spat on Adones.

Guffaws rippled across the crowd as Adones slowly wiped spittle from his face. Then he unsheathed his sword.

I didn't think, didn't feel. I just jumped in front of Bear.

The sting of Hannibal's gaze cut through my bravado with razor sharpness. "You dare defend this brigand!"

"This isn't your fight, Amara," Adones said.

Resisting the urge to tuck and run, I held the general's stare, ignoring how my voice shook as I spoke. "This isn't justice. Killing him in cold blood before he can plead his case will only make you appear a tyrant."

Hannibal studied me for the longest minute of my life before turning his gaze on Bear. "This girl has bought you a stay of execution."

Adones lips curled into a sneer. "Don't get too comfortable. Your day will soon come."

A wet, humorless laugh escaped Bear's lips. He looked down at me through bloodshot eyes. "I shouldn't have let you stop me from slitting this bastard's throat."

Adones stepped closer. "You'll not bait me into killing you. I want to see you die slowly for what you did to me."

He turned his back on Bear and faced me. "Did our earlier discussion mean nothing to you?"

"Of course, it did. Please understand, the Numidian saved my life on the beach, kept me from taking an arrow. I owe him my life."

"You've repaid your debt this day!" the general said.

I gazed at the partially unsheathed sword by his side. Golden symbols were etched around the edge of the blade in the form of stars and moons, surrounding geometric shapes. I gasped. They were the same symbols on the disc that brought me here. Before I could get a better look, Hannibal sheathed the weapon and headed back to Imilce.

"You'd do well to concentrate on returning to your homeland, girl, rather than worrying about that brigand who faces imminent death," the general called over his shoulder.

When we returned to our formation, it took all my restraint not to look back at poor Bear, and the merciless crowd still jeering at him. I never missed home more than I did at this moment, and Hannibal's sword may have held the key to returning me there. Since Ba'al Hammon had given the weapon to the Barcids, I needed to start with him. Yet, finding the god was easier said than done.

Elissa leaned in conspiratorially and said, "You'd be wise to remember that the Numidian's an enemy of House Barcid. This makes him your enemy."

I nodded, cringing at the judgment in her voice.

We cleared the plaza and climbed at least fifty stone steps leading toward the entrance of a theatre. I drew in a deep breath as I took in my surroundings. The Acropolis was just west of us on Byrsa Hill, where the military fortifications stood, and the ruins in my time didn't do it justice. Hundred-foot marble pillars lined a front with large square windows that seemed to watch over Carthage like a vigilant sentry.

The structure was equally as impressive as the one in Athens. I glanced at Elissa. "The Acropolis is incredible."

She shot me a wide grin. "It's been here since before my great-grandmother's birth."

Our formation moved, and I felt very VIP when soldiers escorted our party to the front of a long line and ushered us through the entrance. The theatre was built onto a hillside surrounded by hundreds of tiered seats, descending toward a circular stage. Indistinct chatter echoed through the air.

We passed men dressed in linen tunics with mantles over their shoulders. They punched their chests in a salute to Hannibal. Women in sleeved petticoats with gold earrings and bracelets, and decorative headbands had no shame as they eyed Hannibal and smiled sweetly. The great general didn't acknowledge them. Instead, he just returned the men's salutes.

We stopped before an area close to the stage. This must have been the bougie section of the theatre. Unlike the rest of the audience seated beneath the blaring sun, this area was shaded by a canvas roof, hoisted with tent poles onto a rigging, and the bench seats had cushions.

Hannibal sat in a high-back chair with clawed arms, next to Imilce. Elissa and I lucked out and were seated beside her, while Aurelia and Adones took their places next to Hannibal.

I played with Greg's ring on my finger and adjusted Sophie's bracelet, to center my nervous energy. When would I learn to think before acting? Running to Bear's aid had cast a spotlight on me, but it wasn't like I could just stand there and do nothing.

Drums caught my attention as they echoed throughout the stadium. Elissa sat straighter. There was a hint of pride in her voice as she turned to me. "You won't be disappointed."

About a dozen men in hooded black cloaks, wearing masks with wide mouths and big empty eyes, emerged from a door at the top of the stands. They descended the steps to our right while chanting in ancient Greek about the play's setting before Oedipus' palace in Thebes. Since the play was written in this language, it made sense that the actors spoke it.

"The Chorus introduces the setting before the actors emerge," Elissa said with a wide smile.

Nodding, I bit my lower lip to keep from telling her that I already knew this. Instead, I turned my attention to the cloaked Chorus now on center stage. They held hands and danced in circles narrating how a plague had fallen on the city. Although it was no secret that the Carthaginians had known something about acoustics, the sounds were clear, like loudspeaker clear.

We had just finished applauding the Chorus when Hannibal's guard squeezed past a couple of nobles and whispered in the general's ear. Adones jaw ticked as he listened. I looked around, noticing how other soldiers were talking to many of the noble people behind us.

"Is there a problem?" I asked Elissa.

She leaned in, covering her mouth with her hand. "Master Hannibal's guard reported that a Roman emissary just arrived in the city. They fear he's threatening war for Carthage's role in sacking Saguntum."

I brought my hand to my mouth, hoping my feigned shock was believable. "Oh, that can't be good."

This was unfolding just as it had in my history books. A Roman emissary had brought a declaration of war to Carthage. Though the city would be safe for several years, the same couldn't be said for poor Adones. Hannibal would soon march his elephants over the Alps, and this was the day he had made that decision.

Hannibal let out an exasperated breath, looked at Imilce and murmured in Punic. Although I couldn't understand her whispered words, the frustration and disappointment in her pressed lips as Hannibal bent down and kissed her was evident. Then he departed the theatre with Adones and the guards. Several nobles in the audience followed them. Aurelia moved to the general's seat and rested her hand on Imilce's.

After flashing a friendly smile, Imilce turned her attention to me. "Apologies for the disruption. My husband has urgent business with the Senate."

"Should we return home?" I asked.

Imilce shook her head. "If I left every time my husband was called away, I'd have no social life."

I nodded.

Three actors emerged from behind a shed center stage, wearing costumes resembling those worn by the Chorus. During the play, they used little or no props, but still got the point across. As the hours dragged by, I pondered Oedipus' tale. When his father Laius, the king of Thebes, tried to prevent the prophecy foretelling how the son would kill the father and marry his mother, he inadvertently sealed this fate. If I told

Adones how and when he would die, it was possible that I'd be playing a similar role in his demise.

Imilce's groan pulled me from my thoughts.

"Are you unwell?" I asked.

She leaned forward and winced. "I'm feeling my first pains."

Elissa's hand flew to Imilce's shoulder.

"Should I find a midwife or healer?" Aurelia whispered.

"No, do *not* call attention to me," Imilce said. "Take me home. Melania will know what to do. She delivered me into this world, and I trust no one else with my child's birth."

"What of Master Hannibal?" Elissa asked.

"He's engaged in important matters of state. I will not disturb him unless we're certain the time is near." Despite her pain, Imilce rose from her seat and smoothed her robes as if she wasn't about to push out a baby at any second, then she glided up the steps. I followed her and the rest of our crew toward the exit, praying we'd make it to Imilce's house before she gave birth.

Chapter Eleven

The carriage ride to Hannibal's mansion was tense. Imilce kept doubling over in pain. Elissa's concerned eyebrows were raised so high, they nearly touched her hairline. Aurelia babbled on about her wedding.

Just as she was about to grate on my last nerve, Hannibal's mansion crept into my view. My shoulders relaxed and I smiled. "We are—"

Aurelia gasped and pointed at Imilce's lap. "Your garments, they're soaked."

I'd watched enough *ER* shows to know this was about to get real. "Your child's coming soon."

"Are ... you ... a ... midwife?" Imilce bit her bottom lip.

My AP anatomy and physiology classes back in high school had given me a basic knowledge of the human body and the importance of sterilization. If I let on that I knew these things, they might ask me to help with the delivery. Watching something the size of a cantaloupe squeeze through a pinhole wasn't at the top of my to-do list, so I went into denial-mode.

"No, not a midwife. I've seen this before though. My cousin also lost water just before her child's birth." I hated how easily the lies came.

Aurelia took Imilce's hand. "House Barcid will soon be blessed with a son."

"Hopefully not in this carriage. That would be disasterou—" Imilce's face contorted in pain.

"Hold steady, we're nearly home," Aurelia said.

Moments later, we pulled into Hannibal's drive. Elissa shot out of the carriage like a cannon. By the time the driver helped Imilce out, Elissa had returned with Melania. The old woman stared at the water pooling around the mother-to-be's sandals.

"Stop standing there like a mute. Lady Imilce is suffering," Aurelia said.

Melania glowered at Aurelia before moving into action, speaking consolingly as she tucked her arm around Imilce's waist. Elissa took up the other side.

"Perhaps the driver should carry you," Aurelia observed.

Imilce stopped mid-step. "I'm perfectly capable of walking on my own."

"You are stubborn as a goat," Aurelia said.

"How can I help?" I followed the women into a chamber blanketed with sunlight, creeping in through the front door.

"I have it well in hand, child."

Melania's words contradicted the fear I heard in her voice. Then again, I'm sure that delivering the firstborn child of Carthage's greatest general added additional pressure to an already stressful situation.

Before hastening down the hallway, Melania turned to Aurelia and spoke in Punic. Best I could tell from Aurelia's constant nods and "mhmmms," Melania was instructing her about what to expect during the delivery. Or so I thought.

Once Melania and the mom-to-be had disappeared down the hallway, Aurelia turned her hateful gaze on me, "Lady Imilce has asked me to ensure your comfort."

Before I could respond, Aurelia gave a tart, "Follow me." She sauntered through the dining room and stepped onto a terrace overlooking the city.

I sat on an armless couch next to several vases dripping with flowers. Aurelia lowered herself onto a lounge across from me and folded her hands together. We stared each other down for seconds that passed like minutes. I fidgeted, hyperaware of the chorus of birds trilling around us — how the warm breeze grazed my skin — and the city, with all its flat roofs and temples, shimmered below us in a heat haze.

Finally, I found my voice. "Did Melania decide you weren't needed?"

"No, she'll call for me once Imilce's prepared for the birth." Aurelia's gaze swept over me all judgy. "If nothing else, you and I will have time to talk."

I gave a tense smile. "How nice."

"Indeed. Dear Imilce's weakness for strays has added undue stress on her."

My brow knitted together. "Did you say, 'stray'?"

"I did. Would you prefer I use vagabond or drifter instead?" There was no inflection in her voice. She could've been discussing the actors at the theatre.

What did I do to her? "I prefer, Amara," I said coolly.

"Very well, *Amara,*" she set to pacing as if I wasn't there.

Heat rushed up my neck to my cheeks. "Have I said or done something to offend you?"

She froze and pursed her lips. "Today, you ran to the defense of the very criminal who abducted Adones. Yet here you stand a free woman."

"That man saved my life when I first arrived here. Adones and General Barca know this. I merely tried to return the favor."

"How noble," she crooned. "You may have Adones and Imilce fooled. Yet, I know a scheming street rat, preying on sweet Imilce's sympathies, when I see one."

"You're wrong." My voice shook. "I'm no schemer. Nor am I a street rat. I never asked for the Barcids' hospitality, though I'm nonetheless grateful for it."

"I beg to differ. Adones is a good man, and you've charmed him with your foreign ways and lilting accent. I'll not have it!"

"To what end?" I asked, losing hope by the second for a truce. "I have no claim here. Hannibal's returning me to my father in less than a fortnight. Your imagination has run away with you."

Aurelia's mouth twitched downward. "I didn't imagine that moment in the gardens. Had I not interrupted, there's no predicting what may have happened."

Irritation bubbled in my chest, and I shoved it down, trying to grow as a person, trying to think before I spoke. Exhaling deeply, I said, "You're mistaken. You only observed friendship. Even if I were what you say, which I'm not, you should have faith in Adones."

She stopped pacing and stared me down with such contempt, I shifted in my seat.

"You don't know a thing about me." Aurelia paused. "Perhaps that's the problem." She sat on the lounge across from me and spoke more calmly this time. "My relationship with Adones was forged on the day of my birth. It's politically important to our families and I've been groomed to be his wife. Over the past year, we've spent many days together and I believe that he has grown to care for me as I care for him."

Despite my irritation, part of me felt for her. I could tell she loved Adones, that she was looking forward to their life together. This was so unfair.

I cleared my throat. "Why are you telling me this?"

"A man like Adones with his good looks, power, and wealth has many women falling at his feet. Even those with whom he has given a second glance never concerned me. They were mere dalliances, a way for a man to relieve tension." Aurelia's robes rustled as she leaned forward in her seat. "You, however, are the first woman apart from me he has admired with true longing and respect. This is dangerous to the future of our families and our country."

I blinked several times. "I think you've misinterpreted—"

Aurelia raised her forefinger and clucked her tongue. "Ah, ah, ah, don't insult my intelligence. I observed longing in your eyes as well. So, I appeal to you now, please, before Adones' feelings for you become complicated, leave this house and don't return."

How arrogant! Leaving abruptly would cast more suspicion on me. Hannibal's men would hunt me down and Aurelia knew this.

I shot out of my seat. "I won't leave until one of the Barcids demands it. Whatever glimmer of interest you observed was born from your imagination. I assure you."

"You will leave," Aurelia growled.

"Perhaps we should ask Master Hannibal or Lady Imilce if they agree. Better yet, why don't we air your concerns to Adones?"

"How dare you!" Aurelia stood toe-to-toe with me. Every muscle in her neck tightened as she spoke. "You are a conniving little—"

Elissa ran through the doorway holding an armful of cotton rags. "Lady Aurelia, my grandmother awaits your presence."

Aurelia's expression transformed from Evil Queen to Snow White in a matter of seconds. She wheeled around and glided to Elissa, relieved her of the rags, and disappeared into the house.

I met Elissa in the middle of the terrace. "Is Lady Imilce well?"

Elissa pulled a frown. "She's resting."

"Why the sad face?"

"I — I've been dispatched to the Senate to fetch Master Hannibal." She sighed. "I foolishly volunteered. Lady Imilce was pleased, and I couldn't tell her no while she's suffering. I'm not sure I can face all those nobles and soldiers. What if they mock me?"

Other than offer encouragement, I wasn't sure what I could do. I patted her on the arm, and said, "I understand your fear. If there was a way I could help, I—"

Her hand flew to mine. "Oh, mistress, there is. You're a highborn lady. They'll listen to you. Please."

Although I wasn't sure about the whole 'highborn' part, Elissa made it tough to resist those watery brown eyes staring at me like a lost kitten. "I'll do my best to help."

She flashed a thankful smile. "I-I owe you a great debt."

"You owe me nothing."

The next thing I knew, Elissa was leading me through the house at almost Mach speed. When we made it to the courtyard, the evening sun blanketed the area in hues of burnt orange. She dragged me past a handful of children sword fighting with sticks, to a hitching post where a tall, black horse waited. I'd kept my distance from the animals ever since I was thrown at sixth grade summer camp. The thought of mounting one now caused my stomach to churn.

An elderly man in a long leather apron called out to Elissa while approaching. He met her with a brief hug and gestured toward me. "Amara, this is my grandfather, Pallab."

"Melania's husband?"

Elissa nodded.

Pallab shot me a welcoming smile, and hoisted Elissa into the horse's saddle, which was different from those in my time, with a barely notable bump for a saddle horn and no stirrups.

"You'll ride with me, Mistress, Amara." She gently patted the back of her saddle.

I can do this. For Imilce.

Pallab bent forward with his fingers interlocked.

"Step up with your left leg," Elissa said.

I placed my shaky foot into Pallab's hand. With a slight grunt, he helped me onto the horse behind his granddaughter. We were both thin enough to fit comfortably in the same saddle, which made me feel slightly secure, slightly. I stared straight ahead, refusing to think about the distance between me and the ground.

Pallab handed her the reins and she called over her shoulder. "Fear not, I'm a strong rider."

I fought the urge to ask her to define 'strong.' After I wrapped both arms around her waist, she moved the reins to the right, and off we went. Our horse left a cloud of dust in our wake as we galloped through the courtyard. Her exit shouldn't have surprised me. Since I first met Elissa, she'd done nothing slow, and this spilled into our ride through Carthage.

A veiled woman carrying a basket of pink melons barely jumped out of our way as we cantered by her. We passed stone buildings lined with outdoor baths also made from stone. Aqueducts with narrow inground canals ran beneath five tiers of wide arches. At the bottom of the hill, ten inground holes, about the size of Olympic swimming pools, fed into a cistern that stored water for the city.

After what felt like an eternity of riding through the crowded city, the cobbled streets narrowed to a dirt path. Elissa slowed the horse long enough to point toward the peak of a hill, surrounded by a smaller version of the stone wall that guarded Carthage.

"Bersa. We haven't much farther," she said.

Before I could respond, she kicked the horse into a full gallop, and we began our ascent at full speed. We soon entered through an arched gate and stopped before a large stone building. The rectangular structure sat on a stone base, twice the length of its width. Marble steps led to a porch with tall pillars lining the front. The obelisk across from the building was equally impressive. A pyramid-like tip reached for the sky, and the base, made from smooth marble, was covered in glyphs. I shook my head, blown away by Carthage's melting pot of Egyptian, Greek, and Hebrew architecture.

Our animal snorted and wheezed as I slid off. I could relate. My knees almost buckled when I touched the ground. Pins and needles ran down my legs. Elissa walked the horse to a water trough a few feet away and tied the animal there. She watched me stretch and the corner of her mouth twitched like she was fighting a smile.

"Do I amuse you?" I touched my toes.

"No, you remind me of my grandmother when she has back pain and—"

"I'm not in pain." I straightened. "I'm stretching after a long journey." It was a lie. My ass was on fire. I just didn't like being compared to Melania.

Elissa stepped beside me and took my hand. "We can be brave for Mistress Imilce and her child."

I gave her hand a squeeze and headed for the building. By the time we climbed all the steps and entered through the double wooden doors, I was drenched in sweat. I seriously missed elevators.

Inside was at least twenty degrees cooler than the outdoors. Flames from wall braziers illuminated the empty foyer. Just a few feet ahead, a soldier in a plumed helmet and white tunic stood at attention beside a set of massive wooden doors.

Elissa froze. "What should we do?"

"We'll ask him to admit us," I said, fearing this was easier said than done. I dipped my chin to give off a noble vibe and approached the guard.

He moved in front of the doors with his hand on his sword. "What say you, woman?"

I pressed my lips together to keep the fear off my face. "Good day," I said in ancient Greek. "We request admittance at once. I have an important update for General Barca."

"Apologies, madam. I can't allow a woman to disrupt the Senate. You're welcome to wait by the entrance. Yet, much time may pass before the proceedings end."

The soldier's thick accent made it tough to translate his words. After a moment of interpreting, my body went rigid. No way I endured hard riding that chapped my ass raw, only to be turned away by a damn misogynist. Time to pull out the big guns.

"General Barca's wife is giving birth to his child as we speak, and he has asked to be notified. Perhaps you should reconsider rather than face the general's wrath."

The soldier sucked in his cheeks.

"He'll be most displeased when he learns you're the reason he wasn't informed of his wife's situation. I've no doubt you will pray for death if she takes a turn for the worst."

He swallowed and his Adam's apple bobbed. "With tidings such as these, you make it difficult to deny you."

"I'll inform the general of your cooperation."

The soldier ushered Elissa and I into a small foyer and directed us upstairs. I fought a groan and ascended several more steps to the third-story terrace, overlooking the Senate. Despite my aching legs, I couldn't help but marvel at the piece of history unfolding before me. Flames from wall braziers illuminated a space about half the size of a basketball court. Onlookers in bright white robes, and soldiers in red and purple cloaks, sat on descending marble benches to each side of the stage. Hannibal stood in the center, speaking Punic to a man seated on a wooden throne.

I leaned in and whispered in Elissa's ear, "We should wait until Master Hannibal finishes his speech."

"Agreed. Lady Aurelia's father will be cross if we interrupt the session."

My brow furrowed. "Her father?"

"Why yes, he's the Sufet." She pointed at the nearly chinless guy with long salt and pepper hair on a throne-like wooden chair.

"I see." Aurelia got her looks straight from dear ole dad.

"My grandmother says aside from Master Hannibal, Senator Bomilcar is the second most powerful man in Carthage."

"I believe she's right." If my history was correct, a sufet was a cross between a magistrate and the Speaker of the House.

Excited chatter returned my attention to the white marble chamber below me. A bunch of nobles to the right of the room rose from their seats and pointed accusingly at Hannibal. Men on the opposite side of the arena stood and countered with their fists held high. In no time, it was a free-for-all with Hannibal in the center of it. Although I already knew how these proceedings would end, I couldn't pass up a chance to hear the Senate debate that led to the second Punic War.

"Can you translate?" I asked Elissa.

"Of course." She pointed toward lettering ranging from circles to upside down triangles, engraved in the tile floors on the right side of the arena. "That marks the Peace Party's side." She listened for a moment before continuing. "Rome has threatened war unless the Senate turns Hannibal over to the empire. Senator Hanno is on the Peace Party's side. He's concerned that Master Hannibal's attack on the Roman territory of Saguntum will lead to the city's destruction. He wants to surrender Master Hannibal to Rome."

"Why would they consider such a thing after the citizens had hailed Hannibal as a hero?"

Elissa paused as if considering my words. "My grandfather told me that the Peace Party accused Master Hannibal of buying the people's support when he distributed booty from the raid at Saguntum. Perhaps this undermines the Senate."

"That's not good," I said with feigned surprise. These details were common knowledge among historians in my time.

"There's hope." Elissa gestured toward the left. "The Patriot Party feels the attack on Saguntum helped the people of Carthage and they want Hannibal to go to war."

I nodded. *No shocker there.*

Aurelia's dad rose. His robes of gold glistened against the firelight as he joined Hannibal and signaled the onlookers' silence. Yelling turned to mumbles which finally faded to a hush. The Sufet's deep voice resounded throughout the great hall.

Elissa listened a minute before explaining. "Master Hannibal wants approval to march over the Alps onto Roman soil so he can bring the war to them. I think we're about to get a ruling."

Someone grabbed my arm. I wheeled around, meeting Adones' emerald gaze. "What are you doing here?"

"Lady Imilce," Elissa said.

"She's in labor," I blurted. "Melania sent us to inform Hannibal."

Adones cocked a perfectly arched eyebrow. "This is most unusual. Is my aunt having trouble?"

I was so used to fathers being part of the delivery, I had almost forgotten this wasn't normal here.

"The birth is progressing. Aurelia and Melania are with Lady Imilce, and they sent us to summon Hannibal. This is all we know."

He peered at the stage below. "We'll inform him after the Sufet finishes his speech."

I turned away from Adones and leaned against the rail. Based on the frowns on the Peace Party's side, they weren't thrilled with the Sufet's speech. Hannibal's stony expression wasn't giving much away either. Adones moved closer to get a better look below.

His breath warmed the back of my neck, sending pleasant shivers down my arms and a pang of sadness through my heart. He was so alive and real and vibra—

The Patriot Party and Adones roared with applause, causing me to jump about a foot in the air.

Adones rested a hand on my shoulder. "We have the Sufet's support. Carthage is going to war."

I tried to ignore the sinking feeling in my stomach and forced a smile. Aside from being in a city that was facing the beginning of the end, Adones would soon find death in battle. I needed to warn him, and hopefully it wouldn't cause unintended consequences.

"What of Lady Imilce?" Elissa crossed her arms over her chest and tapped her foot.

"I'll inform Hannibal at once." Beaming, Adones tugged an errant curl by her ear. "Allay your concerns about my aunt. Ba'al Hammon has smiled upon our house, and nothing can tear it down."

Chapter Twelve

By the time we rode into the empty courtyard, the sun had begun to give way to night. Despite our hard-riding, Hannibal and Adones had beaten us to the mansion. Pallab met us. He set a brush on the trough and took our reins while we dismounted.

The minute my feet hit the ground, I rubbed my aching back. At times like these, I missed cars more than French fries, and that was saying a lot. I really, really loved fries.

Elissa greeted her grandfather with a hug while I stretched. After a brief exchange, her smile faded, and she returned her attention to me.

"Is something amiss?" I asked.

"Lady Imilce's labor has proven difficult." Elissa's voice trembled. "The midwife is with her now."

According to the Roman poet, Silius Italicus, Imilce had given birth to a son. It was thought that before Hannibal's trek over the Alps, he had returned her home to Iberia to protect them from the Romans. This knowledge made it easy to reassure Elissa.

Taking her hand into mine, I said, "I know this situation seems dire, yet we must not give up hope. I believe Lady Imilce will give birth to a healthy baby."

She sniffed and nodded.

When we entered the kitchen, two young girls were busy cooking. The thinner one leaned over a hunk of meat with a hatchet. Long, black braids fell over her shoulders and almost touched the bloody board as she chopped away. I fought a gag and turned my attention to the other girl.

"Good evening," I said.

She flashed a dimpled smile while kneading a hunk of dough. "Evening, mistress."

"How is Lady Imilc—"

A high-pitched scream echoed above us.

The girl with the dough stared at the stucco ceiling. "Lady Imilce has screamed like this since you left. Praise Ba'al you found Master Hannibal. I pray he'll bring her comfort."

I considered offering to help, but something told me I'd only get in the way.

"And what of my grandmother?" Elissa asked.

Hatchet-girl regarded her beneath bushy eyebrows. "She's assisting the midwife. Mistress Aurelia fell ill and took abed."

Of course, she did. Freaking Wuss.

Another scream resounded above, followed by Hannibal's indistinct words.

"Fear not, she's under the best care in the city," Hatchet-girl added.

There was a jumble of chatter and laughter above us.

Elissa smiled. "This is good."

"Praise Tinnit," said Dough-girl.

"Don't celebrate too soon," said the girl with the hatchet. "If Lady Imilce were through the worst, wouldn't we hear a child's cry?"

"I don't know," Elissa observed.

A high-pitched shriek above us pierced my soul. It sounded like Imilce. I couldn't be sure.

Hatchet and dough girls kept staring at the ceiling with their mouths hanging open.

Imilce and her baby are okay.

Melania's voice blended with others above us in Punic. Hannibal spoke fast and rumbly, and scrambled footfalls followed. Then, Elissa and I exchanged uneasy glances, bolted down the hall, and headed upstairs. We nearly slammed into Adones along the way. The lines around his mouth were deeper than usual.

Elissa bit her thumbnail.

My heart fell. "Lady Imilce, her child?"

Adones clenched and unclenched his fists. "They're with Tinnit now." Then, he pushed past us and ran down the stairs.

Elissa covered her face and crumpled onto the step. I stood there, stunned, unable to breathe, let alone comfort her. This was all wrong. I closed my eyes, unable to push away the memories shadowed by time. Memories of Dad on the night of the accident nine years ago. I'd stood there like a mindless zombie, barely noticing the blue and red police lights flashing through the kitchen window. The trooper's voice boomed against the silence as he announced Mom had rolled her car and died instantly. There had been no fear or anger, only numbness. That is until Dad dropped to his knees and rasped out a sorrowful cry that pierced my soul. I knew at that moment, my mother was gone. Since then, only an unending void remained in the place I had reserved for her love. I had a sinking feeling that another unbearable night lay ahead.

That night, members of the household gathered in the foyer and watched in reverent silence as temple priests carried the dead past us. Beneath the gauzelike wrap, Imilce's golden skin had paled. Her bluish lips were turned down in a frown as she cradled her lifeless newborn against her chest. Mother and child in eternal sleep. Hannibal didn't shed a tear. He stared ahead. His brown eyes flickered with pain and anger, darker and deeper than anything I'd ever seen on a person's face. It was as if he would never know joy again.

Adones' and Aurelia's washed-out cheeks and puffy skin were the only signs of grief betraying their otherwise emotionless expressions. Elissa and Melania sniffled beside me as the priests passed us carrying the dead. The scene was a breathless reminder of the mother I'd lost, of missed shopping trips, proms, dances, and graduations. Elissa took my hand. Tears streamed down her cheeks as we watched the dead pass over the threshold of the front door, then fade into the night.

Chapter Thirteen

Over the next four days, Hannibal's men poured in by the dozens to offer their support. The only good thing about their presence was Aurelia's father feared her virginal reputation might be sullied and he sent for her. Despite all her insecurities about me and Adones, she returned home without a fight. Probably because she was too shallow to deal with anything heavy.

The house's sorrow served as a reminder of my losses and my need for answers about all the contradictions between this version of Carthage and the one I had learned about in school. According to the history in my timeline, Imilce should have lived. Carthage shouldn't have had magical swords, Shadus, harpies, or mammoths. There had to be a logical explanation, and Ba'al Hammon seemed the only connection to getting answers. First, I needed to help this family through their grief, then I'd locate the god after the funeral. Even if that meant marching up to the temple and holding a priest hostage until he showed.

In the meantime, I kept busy helping Melania and Elissa. This didn't stop Adones' protests about how I made the family look bad by putting a guest to work. I just ignored him and did what was needed, but busting my ass in an ancient kitchen was no joke. Aside from the oppressive heat, all the food was made from scratch. Wring the neck and pluck the feathers off the bird from scratch. After seeing that, I happily volunteered to play server to Hannibal's men.

While waiting for the next food tray, sweat dripped from Melania's brow onto the wooden table as she wrapped a fig leaf around cheese and ground meat. Hygiene issues happened so often, I hardly blinked an eye anymore.

I gestured toward the food. "May I help? You haven't taken two moments for yourself."

"No." She ran her forearm over her brow and resumed her task. "I need to work. It keeps me from going mad."

I grabbed a wooden cup. Then, I filled it with water from a bronze spigot on the wall fountain behind us and handed it to Melania. "Please, you need to drink."

Melania emptied the contents in a couple of gulps, set the cup down, and leaned on the table. "Apologies if I'm curt. Lady Imilce's passing has—" Her breath hitched. "I raised her since she was a babe. It's torture to see one so young move on."

I fought the urge to back away from her, to run and hide from discussing … death.

Fortunately, Elissa interrupted the moment when she entered carrying a basket full of empty cups and plates. Her perky side had packed up and left for places unknown, leaving a more frowny, quiet person behind. She placed the basket on the workstation, moved to the corner of the kitchen, and sat alone.

Melania glanced at the food on the bread board and sighed.

"What is it?" I asked.

She wiped her hands on her apron. "I need another tray."

"I'd be happy to get you one," I said.

She pointed toward a hallway off the kitchen. "They're in the room next to the food cupboard."

I headed down the short hallway to a barred door that was propped open. When I stepped inside, I understood the need for security. Wooden shelves along each side of the rectangular space were filled with silver trays, golden goblets, and candle holders. However, given Hannibal's reputation for ruthlessness, I doubted anyone would be stupid enough to steal from him.

I grabbed a flat silver tray off the shelf and returned to Melania.

She eyed me curiously. "I have a feeling you were a strong-willed child."

I shrugged and helped her arrange the wrapped fig leaves on the tray. "I prefer tenacious. Is it so difficult to accept that I want to make myself useful?"

"No, I suppose it isn't," she finished the arrangement and wiped her hands together. "I should take these to the—"

"I can do it."

"No, mistress, it isn't right."

"Look, I'm off to my quarters after this. Please, this is my last run. You have my word."

With a grateful nod, she handed over the tray and I headed down the corridor before she changed her mind. A couple of minutes later, I entered the bustling hall and maneuvered around bearded men standing along a table filled with food. Some ate quarters of meat. Others downed the contents of their wooden cups. A toothless guy with two hairs on his head slapped my ass with a loud *whap* as I passed.

I wheeled around with tray in hand and kicked him in the shin, yelling in English, "Asshole!"

He and the three other bearded wonders roared with laughter.

I stormed over to Hannibal and his frowning sidekick, Captain Asshat. Placing the tray on the table next to a war board dotted with miniature replicas of wooden elephants and soldiers, I said, "Melania sent these for you."

Adones smiled at me from a chair beside his uncle. "We're most grateful."

Hannibal slowly tore his attention from the war board. The joy I had seen when he had spoken of his unborn baby and gazed at his wife had been replaced by a cold, emotionless man. "I suggest you adjourn to your quarters and get some rest. We rise early for the funeral rite. Ba'al Hammon will be blessing us with his presence, and we must honor him by arriving at the bidden time." He returned to moving the figurines around the board like a bunch of chess pieces.

For the first time since my arrival here, hope flooded my chest. This was it. My chance to engage with the god, to find out if he could help me. With a slight curtsy, I rushed toward the door, mind reeling. Could I just go to Ba'al and say, hey, I'm from the fut—

Someone grabbed my arm. Anger simmered in my stomach. I wheeled around with my fist drawn, ready to throw a punch.

Adones chuckled. "I didn't mean to startle you."

I brought my hand to my chest. "Easily done in this crowd."

"They can be quite unruly." Adones scanned the room, frowning. "Please, allow me to see you safely to your quarters."

If I didn't accept his offer, one of those pervs might follow me upstairs. He was the safer bet, so we left the hall and headed down the dimly-lit foyer.

Adones gave me a sidelong glance. "I haven't thanked you for helping Melania."

I smiled. "It was the least I could do after your uncle's hospitality toward me."

He glanced at the ring on my finger and the bracelet. "Your work here has more than paid your debt for those jewels."

"Absolutely not! I chose to help because I care for your family," I shot back at him.

His mouth twitched upward. "So prideful."

We broke off and ascended the marble stairs to the second floor. I stepped onto the landing, ready to continue my protest about the jewelry when Adones blocked my way.

"I bring good tidings." His words didn't match the hint of sadness in his tone.

My brow wrinkled. "Oh?"

He nodded. "Your journey to Sparta has been expedited. Three sunrises from this day, you will board a textile vessel with my uncle's guards. They'll remain by your side until you're reunited with your father."

My stomach tumbled. This was sooner than expected. If I didn't get momentum with Ba'al Hammon tomorrow, I'd have to run and take my chances on the streets.

Adones studied me for a beat. "Are you displeased?"

The smile I flashed was so tight, my cheeks hurt. "Er, no I'm elated. I — I'm merely concerned about my brother and his partner. They're still lost and alone. Nor am I comfortable leaving your family after—" I bit my bottom lip as the image of Imilce and her baby's lifeless bodies shot to the front of my mind.

Adones stepped closer. I didn't resist, didn't move as he tilted my chin up until our gazes met. I breathed in his scent, fresh as the wild rosemary that grew naturally here, with hints of sweet honey. If we'd met in another world, another time, maybe we could have pursued this attraction. I curled my hand into a fist to keep from touching his broad chest.

His green eyes, with all their differing shades, gazed at me with such promise as he spoke. "Did you lose your mother?"

I let out a shaky breath, feeling like I'd just been stripped naked, like there was no part of me he couldn't see, and I didn't know how I felt about this. "Ho-how do you know?"

He swept an errant curl behind my ear. "You never speak of her."

This was way too personal. I backed away from him stating curtly. "Thank you for the escort. I can see myself to my room." I turned and practically trotted off.

"You're not alone," Adones called after me. "I too lost my parents."

I slowed my pace. This explained why he lived with his aunt and uncle. Yet I couldn't concern myself with such things. My priority was to find Greg and Sophie and return home. Nothing more. Unfortunately, Adones didn't make this easy.

He closed the gap between us, grabbed my arm, and wheeled me toward him. "I mean this sincerely. You're not alone, Amara."

I should have taken my arm back, except the intensity in his gaze kept me glued in place.

"I seldom speak of this."

"You don't have to," I said.

"I want to." His grip on my arm tightened, but not in a way that hurt. It was more like he was afraid to let go. "When I was four and one half, my mother died giving birth to my brother who was also stillborn. The memory's vague, yet it doesn't sting any less. Uncle Hannibal was close to my mother. Although nine years his senior, she was a fiercely protective sister and he took her death very hard, as did my father. I was left as a ward with a warrior who trained me in the way of the sword, while my father fought in various campaigns. Seven years later, he died in an unofficial battle against Roman scum. My uncle Hannibal is thirteen years my senior, so he took me in. I adopted the Barcid name and joined him here in Carthage."

"I can't imagine how difficult that must have been."

Adones took my hand. The warmth of his touch sent a dozen butterflies fluttering across my chest. I'd never met another person who lost a parent, much less two.

"We've both suffered much loss." Adones' voice had become rougher. "Don't we deserve some happiness as well?"

I tilted my head. "What are you saying?"

"I wish to know you better," he said. "I see how this must appear to you, an engaged man expressing interest in another woman. Yet, all is not as it seems. I'm only marrying Aurelia out of duty to my family. Nothing more."

My jaw tightened. I wasn't sure what he expected me to do with this information because it didn't make him any less committed.

Adones raked a hand through his waves. "Unlike Aurelia, you're a woman of depth. Despite being highborn, you work in the kitchen with servants. Not to mention your bravery, how you stand for what you believe. Don't we owe it to ourselves to explore what's growing between us before I go to war?"

The thought of how that war would end for him had my stomach in knots. Adones had been the only constant since I arrived here, the life raft that kept me from drowning in a sea of fear and uncertainty. At the very least, he deserved to be warned, unintended consequences be damned. I opened my mouth to tell him what I knew and closed it. How could I do this without sounding insane? Maybe leaving a letter was the easiest approach.

"Have I poured out my heart for naught?"

I just didn't have it in me to deal with more loss, so I decided to bow out gracefully. "Like it or not, you're engaged to another, and I must return to my father. This, us, cannot be."

At that, I took back my arm and headed down the hall.

"Believe me. I don't love Aurelia, nor do I wish to wed her," Adones called after me. "My family require—"

Tears leaked from my eyes as I entered my bedroom and slammed the door behind me. I hated my insane attraction to a guy who was not only engaged but was also destined to die in battle. Things were getting too muddied, and I needed to get home before I did something stupid. Tomorrow, I'd talk to Ba'al Hammon. Otherwise, my lie would be revealed, and I might land in a dungeon beside Bear or worse.

Chapter Fourteen

The next morning, I descended the stairs to the foyer dressed in a Tyrian purple gown. Although I dreaded all things having to do with death, I had to suck it up and attend the funeral rite if I hoped to speak with Ba'al. All I needed was a minute to request an audience for later.

Elissa met me at the door in tan petticoats with a matching shawl. Her washed-out skin and dark circles beneath her eyes made her appear much older than the bouncy girl I had met six days ago.

"This color suits you, Mistress, Amara," she said in a flat voice.

"Thank you."

She reached for the door and hesitated. "Apologies if I've been out of sorts lately. Lady Imilce's death has been difficult." Her lip trembled, and she bit down on it.

I ignored the stabbing pain in my chest at seeing her discomfort. "Never apologize. I'm sorry this happened."

"Your graciousness is truly appreciated." Elissa opened the door, and we stepped outside to the circular cobbled drive.

The first hints of daylight painted the sky pink and white, and a soft breeze warmed my skin. Several feet to my right, a cluster of mourners had gathered before Hannibal. He appraised them through eyes that were fierce and sharp as the blade by his side. My attention gravitated to Adones. As always, he looked so tall and handsome standing at attention beside his uncle. His white chlamys was etched in purple and pinned with a gold fibula at the right shoulder. Before them, a platoon of foot soldiers stood at attention. Although their hardened faces were lined and scarred from many battles, more than one eye was wet with tears.

Elissa and I filed in at the rear of the formation beside Pallab and Melania. They were freshly scrubbed and dressed in clean, unbleached robes.

"Good day," I said.

Melania and Pallab's pained expressions spoke to the solemnness of the occasion. "Good day, mistress," she greeted.

A woman in the front coughed. When I glanced toward the noise, Aurelia stood with her back to us, acting like she hadn't heard me and Elissa. No shocker there. Immediately I recognized the man in a cap with a top knot as the Sufet. He stepped into formation beside Aurelia and the woman beside her in a veil. The trio chatted with other nobles in robes ranging from bright blues to tones of gold.

A horn blew from the front of the crowd and Elissa elbowed me. "It's time."

Hannibal shouted a command in his deep, booming voice. His men marched toward the front gate followed by the rest of us. Heavy footfalls clapped against flagstone streets. Swords clinked, and axes dangled from the soldiers' hilts as they followed their general. Ahead, the ocean sparkled deep aqua, and seagulls squawked beneath the morning sun. Despite the bright day, a sort of gloom lingered among the crowd of grieving people. Aurelia reached beneath her veil and wiped her tears. Her father's spine bowed. Other mourners emerged from their businesses and took a knee as we marched past them.

After about a half hour of walking, we approached a domed temple with stone columns. Elissa pointed at the symbol of a bearded man with goat horns etched into each corner of the building.

"That's the symbol of Ba'al Hammon."

I fought the urge to say, 'duh,' and nodded instead. I suppose this showed some growth.

The procession stopped before a stone sepulcher behind the temple where two priests in striped headdresses waited. Their embroidered robes with red stars folded into pleats and gathered at their legs as they approached the general. While he kissed each of their hands, my attention gravitated to hundreds of tiny clay urns sprinkled across the field.

"A Tophet?" I said more to myself than Elissa.

She frowned. "Indeed. We lay the ashes of our infants to rest here. Haven't you seen one before?"

"Yes." This burial site was larger than the one at the ruins and I had a tough time looking away.

There had been speculation the Carthaginians had sacrificed their children to the gods during times of strife. Yet, I didn't see the monsters portrayed by history in this procession. Could historians have been wrong? What remained of Carthage's story had been told by the victors who destroyed the city. I also couldn't dismiss that infant mortality was more than fifty percent during this time. Adones' mother and unborn child had died giving birth, just like Imilce and her baby. All the urns could have been the result of stillbirths or crib deaths.

"You should join the nobles." Elissa gestured toward the line of people moving single file into the sepulcher.

I dragged my gaze from the urns, confused. Dad once told me the Carthaginians had conducted funeral rites outside, which clearly wasn't the case. I gave Elissa a once-over. "Aren't you coming?"

She shook her head. "No, only those from highborn families may enter due to a lack of space."

This was unfair. She and Melania loved Imilce. They should have been afforded an opportunity for closure, but this wasn't a day to question their culture.

"Go!" Elissa urged me on. "You're one of them."

Reluctantly, I took my place at the back of the line. The closer I moved to the darkened entry of the sepulcher, the harder my heart thumped against my chest. Pagan rites varied between cultures, and little was known about those practiced by the Carthaginians. Yet, this didn't stop my imagination from running away with me. If Ba'al sacrificed an animal or forced us to drink real blood, I'd tuck tail and run.

I stepped into the small chamber and took my place at the back of the crowd. If nothing else, I was close enough to the door to run if my worst fears came true. The setting did nothing to ease my mind. Flickering flames caused splinters of light to dance across the stone sarcophagus. The rectangular altar in the center of the space resembled those I'd seen in Rome and the ruins of Carthage. They were forged from marble, and the altar had a flat top, with beveled edges and round legs.

The priests escorted Hannibal to the sarcophagus and waited with their heads bowed. I blinked away my tears as this great man rested a hand on the likeness of his wife, carved into the top. Since only four days had passed since Imilce's death, the noble's coffins must have been prepared beforehand.

After a long silence, Hannibal reached toward a small urn on the altar, containing the ashes of his newborn son, then withdrew his hand before touching it. My chest clenched when he tilted his head back and released a mournful, hollow wail from his lungs. The sound echoed throughout the chamber and lingered in the air like a dark spirit, unable to escape a prison of unhappiness.

There was a sudden flash of light in the arched doorway ahead. Hannibal sniffed. When he stepped back, a loud crack like a firecracker followed by thick, acrid smoke drifted through the chamber. I rubbed my nose to filter out the rotten egg smell.

An excited murmur rippled across the crowd, followed by the whispered name, Ba'al Hammon. Hannibal and everyone else, including me, knelt. We all watched in silence as a figure wearing a gold mask with large round eye holes and goat horns emerged through the smokey doorway. How strange that the god covered his face. Did he look like us, or was he different?

Ba'al was hardly the towering figure I expected. Standing about six feet tall, his flowing gold robes shimmered as he raised his arms in the air. Everyone stood as he walked to Hannibal. The great general remained kneeling and Ba'al placed a hand as human as mine on his subject's crown of curls, speaking Punic.

My breath stuck in my throat. Even through the mask, his voice sounded familiar, too familiar. Where had I heard it?

After several minutes of praying over Hannibal, or whatever the god was doing, the mourners knelt again, leaving me standing in the back. My cheeks burned with heat. I dropped to my knees, watching Ba'al like a freaked-out possum about to be hit by a car. Our gazes locked. He fell silent, so silent that after several seconds, some of the mourners peeked over their shoulders in the direction Ba'al was looking. Someone in the audience cleared his throat, pulling Ba'al from his trance-like stare. He returned his focus to Hannibal and stammered a couple of times.

He's shaken.

One of the priests walked to the altar, grabbed a long silver wand with several holes on the end, and brought it to Ba'al. He turned toward the sarcophagus and flicked his wrist. Red stuff splattered out of the top of the wand. I hoped it wasn't blood. Ba'al returned the object to the priest on his left. The other one picked up a golden chalice from the altar and waited as Ba'al stood over the genuflecting Hannibal and looked across the crowd. The god and I locked gazes again. Seconds passed like minutes. My pulse beat thickly in my ears. Perspiration dripped down my temples and, in those seconds, I knew the god recognized me.

Chapter Fifteen

While following the nobles out of the sepulcher, I ran the encounter with Ba'al through my mind. I had not imagined the familiarity in his voice, the glint of recognition when our gazes met, or the stammering that followed. He was surprised to see me. His smoke and mirrors entrance left questions too. The sulphury rotten egg smell during his grand entrance hinted that he had used gunpowder, but this didn't exist yet. He had practically run out of there after the rite, leaving me no closer to getting answers than I had been this morning.

Since I only had three days left in Carthage before Hannibal shipped me off, there wouldn't be enough time for him to request an audience. Plus, he would probably ask a lot of questions I wasn't prepared to answer. If I slipped out of the house tonight and returned to this temple, I'd likely encounter the priests. I doubted they'd let a lowly nobody like me go anywhere near Ba'al. At least not without something to offer. This didn't mean I couldn't try.

On the return trip to Hannibal's mansion, I walked in the back of the procession with Elissa. The bathhouses, and cisterns were metaphorical breadcrumbs to guide me back to the temple. As we rounded a corner and proceeded up a hill, I noticed a guy in a brown hooded cloak standing among the crowd of mourners. I could have sworn he stared straight at me as we passed. When I glanced over my shoulder to get a better look at him, he was gone.

The procession continued in silence until late afternoon when we arrived at Hannibal's house. The journey there had provided time to devise a plan that might tip the scales on my side. However, this required me to do something I never thought I'd consider, until now. Desperate times called for desperate measures.

Acting like I was heading to my room, I crept down the back stairs instead and headed toward the kitchen. I stopped short of entering when I saw a girl with long black braids kneading dough. I pushed away the guilt rising inside me and approached her.

She greeted me with a wide smile. "Can I help you, mistress?"

I wiped my sweaty palms on my robes before answering. "Um, I believe Melania wants you to check on the guests. There are several."

The girl's brow furrowed. "How odd. Aren't the other servants with them?"

"It's very busy. I think she needs your help." Lying had become too easy, and I didn't like it.

She swiped her hands together, ridding them of the residual dough before she stormed out of the room. My heart thundered as I hastened down the short hallway off the kitchen and stopped before the storage closet that housed the Barcids' valuables. The barred door hung open. It mocked me for taking advantage of Hannibal's trust. Not to mention what would happen if he caught me.

I mopped my hands over my face and entered the small closet-sized room, listening for even the slightest sound in the hallway. My gaze darted between the silver trays and goblets. There had to be something small enough to hide beneath my robes, yet valuable enough for bartering. Then the golden candle holders on the second shelf caught my eye.

My breaths came out in erratic huffs as I plucked the items from their homes and shoved them inside my robes. Never had I felt so dirty. Ignoring the hand-sized knots tightening in my stomach, I peeked outside the door into the hall. The coast was clear, so I scurried out of the closet like a rat and ran upstairs to my room. Quickly and smartly, I hid the items in a sack beneath my bed. Tonight, I'd make my move.

When I returned to the great hall, I took in the scene before me, noting how the mourners' interactions weren't much different than the people from my time. Hannibal's soldiers were the ancients' version of college athletes. Engaged in a total testosterone fest, they hung around the tables at the back of the space, swigging wine, laughing, and speaking over everyone.

Aurelia and her posse could have passed for the rich sorority girls, dressed in soft robes with intricate beading, looking down their noses at everyone who didn't fit their mold. And then there was me. If nothing else, I was consistent, even in this century. I stood alone in the far corner, holding up the wall. Mostly, I tried not to stare at the way Adones' white tunic contrasted against his sun-kissed skin. How his wavy black hair touched the top of his collar as he worked the room. If he found out what I'd done, he would hate me.

"He's handsome, don't you agree?" a familiar voice said.

Elissa had taken her place beside me as one of the resident wallflowers. She regarded me through wide, perceptive eyes. Eyes that had busted me watching Adones.

"Um, I suppose. Why?" I asked, feeling all the blood rush to my face.

Her lips curled into a humorless smile. "It's odd that you're admiring him, considering you found it acceptable to steal from him."

She knows! I grabbed her slim wrist. "Come with me now."

Before she could protest, I led her past the crowd of people, sensing Adones watching us as we headed down the foyer and up the stairs. When we entered my room, I closed the door behind us. Elissa made a beeline for my bed. She fell to her knees, pulled the sack from underneath, and turned it upside down.

The golden candle holders fell onto the sheepskin rug as she glowered at me. "Care to explain?"

I balled my hands into fists when I caught a glimpse of my boots protruding from beneath her skirt. "Do *you* care to explain why those are on your feet?"

"This is not about me. First you go to that criminal's aid and now this." Elissa gestured toward the items on the rug. "How could you steal from the Barcids? I thought you were their friend."

My face flushed hot with shame. "If I told you the truth, you wouldn't believe me."

"Why should I?"

"Because I have good reason for what I've done." When she continued glaring at me, I let out a defeated sigh and plopped on the bed. Time to let the chips fall where they may. "My father isn't from Sparta, and we were never robbed by bandits." It felt good to let go of my baggage.

"You purposely lied to the Barcids?" she asked with her lips pursed.

"I didn't lie to Master Hannibal. I'm from the Americas, and my country is far across the sea. The part I omitted was *when* my country was discovered and *how* I arrived here."

The crease between Elissa's brows deepened.

"I know this is confusing, and what I'm about to tell you may sound like the words of a madwoman, but I'm telling the truth. My country won't be discovered for two thousand years."

Her lips parted. "In the future?"

I nodded. Then I told the Cliff Notes version of my journey, beginning with how the disc magically transported Greg, Sophie, and me here, my run-in with Bear, finding the ring and bracelet, and ended on the encounter with Ba'al.

Elissa's mouth was open. "What you're saying defies logic."

I held her gaze and pointed at my boots. "Have you ever seen shoes such as those or garments made from my fabrics?"

"No." She rubbed the sculpted rubber soles on my boots. "Yet, I still struggle to believe you're from the future."

"Why would I lie? There are other stories I could concoct to convince you. Believe me. I'm from a time far more advanced than anything you could imagine."

She blinked. "The odd device in Master Hannibal's possession?"

She had to be talking about my cell. "How do you know about that?"

Her face flushed red. "I overheard him discussing it with Captain Aharim. They'd never seen anything like it."

Of course, her little nosy ass knew what was going on. Still, telling her about texting and the Internet was far too complicated. Asking the location of my cell was also pointless. No way I could get past Aharim or his guards. Best to keep things simple, so I inhaled deeply and continued my explanation.

"It's used to communicate with others over long distances with the push of a button. In the Americas there are ships that fly and carry people between countries. We have establishments that sell meals in the time it takes to set a table, and large insulated, er, crates to keep our food cold."

"Truly, ships that fly?" Her voice held an edge of excitement, but she quickly reined it in and sat back with her arms crossed over her chest again. "How is this possible?"

I shrugged. "Ships have large wings and they are self-propelled by a thing called a—" I searched my mind for the word motor in ancient Greek and replaced it with the modern translation, "Motér and they're spacious enough to fit at least two hundred or more people. My family used to travel in them during the summer solstice."

My chest had constricted at the thought of them.

She frowned. "You miss them."

"I do." My voice trembled and I cleared my throat. "Please believe me. I'm not lying."

A long silence passed between us. "I do. Tinnit, help me, I do believe you, mistress. Your odd clothing and speech, along with the mysterious device, support your story."

My hand flew to hers. "You have no idea what a relief it is to tell the truth."

"I can only imagine," she said. "Although I don't like keeping secrets from Masters Hannibal and Adones, sharing what I know could put you in peril. I'd never forgive myself if they thought you mad and imprisoned you."

I fidgeted. "You'll keep my secret?"

"I will, mistress. You have my word." Elissa picked up one of the candle holders and ran her finger down the golden stem. "What does this have to do with the lie about how you arrived here."

"Er, like I told you, I saw clear recognition in Ba'al Hammon's eyes during the funeral rite, and before you ask, I'm certain we've never met. I planned to use those holders to bribe Ba'al's priests to gain an audience with the god."

Elissa clenched the candlestick. "What if you're mistaken and he didn't recognize you?"

"What if I'm not? Ba'al may hold the key to helping me find my brother and his partner, of returning me to my time so I can help my father through his illness."

"I see. At least you're giving these to my god." Elissa returned everything to the sack and put it beside me.

She could've been the little sister I never knew I wanted. "Thanks for giving me a chance to explain." Then I added. "Why didn't you tell Master Hannibal about the theft?"

A long moment passed between us before she spoke again. "If not for he and Lady Imilce, I might have lost my hand or worse for stealing. They gave me a chance. I thought it fair to do the same for you."

"You had your grandparents. Was their situation so dire that you needed to steal?"

"I barely knew them," she observed. "Since my mother and I followed my father's troop and cooked for them, we didn't have the opportunity to establish roots. After the plague took them, I was forced to make my way to Carthage and find my grandparents. This proved more difficult than I thought. When I arrived here, I had to steal to survive until I found Master Hannibal."

The thought of her alone in the city like some stray dumpster kitty made my heart ache. "That must have been difficult."

She shrugged. "There's no advantage in lamenting the past."

Being a priestess was far better than that fate, unless the Romans invaded before she finished her schooling.

I took Elissa's hand into mine. "There's something you need to know in case the worst happens."

"The worst?" She withdrew her hand and scrunched her skirt nervously.

"Yes. Ten seasons of Spring will pass before Hannibal returns from the war with Rome. Much strife will follow, and eventually, Rome will destroy Carthage to the point that nothing remains of the city or its culture. Since you're studying to be a priestess, I urge you to hide as many of your scholars' codices and scrolls as possible. This way the Romans can't rewrite your people's history. Then, you and your family must leave Carthage. Perhaps move to Athens or Jerusalem."

Her lip quivered. "Are you certain this will happen?"

I swallowed the knot in my throat. "Unfortunately, yes. Historians have written about the atrocities that occurred here. If you see signs that what I've shared will come to pass, flee the city."

"I will." She sat forward. "If you fail tonight, how will you find your way back here without a guide?"

"I took note of the buildings and other markers after the funeral rite." It wasn't like Carthage was LA.

She crossed her arms. "At least allow me to aid your escape from the grounds. I can help you get past the guards, and I'll keep watch until morning."

"That would be helpful."

"In the event you don't succeed, try to return before sunrise as Master Adones rises early."

My stomach sank. I still hadn't told Adones about his future, and he was too good a man to be lost in battle.

"Mistress, are you alright?"

I swallowed hard, hating to dump more stress on her. "There's one more thing I need to ask of you."

Elissa arched an eyebrow. "What is it?"

I entwined my fingers together on my lap to keep my hands steady. Then I told her about the tomb and how Adones died in the battle of Cannae. When I finished, her face was ghostly white.

Tears wet her cheeks. "First, you tell me that the city I've come to love will be destroyed, and now this?"

"It's unfair to lay these burdens in your hands, but given the urgency of my situation, I may not get a chance to warn him."

"Life isn't often fair, mistress." Elissa dried her cheeks, then she rose and smoothed her skirt. "I'll do what I can."

I pointed at her feet. "I need my boots, along with the rest of my clothing."

Elissa's cheeks reddened as she lifted her cover, revealing my clean T-shirt and bra. My mouth hung open. She had no shame.

She rubbed her palm over the bra. "I-It took me some time to understand this garment's purpose. The odd clasps were confusing." She surveyed my chest. "I'd like to keep this. It's not like you need it."

Elissa knew how to throw shade, and like it or not, she was right. My B-cup breasts didn't need the support. Still, was it wise to leave my clothing with her? I might have already changed the future here by sharing what I knew about Carthage and Adones. Fashion would change too. Yet, denying the one person who had agreed to help me wasn't smart so I nodded and said, "You may keep everything except my boots."

A wide smile was her response. She removed my shoes and set them beside me, then slipped on my sandals. "I'll return once the staff retire for the evening."

I glanced toward the shuttered window. The setting sun had given way to night, casting shadows throughout the room. We must have talked longer than I thought.

Elissa headed to the door and lingered a moment. "I won't be long."

She lied. I must have sat there for an hour, maybe longer. Just as I was about to give up on her, the door opened.

Oil lamp in hand, she stepped inside the room. Golden light washed over the space. "Come, mistress." Her eyes were wide and alert. "We should move while the men are otherwise engaged."

I grabbed the wheat sack and followed her down the hallway. As we descended the rear stairs, it wasn't lost on me that the flouncy girl I knew and loved had been replaced by a stealthy little cat, hunting prey. My step creaked. She froze, listening for movement against the muffled sounds of men's laughter coming from the great hall. After a moment, she resumed the journey, moving slowly and surely down the steps.

When we entered the kitchen, it was odd to see it empty. Beams of moonlight streamed through the open windows. Dozens of hanging spices swayed against the breeze. Elissa set the oil lamp on the table, blew out the flames, and walked to the arched entry. She cracked the wooden door enough to slip out. Following behind her, I glanced over my shoulder at the empty room, fighting the sinking feeling that this was the last time I'd see this place.

Chapter Sixteen

Hannibal's mansion loomed behind us as Elissa and I crept across the gated grounds like a couple of thieves in the night. We crouched behind flowering bushes and scurried between palms until we reached a flat-roofed stable, blanketed in light from the full moon. Horses whinnied from inside and I instantly realized how Elissa planned for me to escape.

"I can't ride. You know this," I whispered.

The sound of crunching rocks resounded behind us. I sucked in a deep breath when I spotted a shadowed figure heading in our direction. Elissa grabbed my hand and pulled me inside the stable. Mildewed hay and the pungent scent of horse manure wafted by my nose. Silver light shone through small, square windows running along the wall beside the door.

I pointed at the stall ahead. "We should hide in there."

"No, we'd alarm the horses, and they'd stomp us."

Heavy footfalls grew louder by the second. Elissa pushed me against the wall beneath the windows. She brought a finger to her lips, gesturing my silence. I clutched the wheat sack against my chest. My heart jackhammered as the door creaked open.

This was it. I was about to be busted. I didn't have an active enough imagination to lie my way out of this one. And what about Elissa? I needed to keep her out of it. Guess I could say

I ordered her to come with me, and she didn't know anything about my plans.

A masculine figure stepped inside. His face was shadowed. "Elissa," he called out.

Relief and anger coursed through my veins all at once. I slowly turned my head toward the little sneak beside me. "You told him?"

"You left me no choice." Elissa stepped out of the shadows. "Here, Master Adones. We're here."

He closed the gap between us and pried the sack from my hands while I stood there like a loser-shoplifter busted by store security. Without taking his eyes from me, Adones loosened the ties, reached inside, and pulled out a candlestick. "Why did you appropriate these?"

I waved a hand toward Elissa. "Didn't she tell you?"

Elissa wrapped her arms around me. I resisted the urge to push the little traitor away. "Oh mistress, forgive me. I couldn't have you walking the streets alone at night. They're too dangerous. I had to trust Master Adones with your plan to go to the *temple* and find Ba'al Hammon."

Since Elissa made it a point to tell me specifically what she shared with Adones, maybe she hadn't given up my time travel secret.

Adones glowered at me. "You're here because I wanted to hear your explanation away from prying ears. How will these candlesticks grant you an audience with my god?"

"Er, I planned to use them to bribe one of the temple priests. After witnessing Ba'al's greatness at the funeral rite, I hoped he could offer advice about how to return to my father. Perhaps he could tell me what happened to my brother and his partner, as well."

"Amara, one doesn't march into a temple and demand an audience with a *god*. There are protocols. We must submit a request through a high priest."

"I knew you would say this. Thus, the reason I planned to go tonight. I haven't the time to await the response to a written request. Your uncle plans to ship me to Sparta soon. With so much uncertainty surrounding my loved ones, I need answers now."

Adones bent until he met Elissa at eye level. "Can you ready my horse without a lamp?"

She flashed a wide smile. "I already have. In case you decided to escort Mistress Amara. Would you like me to bring it to you?"

He nodded and she took off like a shot.

Elissa had to be one of the most energetic people I'd ever known. Good thing she didn't live in my time. She would've lost it after a couple of iced coffees.

When she disappeared into a stall at the end of the walk, Adones said, "Since you insist on visiting the temple this night, I'll see you safely there. Be warned, it's unlikely you'll find the answers you seek."

"I must try. If you were in a similar position, wouldn't you do whatever it took to return to your family, to find your friends?"

"I suppose I would," Adones held up the wheat sack. "These candlesticks are a trivial offering and would likely insult Ba'al Hammon."

"What do you suggest?"

He shrugged. "I'm a Barcid. This may give us an advantage."

My brow creased. "I thought your position wasn't high enough to speak to your god."

Adones shook his head. "It's not. My uncle, however, has close ties with Ba'al Hammon and this may be enough to grant me an audience. If not, we'll return home and send a formal request."

"Won't that spark questions?"

"Perhaps," Adones observed. "Let's deal with that if the need arises."

Elissa emerged from the stall and ran toward us with a giant black horse plodding behind her.

Adones took the reins. "Thank you. You've done well."

Elissa beamed.

Although it was tough to admit, I was relieved to have an escort.

Adones handed Elissa the wheat sack. "Return this to the house. We have no need for it." He hopped onto the saddle in one lithe swoop and adjusted his sword and cape.

I wrapped my arms around Elissa and whispered. "Thank you for keeping my secret."

She nodded. "I'll take it to my grave."

"It's time." Adones extended his hand toward me.

His palm was warm and calloused against mine. With a slight grunt, Adones pulled me up until I was seated in the saddle in front of him. Then he slid an arm around my waist. His chest and abs were rock solid against me. I fidgeted uneasily, falling further and further into an abyss of unwanted emotions. I needed to find a way out before this non-relationship with Adones went way beyond complicated.

Elissa smiled. "I'll see you soon."

I took in the loose curls falling around her face. Somehow, she'd weaseled her way into my heart, and there, she'd always stay.

Adones shook the reins, and our horse carried us toward the door. Elissa beat us there and opened it. Breathless, she waved as we passed. "Take care."

We made our way through the streets of Carthage, illuminated only by the fire from freestanding braziers along our path. Our horse's hooves clacked against the pavers, a ghostly sound in the night. We passed an ancient pub, bubbling with voices. A lone man in a heavy hooded cloak staggered out from between two buildings. I did a double take as he disappeared into the shadows across the street. He was the second person today I had seen in a heavy cloak. What were the odds?

Dogs yelped from somewhere close by. Two young boys rang bells in front of a bathhouse door as we passed. People with baskets on their heads barely looked our way.

Curiosity about Adones' motives finally got the best of me, and I broke the silence. "Why are you helping me?"

He leaned in and whispered in my ear. "I couldn't pass up the chance to be alone with you."

I shrugged him away. "Like I said before. You're engaged."

"Amara, I—"

A gasp escaped my lips as something moved in my periphery. I glanced toward a shadowed courtyard to our left. Rows of bushes sprouting with white flowers shined beneath the moonlight. I sat straighter and scanned dark yards and tall buildings to each side of us, seeing nothing but shadows. Ahead, domed roofs cascaded toward a massive lake divided by stone barriers. The water glistened and twinkled silver beneath the starry sky. Carthage's walls towered in the distance. Nothing was out of place.

Adones wrapped his cloak around me, and I inhaled his familiar scent of honey and rosemary.

"You're shaking. Are you warm enough?" His voice was barely a whisper.

"Yes, thank you." *Why did he have to be so damn sultry and handsome?* I leaned forward to put a little distance between us.

"Is something amiss?" he asked.

"If someone sees us, could it compromise your engagement to Aurelia?"

"I'm not thinking of *her*." He let out an exasperated breath. "Ba'al's blood! How many ways must I tell you how I feel before you understand?"

After losing so much with Mom's death, and now Dad's cancer, there was no way I'd let myself get pulled in by an engaged warrior who found honor in battle. A pang of sadness pierced my lungs as I thought about his end. He could have turned me in for the candlesticks, and instead, he decided to help. He was kind and supportive, and he deserved to know the truth, regardless of how he might take it.

"Adones, there's something I need to tell you."

"I'm listening." His thighs shifted as he guided the horse toward a garden fountain surrounded by lit braziers. The statue of a mermaid in the center of the pool watched our approach through bulging eyes. Her fish-like lips, flowing hair, and long torso fin looked so real, I half-expected her to swim away.

I leaned into Adones, couldn't help myself. "What I'm about to share may sound mad—"

A twig snapped in the garden. There was movement in the shadows between two palms. Possibly an animal. Adones tightened his arm protectively around me. Water trickled from the mermaid's mouth into the babbling pool. Palms rustled mysteriously in the breeze.

Then, a handful of hooded men emerged from the bushes with their swords drawn. Our horse tossed its head. I held onto the almost nonexistent saddle horn. Adones drew his blade, jiggled the reins, and spurred the horse forward.

"Ha'ah!"

Three men ran in front of us, gesturing wildly with their swords. They were yelling in Punic. Our animal reared. My full weight fell against Adones, and we slid backward off our mount. Then his sword went flying and I fell onto Adones. He hit the ground with a thud, and I rolled off him.

The horse galloped away. Adones scrambled toward his blade, grabbed it, and was on his feet in a blink. A short guy shouted at us. His face was shadowed beneath the hood.

Adones struck first. He swung his glistening blade at one of the attackers, and the man ducked sideways. This wasn't fast enough to prevent Adones from slitting him from naval to chest and spilling his guts like a fish. Short man yelled while waving his hands at us, like he wanted us to stop.

"Run, Amara. Now!" Adones yelled.

Fear jolted through my body like an electric current. I came to my senses and hauled ass toward the buildings. The short guy grabbed my robes from behind. I shrieked, twisted toward him, and clawed at his face. Blood rolled down his cheeks. He growled under his breath and tackled me to the ground, landing on top of me with all his weight. The back of my head slammed against the pavers. Voices faded into the background and then there was nothing.

Chapter Seventeen

I groaned and my vision blurred. My head throbbed, but not in a headache sort of way. More like a constant soreness radiating from the back of my scalp to my temples. Then, the sword fight and the chase slowly materialized in my mind like the aftereffects of a bad dream. I tried to rub my eyes and jolted to full consciousness when I realized my back was against a stone column.

"Are you awake?" called a whispered voice.

Something warm rubbed against my fingers, and I curled them into a fist, trying to jerk away.

"Amara, it's me, Adones," came from the other side of the column. "Our hands are tethered together."

I tugged at my ties.

"It's futile. Preserve your strength."

Our room couldn't have been much bigger than a classroom at Harvard. Flames danced in a freestanding brazier by the door. Fluted columns in each corner of the space rose toward gold-plated domed ceilings surrounded by rough marble walls. All things I could mark off the *I'm still in Carthage* checklist.

"Do you know where we are?"

"The temple of Ba'al Hammon, I've been here twice with my uncle. What I don't understand is why his men ambushed us, or how they knew where to find us."

I straightened. "Those men you fought—"

"Temple priests," he said. "They're like none I've encountered before. Had I known who they were, I wouldn't have killed one."

Since I was tied to a column, I doubted Ba'al intended to have a nice talk. "Why do you think they took us?"

"I don't know. They must want us alive since we're not dead."

"We can't be certain." The thought made my heart amp up. I tugged at my ties again. Nothing. "Dammit!" I screamed and beat my feet against the mosaic tiles. The meltdown only made me feel worse.

"Calm yourself. Ba'al Hammon and my uncle have a close relationship. Our god would never allow any harm to befall me."

"That doesn't mean he won't hurt me."

No response. If Greg were here, he would've told me to quit being such a wuss and figure a way out of this. I glanced at the arched opening on the opposite side of the chamber. "Any thoughts about where that doorway leads?"

The words had just left my lips when two bald men in white chitons entered. Their garments draped over their shoulders and were fastened in place by brooches. One untied my binds and yanked me to my feet. I kicked and punched him. "Let me go. Asshole!"

"Don't fight," Adones yelled.

I barely glimpsed the other guy standing over Adones as I clawed at my guard. He brought a dagger to my throat with such speed and precision, I barely saw the movement. I froze. Sweat trickled down my back. My breathing was erratic. Without looking away from me, the guard reached into his waist belt with his free hand and pulled out a strip of cloth.

Tears rained down my cheeks as he pressed the blade deeper into the skin of my throat; a silent warning not to move. I didn't swallow, didn't breathe. After a long silence, the guard sheathed the dagger and blindfolded me. Then a hand gripped my bicep and shoved me forward.

"Stay strong, Amara." Adones' voice echoed behind me.

My legs were like rubber as I stumbled alongside the guard, realizing if Ba'al planned to kill me, he wouldn't have bothered covering my eyes.

I once read when one sense was lost, the others took over, and this was true in my case. The spicy scent of my guard's body oils became stronger. Every rustle of fabric hung in my ears. Musical chants echoed ahead, rising and falling in a soulful chorus. After several twists and turns, I was guided down a bunch of steps. The further I descended, the damper, staler, and moldier the air became.

When we finally stopped, something buzzed behind me. The sound reminded me of the electric bug lamp Yia Yia used last summer, a constant zzzzzz. A hand rested on my arm, and I spread my feet apart, steadying myself.

Fingers fumbled on the back of my head, and the blindfold slipped off my face, revealing a windowless space alight by wall braziers. I let out a startled breath when I noticed a hooded figure a few feet away, standing before a long stone altar table. Based on the broad shoulders and above average height, at least six feet tall, the figure was a man.

The guard knelt.

Without facing me, the cloaked guy gave a short and snappy command in what sounded like Punic. I immediately recognized the voice from the funeral rite as that of Ba'al Hammon.

The guard rose, brushed past me like I was invisible, and walked toward the narrow opening. When he faded down the hallway, Ba'al slowly faced me and pushed back his hood.

Chapter Eighteen

I stood in the underground temple for at least a minute, mouth breathing like a Neanderthal until my brain finally became functional enough to spit out, "Dr. Hamad!"

"Jasim, you may call me Jasim," he responded in English.

The buzzing behind me barely registered as I continued staring at him in disbelief.

"You're a difficult person to get alone." He gestured toward the altar where two shirtless men in pleated skirts stood. Firelight cast a soft glow on their upper bodies, revealing weird triangular and star-shaped symbols tattooed vertically down their spines. "My guards have been following you since the funeral rite."

The cloaked man I had noticed this afternoon and the guy near the pub tonight came to mind. "Why were they tailing me?"

"I asked them to discreetly bring you here so we could talk and—"

"They attacked us."

He regarded me for a measured beat before responding. "From what I understand, Adones sprang into action before my priests could plead their case."

"Maybe their swords had something to do with that." His intense brown gaze cut through my display of strength, but I stood my ground. "And where is Adones?"

"Safe and unharmed," Jasim said in a clipped voice.

"Good." I stood taller; despite the way he looked down at me like a bug he could easily squish. "Mind telling me how you're here?"

An emotion, possibly irritation, tightened the lines around his mouth. "Basically, you and the others accidentally activated a portal key that I had planned to use later."

He paused, as if gauging my reaction to his vague answer.

I hoped the mask of calm I was trying to put off wasn't betrayed by my voice as I said, "How could you be connected to a key that was hidden in a tomb for two thousand years?"

"The key is linked to me, and I had control over when and where I wanted to be transported."

I crossed my arms over my chest. "I take it that would be here." He still hadn't answered how the key landed in the tomb.

"Indeed, and when none of you arrived with me, I thought the key had returned you to Tunis. Imagine my surprise when I saw you at the funeral rite."

"Oh, I can but why her—"

"Where are Greg and Sophie?" Jasim asked.

"I'm not sure." I pulled back my sleeve, revealing their jewelry pieces. "This is Greg's ring and Sophie's bracelet. I stumbled on a vendor at the marketplace after he'd bought them from a nomad."

"Well, they obviously came through the portal." Jasim waved a hand in the air. "Yet they could be anywhere."

I opened my mouth to ask if there was a way to find them and closed it when Jasim snapped his fingers, and two guards emerged from behind the altar. One held a leather-bound book about the size of a laptop, and the other man handed Jasim a small box.

"This holds one of the most powerful forces in the universe."

The access Jasim had to portal keys, and now a universal force, clearly suggested that he was a powerful being. "What are you?"

He shrugged. "I'm a sentient being, capable of emotion and feelings. I speak multiple languages and—"

"I noticed your accent's gone," I blurted. "Your English is better than mine."

Jasim went rigid. "You're a human of nineteen years. You can't compare yourself to me, a being who has lived since the dawn of time. My kind have explored other dimensions and watched worlds rise and fall."

His words hinted that he was a god, but this wasn't what stood out to me. "Did you say, dimensions?"

Jasim sighed like it was a chore to explain things to the dumb human. "We happen to be in an alternate or parallel version of the ancient Carthage from your history books."

I crossed my arms. "Why an alternate version?"

"Because there are forces here unlike anything you've ever seen and they're important to my plan." He pointed over my shoulder. "What waits behind you, is one of them."

When I turned around, my lips separated as I took in four human-sized cages enclosed by flaming prison bars. Smoke funneled inside each one, scattered into long streaks and bonded together again, as if trying to assume a dense shape.

"Wh-what are they?"

Jasim moved beside me with box in hand and raised the lid. The buzzing sound immediately stopped. Each of the smoke beings and the fiery bars on their cages froze in time. He reached inside the box and retrieved a bracelet that could've passed for a dull gold watch. Instead of a face with hands and numbers for telling time, the bracelet had a flat, black star-shaped stone, almost the size of my wrist.

"Have you ever heard of a species called the djinn?" he asked.

My first impulse was to respond with, "Yeah, like *Aladdin* with Robin Williams?" Except Jasim didn't strike me as one who appreciated dry humor. Instead, I said, "I've read stories about them. They're mythical, angelic-like creatures, right?"

"Not quite. Djinn are a highly intelligent warrior species, endowed with abilities beyond your imagination." Jasim gestured toward the cages. "These four are in a non-corporeal state. In their true form, each djinni is something to behold."

I stared past the flaming bars at the smoke beings, now frozen in time, ignoring how my pulse thudded thickly in my ears. "How did they wind up here?"

"That's a story for another day."

Of course, it is. I forced my gaze away from the cage. "How do you control them?"

Jasim held up the bracelet. "With this. Each djinni is bound by a stone. Whomever wears this bracelet becomes one with the creature, and they rule it."

I glanced at the other cages before returning my attention to Jasim. "Do you have more stones?"

"Yes, and they're stored in a place where no one can find them," he said with the casualness of telling me what he had for dinner.

"What keeps the djinni from killing the bearer of the stone?"

"Doing so would also kill it." Jasim spoke to the guards in Punic. They gave a compliant nod, approached a waist-high stone pedestal in front of the cages, and set the leather-bound book on it.

"That book contains incantations to ward against theft and to kill anyone who wears the bracelet without my authorization."

I could no longer ignore the question that kept pushing to the front of my mind. "What does any of this have to do with me?"

Jasim held up the bracelet. "I need *you* to take this and," he pointed at the cage closest to us, "that djinni to Hannibal's camp in Saguntum."

"Me?" I stepped back, shaking my head. "I just want to find my brother and Sophie and go home. My dad needs us. Can't *you* take the journey?"

His jaw ticked as though considering his next words. "Perhaps I could, if I wasn't hunted."

I wasn't sure what I had expected to hear, but this wasn't it. "Who is hunting you?"

"The Seekers." His features had become hard as stone. "Think of them as interdimensional marshals. They tracked my portal key when I entered this dimension, and I can't risk exposing myself and getting caught."

"You attended the funeral rite," I observed.

"Yes, and I wore a mask and moved through a series of underground tunnels to get there."

I was pushing my luck with all the questions but couldn't stop myself. "Why are the Seekers after you?"

His lips curled into a cruel sneer. "Because a dictator from my dimension perceived my choices as a crime against mankind."

He must have read the confusion on my face because he let out a breath and said, "It's a long story that occurred centuries ago. Back then, I was sent to observe the people from Carthage in your dimension and log their evolution. Unfortunately, my portal key malfunctioned and I was stuck there. After some time passed without a rescue, I assimilated with the people. They were so caring, and eventually, I reciprocated those feelings. I shared a small fraction of my knowledge and technology with them and they came to revere me as a god."

I knew he wasn't a real god. What an ego.

"My *king*," the word came out like a curse, "felt my actions had interfered with man's natural progression. This is a high crime among my kind, so he sent his Seekers to arrest me. During this time, the second Punic War in your dimension had begun. Although I was in hiding, I secretly advised Hannibal on his battle strategies, and he was unstoppable."

"Was his sword with the strange markings used in the Carthage from my dimension as well?"

Jasim stilled. He watched me with such intensity it was difficult to hold his gaze. "No," he said finally. "The weapon is only in this dimension. Sometimes events differ between parallel timelines."

Before I could ask how this was possible, he said, "Anyway, many good men were lost in that battle, and this included young Adones. When I learned that the Seekers were closing in on me, I repaired my portal device. Then I ordered my guardians to hide it in Adones' sarcophagus just before his funeral rite. However, before I could make my escape, the Seekers captured me."

"I'm confused. If the Seekers were closing in on you, why didn't you leave immediately after repairing your device?"

He raked a hand through his hair. "An incredible amount of power is needed to shift between dimensions. Even though the device is nuclear powered, it takes time to charge. Time, I didn't have.

"Centuries after my capture, I broke out of my prison and traveled to your time with hopes of finding the portal key in Adones' sarcophagus. Only I had no idea where to look more than two thousand years after his death. Out of desperation, I posed as an official with the Tunisian government and waited. The rest you know." He paused. "Now that you know why the Seekers are pursuing me, I hope you'll help me."

"Look, I can appreciate your dilemma, but what you're asking is impossible. I don't speak the language, nor do I know the terrain. I don't belong here."

Jasim stopped mid-step. "That's exactly why you're the only person who can accomplish this mission. Since you're from another dimension and don't exist in this time, you don't have an aura, and before you ask, it's an electromagnetic signature that can be tracked. When the Seekers look for the bearer of the stone, they won't find you."

"If the djinni's so powerful, what's to stop me from using its magic to return to my time?"

Jasim's lips curved into a thin smile. "Apart from the fact I'd use my book of incantations to turn you both to a pillar of salt, a djinni doesn't have that ability. Only a portal key can transport matter between dimensions."

"Can you at least explain why you need me to take the djinni to Hannibal's camp?"

Jasim shook his head. "If you don't know my plans, you can't betray them."

"What about Greg and Sophie? I won't leave without them."

"Finding them is akin to finding a needle in the proverbial haystack."

Desperation gripped my chest as I spoke. "I-If the djinni's as powerful as you say, it can help us find them?"

"No," Jasim said flatly. "Djinni's aren't omniscient. They may have a heightened sixth sense, but without a metaphorical scent to follow, they wouldn't know where to begin."

I pointed at my wrist and finger. "Wouldn't this ring and bracelet be enough?"

"How long have you had them?"

"A few days."

"It's been too long. They'd have to be close for a djinni to pick up their scent, if your party is even alive." Jasim rubbed his forehead. "I hate to sound callous. Perhaps you should concentrate on something less hopeless, like seeing your father again, and on accepting the deal I've offered."

The truth of his words stabbed me like a knife in the chest. Greg and Sophie had to be alive, just had to. Still, this was an impossible choice. The longer I remained in this dimension, the more likely Dad's situation declined. With Greg and me thought dead, he was likely hitting the bottle instead of treating his cancer. Refuse Jasim, and there was no way he'd free me. I knew too much.

I held up my forefinger. "If, and this is a big if, I agree to the mission, how do I know you'll keep your word and return me home?"

"You don't, but I have no reason to keep you here."

Agreeing seemed my only option. Jasim's word's about keeping me here caused an idea to materialize in my mind.

I met his stare. "I'll help you, on one condition."

His body stiffened. "Go on."

"When I first arrived in Carthage, a Numidian named Tanno helped me. He had kidnapped Adones to use the ransom and free his brother from Roman slavers."

"Your point?" Jasim said.

I squeezed and released my robes to ease my tension. "Tanno's a pirate with access to a ship. I saw it, and I'd bet money he knows how to avoid Roman trade routes."

"Why would he agree to this journey?"

"I doubt he'd choose a chopping block over helping you," I said. "Plus, you're a god to him. He'd do as you ask."

Jasim rubbed his five o'clock shadow of a beard. "I'm unsure how Adones would take traveling with his kidnapper."

My fingers halted their fiddling. "Adones is taking the journey?"

"Yes," Jasim said. "He knows where Hannibal will be camped, and he'll get you past the guards. If what you say about Tanno is true, he *could* also prove useful."

"Are you saying you'll help him?" I asked.

"I will. If we have a deal."

I nodded, fighting the sinking feeling that I had just climbed into bed with the devil.

With the bracelet in one hand, Jasim picked up the box, pulled out a small scroll, and handed it to me. "This contains the spell that bonds you and the djinni to the bracelet."

I unrolled the thin parchment, revealing two lines of black script I couldn't begin to decipher. "This might as well be gibber—"

The squiggly letters blurred in my vision, then transformed and moved on the parchment until the script was written in English. I shot Jasim a questioning look.

He responded with a foxlike smile that showed all his teeth. "The spell converts to the language of the person who opens the scroll."

This situation was ... surreal, and it was all I could do to stay focused. "Okaaay, now what?"

"You don the bracelet. My guards will recite the transformation spell from my book to make the djinni appear human, while you read the incantation in the scroll aloud. This must happen simultaneously to seal the bond between you."

I scanned the cages in front of me, the guards on my right, and the scroll, then I gulped. All I knew was the djinni couldn't harm the bearer of the stone without posing a risk to himself, and that he had a heightened sixth sense. This wasn't much to go on.

"I'm not sure I can do this."

Jasim set the box on the floor and grasped my shoulders. "I wouldn't jeopardize your life or this mission. Trust that I know what I'm doing. Just. Take. Command." He grabbed my hand and shoved the bracelet into my palm. "Put it on." His voice boomed through the chamber.

I flinched, and reluctantly slipped the bracelet over my sweaty wrist, gasping as threadlike tendrils grew out of each side of the clasp and embedded into my flesh. I groaned as a sensation like thousands of needles pricking me at once burned my arm. A scream escaped my lungs. I yanked at the bracelet, but it was attached to my wrist.

As the guards recited from the book, their voices rose and fell in perfect harmony. The flaming bars on the cages shimmered back to life, licked the air, and hissed with heat. Gray puffs of smoke danced and twisted inside each prison.

"Prepare yourself, Amara, you may feel more discomfort."

The star-shaped jewel on the bracelet liquified into a reddish pool. A sudden wave of nausea washed over me. I staggered back.

"Fight through it," Jasim's voice sounded like he spoke under water.

I caught my balance and almost fell over again when the black symbols on the guards' backs crackled like red embers. My arm shot into the air, uncontrolled by me. A scarlet beam radiated from the stone and fired toward the cage closest to me. Upon connecting, the flaming bars turned to ash and fell to the ground.

In those weird, disorienting seconds, streaks of smoke funneled together and transformed into a male, snow-white being. His humanoid body was chiseled with muscle. A crown of four thick steer-horns sprouted from the top of the creature's head. The whole time, it watched me with startling red eyes. Mighty, translucent bat-like wings unfurled from the thing's shoulder blades, flapping and beating against the air.

I shivered. Cold, I was so cold, and the emptiness ... Never had I felt such loneliness and isolation. Was I picking up on the creature's emotions?

"Take control, Amara. Hurry, before the transformation is complete."

I tore my gaze from the djinni, unraveled the scroll and read the incantation aloud in English. "With permission granted to me by Jan-Ib-Jann, the first of your kind, the leader who bestowed this stone upon man, I command thee, Moqerhe, do my bidding, accept me as master of thy soul or perish."

When I looked up, the creature glowered at me while responding in a guttural voice. "By the order of Jan-Ib-Jann, I'll obey your command."

The guardians' chants thundered through the chamber.

The djinni shimmered like a hologram. Translucent wings flapped then retracted. Marble-white skin transitioned to a smooth olive, and woolen robes appeared on his body. The crown of horns dissolved and were replaced by shoulder-length hair, black as the darkest night. His goat-like mouth morphed into a set of full lips, shadowed by an Aquiline nose. Yet, his most striking feature was his eyes, which shimmered to a beautiful golden brown.

The djinni was now human. Jock meets biker-boy human.

The red beam retracted into my bracelet and the room fell silent as I stood there hunched over, gasping for breath.

"You did well," Jasim said.

Moqerhe stood up and glowered at me. *"Now, we're both prisoners,"* ran through my mind in English.

My breath caught.

"Yes, I'm speaking to you, human!"

"Are you alright?" Jasim asked.

I nodded, unable to decide whether I was more freaked out by the djinni's telepathic abilities, that he spoke English, or the fact that I had no clue who to trust. The djinni was a prisoner to my stone and he would say anything to gain his freedom. Jasim had enslaved him and used my desire to return home against me so they both were probably shady.

"Very well. I still have to prepare for your journey, and I'll need to free your Numidian friend from prison." Jasim extended his hand. "I'll take the scroll now."

I placed it in his palm. "What's nex—"

Jasim gave an order in Punic. One of the guardians snapped to attention and headed toward us.

"In the meantime, I've arranged a bed for you. You should rest while you can," Jasim said.

"What about Adones? When will I see him?"

"Soon. First, you should get to know—"

A guard spoke Punic as he took his place beside Jasim.

I pointed at the blindfold in the man's hand. "Is that necessary?" The thought of losing my sight again had my heart jackhammering against my ribs.

"There's too much at stake to allow you or anyone outside my circle to know this location."

Jasim jutted his chin toward me. I stiffened, feeling helpless as a baby bird in an evil man's hand as the guard slipped the blindfold over my face, plunging me into darkness once more. A lot of back and forth between Jasim, the djinni, and his guards followed. Then, a hand clenched my arm hard, urged me forward and into the unknown.

Chapter Nineteen

"Where are you taking me?" I asked.

No response. If not for the occasional grip on my arm, helping me up steps or guiding me around corners, I wouldn't have known my guard was there. When we finally stopped, he removed the blindfold. As my vision focused, the dim yellow glow from a clay oil lamp on a corner table came into my view. Huge cushions in rich burgundies, blues, and reds were clustered against the adjacent wall. Two mattresses with woolen blankets lay next to them.

Was the second one for Adones?

When I wheeled around to ask Jasim's guard, he was already heading out the door. "Hey, what am I supposed to—"

Moqerhe stepped out of the shadows to my left, surveying me with those golden eyes. I stepped back. My heel hit a cushion and I lost my balance. The next thing I knew, my ass was on the floor. Heat rushed to my face, and I leapt to my feet.

He smirked.

I clenched my fists and said in my most confident ancient Greek, "What are you doing here?"

"You're the bearer of the stone," he replied in perfect English, English that clung to every syllable.

I pressed my lips together to keep the shock off my face. This was the third time he had spoken my language. "How do you know English?"

There was something disturbingly intimate about the way he gazed at me, like he knew all my secrets, like there was no place my thoughts could hide from him.

He pointed at the bracelet. "Our bond allows me to communicate with whoever commands me."

My stomach lurched. There was only way he could know what I knew. "Can you read my mind?"

The corner of his mouth curled up. "Would you believe me if I told you I cannot?"

"No." This wasn't going well so I regrouped and tried again. "Look, it's been a long night. You should head to your quarters, and we'll talk tomorrow."

I was proud of the way I had subtly told him I didn't want him sleeping here, if djinnis even slept. Since he was now human this might have been the case.

The elegant contour of his mouth tightened as he frowned, causing the creases along the corners to deepen. "These are *my* quarters. If you're unhappy staying here, perhaps you should take it up with *your* god."

Hot anger simmered within the pit of my stomach. My next words came out through clenched teeth. "Newsflash, Jasim is not *my* god, and if he was, I'd be an atheist. Now you need to leave because there's no way I'm sharing a room with a guy I don't know."

"I'm a guy? Interesting." He sneered so wide I saw his molars. "I have a newsflash for you, *human*. If I wanted you dead, you'd be dead. Even if it meant breaking my bond with that stone and ending up in the nether regions. Your choice to help that abomination, Jasim, as you call him, has enslaved us both. Now, we must do his bidding, and there's no telling what awaits us."

My neck was so tense, I could barely swallow. "This isn't my fault. If I refused him, I'd never see home again."

"This is no surprise." Moqerhe's voice was a guttural rumble. "Your kind knows nothing of self-sacrifice. You only thought of progressing your future."

"Why wouldn't I? I owe you no loyalty. My father's ill and I need to get back to him. Agreeing to help Jasim ensured this would happen, and it also saved my friend from certain death."

He clapped his hands. "Bravo for saving the little humans in your little world."

"I saved you too," I tried to keep my voice even. "You're free from that cage, so you're welcome."

Moqerhe closed the gap between us in an instant, standing so close, my nose almost touched his impeccably chiseled chest. "Free! You call this free? In my prison, I had honor. I was among my brothers-in-arms, an immortal warrior djinni imprisoned by a dictator with whom we refused to serve. Now, now, I'm caged by this pathetic body and enslaved by an inferior being."

The arrogance! "Take a look in the mirror. All I see is a narcissistic, self-centered being who thinks his shit doesn't stink. From where I'm standing, you're no better than Jasim."

The second the words left my mouth, my legs shook, and my underarms broke into a hot sweat. I just told off an ancient being who could probably break me in half with the snap of a finger. If he did, he'd break himself in half too. Given the way his nostrils flared, he might have done it to spite me.

"You foul-tongued fool. How dare you compare me to him!"

"How dare you look down your nose at me! You have no idea who I am or what I've been through!" My breathing was shallow.

Moqerhe studied me for one of the longest minutes of my life. When he spoke again, his voice was smooth as silk. "Perhaps there's truth in your words. Yet, it doesn't make our situation any easier to accept." He pointed at the mattresses. "I intend to lie in the bed you've made for us. If you have any intelligence, you'll push me no further." He headed for the bed, then stopped mid-step and looked at me. "You best get some sleep. Like it or not, we're in this together."

The tone of Moqerhe's voice told me he meant business, but I refused to show any weakness. I stormed to the hay-filled mattresses, picked one up by the corner, and dragged it to the other side of the room. The whole way, he glared at me like a snake watching a mouse. I pretended not to notice and crawled beneath the woolen blanket. Now under a cloak of darkness, tears rained down my cheeks and my chest eddied in a tornado of fear and anxiety.

What had I gotten myself into? I now wore a bracelet that controlled a supernatural creature. Moqerhe's slick black hair, chiseled cheekbones, and full lips made him seductive. I'd seen the horned creature who hid behind a handsome mask, and I couldn't allow myself to forget it. Not for one second.

Jasim hadn't been forthcoming about how to control Moqerhe or what his powers were, and I'd been too stunned to ask. What kind of idiot forgot to ask such an important question? Well, this wouldn't happen a second time. I sniffed and allowed my head to sink into the soft mattress. My muscles slowly relaxed and my eyes fluttered closed despite my efforts to keep them open. Then, before exhaustion took me, I thought, tomorrow I'd get answers, or I wasn't going anywhere.

The next thing I knew, a familiar voice calling, "Amara," stirred me from sleep. I pushed the covers off my head and sat up, squinting through the dim light.

"Afternoon." Moqerhe sprawled over the pile of throw pillows across from me. Firelight from a lamp danced over his smirking mouth. "Plan to sleep all day."

"Did you say afternoon?" My voice was groggy.

He gestured toward a tray filled with dates and bread beside him. "Come, eat. This is your half. I saved it for you."

Did he really think I was stupid enough to fall for his Mr. Nice-Guy act after last night? "What, are we best friends now?"

Moqerhe pulled the tray back and picked up a piece of bread. "Starve for all I care." He bit into my breakfast.

My stomach growled in response. If it was afternoon, that meant I hadn't eaten anything since yesterday, and I was starving. Like hungry, hungry hippo starving. I flopped back on the mattress, refusing to let him know he got to me. "I wasn't aware that djinnis ate."

"In this form we do." He bit into another piece of bread, slowly chewing it as if savoring the bite. "And it tastes—"

The sound of approaching footsteps drew my attention toward the door.

"Good day," a woman with long black hair said as she entered the room carrying a basket of fabrics. "I've brought fresh robes. You should dress quickly, madam. Ba'al Hammon will be here soon."

"Here, in front of him?" I angled my head toward Moqerhe.

His shoulders shook with silent laughter while chewing another slice of *my* bread. "You think too much of yourself. I have no desire to look upon your nakedness."

"And I have no desire to look at your mouthful of chewed-up food. Clearly, time hasn't taught you manners."

The woman glanced between us. Although she didn't understand the exchange, I had no doubt my expression and the frustrated tone in my voice gave away our conflict. She handed Moqerhe robes from the basket and spoke in Punic. He nodded, tucked the clothing under his arms and grabbed the tray of my food. Then he winked at me as he carried it from the room.

Prick!

When he disappeared down the hall, the woman handed me light tan robes made from a thick, woven material, and a rope belt tied around the waist. She then unfolded a shawl and showed me how to place it over the top of my head, while pulling the longer piece over my mouth and nose. Although I already knew how to wear the headdress, I didn't want to insult her. She seemed to take great pride in helping me. Afterward, she pulled a couple of animal skin boots from her basket.

"Allow me to assist you with these."

"Gratitude," I said, smiling.

She held the boot open, and I let out a shocked breath when my foot slipped into the soft leather lining.

"They'll protect your feet from rocks and sand." The woman tied them off just below the knees with a thin leather string.

"When shall I expect Ba'al?"

"Soon."

My stomach growled and I put a hand over it. "Apologies. Moqerhe ate my food."

The corners of her eyes crinkled thoughtfully. Then she reached into her basket and handed me an item wrapped in cotton. "Some bread for you."

My eyes snapped toward her. "Is this your food?"

"I have more." She pulled out a leather waterskin, set it beside my feet and headed out the door.

"I appreciate your kindness." Her nonresponse was a clue she hadn't heard me. I quickly unfolded the cloth and plucked out a piece of crispy pita-type bread and bit off a chunk.

Seconds later, Moqerhe sauntered in wearing robes like mine. His eyes swept over me all judgy. Of all the people to see me stuffing my face, why did it have to be him? I grabbed the waterskin and took a sip, trying to wash back most of the bread.

"Perhaps I'm not the only one who needs a course in manners." He plopped down on the throw pillows and stretched his arms toward the ceiling, like a cat who was pleased with himself.

I almost choked on my food. Irritation bubbled inside me. At this rate, we wouldn't make it to Saguntum without killing each other. Someone had to be the bigger person and it clearly wasn't him.

With a loud sigh, I said, "Look, can we call a truce? I don't like this situation any more than you, but we're in it together."

His lips curled into a sneer. "Thanks to you."

"You're right," I admitted. "I-I can't begin to imagine what you've been through, what you're feeling. We've both been placed in impossible situations by Jasim." I set my bread down and approached him. "Can we at least try to be civil?" I extended my hand, waiting for him to shake when the sound of more approaching footsteps interrupted us.

I faced the doorway just as Jasim entered with two torch-carrying minions in tow. Their tattooed heads glistened beneath the firelight.

Jasim glowered at Moqerhe as if waiting for him to speak.

The djinni snapped to his feet and bowed his head. "Good day." Whatever Jasim held over Moqerhe that made him submit must have been serious since the djinni seemed to loathe the false god.

After a moment, Jasim turned to me and spoke in a sunny voice, like we'd known each other forever. "Hello, Amara. Did you sleep well?"

"Yes," I bit out, gesturing toward the djinni, who now regarded me with his brow quirked curiously. "Moqerhe and I were just getting to know each other."

"Splendid," Jasim said. "Moqerhe will be by your side for the next few weeks, maybe a month, depending on the weather and number of stops you make, so it's best if you get along."

I leaned in and whispered while pointing at the bracelet, "I don't know how this thing works or what Moqerhe is capable of."

"I'll explain everything in a few minutes."

I cleared my throat, knowing I was pushing my luck and unable to stop myself from asking more questions. "Um, were you able to free Tanno? Did Adones agree to come?"

Jasim stiffened. "Like. I. Said. I'll explain everything soon."

He turned to his minions and spoke in their common tongue. They proceeded past me to a wall at the back of the room. The taller of the two rested his fingers against a brazier and pushed. A hissing sound followed as a section of the wall silently slid back, revealing a dark tunnel.

Jasim said something to Moqerhe in Punic.

Despite the hatred in the djinni's glare, he joined the guards at the door.

Jasim gestured toward it. "Ready to begin your journey?"

I peered into the dark tunnel then at Jasim. "Now?"

"Yes. The sooner you start, the sooner you can return home."

It wasn't like I could tell him no, so I just nodded in agreement.

Both guards entered the tunnel with torches in hand, illuminating the way for Jasim and Moqerhe. I silently followed in the back of the line as we navigated several twists and turns that led to a gate engraved with a crescent moon.

After placing their torches in wall sconces, the guardians unlocked the gate. It opened with a creak, inviting white light through the opening. Birds cawed in the distance as I stepped outside and into more uncertainty.

Chapter Twenty

Moqerhe and I followed Jasim and his guardians onto a path that opened to a valley outside the city. The afternoon sun streaked the dry plains before me in hues of burnt orange. I shrouded my eyes with my hand to protect them from the brightness.

"It's been centuries since I've felt such warmth," ran through my mind in Moqerhe's perfect English.

I glared at him, but he just gazed longingly at the sun. While I was open to forming a civil relationship, this didn't include allowing the djinni to invade my head space.

My thoughts were interrupted when two men on horseback approached with three horses in tow.

When I got a look at them, my heart practically leapt out of my chest. "Adones, Tanno, you're—"

Without acknowledging me, Adones dismounted, knelt before Jasim, and punched his chest in a salute.

Jasim raised his palms toward the sky and spoke in Punic. Adones stood up.

Unable to watch my friend get sucked in by an imposter, I turned my attention to Bear. I bit my bottom lip to keep from gasping. His plaits had been shaved, and judging the nicks and cuts on his scalp, his captors had used a dull razor.

"Are you alright?" I asked.

Moqerhe stared at me like a researcher studying a lab rat.

"Allay your sympathies. The gods are not ready for me." Bear dropped his horse's reins, turned to Jasim and bent at the waist, wincing slightly. "As promised, I've come to repay my debt to you."

After giving him a quick nod, Jasim gestured toward the djinni a few feet away. "This is Moqerhe, one of my most trusted priests. He'll guide you to Hannibal's camp."

The djinni's face tensed as he sketched a bow and spoke in Punic. Bear returned the gesture, and they continued talking while moving to the packhorse. Adones shook his head, plucked a leather scroll from his belt, and unrolled it. By the way he studied the thing, it was probably a map.

Jasim turned to me and spoke in English. "I've given Adones enough to finance your journey and he grasps the geographic challenges. The Numidian will first guide your party to the marketplace where he'll meet with a suitable smuggler. Then, you all will board the ship. Once you reach Saguntum, the bracelet will be removed, and you'll return home."

The word *home* made my stomach jump. This was my only chance of returning to Dad and Yia Yia, but could I leave without knowing what happened to Greg and Sophie or would Jasim even give me a choice?

"Amara, are you listening?"

My head snapped toward Jasim. "Yeah, of course."

"Good, because this is important. If your life is threatened, invoke the magic of the stone in that bracelet. It will save you and the mission."

It wasn't like the bracelet came with an instruction manual. "And how do I do that? I don't know much about the djinni's powers or how to summon them."

Jasim's jaw hardened. "To put it simply, Moqerhe's basic abilities are psychokinesis and compulsion, but they don't require the use of magic. Shapeshifting, the power to heal, teleportation, and his powers of mass destruction—"

"Wait. You attached me to a ticking time bomb? Wh-what's to keep Moqerhe from hypnotizing me, stealing the bracelet, and doing his worst?"

"Calm down," Jasim said dismissively. "Now that Moqerhe's bound to the stone, he can't make a magical move without your permission, or his life will be sacrificed. Your bracelet makes you immune to his powers of hypnosis."

"Okay, this doesn't explain how to summon the djinni's magic."

"Just recite the incantation that bound Moqerhe to you, then state what you need at the end. Do you remember the words?"

"I'll never forget them," I said flatly.

Jasim nodded. "Here's something else, and this is important. If you invoke the djinni's magic twice, the residual energy coming off Moqerhe and your bracelet will act like a beacon, making it easier for the Seekers to track you. They'll do whatever it takes to get their hands on the stone, even if it means killing you in the process."

"So, you're saying don't use magic?"

"Shouldn't have to, but if a life and death emergency requires it, put considerable distance between you and the area where the event occurred."

Jasim turned his back on me and walked to the gate where his guards waited. "See you at the end, Amara."

He followed his guards into the tunnel we had just walked through. After the gate slammed shut behind them, our ragtag crew stared at each other like a bunch of strangers on the first day of college.

Someone had to take charge, so I broke the silence and turned to Bear. "We should leave if we hope to board the ship before nightfall."

Bear nodded. "Agreed. We'll need to first stop at the market."

Since I wasn't a strong rider, I wound up mounted behind Adones. Moqerhe took up the rear with the packhorses, while Bear led us single file into the plains. In the distance, the outer walls of the city shimmered beneath the sun like a heat haze. We passed leafless bushes sprinkled across the landscape and weaved around sharp rocks sprawling toward the surrounding tree-covered hills.

Adones pointed at a snake slithering down a large boulder about ten feet away. "Look, Tanno, one of your family members is basking in the sun."

I sighed. "God! I refuse to listen to these barbs for the next month."

"Judge me if you must, Adones." Bear's low and even voice was laced with vitriol. "My choice to abduct you was born of necessity, to spare my brother's life."

Adones tensed. "Why have you waited till now to mention this?"

"We only met last sunrise," Bear said. "General Barca and Ba'al Hammon's guards kept us busy. I didn't have time to prattle on about my past."

"Now you do, and I'm interested to hear your story," said Adones.

Bear paused as though gathering his thoughts. "This all began when my brother and I chose to join General Barca's campaign against Saguntum."

Adones sucked in a breath.

"While in route, Roman slavers ambushed and captured us. When they learned of our intention to join the general, I was given an ultimatum: capture Adones and they would release my brother. Refuse them, and he would wish for death." Bear's voice cracked, and he cleared his throat. "After I failed my task, all hope of saving him was gone."

"You could have asked for my help instead of abducting me," Adones said.

"Spoken with the arrogance of a high-born Carthaginian." Bear spat on the ground. "You wouldn't have granted me an audience."

Adones shook his head. "You know not what you speak. I've fought alongside men from many countries and many classes, and I would have given my life for some. Believe me when I tell you, I would have listened to your plea. Instead, you thought it best to take matters into your own hands. Now, you're angry because the law demands justice."

"How could you possibly relate to my plight?" Bear said. "No member of your family has endured the sting of a whip. They haven't been imprisoned in a cell with flies, feasting on their bloody flesh."

Adones tightened his grip on the reins. "True, I can't relate to what you've endured, and I now see the reason you chose to abduct me. Nevertheless, this does not excuse your cruelty while I was your prisoner."

Bear scoffed. "Should I have bathed you in oils and fed you cakes? I'm sure this is how you and the general treat all your prisoners." Bear pointed at his nicked and cut scalp. "You have my gratitude for the friendly shave, by the way. It's most refreshing without my hair."

Adones sneered at Bear, "You deserved—"

"Enough! We must work as a team. Your god demands it," I said.

A long stretch of silence passed. When Adones spoke again, his tone was calm. "Amara is correct. I serve Ba'al Hammon, and he has entrusted us with this journey. From here on, I'll do my best to cooperate with you."

Bear dipped his chin. "As will I."

We soon arrived at what I assumed was the market. Judging by the rows of dilapidated wooden stands blanketing the valley before us, it seemed sketchier than the one behind the city walls. The scent of smoked meat lingered in the air. Tambourines and drums echoed in the distance.

Our group stopped before a hitching post and dismounted. My numb ass thanked me as I walked in circles to get the circulation going again.

"I'll see to the horses." Perspiration beaded across Bear's bald head and ran down a cheek lined with too many scars and cuts. "It will take time to negotiate the final details before we board the vessel. Perhaps you should take in one or two matches, then meet me back here."

Before I could respond, Bear disappeared into the crowd with our horses in tow. "Shouldn't we accompany him?"

"Leave him be," Adones said with a dismissive wave. "I have no desire to associate with his companions from the underbelly of Carthage."

Thunderous applause and cheers caught my attention. To the right of the market, a bunch of wooden scaffoldings with rows of seats that stepped down glistened under the sun. "What is that?"

"The games, where warriors fight to the death," Adones said. "They're not for the faint of heart."

Adones clapped the djinni on the back. "Shall we have a look?"

Moqerhe's amber gaze slid to mine. There was something mischievous in it. "Perhaps we should."

I huffed and headed through the gate. Adones and Moqerhe soon caught up and strolled beside me down a path flanked by wooden stalls. Laughter and voices jumbled through the air as we navigated the crowd of shoppers, looking at clay jars, and bartering over jewelry. I twirled Greg's ring on my finger with my thumb, missing him and Sophie more than words could say.

A guy with pockmarked skin and beady brown eyes held a green melon in the air, trying to entice us to his stand.

Moqerhe sneered at him and pushed ahead. The more we blended with the crowd, the heavier the stench of *onion a la sweat* became. I let out a quick breath, wishing I had a can of air freshener or a gas mask handy. Then again, what did I expect in a time that didn't have toilet paper or deodorant?

We passed a vendor displaying a crocodile, and a guy playing a lute. Just a few stands down, a handful of belly dancers in harem pants shook their tambourines. The fringes on their hip scarves swayed from left to right as they danced, and their veiled faces hinted of mystery.

"It's a house of ill-repute." Moqerhe watched me with his brow raised, like he was trying to get a rise out of me.

"Obviously," I said in a flat, bored voice.

Adones dragged his gaze from the women's sheer tops. "We should move on."

When we rounded a corner, several onlookers were huddled before a huge square object covered in tanned leather tarps.

"It's a cage. You may not like what you find," ran through my mind in English.

I glared at Moqerhe, but he just shrugged. Clearly, he was baiting me, but my curiosity was piqued. I pushed past the onlookers until I made it to the front of the cage. What I saw stole my breath.

"Sophie!" I grabbed the bars – half-dazed, having a full out-of-body experience – watching myself observe her crouched in the back. The Shadu was chained beside her, and its master, Vicram, whom Adones and I had met at the market not more than a week ago, sat beside it. When the creature locked gazes with me, it roared and lunged at the bars, shackles tightening.

Loud applause followed. Vicram, who was unrestrained, moved to the Shadu and whispered in the animal's ear, sneering at the jeering crowd.

Sophie stared vacantly at me a second before her brown eyes widened. "Amara?"

I nodded, holding back a sob, and reached for her through the bars.

She clenched her torn tunic to cover her barely hidden breasts and ran to the front of the cage. "I've never been so happy to see anyone in my life."

Tears streamed down my cheeks. "I thought you were ... Is Greg here too?"

Sophie's mouth quivered. "Yes, but—"

A wrinkled old man in dusty robes snarled at me in his language and pulled us apart. I fell back and hit the ground with a jarring thud.

Adones pushed the man away and helped me to my feet. "Are you harmed?"

"No." I gestured toward the cage. "Please, Sophie is my friend. Help her, help them."

Adones' gaze landed on the dusty old guy. "I cannot. You've no right to touch the girl."

"Are you mad?" I was shaking. "Those are human beings in that cage, and the Shadu is a beautiful creature. I won't leave until they're free."

Moqerhe stood straighter.

His warning, "You may not like what you find," flashed through my mind.

I clenched my teeth so hard, my molars could have cracked. "You — you *knew* Sophie was here!"

Moqerhe looked at Adones and threw his hands up as though he didn't understand me, while simultaneously sending a mental message my way. *"Don't assume to know my mind, human. That trinket you wear alerted me to a familiar presence. Yet, I couldn't be certain about who it was until I saw her."*

"You should have told me."

"I owe you no loyalty apart from what your stone requires."

Despite the anger in Moqerhe's telepathic words, I could have sworn I saw sadness flicker in his golden eyes when he gazed at Sophie, the Shadu, and Vicram.

I turned to Adones, who watched me with his brow creased, and it hit me that I looked like I was talking to myself. I shrugged off my embarrassment. Right now, Sophie, Vicram, and the Shadu needed my attention. "Do you have spare coin to buy their freedom?"

"I do not," Adones tone was compassionate yet stern. "We have a long journey ahead, and we must conserve our funds."

I held up my arm, revealing Sophie's bracelet and Greg's ring. "I can use these to negotiate their freedom."

Adones shook his head. "Those won't be enough to—"

"Amara," Sophie said.

I faced her again. "Are you okay?" No, she wasn't okay. Why would I ask such an idiotic question?

"Listen, this is important," Sophie said in a hoarse voice. "Greg is here but they took him away this morning."

My grip tightened on the bars. "Where, where did they take him?"

Sophie pointed toward the sound of the cheering crowds on her right. "To the games. He's been fighting since our arrival three days ago. I'm not sure how much he can take. You gotta help him before—"

"Don't say it!" A sick feeling welled in the pit of my stomach. If every second counted, I'd have to leave Sophie and help Greg. Except, how could a person from another time with no money or power pull off a Get-Out-of-Jail-Free Card? The answer came to me when I glimpsed Moqerhe studying us.

"Be right back," I told Sophie.

"Where are you off to?" Adones asked.

"One moment."

I grabbed Moqerhe's arm, pulled him aside and whispered in English. "You have powers of compulsion, right?"

"What of it?" his voice held an edge of irritation.

"My brother is forced to fight in the games. If you could hypnotize his slaver, make him release—"

"And what about the girl — the Shadu — its master?"

I pointed at the cringy slave owner beside the cage. "Once we free Greg, we'll return here, use compulsion on that awful man then we'll rescue our friends."

Moqerhe's eyes narrowed on the bracelet that bound us together. "You wear the stone that keeps me enslaved. I see no difference between you and the man who owns your brother and your friend."

I grabbed his forearm hard. "How dare you compare me to that horrible man! You know I didn't ask for this."

He yanked his arm away and rubbed it. "Do I?"

"Please, I'll do anything to free my brother and Sophie."

"Anything?" He eyed my bracelet.

"Except release you. If I tried, I suspect Jasim would somehow know, and he'd use the book of incantations to destroy us both. I can't take that risk."

Although Moqerhe's face had the smooth chiseled features of someone my age, the fine lines around his golden eyes gave away the ancient being who stared at me. After an uncomfortable beat, he said, "I'll help you."

That was quick, too quick. I waited for a caveat. When it never came, desperation took over and I said, "Let's go."

We hadn't made it far when Adones met us head on. His gaze moved from Moqerhe to me. "I sense a plan's afoot."

Moqerhe nodded. "Indeed, we've just learned that Amara's brother is here."

Adones rested a hand on my shoulder. "Are you certain?"

"Yes." I brought a hand to my chest. "He has been forced to fight in the games and I fear more for his life with each passing second."

"Gods!" Adones said. "I wouldn't wish that fate on my worst enemy."

"I agree." Moqerhe gestured toward me. "While we've devised a plan to free the boy, we could use your help to put it into action."

Adones' brow shot up.

"As a member of House Barcid, you have more influence than you know," Moqerhe said. "If you can arrange a meeting with the slave owner, we may yet save Amara's brother."

Adones regarded us curiously. "What's your plan once you speak to the owner?"

Moqerhe and I exchanged uncomfortable glances.

"Greg could be preparing to fight at any moment, and we need to move quickly. Trust that we have a plan."

The tension left Adones' face. "I'll do what I can. Please don't make me regret this."

"Give me a moment." I rushed to Sophie. She had a death grip on her prison bars as I placed my hand over one of hers. "We'll find Greg. If he's here, we'll save him."

Sophie frowned. "I hope it's not too late."

Chapter Twenty-One

By the time I arrived at the games, my body was so tense it would have snapped in two if I bent over. Moqerhe and I followed Adones through the sea of people. The whole time, I scanned the crowd looking for a sign of Greg. We passed soldiers in leather armor laughing and socializing. Kids in threadbare tunics begged for coins, and Adones waved them off.

We passed wooden stands, which stepped down like bleachers, and were packed full of onlookers. Then, we stopped before a waist-high rail overlooking a rectangular depression about twenty feet below us. The area was the size of two tennis courts and surrounded by stone walls. I exhaled when I saw it was empty, unaware I'd been holding my breath.

A soldier in the crowd greeted us. After a short exchange in Punic, Adones turned to me. "He speaks of a giant gladiator with hair the color of bronze. Could this be your brother?"

I grabbed his arm, clenching harder than intended. "Yes! We must find him."

Moqerhe pointed at a gate built into the stone wall of the arena. "He's likely there."

"Agreed. That's where they hold the men before the games," Adones said. "We should make haste. The soldier said your brother will fight at any moment."

He then took my hand and gently pulled me with him as we followed Moqerhe through the crowd. Along the way, a boozer held his dark wineskin toward me and laughed. Adones shouted in Punic, and the guy backed off. A vendor held up a small wooden carving of a gladiator holding a sword. When we reached the opposite side of the arena, a loud horn penetrated the chattering crowd. People trotted past us and gathered around the rail. A guy with a long, crooked nose stood on a box, taking bets.

"We're too late. The games are about to begin," said Moqerhe in ancient Greek.

"No," I said. "Maybe it's not Greg." I pushed past the spectators until I made it to the rail.

Moqerhe moved to my right and crooked nose stood beside him. Adones took his place on my opposite side.

My heart tumbled when I saw Greg running toward the center arena, holding a shiny bronze sword. His leather armor gapped at the waist and rose above his belly button. The shin guards fit halfway up the front of his stilt-like legs. Although Greg's metal helmet covered his nose and cheeks, I read the concern in his eyes. He watched two men in loincloths standing next to a trapdoor in the ground, and whatever awaited beneath, screeched and rammed against it.

A loud horn echoed through the arena. On cue, the guys in loincloths pulled a chain above the trapdoor taut until it yawned open. When it flipped back and hit the ground with a thud, the duo hauled ass to the gate in the wall and scrambled inside.

I held my breath as a diamond-shaped head about the size of a tractor tire poked out from the ground, followed by a massive tubular body at least six feet wide and three times as long. The creature slithered into the arena. Silver scales along its back gleamed beneath the sun as it unfurled a scorpion-like tail and glowered at Greg through glowing red eyes.

The crowd roared with applause.

I gasped. My shoulders ached from the weight of my brother's situation. No way he could beat that thing.

"This is not good," Adones said. "The demi-hydra is among the fiercest of all the beasts, and the most difficult to kill."

"Wh-why?" I asked.

"C'mon!" Greg yelled, pulling my attention back to him. He grabbed a rectangular shield hanging off the back of his shoulders and held the sword in his other hand.

The demi-hydra's jaw opened wide, revealing razor sharp fangs as it snapped at Greg. He lurched away. The creature twisted to the side and shot a flame from the tip of its scorpion-like tail. It was an orb of death torpedoing toward the target.

"Move!" I screamed, even though Greg couldn't hear me.

Greg pivoted seconds before the fireball missed his cheek. The serpent snapped at my brother again. This time, he jabbed the sword into the creature's reptilian throat. The demi-hydra recoiled with a bone-chilling shriek. Greg withdrew the blade and held his shield protectively in front of him.

The crowd erupted with cheers. "Your brother is quite skilled with the sword," said Adones. "Perhaps you worried for naught."

I wasn't surprised. Clearly Greg's years of fencing had paid off.

When the demi-hydra approached for a second strike, Greg was ready. He wheeled around and swung the blade across the creature's neck, slicing through thick tissue like butter. Crimson blood trickled down the demi-hydra's scaled chest, just as the creature's head fell off and rolled away. The body smashed to the ground with a loud thud, sending a huge cloud of dust billowing into the air.

I cheered so loud they could've heard it back in my time. Greg bent at the waist and rested his hands on his knees, trying to catch his breath.

Moqerhe's words echoed in my mind. *"This isn't over."*

My eyes snapped toward the arena. Dread hung thickly in the air. The demi hydra's tubular body twitched and rolled into an upright position. Then, a monstrous diamond-shaped head grew from the creature's neck, followed by a second one. Clear venom dripped from the beast's sharp fangs. The scorpion-like tail uncurled, now revealing two pointed tips, moving independently.

Greg stood there, owl-eyed, with the sword dangling at his side. The creature slithered toward its prey, one head snapping forward while the other retracted. Greg swung the sword, using right-handed strikes.

My heart thundered. I looked at Moqerhe. "You gotta help him. Th-that thing will kill him," I said in English, no longer caring if his magic attracted the Seekers. I needed to save my brother.

Moqerhe scrutinized my bracelet as his words rang in my mind in English, *"I must do as you command. Be warned, you're asking me to spare your brother from certain death and this will interrupt the natural order. If you invoke my powers to spare a life, you may not like the consequences."*

"What kind of con—"

The creature let out an angry, high-pitched screech. Greg stumbled and fell onto his back.

Desperate tears rained down my cheeks. "Okay, I'll do whatever it takes. Just save him!"

The djinni's voice was low and silky in my mind, *"You must state that you accept my conditions when you invoke my powers."*

I gave a hesitant nod, unable to shake the feeling I was making another deal I'd regret but I couldn't let Greg die, just couldn't. The stone warmed against my skin and swirled red.

Adones regarded my bracelet curiously.

Recalling the incantation Jasim had taught me, I chose my words carefully and said, "With permission granted to me by Jan-Ib-Jann, the first of your kind, the leader who bestowed this stone upon man, I command thee, Moqerhe, to do my bidding. I call upon your power to spare my brother, and I accept the consequences." My arm tingled like a thousand pins were stabbing it. A hum sounded in my ears.

My arm flew into the air, no longer controlled by me. Everything went funeral quiet. Then Adones, along with the rest of the crowd, froze in time. In the arena, the two-headed snake hung in mid-air, both jaws wide, fangs ready to strike. Greg lay statue-still on his back, sword extended above his chest toward the creature hovering above him.

Moqerhe's body shimmered. Great bat wings sprouted from his back. His skin turned paper white. Four thick horns protruded from the top of his head, and his golden eyes resolved into red. He funneled toward the arena like a large tornado, leaving a space between me and crooked-nose guy, who now stood frozen with his fist raised.

The gray funnel encircled Greg and faded into a mist until they both disappeared. Moqerhe's voice rushed to the front of my mind, *"Your brother is safe. Bring Adones and meet us at the arena entrance. If we make haste, we may save four souls this day."*

My arm fell to my side. The stone returned to a normal temperature against my skin. I jumped when the crowd roared back to life. Dazed, I glanced at the arena and gripped the rails when I saw two legs dangling from one of the demi-hydra's mouths. If Moqerhe had Greg, who was with the creature? Blood rushed from my face as I became acutely aware of the vacant space beside me. I searched the crowd for Crooked Nose, seeing no sign of him. My heart fell. Moqerhe must have switched him out for Greg. This meant I had unconsciously agreed to swap one life for another. Why didn't I push Moqerhe about the cost? Crooked Nose was someone's son, maybe a husband and father.

A hand rested on my shoulder and a familiar voice asked in ancient Greek, "Where is Moqerhe?"

My teeth trembled so hard they almost chattered out of my head.

"You're pale as marble." Adones' mouth turned down in a frown. "I'm sorry for your loss, truly."

The sincerity in his words nearly choked me. He thought the man in the arena was Greg. How would I explain my brother's sudden appearance? How would I live with my choice? Images of the man's legs dangling from the serpent's jaw played repeatedly in my mind. My mouth watered and I swallowed hard, trying to keep from vomiting. When Adones pulled me into his arms, the sobs erupted from me.

"I'm sorry this happened," Adones stroked my back.

I should have pushed away and headed to Sophie, but the warmth of Adones' embrace and the kindness of his words were too much. In this place of death and horror, I needed to be comforted.

When Adones and I finally parted, I had no tears left. He tilted my chin up and dried my cheeks, gazing at me with tenderness as he spoke. "Where is Moqerhe?"

I instantly sobered. With all the emotion, I almost forgot about the djinni. "A-at the entrance waiting for us." I still had no clue how I'd explain Greg's presence.

Adones scratched his head. "It's the strangest thing. I never saw him leave."

Still too emotional to come up with a believable answer, I grabbed Adones' hand and pulled him after me. "Come, Moqerhe's expecting us."

A few minutes later, Adones and I made it to the entrance of the games. A smile touched my lips when I saw Greg's red hair above the sea of people.

"Amara." Greg waved his hand, grinning.

Moqerhe stood beside my brother, straight-backed and alert, scoping out everyone who passed.

I left Adones in the crowd, ran to Greg, and wrapped my arms around him. He was my beacon of hope, a piece of home. "You have no idea how good it is to see you."

Greg tightened his arms around me. "Same. I thought I was a goner."

I stepped back and gave him a once-over, taking in his wind-chapped cheeks. Yet, his eyes stood out the most. They held a sort of hardness, like a soldier who'd experienced too much battle. I tried not to focus on the fact he now wore a full-length robe that fell barely below his knees. Moqerhe must have switched out Greg's clothing with Crooked Nose Guy. I imprisoned my mounting guilt in an invisible cage in my mind. If I had another meltdown, it would paralyze me. I owed it to Sophie to keep it together.

Moqerhe stepped between us, grabbed my arm, and looked at the stone, which had now solidified.

I pulled at my arm. "What are you doing?"

The djinni released me and stepped back, as if realizing he'd invaded my space. "Don't you understand the words 'make haste'? That stone will come to life if the Seekers are nearby. We're vulnerable and should leave now."

Jasim never mentioned anything about that. What else had he omitted? "I thought you and I were cloaked to them."

"Care to wait and see?" Moqerhe said.

Greg's gaze flitted from Moqerhe to me. "What about Sophie?"

I glowered at the djinni. "You promised to help me free her. I don't give a damn who's after us, I'm not leaving here without my friend."

Moqerhe pressed his lips together and shook his head. "Stubborn, stubborn girl."

"Can't you use your djinni powers to save Sophie?" Greg asked.

"You know what he is?"

"Yeah, after I practically pissed myself watching him transform into a human." He turned his attention to Moqerhe. "Please, help us."

The djinni let out a long breath and gazed up at the sky as though asking, 'why me?' "All right, if we go to the girl, now."

Adones approached us and gave my brother a once-over. "Who is the newcomer?"

Best to pull the band aid off. I gestured toward my brother. "Adones Barca meet Greg."

Adone's jaw went slack. "Your brother, how?"

Greg's green eyes widened as he asked in English, "Hannibal's nephew?"

I nodded at them both and responded in ancient Greek. "I'll explain later."

"Enough talking, more walking," Moqerhe said in ancient Greek.

We all practically had to jog to keep up with the djinni as he headed down the path that led to Sophie's cage.

"Why are we so rushed?" Adones asked.

"It's best you don't know," Moqerhe called over his shoulder.

Adones stopped at the gate that led outside the market. When we continued following Moqerhe past it, he called out, "Where are you off to now? Tanno has likely returned, and he'll be looking for us."

"Find him and let him know we'll be along soon," I called over my shoulder.

"Amara!" Adones yelled from behind, but Greg and I just kept going.

With Adones out of earshot, Moqerhe spoke in English while fast walking. "Is the stone on your bracelet still solid?"

I glanced at it, exhaling loudly. "Yeah, so far." Maybe we dodged a bullet, and the Seekers haven't traced the magic.

We ran between two tents and turned down a path lined with more vendors. I kept scanning the sea of people in colorful tunics. Some covered their faces with hooded cloaks. Others wore shoulder-length headdresses. Any one of them could've been a Seeker.

After turning a corner, we followed Moqerhe toward Sophie's cage. The crowd had thinned to a couple of sadists who watched her, the Shadu, and Vicram like they were freaks on exhibit. When I ran to the cage, the dusty old slave owner cut me off.

"Let me pass!" I said through gritted teeth.

Moqerhe approached the man and spoke in measured Punic. The pair laughed together and struck up a conversation. Then, the djinni inched the guy toward the side of the tent where no one except us could see their interaction. Moqerhe whispered in the slave owner's ear. When the man's eyes widened into a 'lights-are-on-but-nobody's-home' expression, he pulled a key from his belt purse and led us to the cage. Before turning the lock, he shooed the gawkers off, and luckily, they left without a hassle. The man opened the gate and freed my friends.

Sophie pulled at the front of her torn tunic as Greg made a beeline to her, swept her into his arms, and kissed her full on the lips.

Her dirt-streaked face was wet from crying. "I thought the worst."

"I'm here, I'm okay, you're okay, that's all that matters," he spoke into her hair.

My lips curled into a smile. Despite all that had happened to them, I was thankful they had each other.

A blood chilling roar echoed through the cage. My heart jumped in my chest. I wheeled around and found the Shadu staring down at the slave owner through wild yellow eyes.

My head swiveled toward Greg. "Get Sophie out of here."

"What about you?" he asked.

"I'll be right behind you."

"You'd better be," Sophie said.

At that, Greg grabbed her hand and hauled ass out of the cage.

The slave owner stood stock still, staring ahead with a deadpan expression while the Shadu circled him. The animal's powerful leg muscles shifted with every step. Although that douchebag deserved to die a horrible death, I couldn't allow it. One murder was enough today.

"Call off your animal," I said to Vicram.

"Why should I? This turd has no respect for human life. He deserves whatever fate the Shadu chooses."

Moqerhe moved beside me. "If the Shadu mauls this man, you and the animal will be forever hunted, and he's not worth your lives. Leave now, before it's too late."

Vicram rubbed his beard as though considering Moqerhe's words. After a long beat, he sighed and spoke to the Shadu in a foreign tongue. The animal submitted with a guttural growl and padded through the gate. Once the rest of us made it out, Moqerhe turned the lock, leaving that asshole slave owner to rot in his own prison.

Vicram ran a tattooed hand down his robe and smoothed it before speaking to me. "I owe you a great debt."

"You owe me noth—" The skin on my wrist went ice cold, and the stone on my bracelet glowed neon blue.

A crackling noise resounded behind Moqerhe. Without flinching, the djinni slowly faced a glowing dot hovering at eye-level about six feet away.

I gasped. "The hell?"

"What is that?" Greg asked.

"Nothing good," Sophie said, backing away.

Vicram stared at the growing dot, transfixed. "Tannit's Blood!"

Bone-numbing cold moved from my wrist and rippled up my arms, sending an icy shiver through my body. The floating dot before Moqerhe elongated into a glowing crack, expanded an inch, and grew wider with each passing second until it became a dark and swirling vortex.

"Go!" Vicram pointed toward the path ahead. "I'll delay whatever awaits beyond."

"You can't!" I gestured toward the Shadu, now watching the expanding vortex like a predator ready to pounce. "You could be imprisoned again or worse."

"I've made my choice," Vicram said. "If the worst happens and the gods choose to take me, it will be on my terms, not by the hands of a cruel taskmaster." He waved me off. "Go! Allow me to repay my debt to you."

Moqerhe's brow furrowed. I could have sworn I saw a glint of admiration in his eyes as he pulled a dagger from his belt and handed it to Vicram.

"Amara, we need to run," Greg said.

I glanced at Moqerhe. "C'mon."

He waved me off and faced the vortex. "Time to atone for my past."

My face twisted in confusion and frustration. "Are you crazy?"

Moqerhe gestured toward Vicram, who stood before the expanding hole with dagger in hand. "This man reminds me of the value of honor."

If Moqerhe was caught, the whole plan would fall apart. No telling what Jasim would do to me, Sophie and Greg, not to mention poor Bear. I had to convince Moqerhe to continue this journey, so I looked him square in the eyes as I spoke.

"I could command you to come with me, but that's not what friends do. If you stay, I'm staying." I prayed Moqerhe's honor would force him to do the right thing and save me.

"Amara, c'mon!" my brother yelled.

My hand shot up without averting my gaze from the djinni. "Shut up, Greg!"

Moqerhe narrowed his eyes. "Truly, you'd allow yourself to be captured, for my sake?"

The vortex crackled and zapped. I forced myself to hold Moqerhe's stare. "Yes, I would. If that's what it takes. I'm not your enemy." The air continued buzzing. I was hanging on by a thread.

After a long beat, Moqerhe said. "Damn you, girl!" He grabbed my hand and yanked me away.

Our group ran as fast as our legs would carry us. Something boomed behind me. While running, I peeked over my shoulder. The vortex had disappeared. Thousands of black specks buzzed in a tight circle and divided into two sections. A loud hissing noise followed, and the specks diffused and spread until they formed the outline of two humanoid figures. Vicram stood beside the Shadu, dagger extended and ready to fight as the specks shimmered between full human bodies and nothingness.

Greg and Sophie sprinted between the tents while Moqerhe followed with me in tow. I barely kept up as our group plowed past the exiting shoppers like a bull on stampede. The more distance we put between us and those black specks, the more the stone warmed against my wrist. I tried to look at it and stumbled.

"Keep up," Moqerhe hissed, jerking me forward.

By the time we made it to Adones and Bear, my legs were like jelly. "Where are our mounts?" I was hacking like a chain-smoker.

"Tanno sold them as payment aboard the ship, just as Ba'al Hammon instructed." Adones grabbed a large leather bag off the ground and slung the strap over his shoulder.

I took in the crowd of robed men and women. No way we could outrun supernatural creatures. No one even glanced our way.

"We must leave, now," said Moqerhe. He gestured toward Sophie. "The girl's owner didn't take kindly to losing his prize spectacle, and his men gave chase."

He lied better than anyone I knew.

Adones' face flushed red. "I knew better than to leave you to your own devices. We don't need this attention!"

Bear muttered under his breath and glanced toward the gate. "You certain her owner gave chase? Nothing looks amiss."

I shrugged. "They may have lost us in the crowd."

"Clearly, I'm among more fools than wise men," Moqerhe said. "You wag your tongues when you should be fleeing."

Bear turned a fierce gaze on Sophie and Greg. "If they slow us down, I'll leave them behind."

Chapter Twenty-Two

My lungs burned and my robes were drenched in sweat as we put some distance between ourselves and the market. About a half mile out, the stone on my wrist had solidified. I hoped that meant the Seekers lost our trail. Since I couldn't tell Adones and Bear who we were really running from, I had to endure the torturous trek until one of them called it quits.

When we ascended a hill dotted with firs and parched brown bushes, our group slowed their pace. Greg, Sophie, and I fell about ten feet back while Bear and Adones continued in silence up ahead, leaving Moqerhe between them.

"I'd kill for a cold beer right now." Greg's tomato-red face and cracked lips were telltale signs he was wearing down quicker than the rest of us.

I cringed, picturing my ten-year-old self watching Dad passed out on the couch with throw-up on his shirt. "Why beer? Water's better for you, especially after all the energy expended on that demi-hydra."

Greg's jaw ticked. "I'm not Dad. A beer in moderation can be refreshing. Why does everything have to be so black and white with you?"

"Excuse me for caring."

Sophie clutched the front of her shirt to prevent a peep show. "Er, what's a demi-hydra?"

Greg shot me a dismissive sidelong glance before turning his attention to her. "A two-headed snake with a scorpion tale that shoots fire."

"That's crazy!" She touched his arm. "I'm just glad you're okay."

"Me too," Greg said.

"And what the hell was that vortex back at the market?" Sophie asked.

"It's a portal," I said. "The Seekers use it to travel between dimensions, but we lost them, for now."

Her deer-in-the-headlights expression told me I had gotten ahead of myself. I recapped from when I first landed on the beach, then explained how I wound up at Hannibal's mansion, coincidentally found Sophie and Greg's jewelry at the market and ended with Jasim and our mission.

"A djinni, that's incredible. It's all incredible," Sophie said.

The others had put some distance between us, so we picked up our pace.

"Well, now that we're together, can I have my ring back?" Greg asked.

"Gladly." I returned their jewelry.

Sophie teared up as she slipped the bracelet over her wrist. "I thought I'd never see this again." She swallowed before continuing. "Those assholes took everything from us. Thanks for grabbing these."

"Of course. I thought your jewelry was all I had left of—" I choked and glanced at the ground.

A long silence passed before Greg said, "Dr. Hamad, huh? I would have never pegged him as an interdimensional traveler posing as a god."

"If the djinni's as powerful as you're saying, Dr. Hamad — Jasim — Ba'al or whoever he is, must be planning to use him for something big," Sophie said.

I shrugged. "I don't know. It wasn't like we bonded over a caramel latte and shared our darkest secrets. If I didn't go along with his plan, I'd never see Dad or Yia Yia again."

"Now, that we're together, do you think Jasim will send us home too?" Sophie bent forward as we climbed the hill.

"He'd better. Our chances are increased if this mission goes off without a hitch."

"Screw the mission." Greg waved toward Moqerhe who was walking several feet ahead and whispered. "He's magical, why can't he zap us home?"

"Moqerhe can't help," I said. "Jasim told me djinn need a portal device to move between dimensions."

"That's just our luck," Sophie said in an exasperated voice. "I miss my parents, I miss home." She blinked several times.

"I can't imagine what Dad must be feeling, thinking he lost both of us," Greg said.

Guilt seized my chest as I pictured Dad in the tomb, telling me he loved me. Now, he thought I didn't care.

"Doing okay?" Greg said.

He'd always read me like a book. After all Greg had been through, I didn't have the heart to tell him about Dad's drinking and the tumor. It wasn't like he could change anything. If we made it to Saguntum in one piece, I'd tell him before Jasim sent us home.

I shrugged. "Just thinking about Dad and Yia Yia."

"Don't!" Greg said. "It'll drive you crazy. Focus on the present and getting out of here instead."

Sophie let out a skittish laugh. "If we survive."

The sadness in their voices made my heart ache. I needed to change the subject. "I haven't heard how you got here yet."

Greg swept his sweaty locks away from his forehead. "It's only been a little over a week since we arrived here, but it seems like a few years, you know?"

"Yeah, I hear you." I stared at the rocky ground as we descended a small hill.

"One second we were in the tomb. The next, we were sucked into that vortex. When I came to, Sophie and I were in the middle of the Sahara."

I cocked my head to one side. "The Sahara?"

"Yeah, like miles and miles of sand, and we didn't have a drop of water to drink," Greg said.

"I'm glad you had each other," I observed. "Still, that doesn't explain how you wound up at the market."

Greg and Sophie separated as we all crested another hill and navigated through a copse of cedars and firs. I was grateful for the shade, and the peaceful trills coming from unseen birds.

"That's a long story." Sophie let out an exasperated sigh as she switched the hand that was holding her tunic together. "Long and short of it, just as we were on our last legs, we spotted a caravan of nomads on camelback. We approached them and freaked out when we saw several men in a cage."

"We tried to run, but one of the slavers pulled his sword and—"

"Chased us down." Sophie's voice shook. "A man caught me first and held the blade to my throat."

"Aside from facing off with the demi-hydra, that was the scariest few seconds of my life." Greg swallowed hard. "After they captured us, we were forced to live on a diet of glue-like porridge and gritty water. Sophie, um ..." He glanced at her.

"It was tough," she said.

Clearly, they were holding back. If I pushed them, they might shut down. Instead, I decided to let it play out, for now. "When did you realize you were no longer in our dimension?"

Sophie gave a humorless chuckle. "When our caravan arrived at ancient Carthage, we knew we weren't in Kansas anymore."

"Our guards pitched camp at the marketplace where you found us, then they threw us in a cage like a bunch of circus freaks." Greg released a long breath from his lungs. "A couple of days later, the winged lion showed, and that had us questioning everything about this period."

Guilt tugged at my chest. "It's a Shadu. I hope he and Vicram are alright."

"Look, I understand your concern, but he made a choice," Sophie said. "Besides, for all you know, they might have escaped and you're worrying for nothing."

Greg nodded. "Ignorance really is bliss."

If only this were true. I decided to change the subject before my emotions got the best of me. "Uh, so you didn't finish your story, about your arrival at the market."

Sophie's face was unreadable. "Well, our slavers auctioned off the men who were with us, including Greg. There were a couple of times they pulled me out of the cage and marched me around in front of a bunch of perverts. Luckily, no one bought me."

Greg's hands balled into fists. "I hope they all die a slow and painful death."

"You're both lucky to be alive," I said.

"For sure. I should have been dead twice. Assholes forced me to fight a lion, and safe to say, that cat was no match for my sword. Afterward, they threw me in with the demi-hydra." Greg had a far-off look in his eyes. "It was tough not to give up hope."

Sophie took Greg's hand into hers. "We're okay now, as long as we stick together."

I wanted to promise that things would be okay, but I couldn't lie. We'd be lucky to make it out of this hellhole in one piece.

We cleared the trees and followed Bear to a flat ridge overlooking a marina. A city wall, about a mile wide, horseshoed the harbor. Seafoam sprayed against hundreds of massive ships, each docked in individual bays.

A high-pitched trumpet resounded below us. When I looked that way, a caped man stood before a white, one-story stucco building in the middle of the dock, holding a horn.

Adones pointed toward a handful of incoming ships. "He signals their approach."

Greg wrapped his arms around Sophie and smiled. "They're more impressive than I could have imagined."

I nodded. "They are."

I'd never tire of looking at those ancient ships. Each stood at least four stories, with square sails and three levels of oars, and horsehead bows. When passing through the harbor entrance, they were greeted by an imposing statue of Poseidon, erected on the edge of the dock. The Greek god held his trident toward the sky like a beacon of hope for all those who navigated the seas.

Greg pointed at soldiers in leather armor loading clay containers onto the rear of a black ship. "The security down there makes Fort Knox look vulnerable. I hope your contact is reliable."

He made a good point. One I hadn't considered until this second.

I turned to Bear. "What's the plan?"

"That war galley is destined for Saguntum, so we'll wait till nightfall until my contact signals we are clear to sneak aboard."

I gasped. "We're stowaways?"

Bear crossed his arms over his chest. "No, we're mariners. You'll be disguised as a man and work above with the rest of us."

Greg laughed. "I'd like to see that."

I shot him a shut it look. "What about my brother and Sophie?"

"What about them? You've yet to explain how you freed them without coins or weapons," Bear eyed me dubiously. "Despite your warnings, no one gave chase. What caused such alarm back at the market?"

Raising my shoulders in what I hoped was a nonchalant shrug, I said, "It was simple. Er, Moqerhe ambushed the girl's owner and knocked him unconscious. Then we freed Sophie."

Bear shook his head. "You risked our hides to save—"

"My brother and a friend," I said. "I would have done the same for any of you and I expect them to continue this journey with us."

Adones crossed his arms. "You haven't answered how you saved your brother from the demi-hydra?"

"I'm standing right here," Greg said in ancient Greek.

I held up my hand in a hold on a second motion, buying time to think how to answer. "Er, it happened that Greg wasn't the one fighting the demi-hydra after all. During the games, a spectator informed Moqerhe of a man fitting Greg's description, awaiting battle in the lower chambers. Moqerhe feared raising my hopes, so he asked me to meet him at the gate after the match."

Moqerhe gestured toward Adones. "You were engrossed in the games when I secreted away to check. It seemed luck was on our side and I found Greg and brokered a deal for his freedom."

Adones pulled a face. "How, without coin?"

I pursed my lips wondering why Moqerhe was suddenly so helpful when Bear chimed in. "Brother or not, my contact won't agree to additional sailors."

"Surely you don't expect me to leave them behind," I said. "You'd have been imprisoned or beheaded if I hadn't intervened on your behalf. I'm asking you to return my kindness and ensure they sail with us."

"And you'd be food for the sea birds had I not come to your aid," Bear sneered. "Dare not lecture me about the requirements of kindness."

"Sophie won't need much," Greg said. "You could add me to the manifest, and she could dress like a man."

Adones and Bear gave Sophie a once-over. She fidgeted under their scrutiny. "She will never pass for a man," Bear said at last.

They had a point. Aside from being super short, her D-cup breasts would be tough to cover. "Can you hide us below deck? I'll share my rations with her."

Moqerhe cleared his throat. "When Ba'al Hammon first met Amara, he asked after her brother and the girl, even expressed concern for their well-being."

I nodded, quickly picking up on where he was going with this. "If we leave them behind, I fear your god's wrath."

Adones passed the skin to Sophie. "It is dark and cramped beneath a ship and you won't see daylight for the entire journey. Apart from that, if you are discovered, the captain will show no mercy."

Historically, Saguntum was in what I knew as Valencia, Spain, which was about sixteen hundred miles from Carthage. Travel aboard a trireme war galley could take a few weeks to a month. The thought of being stuck in a small dark space for this long caused my chest to constrict. I breathed through my mounting anxiety, realizing that my options were limited. If stowing away was the only option for Sophie to come along, I'd suck it up and live in the dark.

"I understand," I said finally.

Greg and I explained everything to Sophie. Her instant nail-biting told me she wasn't keen on this either, which wasn't surprising since she was claustrophobic as hell.

"Ba'al Hammon's temple guard has spoken," Adones said. "Amara's brother and the girl will accompany us."

Bear sneered at Adones. "*If* I successfully negotiate the extra passengers on board the ship, don't complain when most of our purse is lost."

With a grunt, Bear snatched the waterskin from my hand and stalked toward the wooded area behind us. Sophie and Greg followed him, sat beneath a tree, and held hands.

Adones rolled his eyes and the edges of Moqerhe's lip twitched upward.

"Speaking on behalf of my brother and Sophie was too kind," I said.

"It was my pleasure," Adones responded in a silken voice.

I extended my thumb toward Bear, now sitting beneath a tree several yards away. "Perhaps we should join the others and rest." I turned and had only walked a few steps when Adones grabbed my shoulder and wheeled me toward him. "Yes?"

He reached into the leather satchel he'd been carrying, pulled out an off-white cloth and handed it to me. "For your friend."

The crease between Moqerhe's brow had deepened as he watched our exchange.

I unfolded the cloth and looked at Adones. "Is this your tunic?"

He nodded. "To spare your friend further embarrassment in her torn robes."

"This will help, more than you know." I quickly joined Sophie and Greg beneath a mature tree across from Bear.

"Glad you could join us," Greg eyed Adones' back as he walked away. "Did you tell him how he'll die?"

I shook my head. "No. Every time I tried, some catastrophe happened."

"Good, don't. Since this is an alternate version of Carthage, it's possible that he won't die in battle. Telling him might complicate our situation," Greg said.

"Adones deserves to know. He has a great life waiting back at Carthage."

Greg shook his head. "What if he tells his uncle, and we're detained. They'll imprison us until we confess all we know. It's best to keep our heads down and our mouths shut. Our priority should be returning home."

I glowered at him, ready to unload about his callousness when Sophie chimed in.

"What's that?" She eyed my hands.

"It's a tunic. Adones thought you could—"

"Thank you!" Sophie snatched it, leapt to her feet, and ducked behind an adjacent bush.

I decided to wait until I had a handle on my emotions before bringing up Adones' demise to Greg again. Otherwise, we'd just blow up at each other and nothing would be accomplished. Instead, and for reasons I didn't understand, I glanced over my shoulder at Moqerhe, now under a tree beside Adones. It was tough not to compare the two. Adones was muscular and broad shouldered with high cheekbones set off by a Roman nose and square jaw. All traits that could have landed him on the cover of a fashion magazine. The djinni, on the other hand, was taller and leaner, with sharper features, including a high forehead, aquiline nose, and dimpled chin. However, Moqerhe's eyes stole the show, gold as the sun and just as ancient and mysterious.

Although the djinni stared at his nails like he didn't have a care in the world, his behavior at the market told me otherwise. What did he mean by "I have much to atone for"? Since he was ready to face the Seekers, they could have been connected to his past. Also, what caused him to change his mind and leave with me?

My face flushed with heat when Moqerhe busted me staring at him. A slow smile crept across his lips. *"Like what you see?"* His annoyingly smooth voice resounded in my mind.

I jolted and curled my hands into fists. Arrogant ass! If Sophie hadn't emerged from behind the bush, I would have marched over and told him to stay the hell out of my head.

Sophie smoothed the wrinkles out of Adones' tunic, which hung midcalf. "Man, I miss my jeans and tees."

"Me too." The fact she hadn't complained before now was a small miracle.

"The stripper look was nicer," said Greg.

Sophie sat between Greg and I and slapped his knee. "Perv."

"Get a room," I said.

"I wish. Even a roach motel with a *real* bed would be better than this place." Sophie sighed and took my hand into hers. "Greg filled me in about the ship."

"I'm concerned, Sis. If we can't, then what?"

"I'll refuse to go. Since Jasim made it clear that me, Moqerhe, and this bracelet had to make it to Saguntum in one piece, Bear and Adones will find a way to board us all."

Sophie leaned against Greg's arm ponderously. "I hope you're right."

After a while, she and Greg settled in and caught some z's, as did Bear. His snores resounded from across the way. Adones napped under an adjacent fir with Moqerhe beside him, staring at the sky. Too keyed-up to sleep, I walked to the edge of the ridge, sat down, and pulled my knees to my chest. The port below bustled with soldiers and sailors. How would Sophie and I keep from going crazy in the dark cramped space?

A shadow fell over me. I gasped. When my eyes darted upward, I met Moqerhe's amber gaze.

"May I join you, Amara?"

I bit my bottom lip to keep the surprise off my face. "Su-sure have a seat."

Moqerhe lowered himself to the ground beside me in one graceful move. He paused a moment as though gathering his thoughts before speaking, "I'm curious about something."

"Oh, what's that?" I asked.

"Why did you risk your safety at the market? I've been less than amiable since we met."

"Don't you know? You're in my head enough."

He sighed and pointed at the bracelet on my wrist. "That *trinket* has tied me to your emotions, and it allows me to speak the language of the bearer of the stone. Although I can communicate telepathically, I can't read your mind without your permission."

"That won't happen." I was relieved he didn't know my thoughts.

"Fair enough." He paused. "You still haven't answered why you risked your hide at the market."

It had taken Moqerhe centuries to hate and distrust humans. If I wanted to win him over, I needed to be honest. "I'm not sure why I decided to stay. Maybe part of me felt like the mission would be lost and I'd never make it home if you were captured, so I took a chance."

"And what of the other part?" he asked with a quizzical glint in his eyes.

"Guess I needed you to know not all humans are bad, that I'm trustworthy."

Moqerhe's silky black hair hung loosely below his chin, and he tucked it behind one ear before speaking. "I nearly called your bluff, you know."

"I wasn't bluffing," I said. "What made you come with me?"

He waved a hand over his upper body. "This vessel has given me insight into human emotions. My instincts told me you spoke the truth and I didn't want to risk your life."

Despite how he annoyed me, I felt bad for him. "I'm sure this is hard. Once we arrive at Saguntum, maybe Jasim can return you to your true form."

"If only." Moqerhe's voice was laced with malice.

"What do you mean?"

He leaned back on his hands. "Essentially, the transformation spell you recited for *Ba'al* was created centuries ago by my king, Jan-Ib-Jann. When my kind first arrived on this plane, the spell was intended to make djinn appear human so men wouldn't fear us."

"That's smart," I said.

Moqerhe shook his head. "As it turns out, there was a flaw in the spell. After two full days in human form, the change became permanent."

"How did the king find out about this?"

Moqerhe stilled. "He once used the spell on two of his high-ranking ambassadors, enlisted to meet with a human monarch for one night at most. When they reported for duty two days later, they discovered the flaw. The ambassadors could only maintain their true djinni forms when their powers were summoned, and if they pushed it, they held on for several hours. Unfortunately, the energy it took to maintain their true forms for much longer proved too tasking and they became human once more. After their transformation, they also had to rest to regenerate their powers. Distraught by this turn of events, the king called upon his most talented mages to reverse the spell, but his efforts were for naught."

"What happened to the ambassadors?" I asked.

"Unable to cope with their hybridforms, they called upon the full potential of their remaining powers until their auras burned out and they died."

I shuddered despite the warm breeze. "How can using their powers burn them out, aren't djinn an immortal species?"

Moqerhe nodded. "Yes, except in human form, we must regenerate after expelling too much energy, otherwise we burn out like the ambassadors did."

"After that tragedy, the king should have destroyed the spell. Instead, he placed it in his private book of incantations. As you now know, *Ba'al* has since taken possession of it, made me human, and enslaved me to your stone." Then he added, "Not to worry, I won't take my life. Perhaps someday, I'll find a mage who can reverse this spell."

"For what it's worth, you're still one of the most powerful beings I've ever encountered."

"I'm but a shadow of my former self." Rage twisted Moqerhe's features and disappeared just as fast. "Once, I was the strongest and most powerful djinni in my realm and my powers had no bounds. Now, I've been reduced to a hybrid — a magical creature in a human body — with feelings I struggle to comprehend. The way a mere touch causes my skin to shiver, and my face heats when ... I shouldn't be experiencing such things. I shouldn't exist in this form."

"I'm sorry." And I meant it. "If I'd known, I would've tried to talk Jasim out of—"

Moqerhe touched my leg, pulled away, and folded his hands in his lap. "You couldn't have stopped it. I was angry with you. I now see this emotion was displaced. You're as much a victim of circumstance as I."

"I imagine you're feeling a lot like me," I said. "Out of sync in this time, afraid of the unknown, of being different." At least I had Sophie and Greg for support. He had no one.

My statement brought a hint of vulnerability into the djinni's gaze. "You're quite insightful for a human."

"Thanks, I think."

"It's a compliment." He stared at the sea as though contemplating his next words. "I sense you're struggling with our bargain at the games, to save your brother."

I stared at my hands, hoping he didn't see the emotion on my face. "I wish I would have known the full consequences before agreeing."

He studied me for a moment. "Would you have made a different choice?"

That was a question I couldn't answer aloud because hearing myself say *no*, would make me complicit in a stranger's murder. This knowledge somehow tainted me. Instead, I shrugged and said, "It doesn't matter. What's done is done."

The image of the man's legs dangling from the demi-hydra's mouth came to mind. I brought my hands to my face to cover the tears threatening to fall.

Moqerhe gently, tentatively touched my arm. "It's the rule of the stone, a life for a life. I — I wish I could've spared you this pain."

I was drowning in my hypocrisy and guilt, trying to fight my way toward the light, and Moqerhe was there, consoling and warm. I leaned into his chest, and he tensed for such a long beat, I almost pulled away. Slowly, he inched his arms around me until my head rested on his chest. His heart thrummed in my ear and his breathing had become shallow. This was unexpected for such a force of nature. Even the scent of him was a combination of earth and freshly fallen rain. I squeezed my eyes shut, trying to hold in my tears. They fell in a river of pain and Moqerhe tightened his arms around me. Maybe, just maybe, I'd misjudged him.

Chapter Twenty-Three

I must have fallen asleep in Moqerhe's arms because the next thing I knew, he was shaking me awake. His slight grin made me acutely aware of the slobber dribbling from the corner of my mouth. My hand flew to my face, and I wiped away the saliva, trying to get my bearings. I must have slept longer than I thought because night had fallen. The full moon hung amidst thousands of stars shimmering across the sky like diamonds, silvering the ground.

Adones stood over us with his arms crossed. "You both look comfortable," he said with a hint of condescension in his voice.

Under his scrutinizing gaze, I sat up, self-conscious about how close I was to Moqerhe.

"One of us was," Moqerhe watched me beneath creased brows. "You were snoring quite loudly."

Something territorial crept into Adones' gaze. "Snoring on a stranger's lap."

"I'm not a stranger anymore," Moqerhe said in a silken voice.

I glanced between them, irritation bubbling in my chest. Could they be anymore Cro-Magnon? "A betrothed man needn't be concerned about where I sleep."

Adones opened his mouth to speak then stopped. The emotion on his face faded to careful blankness. "Perhaps you should concentrate less on *personal* relationships, and more on readying yourselves for the journey ahead." He pointed to our left, where everyone was huddled together at the edge of a trail that led down to the port. "Tanno's contact should signal us at any moment." Before I could respond, he turned his back on me and stalked toward the others.

"He's jealous, you know." Moqerhe studied me as if awaiting my response.

"I can't worry about that. My priority is getting home to my dad. He's ill, and—" I swallowed back my mounting emotions at the thought of him alone, probably drinking his grief away. "And he thinks Greg and I are dead. The longer I'm here, the worse he gets."

Moqerhe stood up and offered his hand. "I'm sorry to hear about your father, truly." His grip was strong, yet gentle as he helped me to my feet.

"Thank you." I brushed the dust off my robes.

"You still look tired," Moqerhe observed.

"It's been a long day." He, on the other hand, was clear-eyed and fresh as a morning flower. "Do djinnis sleep?"

Moqerhe shook his head and headed toward the others, forcing me to hurry to keep in step. "No, they remain in a meditative state. However, now that I'm *human*, fatigue sets in and I need rest."

I silently kicked myself for bringing up a reminder of all he'd lost. Luckily, Sophie and Greg rushed toward us, saving me from putting my foot in my mouth again.

"Good, you're awake," Greg said. "Tanno isn't much for conversation and—"

"Adones seems pissed," Sophie said.

Greg gave an agreeable nod. "What did you say to him?"

My face twisted in frustration. "Why do you assume it's me?"

Moqerhe let out an exasperated breath. "By the gods, it's exhausting watching you both cluck like two hens."

Greg chuckled and clapped him on the back. "C'mon, brother." They headed toward the others while Sophie and I lagged.

She gazed at Moqerhe's muscular back, grinning. "You and the djinni, eh?"

My head snapped toward her. "No. We caught a few z's. That's it."

Sophie snorted. "For you it was a few z's. To him, I believe it was something more."

My stomach did a little flip. "What do you mean?"

"He watched you sleep, Chica."

I shrugged. "You can't know what a supernatural being is thinking. Maybe he's never seen a human sleep, or he could have been meditating."

"I don't think so."

When Greg and Moqerhe reached Bear, he handed over his waterskin.

Bear approached Sophie and me with his lips pressed into a tight line. "Pleased you could join us."

"Should I have stood around twiddling my thumbs until you deigned me with your presence?" I asked.

"Look." Adones pointed at a ship on the port below. A lone man stood on the top deck waving an oil lamp. "Is that your contact?"

Bear walked to the edge of the ridge and whistled three times.

"He's responding to the guy's signal," I said to Greg and Sophie.

She sighed. "Thank you, Captain Obvious."

Wanting to show growth, I fought the urge to flip her the bird. "Whatever."

Bear led us down the hillside. When we reached a port surrounded by the city walls and illuminated by braziers, a soldier with dark brown, shoulder-length hair waited with two oil lamps in hand. He gave one to Bear. Adones responded in Punic and placed three silver coins in the man's palm. Then the guy opened the gate and waved us through. Warm winds rustled in my ears and the sea swished against the dock as we approached the port.

"Damn, this is spooky," Sophie whispered.

I glanced at Bear, walking beside me, so tall with oil lamp in hand. "Where are all the men?"

Greg said in ancient Greek. "There are no beds aboard a trireme, so they are home resting before the voyage."

"During the journey, the ship anchors near land and the crew sleeps ashore," Adones added.

A few minutes later, we stood below a ship. It was even more impressive up close — at least a hundred feet long with three decks of oars. The cool breeze blew against the retracted sails, causing them to clink against the masts. The horsehead bow, carved from dark wood, stretched beyond the ship's round-bellied hull.

Bear let out a low whistle that could've passed for a bird's trill. A couple seconds later, a guy leaned over the ship's rail, oil lamp in hand.

"Who is he?" I asked.

"A friend of a friend who is helping us board," Bear said.

The man waved us on. Bear quickly walked the wide plank running from the dock to the ship's empty deck. Then the rest of us followed. Up top, the wind blew, and the vessel creaked and swayed beneath us, making it tough to get our footing. If the rocking was this bad while docked, I didn't want to consider what to expect at sea.

Greg gestured toward the large clay urns dripping with olive oil, and the covered baskets packed tightly together. "Wow! They really do tie the cargo down. I've read conflicting theories about how the Carthaginians packed cargo."

I scoffed. "That's what you're getting from this? You should be worried about whether we can board."

"Why, we're already on the ship."

He must have jinxed us because Bear's contact eyed Sophie and me while babbling in Punic. Adones pulled coins from his leather pouch and extended them toward the guy. He just shoved the money away and shook his head.

"The way Captain Ahab's going off, maybe we should take our chances on land," said Sophie.

Greg rubbed his chin. "He's acting awful squirrely."

"Superstitions," Moqerhe whispered in English.

I whipped around. He'd been so quiet, I nearly forgot he was behind us.

"The sailor expected Amara to dress as a man and work with the crew. He fears that two female stowaways will bring bad luck and cause the ship to sink."

"Seriously, you caught all that from here?" My voice was high and thin as I stared at Moqerhe.

He shrugged. "I have exceptional hearing."

This ship brought us one step closer to the completion of our journey, to getting home. "We need to take this voyage. Can't you hypnotize that mariner?"

"Great idea," Sophie said.

Moqerhe glowered at the bracelet. "Despite the power your bauble holds, I'm not a magical trinket to be used on a whim."

"You're right," I admitted. "I don't want to order you around, and I'd rather you helped because it's the right thing to do—"

Moqerhe closed the gap between us, standing so close, his breath caressed my face. I crossed my arms over my chest and lowered them to my sides. *Why am I so anxious?*

"I will do this, for our budding friendship," he said.

My breath caught. The glint of tenderness in his eyes was unnerving. Without another word, he approached Bear and the sailor.

Sophie held up her hand. "Can't believe I'm saying this, but fingers crossed."

Moqerhe inched the sailor away from Adones and Bear and whispered something. The sailor's face went blank, and he stared straight at us. Seconds later, the guy nodded in agreement. Moqerhe's mouth curled into a satisfied smirk as he led the sailor back to Adones, who dropped a couple of coins into his hand. All the men had a brief exchange with lots of nods.

"Looks like it worked," Greg said.

Bear approached me. "You and the girl will stow away below deck where you'll remain silent and hidden. If you're discovered, it won't end well." He pointed at Greg. "You'll work with me."

"I'll do what it takes." Greg turned to Sophie and me. "Hope I can Gump my way through this."

"You'll be fine," I said.

"Look on the bright side," Sophie said. "At least you'll get fresh air. We won't see daylight for a few weeks."

Bear cleared his throat. "Let's get you below deck before the crew boards."

Our group followed Bear's contact past more jars and crates until we made it to the ship's forward. We stopped before a ladder in front of the horsehead bow. The sailor descended first with lamp in hand, followed by the rest of us.

The ladder's rungs moaned beneath my weight as I descended to the third and lowest deck. I let out a loud "phew," as the stench of fish and sweat wafted past my nose.

"It reeks down here," Greg said.

Sophie crinkled her nose. "That's putting it lightly."

Firelight from Bear's lamp revealed benches for rowing, lining the left and right side of the hull. Given the lack of space aboard the ship, I could see why it had to dock each night.

We bent at the waist and followed the sailor down the narrow center aisle between the rowers' benches. Although he was sure-footed as a goat, I struggled to keep my balance with all the swaying. We finally stopped before a small door at the aft of the ship. Inside, the space within the hull was no larger than eight-by-eight, with a hatch in the floor. When the sailor opened it, the air left my lungs when I saw the dark hold or keep below with a ladder.

Sophie's brow nearly touched her hairline. "I'm not sure I can stay down there for two to three weeks."

"You can do this. I'll be with you the whole time," I said.

She bit her thumbnail.

Greg gently lowered her hand. "This is our only option if we want to go home."

"What if I lose it down there?" Her voice was a thin rasp.

He kissed her forehead. "That won't happen. You're one of the strongest people I know, and you can do this."

Bear handed me a waterskin. "Stay below at all times. You'll be fed once a day and your chamber pot will be emptied by a cleaning boy, after the crew leaves the ship each night."

I nodded. "If they're gone, can we come up for air at night?"

Adones shook his head. "Someone always remains aboard to guard the ship. If one of us is on duty, we'll bring you to deck."

That didn't sound very promising. I pointed at the lamp in Bear's hand. "Um, can we take that below?"

Bear clenched his jaw. "I warned you it would be dark. Fire on a ship is dangerous."

"Sophie struggles in enclosed spaces," Greg said in ancient Greek.

Bear gaped at him. "Perhaps you should have considered this before agreeing to your accommodations."

"Give her the lamp." Moqerhe rested a hand on Bear's shoulder "It will keep them from going mad."

After considering his request, Bear turned to the sailor and spoke in Punic. A long exchange followed then Bear handed me his lamp. "I'm told oil is stored below. Be sure to keep this filled."

"If the flame dies, you'll be in darkness until your food is delivered," Adones said.

"How can we be sure no one will come below?" I asked.

Bear gestured toward the sailor. "He's in charge of the area, and there's no reason anyone should need to. The crew's stores are above. You'll be safe."

"Alright." I turned the lamp on Sophie, which cast long, spectral shadows across her features. "Wanna go first, or should I?"

Her eyes shined beneath the lamp light. "At least I don't have to worry about cave-ins. Maybe I'll drown down there."

When Greg reached for her, she turned away and climbed onto the ladder. I admired her bravery as I handed her the oil lamp.

"This is hell." She descended into our hidey hole.

"Right behind ya." Just as I was about to climb down, Adones stopped me.

He took my hand into his and placed a sheathed dagger in my palm. "For your safety and protection."

The dagger fit perfectly in my hand. I had never considered the possibility of using deadly force. Then again, old Amara would've never agreed to stowaway in a dark hole aboard a ship full of sailors. This place had changed me into someone different, better.

I stuffed the knife into my boot and gave a thankful nod before heading below.

About halfway down the wobbly ladder, the hatch slammed shut with a bang. I continued my descent to the bottom of the ship's hull and landed in front of Sophie. The space was too short to stand, forcing me to hunch over.

"I was right. This is hell." Sophie held the oil lamp above her head and scanned the space with her mouth agape. The flame cast dim light across the floorboards that expanded the length of the ship. Motes of dust swirled in the air. Cobwebs hung in about every corner.

"Okay, it's not a palace, but we can do this." I didn't believe a word I said. This was horrible.

The hot salt air hung heavily in our throats, and the space was crowded with all the makings of war. Rows of baskets containing bows, arrows, animal furs, and small clay jars smeared with oil ran along one side of the hull.

Sophie turned her back on me, to hide her emotions. She pulled a few of the furs from a wooden container and disappeared between two man-size baskets. By the time I squeezed between them, she had spread the fur on the floor, and made a nice pallet.

She sighed. "Might as well have a seat. This'll be our home for the next few weeks."

Chapter Twenty-Four

Although our journey was a little more than a week in, it felt like months had passed in the dark compartment below the ship. Oars scraped against the hull, and we often bounced around during large currents. This made Sophie too sick to obsess about being trapped or she had just kept her fears to herself. On days with gentle seas, we kept from going nuts by trying to guess if we heard Bear, Adones, Moqerhe, or Greg among the jumble of men's voices above us.

Yet, the boredom wasn't the worst of our journey. On hot days, our sweat and Sophie's puke hung thickly in the air. Flies buzzed around our chamber pot toward the aft of the ship. Our only solace was sleep. At least the vessel's constant rocking and swaying helped with that.

After waking from a long nap, I immediately noticed how the ship had quieted, which signaled that the crew had disembarked for the night.

Sophie had collapsed on her belly after her second push-up and turned toward me. "I'm going nuts down here."

"Uh huh," I said, half-listening.

Sophie glanced up at the ceiling. "Ugh. You're obsessing about Jasim's end game *again*."

My gaze darted to hers. She knew me too well.

She sighed. "How many times do I need to say this? What happens here isn't our concern."

"Isn't it? There are people here I care about, and Jasim can't be up to any good. Think about it, Hannibal camped at Saguntum just before he marched over the Alps. If he gets his hands on the bracelet and Moqerhe, he'll—"

"Have the magical equivalent of a nuclear weapon. Yeah, you've told me a thousand times. We've discussed scenarios like escaping the ship, trying to figure out how to free the djinni, blah, blah, blah. None of them are doable."

"If only Jasim didn't have that damn spell book."

Sophie sat forward. "Well, he does, and if you don't want to become a pillar of salt, you'll finish this mission so we can get home."

A sort of heaviness weighed me down as I considered for the hundredth time that I was no longer solo. I had her and Greg to worry about, and deviating from Jasim's plans would put them at risk. "You're right. Home should be our priority."

Sophie handed me a piece of flat bread from the basket.

I took a bite. "Yum, a little more saliva and I'd have glue."

A low chuckle escaped her as she slid the waterskin toward me. "There's not much left. That little brat better come tonight." She pointed behind us, past a bunch of wooden boards stacked along the hull of the ship, where our chamber pot sat. "That's getting ripe."

"He'll show," I said reassuringly. "I'm sure there's good reason he didn't come last night." Though I couldn't imagine what it could be. I had to believe if the guys were in trouble, they would have warned us.

As though on cue, a clanking noise resounded above, followed by a swish as the hatch opened. "It's me, Maego. I have your meal." His clothing rustled as he descended the ladder.

A loud breath rushed from my lungs. "Finally."

Sophie crawled to a crack between two large baskets that hid us, pulled a lit oil lamp through, and passed it to me. She also handed over a clean chamber pot, fresh wine, a filled waterskin, and a small basket of food. Maego then slipped through the crack with ease, which wasn't surprising for a twelve-year-old with a skeleton body.

"What tidings do you bring?" I asked in ancient Greek, feeling like a character from *The Odyssey*.

Maego smiled. "Gregory is an excellent oarsman. He even kept pace with Tanno."

I sniggered. "I'm not surprised. He's good at everything."

Sophie elbowed me. "What's he saying?"

I repeated Maego's words in English.

"Yeah, no shocker there."

"You're pleased with my report?" Maego asked.

"It's a relief," I said. "When you didn't visit last night, I feared the worst."

His long lashes cast shadows over his cheeks as he searched the floor. "I — I made a mistake. Er, after the lower deck was cleared, I decided to bring your food, but this was an error in judgment since the navigator was still aboard. He found me below deck and accused me of stealing. If Tanno hadn't intervened on my behalf, I'd be hanging from the ship's bow. He told the navigator that my weight was a concern, and he had ordered me to take the food for later. Unfortunately, the navigator departed with disbelief in his eyes. We were concerned so Tanno advised me to wait a day before attempting another delivery, in the event spies were watching."

My blood chilled. If the navigator found out about Sophie and me, we'd be walking the plank or worse. "Do you think he suspects anything?"

Maego scratched his head, rumpling his long black curls. "I cannot say. He's been on high alert ever since our crew saw the water djinn. Now, he believes our ship is cursed."

"Water djinn?" Very few things about this dimension surprised me anymore.

"Indeed, they're vicious sea creatures who'd rather kill humans than look at them."

My breath hitched. "Are they still out there?"

He shrugged. "We haven't seen them since last evening." A jagged breath escaped his mouth. "Perhaps they grew bored and swam elsewhere."

Sophie spoke up. "Kid looks like he's about to cry. Care to share?"

I kept the sea djinn part to myself. Dropping two bombs at once would totally wig her out. "He was almost caught bringing our food last night and had to lay low until the coast was clear."

Sophie's face was shadowed, so I couldn't read her expression. However, the hitch in her voice spoke to her nervousness. "Why didn't Moqerhe inform you telepathically?"

I shrugged. "Maybe he can't unless he's close." I returned my attention to Maego. "Are you certain you weren't followed?"

"Yes, I was careful." Maego collected our chamber pot, the old food basket, and put them into a wooden bucket left from his last visit. "Do you require anything else?"

"No," I said.

With a slight nod, Maego pushed all the used items through the crack between the baskets then squeezed through. I peeked after him and said, "Will you return tomorrow?"

He stopped and spoke in a thin voice. "I intend to. Be well, madam."

I plopped onto our fur pallet while Sophie poured herself some wine. She had drunk the bulk of it since we set sail. Though alcohol triggered me, I also understood that she used it to hold off her nightmares, but this only worked half the time. On the nights she awoke in a cold sweat, I tried to get her to talk except she wasn't having it.

"I'm starving, what's in the basket?" Sophie asked.

I lifted the cloth from the food. "At least they're consistent. We've got about six pieces of lamb jerky, cracker bread, a side of dates, figs, and some olives. What sounds good?"

Sophie's lip curled like she was grossed out. "Guess it's the bark, I mean, jerky."

I chuckled and handed her the basket, ignoring how my belly rumbled. Such meager rations kept me in a perpetual state of hunger.

She plucked a piece of meat out and bit into it, pulling a chunk away and chewing hard. "Glad Greg's hanging in there."

"Me too." I grabbed the waterskin and took a sip. "Is this a me thing or does Greg seems more serious? I mean he hasn't smiled since we found him."

"It's this place," Sophie said mid-chew. "The constant life and death stressors have changed us. Some of the people here, they're—"

"Evil and awful." The boat creaked and moaned beneath us.

Sophie washed back the remains of her food with a sip of wine. "When I think about that cage and where I might be if you hadn't—"

"Don't." Something moved in my periphery. "It's that stupid rat." As the words left my mouth, I realized a lot had changed. At first, the creatures freaked me out. Now, I didn't even blink when I saw one.

The rat inched toward us. Its beady red stare glowed in the dim light as Sophie tossed a piece of jerky on the floor.

"Stop feeding it," I said. "Rats aren't pets. They carry diseases. It's not like we have loads of hand sanitizer laying around. We need to keep our distance."

"It's cute."

The rodent grabbed the meat with its tiny hands and retreated behind the planks stacked against the hull.

A clank from above rattled me. I froze as the hatch opened. When Maego's call didn't come, Sophie blew out the flame in our oil lamp. The ladder whined as someone descended. Golden light from the intruder's lamp caused shadows to scrabble along the ceiling like menacing spirits. I crawled to the crack between the baskets and peeked toward the ladder. Large boots, made from animal fur, descended the rungs one at a time, followed by loud grunts, a man's grunt.

My heart flew to my throat. I pointed toward the pile of wood along the hull, gesturing for Sophie to hide behind it. She quickly squeezed between the wall and the pile. I tried to follow. The space was too small. Footsteps shuffled closer. Someone pushed the baskets apart, expanding the crack between them. I scanned the hull, desperately searching for somewhere to hide. Anywhere. I scooted back against the hull, cowering in the shadows.

Be still as air.

A man crouched. Firelight from the oil lamp outlined his hawk-like profile as he examined our pallet. He turned in my direction and moved toward the aft. Each shuffle of his feet grew louder and louder. I didn't breathe, didn't move.

Then he saw me.

Maybe his narrowed stare wasn't as creepy as I thought. Maybe it had to do with the way the shadows fell over his unshaven face, but when that deep voice whispered in Punic, chills ran down my spine.

His mouth curled into a horrible grin, revealing a mouthful of brown teeth.

If I screamed, we'd face a lot worse than this crew member. Moqerhe, I could summon Moqerhe, but what about the Seekers?

Just as the thought entered my mind, the bracelet glowed red and burned hot against my skin. Pinpricks tingled up my arm. I pressed my back against the hull, watching the dirty stranger stare at me like a wolf about to pounce on a bunny.

I held my chin high, praying he bought my show of strength. "Keep silent about me, and my father will reward you well," I said in ancient Greek.

The stranger set the lamp aside and took a knee before me. "A woman with a wealthy father has no need to stow away." He responded in the same language.

"I assure you—"

He grabbed my arm. I clenched my teeth to keep from screaming. "The captain will be quite pleased with my find. Stowaways are bad luck, and you'll undoubtedly get a good price at market."

I pulled against him, drowning in desperation. "Please, don't do this."

"Stop your begging, girl." The stranger tried to drag me toward the basket, and I clawed at his hand, drawing warm sticky blood.

He bared his teeth and slapped me across the face, hard. My cheek stung as he flung me on my back, crawled on top of me, and slammed my head against the floor.

My vision blurred. I screamed and beat his chest.

The ship groaned against the stillness. A mocking sound, telling me no one heard me. And then, I felt the dagger shift in my boot.

Thank you, Adones.

The stranger grabbed my wrists. "Learn your place, girl!"

I spat in his face. He recoiled long enough for me to wriggle my arm free and reach into my boot. With dagger in hand, I went straight for his neck. The stranger grabbed my hand and beat it against the floor. Stabs of agony surged up my arm. I shrieked and released the weapon, watching the only hope of saving myself slide out of reach.

The bracelet burned hotter against my wrist, bidding me to summon Moqerhe. The heaviness of my attacker's body crushed me to the point I could barely breathe, much less speak.

Then a shadow fell on my face.

A loud crash followed. Oil splattered on the man and me. He hissed and rolled off me. I gasped for air. Sophie crouched over us, holding the remains of a clay pot. My attacker muttered under his breath, moved onto all fours, and scrambled toward her. She stumbled and landed on shards of pottery. I jumped up, grabbed a small plank of wood, and clocked him on the head with it, twice. The stranger's mouth formed a perfect O as he rolled onto his back. I raised the plank again, ready for an encore, when Moqerhe grabbed my arm.

Chapter Twenty-Five

Moqerhe peeled my fingers away from the board and tossed it aside. "It's over. He can no longer harm you."

"Is-is he dead?" Sophie asked. All the color had drained from her face.

Moqerhe rested a hand against the man's neck, checking for a pulse. "His heartbeat is faint."

A sour, nauseated feeling welled in my stomach. My mouth watered, and I vomited. I wiped perspiration from my forehead and looked at Sophie hazily. "You saved me."

She let out a shuddering breath. "Sorry. I — I froze."

I pulled Sophie against me and stroked her tangled hair. "We're okay now," I said, unconvinced, crying like a baby.

We must have held each other beneath the ship's moaning deck for a while, because when I released her, Moqerhe had plucked a piece of fabric from one of the baskets and gagged the unconscious man.

"Do you know him?" I asked, calmer now.

"Callan. He's the navigator." There was something totally disarming about the softness and compassion in his voice.

Despite all the pain and fear, I couldn't help noticing Moqerhe's sculpted cheekbones and full bow-like lips. He was beautiful.

Sophie wiped her tear-stained cheeks. "How did you know about the attack?"

Moqerhe pointed at my bracelet. "Amara and I share a connection through the stone."

"Oh, I see," she said.

It was hard not to notice the way his eyes had shifted from a golden brown to amber beneath the dim light. Needing to get a grip. I shot him a thin smile. "For once I'm grateful for our connection."

"We need to get rid of him." Sophie was pointing at the navigator. "Can you zap him out to sea or something?" The pulse on her neck fluttered so fast I could've spotted it from a mile away.

Moqerhe shook his head. "No, magic might draw the Seekers. Plus, he'd be missed."

"You just teleported down here? Isn't that magic?" Sophie asked.

"It is," Moqerhe observed. "Teleporting myself is far different than teleporting an unwilling target like Callan. That would demand exponentially more power, which could draw the Seekers' attention."

"Well, what are we supposed to do?" I asked. "He can't stay here forever."

"Can you hypnotize him?" Sophie asked.

"Yes, that seems our only option," Moqerhe observed. "For all we know, he may have shared his suspicions with others aboard and they may choose to explore here as well. We'll need to make our escape tomorrow night."

"How are we supposed to do that?" Sophie asked. "We're miles from shore."

Moqerhe shook his head. "No, we're not. The ship travels close to land in case of an accident, and at night, the crew goes ashore to refill water stores and eat and sleep. I'll inform the others of what occurred here then we'll volunteer to stay behind tomorrow. Once everyone disembarks, we'll make our escape and take the remainder of the journey by land."

Sophie mopped her hands over her face. "I hope this works."

Moqerhe's lips pressed into a pained line as he glowered at Callan's unconscious body. "He deserves to die."

"No way." I shook my head. "Living with one murder is hard enough. Two would do me in."

The djinni's face creased curiously. "It's a rare human indeed who doesn't seek revenge when wronged."

"We're not animals," Sophie said. The only evidence of her shock showed in her trembling hands.

Moqerhe's cheeks flushed red as his eyes slid to me. "No, you're not."

We dragged the navigator to the ladder, sat him up and threw water in his face. He groaned and blinked as if trying to focus. When he saw me, he sneered.

Kneeling before him, Moqerhe looked into his eyes, and spoke in Punic. Callan's pocked face went blank, and he nodded. After a moment, the navigator climbed up the ladder without looking our way.

"What did you say to him?" I asked.

A devious smile spread across Moqerhe's lips. "He won't remember you, this ship or anyone aboard, and he's about to swim ashore."

I gasped. "After I asked you not to harm—"

"Calm yourself." Moqerhe gave dismissive wave of his hand. "We're not far from shore. Unless fortune smiles upon us and Callen becomes a shark's next meal. Otherwise, he should make it to the beach unharmed."

Sophie picked up my dagger and eyed it. "He deserves this and worse."

"He'll get what's coming to him someday." I gently reached over and took the blade from her, then sheathed it in my boot.

"Indeed." Moqerhe's gaze slipped from Sophie to me. "You've suffered much. Just stay the course one more day, and we'll be off this ship."

We nodded and took a seat on the pallet. After the trapdoor shut behind him, Sophie and I sat together in tense silence. My neck ached from where the navigator had choked me, and my hand throbbed from being slammed against the floor.

I grabbed the water container, took a few gulps, and extended it toward Sophie. "Want some?"

"No, thanks." Her voice was as flat as her expression.

"You okay?" I already knew the answer, but I hoped the question would get her to share her feelings.

"I'm not sure."

Short but honest. I could work with that. "Look, I know the attack—"

"Freaked me out? Well, it did, and not for the reasons you think." Tears shined in Sophie's eyes. "Remember how I told you Greg and I were captured by slavers?"

"Yeah."

"Well, I left out a couple of things. I got sick one night, and one of the slavers snuck into my tent." She pressed her lips together.

My hand flew to hers like it had a mind of its own. "How awful."

"It *was* awful." Her voice quivered. "Like tonight, except my attacker tried..."

I wasn't sure how to respond. I'd never felt more uncomfortable, and yet, I needed to force myself to be present. "I wish I could say or do something to make it better."

"It is what it is. Anyway, Greg heard my screams, and he intervened before the guy could do ... well, you know. I've never seen your brother that angry. It took three men to pull him off my attacker. The head guy was pissed. I guess testing the merchandise was a no-no, so the guy slit my douchebag attacker's throat in front of us."

I brought my hand to my chest. "God!"

"They made Greg pay. He was beaten and chained to the back of the wagon, made to walk the whole way." Sophie sniffed. "It was horrible. He fell several times. Too sick to help, I kept passing in and out of consciousness. If not for one of the other slaves who was a healer, we would've died. When we finally arrived at Carthage, they sold Greg to the people who ran the games and threw me in a cage. The Shadu showed up shortly before you found me."

My chest ached. "Why didn't you tell me?"

She shrugged. "Talking about it won't change anything."

"You were attacked by an evil man, Sophie." No wonder she was having nightmares. "You didn't deserve any of this. You know that, right?"

"None of us do," Sophie said. "When I saw the navigator attacking you, all my rage just came out and—"

"And I'm alive because of you."

"I don't regret anything. In fact, I wish I'd killed him." She covered her face with her hands and cried. "I can't believe I just said that."

I gently moved her arms to her lap. "You're one of the kindest people I know."

Sophie squeezed her eyes shut and shook her head. "I'm just so, so tired."

"Why don't you get some sleep." I patted my lap. She laid her head down and I stroked her hair, praying she'd be okay, that we'd be okay.

Chapter Twenty-Six

In the hours after the attack, I tossed and turned, falling in and out of sleep. Although my fear had dulled to a slight anxiousness that followed a horrible nightmare, the reality of how vulnerable we were had sunk in. I wouldn't feel safe again until we were off this hellhole of a ship.

A clanking noise from above distracted me from my thoughts. Sophie jolted upright, scanning the area with dazed and glassy eyes.

I blew out the lamp just as the hatch swished open. "Amara, Sophie," Greg stage-whispered from above.

"Lower the lamp a little so we can see," I said.

The second the flames flickered on the ceiling, Sophie and I bolted from our pallet. I squeezed between the baskets and hurried up the ladder with her on my heels. When I emerged, the deck was empty and dark as the night we first boarded. Greg was bent over. He set down his oil lamp and helped Sophie and I climb to the first and lowest deck.

Greg dropped to his knees, pulled her into his arms and kissed her longingly. "God, I've missed you," he spoke into her neck.

"Me too," Sophie rubbed the patch of red hair on his chin. "You look like Shaggy."

"Thanks, that's what every guy wants to hear."

I cleared my throat, feeling like a third wheel. "Um where's everyone else?"

"Waiting up top." Greg pulled me in for a bone-crushing group hug. "Thank God you guys are okay."

I pushed away. "I can't breathe," I said with a slight chuckle.

He laughed and picked up the oil lamp with calloused hands, "C'mon, we need to get going."

Greg didn't need to ask me twice. I scrambled down the middle aisle between both rows of benches and ascended the ladder. Up top, I sucked in a lung full of fresh salt air. It felt like years had passed since I'd been outside.

"Damn that breeze feels good," Sophie said.

I nodded. "For sure. Especially after living in that dark and stinky hidey hole."

Sophie stepped beside me, gazing at the horizon with a slight smile on her lips.

I stretched my arms overhead while taking in the view. About a half mile out, light from the crescent moon blanketed the rolling hillsides in wide shadows.

Someone tapped me on the shoulder. My heart jumped and I wheeled around, meeting Adones. His green eyes twinkled beneath the glow of his oil lamp, and the beginnings of a beard covered his square jaw. He clenched his teeth and touched my throat. "Callan should be impaled and fed to the sharks."

"I wish."

Adones passed the lamp to Sophie and hugged me. "I'm unsure what I would've done if you had been harmed."

I slowly wrapped my arms around his waist and breathed in his scent, a mixture of salt and sweat. When I noticed Moqerhe watching us, I backed away, realizing he sensed my affection for Adones, which shouldn't have mattered.

Bear stepped up and flashed a grin that deepened the long scar on his face. A scar I'd come to love. "I see the rats haven't eaten you."

I snorted and hugged him. "Miss you too."

Bear scrunched his nose and backed away. "You're riper than a bucket of fish guts."

A smile played on Moqerhe's mouth, and my face flushed. I squared my shoulders, determined not to let him see my embarrassment. "All the reason to get to land so I can bathe."

"Indeed." With a slight nod, we followed Bear to the center of the ship, where a cluster of tall urns and baskets were located. Moqerhe walked to the rail and helped Bear untie the pulley rope that lowered the skiff. The moment it hit with a splash, about fifteen men emerged from behind the cluster of urns and the small shed where the captain steered the boat. Two men with longbows flanked Sophie and me with strings pulled tight. Their arrows were aimed straight at our heads.

"Shit!" Sophie said.

A man stepped to the front of the group. His ruffled black hair and missing front tooth were enough to distract me from the sharp sword in his hand. The blade shined silver beneath the moon, a reaper ready to take our heads. Men stood behind him, watching us like a bunch of hungry animals.

"He's the captain," Moqerhe's voice ran through my mind as he moved to my side.

The captain pointed a bejeweled finger at me and spoke in ancient Greek. "I've been told you're at the center of this deception."

I blinked. How did he know to speak ancient Greek? Was there a traitor among us?

Bear, Greg, and Adones unsheathed their swords and stood with Moqerhe. Words were exchanged in Punic.

The captain's gaze returned to me. "It's over. Instruct your friends to lower their weapons before they lose their heads."

"Never!" Bear spat.

"You're outmanned and outwitted," said the captain in a deep voice.

Adones lowered his weapon. "General Hannibal Barca's my uncle. He'll pay a high price to see us safely returned to him."

The captain threw his head back and laughed, loud and haughty. "If that were true, you'd be on campaign instead of keeping company with these sea urchins."

Although Adones' face was the picture of calm, the venom dripping from his voice betrayed him. "He *is* my uncle. If any harm befalls me, you'll lose your head."

Still staring at Adones, the captain whispered to a thin, scruffy man beside him. The guy nodded and moved to the back of the crowd. Seconds later, he emerged with the boy, Maego.

He's the traitor.

"The boy told me everything." The captain pointed a knobby finger at Sophie and me. "Those stowaways have brought bad luck. My navigator has gone mad. He can't remember his own name. We've seen water nymphs and veered off course. Justice must be served."

"Those issues could occur on any ship. You've no right to hold us," I said.

The captain scoffed. "I can execute or enslave any man or *woman* stowed aboard." He rested a gentle hand on the boy's shoulder. "Maego here, and the rest of these men, will be my witness should any legal issues arise."

"If you knew about the women," Moqerhe jutted his chin toward Sophie and me, "why wait till now to act?"

"And miss catching the whole gang, where's the fun in that? Sailing the ocean can be quite tedious. My men need a good game of cat and mouse." The captain shoved the boy aside. "You have to the count of three to lower your weapons or die."

Adones looked down the line at Moqerhe, Bear, and Greg. "Together then."

Sophie grabbed my hand, and she shot me a questioning look.

"We — we've got to the count of three to give up," I sputtered.

"One," said the captain.

The word set my teeth on edge.

Moqerhe's voice rushed through my mind like a runaway train. *"Invoke my powers. Do it now."* The bracelet heated up and the jewel glowed red as if it heard his plea.

"Two." The captain's deep voice echoed across the deck.

I couldn't die like this. My heart somersaulted against my ribs as I recited the incantation Jasim had taught me. "With permission granted to me by—"

"Three."

The arrows whirred toward Sophie and me. She screamed. I covered her body with my own. Then, everything went quiet. Funeral quiet. When the death blow never came, I inched away from Sophie. She was frozen in time with her mouth gaping open, along with the crew and everyone else. The arrows hovered about four inches from Sophie's head as I separated from her.

"No!" My heart sank when I saw Moqerhe in his true form, collapsing a few feet away. I weaved between my statue-still friends and dropped to my knees beside him. Moqerhe's bat-like wings were withered. He slowly turned his head toward me. I choked back my mounting desperation. "How did you do this without my permission?"

Moqerhe gazed at me through dull red eyes.

"I defied the rules and used my powers." Moqerhe's voice was barely a thread. "There's always a sacrifice. Death is my price."

Did he sacrifice himself for us or was this a suicide attempt to get out of his misery? Just like the ambassadors he had told me about. Regardless of his reasons, we were safe because of him, and I couldn't let him die here.

"Board the others on the skiff." His cough was wet. "Before my spell fades."

"You're part of our team and I won't leave you." I clutched his clawed hand against my tightening chest. His skin was cold.

Moqerhe's pale lips curved into a thin smile. "Stop being … so obstinate. You must accept … It's too late for me." A strong wind blew my hair over my eyes. As I raked it away, tentacles of fog slithered over the rails like hundreds of octopi, and coiled us in a thick, gray mist. Fear hollowed out my chest. "Don't die on me."

"No one ever truly—" A deep, sucking breath interrupted his words.

The stone faded to a dull red. I inched my hand toward Moqerhe's chest. *Please don't be dead. Please.* A loud breath released from my lungs as his chest barely rose and fell beneath my palm. "Thank Go—"

A warbled tone, like a whale's song, except harsher and louder, echoed from the sea. My body rose without permission, and I walked to the rail with heavy legs. The rising and falling whale-like hums echoed across the deck, luring me in with their haunting melody. Through the dense, gray fog diffusing from the ocean, two figures with bright yellow eyes emerged.

Adrenaline pumped through my veins.

Run, get the hell out of here!

My body wouldn't obey.

In those heart pounding seconds, I knew beyond a shadow of a doubt, we were all going to die.

Chapter Twenty-Seven

Two figures shimmered in and out of my view and floated toward Moqerhe like ghosts in the fog. Frozen in place by an invisible force, it took every muscle in my neck to slowly turn my head in their direction. The mist retreated from the figures, revealing human-like creatures standing almost seven feet tall. Their scaled skin sparkled with the brilliance of a thousand diamonds. Fins fanned down their cheeks, and they stared at the frozen crew over thin noses. One was clearly female with slim hips, small breasts, and long silver hair. Her male companion was slightly taller with a thin, muscular frame, and he held a silver trident.

The male stood over Moqerhe and hit his trident against the deck three times, clack, clack, clack. Thunder roared and rumbled overhead. A blue flash rippled down the handle and connected with Moqerhe's chest. The djinni's eyes snapped open, and he sucked in a loud breath. Streaks of electricity crackled and branched along his body, enveloping him in a glowing nimbus.

My heart thundered as the female's mouth opened wide, revealing a mouthful of shark teeth. She released a screech that was so high and shrill, it rose above the claps of lightning. My bracelet warmed against my skin. Heat rushed up my arm and

I stumbled backward. It took a second to realize that I was the only person who wasn't frozen.

Slowly, I searched through the fog. My knees almost buckled when I spotted the male creature aiming his trident at the captain. Blue streaks of electricity rippled from the weapon's forked end and connected with his back. Then the captain magically rose into the air. The spell must have been broken because the captain kicked and flailed like a crab on a spit as the creature flicked the trident upward. The captain propelled about twenty feet in the air, before plunging into the sea with a horrible splash.

My hand flew to my mouth to stifle a scream.

The creatures moved to their next victims. High-pitched cries dissolved into the fog. I skimmed the urns and baskets looking for anywhere to hide but couldn't get to them unseen. The female's shrill laugh trilled against the silence, drawing closer with each life she claimed. I inched backward toward the rail, gripped by fear, when a hand covered my mouth. I recoiled and struggled beneath my captor's grip.

"Relax, it's me," ran through my mind in perfect English. After removing the hand from my mouth, Moqerhe moved in front of me. He was in human form, smiling through pale lips.

Cheeks wet with tears, I pulled him against me and wrapped my arms around him. "I thought you were dead."

Moonlight danced along his sharp features. "I know."

"Those things, they're killing everyone," I sputtered.

He took my hand. "We need to leave before the Seekers track the magic."

I tore my hand away, nearly panting. "Not without—"

Moqerhe grabbed my shoulders. "I won't abandon our friends."

Wow! We'd come a long way if he called them that. My breathing slowed a little. "How will we get them off the ship?"

Pale as a corpse, he opened his mouth to speak, and closed it when a shadow fell over the floorboards beside him. My stomach took a nose-dive. The creatures, now standing on each side of Moqerhe, both regarded me with yellow-eyed fury.

He gestured toward the male. "This is my former brother-in-arms, King Himilco, and his sister, Princess Anath of the sea djinn. They've ruled the waters since the great war."

My dry mouth forced out a, "Hi."

The female djinni hissed and bared her pointed teeth. I sucked in a lung full of air. One bite from those suckers, and I was a goner. She clucked her tongue at Moqerhe, then the male joined in. Together, they interacted like a bunch of arguing Klingons.

Moqerhe returned his attention to me. "Since I'm still weakened, the king will ensure our team boards the skiff."

I licked my dry lips. "Thank you."

The female continued sneering as she spoke in ancient Greek. "Save your gratitude, *human*."

Contempt flickered in the king's eyes when he spotted the jewel on my bracelet. "Moqerhe's a fool to form alliances with those who enslave us. How the centuries have changed him."

I shook my head. "No, no, I don't want to hold anyone against their will."

"Then give us the jewel in that bracelet and release Moqerhe." The princess' voice was high and raspy. "Allow him to *choose* how next to proceed."

I needed to *choose* my words wisely if I wanted to walk away from this. "If I do as you ask, the one known as Ba'al Hammon has an incantation that would kill us both."

"You're in league with *him*!" the king snapped.

"Not by choice. He threatened to kill everyone I love unless I complied with his request."

The king's webbed hand tightened around the handle of his trident. "Always the same. Human life means more than djinn life. I could cut off your hand, take that jewel and free our brothers-in-arms now held in Ba'al's prison." He glowered at Moqerhe. "Join us. Let's finish what we started."

Moqerhe clucked his tongue. King Himilco responded in like, only more animatedly.

After an uncomfortable minute of me pretending to ignore the princess' murderous glare, Moqerhe's voice ran through my mind. *"Forgive them. Their anger is well earned. Over the centuries they've avoided man, fleeing deeper into the seas as your kind took over the waters. Himilco's children have fallen prey to fishermen's nets and hunters seeking to confirm myths of the ancients. They'll always see humans as evil."*

The king's yellow eyes narrowed. "Despite my protests, Moqerhe won't allow any harm to befall you or the rest of his *pets*. I owe him a great debt, and this is the only reason you still breathe."

A light flashed in the center of the ship, followed by a buzzing sound. Golden dots appeared from nowhere and began elongating.

"Seekers?" I yelled.

Moqerhe pulled me against him. The glowing dot expanded into a circle about the size of a trashcan lid. Something buzzed like a hive of bees and grew louder with each passing second.

The king banged his trident against the deck three times. A silver bolt flickered. Then my surroundings faded to black. There was a sucking feeling at the top of my head. The next thing I knew, Moqerhe and the rest of our friends were in the skiff, unfrozen now, with their mouths agape. Our leather packs and a couple of waterskins rested at our feet.

Bear's wide eyes scanned our surroundings. "How is this possible?"

Adones shook his head. "I don't know."

The buzzing sound had become a loud crackle on the ship above us.

Sophie's voice was shrill. "What's going on?"

"The hell?" Greg rose a couple of inches from his seat and pointed at the ocean ahead where hundreds of yellow eyes peered through the fog.

Dagger blades swished as Bear and Adones unsheathed them.

Moqerhe yelled, "Stop, they won't harm you."

No more than ten feet away, King Himilco hovered before us. He aimed the forked end of his trident at our skiff. A long sliver of blue electricity hit our outer hull, causing our vessel to rock.

My friends' screams barely registered when a wave, the size of a mountain, connected with a loud crash. The skiff shot forward. Salt water assaulted my face and entered my lungs. I coughed and gagged, unable to see or breathe. And then, as quickly as it had begun, the wave subsided, and the rocking slowed.

Between my coughs, I deduced that we were beached along the shore next to a tall palm.

Bear glared at Moqerhe and caught his breath long enough to spit out, "How did you know the sea djinn wouldn't harm us?" He hacked a couple of times. "What have you pulled us into, sorcerer?"

Moqerhe leaned close, looked Bear straight in the eyes and spoke softly. I was too busy expelling the water from my lungs to hear what he said.

Bear nodded, then stared ahead with a distant gaze in his eyes. Clearly, Moqerhe had just used compulsion on him. I would've bet a day's rations he was told to forget everything he saw.

"Did he just do what I think?" Greg asked between gags.

"I did." Moqerhe climbed out of the skiff and grasped the edge. Once he had steadied himself, he walked to Adones who was now holding his knees near the shore. When he straightened, the djinni leaned in and whispered into his ear. Moments later, Adones' expression became vacant.

"Our friends have had a long night." Moqerhe pointed about a quarter mile away, toward a couple of palms swaying beneath the moonlight. "Would you and Greg help them settle in?"

"Uh, er, okay," Sophie rasped.

Greg hopped out of the skiff. "Was hypnosis necessary?"

Moqerhe took a deep breath. "Words cannot express how much I detest interfering with free will. If Tanno and Adones knew about me and King Himilco, their fear may interfere with reason. This could lead to discord among our team, and we must finish this journey. They'll awake tomorrow with no memory of how we landed here but will otherwise be well."

"Good," Greg's voice held an edge of relief.

Sophie looked at me. "You coming?"

I glanced at Moqerhe. His skin was pale, and he was grasping the edge of the skiff again. I couldn't leave him like this, so I waved her on. "I'll be there in a sec."

Greg's gaze moved between Moqerhe and me. "Okay, I'll be at the palm if you need me." He grabbed a tranced-out Bear by the arm and Sophie did the same with Adones and they headed toward the tree.

"Are you alright?" I asked.

"I will be after this weakened human vessel regenerates."

I thought about the djinni ambassadors who took their lives rather than live as humans. "I know this situation's difficult but sacrificing yourself back there wasn't the way."

Moqerhe's nostrils flared. "You think I wanted to die?"

"Didn't you?" I said with more venom than intended.

"No! I'm a warrior, Amara. To die saving others is an honor among my kind."

I combed a hand through my ratty curls. "I didn't know. For what it's worth, I'm glad you were spared. What you did back there—" I cleared my throat.

The corner of Moqerhe's full mouth curled up. "You do care."

Heat rushed up my neck and I looked away.

"No retort?" Moqerhe watched me like a jungle cat hiding in the trees, studying in his prey.

"Why should I respond when you're obviously trying to bait me?"

Moqerhe slicked his wet hair away from his face. "I don't understand you, or any humans for that matter. Don't get me wrong, fear and anger are easily discernable. It's the feelings of the heart that keep me confused."

I suppose his struggles were a lot like going through puberty. He had to adapt to his new body while navigating raging hormones and a ton of foreign emotions.

Moqerhe gestured toward me. "Take you, for example. You blush, and your heart flutters every time you look at me or Adones. Yet, your face and your words betray you."

My ears burned, and I suddenly felt emotionally naked. "This is getting too personal."

"Our connection *is* personal. Why the reluctance to discuss your feelings?"

I huffed. "Because you don't have the right to invade my head space or interpret my emotions, particularly those relating to you and Adones."

Moqerhe pulled a frown. "Share your feelings and I won't have to interpret them."

I'd never been good at discussing my emotions and putting me on the spot wasn't helping. "What do you want me to say?"

"What you feel. How else can we become friends if you're this guarded?"

He wasn't the first person to call me that. My ex, Dad, Greg, Sophie, had all mentioned it over the years. If I wanted Moqerhe to trust me, I had to give him something. Being vulnerable was easier said than done.

"Okay," I said finally. "If you must know, I appreciate how you've saved me and our team more times than I care to count. Especially since I wear a stone that enslaves you. You're smart and compassionate, and if I weren't returning to my time, well, who knows?"

Anger, possibly hurt flickered across Moqerhe's pale features? "Is your concern for me born out of fear that you won't return home?"

"No!" My voice held more frustration than intended. "I really care, but I need to get home too. Without you, the mission would fail, and many lives could be lost."

"So I'm clear, Amara, returning home is your foremost goal, and anything outside of that is unlikely?"

"No, why are you putting words in my mouth? I care about you, and everyone on this mission."

Moqerhe looked me in the eyes. "I'm sure Adones will be pleased to hear that."

The condescension in his voice cut through me. "You say human feelings are complex but it's not like you've been pouring your heart out to me."

He shrugged. "Apparently there's no need."

Desperation bubbled inside me. I didn't want to lose his friendship. "Let me help you to the camp."

"No, I'm quite capable of walking on my own." He stumbled a couple of steps, steadied himself and shuffled toward the palm where Sophie and Greg waited.

I walked beside him. His silence was hard to take. I hoped small talk would ease the tension. "Er, what should we say if Tanno and Adones ask questions tomorrow?"

He kept staring ahead. "Simple. The captain's men knocked them unconscious, and we narrowly escaped the ship with our lives. Just follow my lead."

"Do the Seekers know we're here?" I wanted to break through his wall.

Moqerhe shrugged. "I've expelled my energy twice. This exposed my aura and now I'm easier to track." He took a couple of labored breaths. "King Himilco and Princess Anath promised to move the vessel. Perhaps the Seekers will follow their energy instead. This should buy enough time to determine our location so we can finish this journey."

"I really do appreciate all you've done for us."

He threw up a hand to silence me and walked ahead. Not that I blamed him. Moqerhe had already given too much. It was my turn to step up and figure out a way to Saguntum before the Seekers found us. I glanced at the jewel on my bracelet, which was now solid. A good sign we'd lost them, but for how long?

Chapter Twenty-Eight

My calf stung like a red-hot poker had touched my skin. I jolted awake, pulled my robes up and swatted away several horseflies corralled around a scab on my leg. Whoever said camping on the beach was fun, never tried it. Sand had invaded every crevice of my body. My neck cramped, and my back ached. I stood up and stretched my arms beneath the pinkish light of dawn, wishing I'd taken Sophie and Greg up on their pallet of palm leaves. The way they were hugged together snoring peacefully, made my exhausted side a little envious.

I scanned the wooded area behind me and saw no one. Since we had left our supplies on the skiff, I decided to check there first for the others. I trudged across the sandy beach. While admiring how the sun reflected off the sparkling waters, movement on the surface caught my attention. A sea djinni with white hair hovered just above the surf about a quarter mile out. The creature's yellow eyes glowed against the blue ocean. From my vantage point, it was tough to tell if it was the princess. After a moment of staring at each other, the sea djinni submerged. It could have been monitoring our crew in case Moqerhe needed help again. I made a mental note of it and approached the Three Amigos sitting with their backs against the outer hull of the skiff, chatting in Punic.

Adones sat straighter when he saw me. His black waves were matted against his head as though he'd just awoken, and his sword was unsheathed beside him. "Morning. Did you rest well?"

I rolled my stiff shoulders, wincing. "Define *well*."

Adones chuckled.

Moqerhe tore off a piece of jerky with his teeth and chewed it with zeal, a good sign he was on the mend.

I shot him my brightest smile.

When he didn't acknowledge me, my stomach clenched. I could ignore him too. Turning my attention to Adones and Bear, I asked, "Did you both have a restful sleep?"

"Define restful." Adones winked. "Where are Sophie and Greg?"

"At the camp. I thought it best not to wake them."

He handed me the waterskin. "Have some."

My brow knotted together as I squeezed the soft leather bag. "I thought we had more water than this."

Bear rested a hand on his sheathed sword across his lap. "Moqerhe tells me I was dazed and unconscious last night, so I cannot speak to our supply."

Adones tore a piece of jerky in half and offered it to me. "It'll give you strength for our hike."

"What hike?" I fingered the stiff meat. If I never had jerky again for the rest of my life it'd be too soon. I turned up the skin and sipped the contents before returning it to Adones.

"We're about to search for water," he said. "The more eyes, the better. We won't get far without it."

Bear sat straighter. "Amara, perhaps you can fill the gaps in Moqerhe's tale. He's the only person among us who remembers what occurred aboard the ship."

I bit off a sliver of jerky to buy some time, trying not to gag at the salty, bark-like texture. "What do you remember about last night?"

Adones held a piece of jerky in front of his face while thinking. "The captain threatened to kill you and Sophie unless we withdrew. Thereafter, I have no memory."

"Nor I," said Bear. "How odd that Adones and I suffer the same lapse in time."

I shook my head. "No, it makes sense that the captain would overcome our strongest fighters. If Moqerhe and Greg hadn't reacted quickly and carried you to the skiff, there's no telling what might have become of you."

Bear cocked his head to one side. "You and Moqerhe's stories align. Yet, I've never had such a lapse in memory."

I stepped forward, buying enough time to change the subject. "We can explore the possibilities later. Have you any idea of our location?"

Adones rubbed his shadow of facial hair. "Before our confrontation aboard the ship, the captain believed we were near Gades, which is approximately five hundred mille from Saguntum."

Moqerhe's voice rang through my mind, *"Converting the math is difficult so try to keep up. One mile is a thousand paces. That comes to—"*

"Duh," I said in English, glaring at Moqerhe's smirking face. "A thousand steps is equivalent to a modern mile. I've had several years of Latin. Not to mention that I'm good at math." I should've stopped there, but I was on a roll. "Seeing as calculus won't be invented for two thousand years, Greg, Sophie, and I are probably the greatest mathematicians alive today. Feel free to let me know if you need to know how a derivative or integral works."

"I don't understand," said Adones.

Moqerhe sniggered. "Nor I."

My fists worked, and it took all I had not to throat-punch him. Instead, I gazed at the blue ocean to calm myself, half searching for signs of the sea djinni. Only clear waters came into view.

With an elbow to Bear's ribs, Moqerhe glanced toward the treeline. "We should begin our search before the heat becomes unbearable."

All three of the men rose and sheathed their weapons. "Let's separate into two groups." Adones shot his thumb toward me. "Amara and I will look to the east."

Disappointment poked at my ribs. Some alone time with Moqerhe might have mended fences.

"You and Moqerhe assess the western portion of the island," Adones continued. "Regardless of what we find, report to camp at midday."

Moqerhe sneered. "You and the girl alone. What of the others?"

"I plan to fetch them from camp," Adones said.

"I'm sure." Moqerhe stormed toward the copse of trees, leading inland.

Bear reached into the skiff and pulled out two empty goat skins. He tossed one to Adones and took the other. "May the gods guide us."

Without another word, Adones and I headed toward camp. Along the way, he glanced down at me. "I haven't expressed my gratitude for your care last night. I'm sure you had something to do with ensuring my comfort beneath a palm."

"You would've done the same for any of your friends."

Adones stopped mid-step. He gently tilted my chin upward, regarding me beneath a fan of lashes. "Do you still intend to return to your father?"

"Why wouldn't I?"

He studied me for a breath. "Wait for me in Carthage instead."

Is he asking what I think he's asking?

I noted how his tanned face contrasted against eyes that were green as a leaf, but I no longer felt an attraction. When did this happen? Could all the stress of our mission have caught up to me and I just didn't have anything left.

Regardless, the intensity of his stare told me he needed an answer. I sighed. "While I appreciate the offer, I don't think it's a good idea to remain in Carth—"

Adones moved so close, I felt the heat coming off his body. "If you're concerned about your father, I could dispatch my men to Sparta to find him. Once I return from my campaign, Aurelia will become my wife in name only. Then you and I can explore what's between us. You'll want for nothing, and I'll ensure you and your father are cared for."

My nails bit into my palms as I stepped back, internally warring with the side that fixated on the word *campaign*, the need to warn him about what I knew, and the feminist part. Although I understood that a mistress was commonplace in this time, my ego wouldn't let me dismiss the crass of it.

The feminist part won, and I brought my hands to my hips. "Wait, you want me to be your—" I searched my mind for side piece in ancient Greek and spit out, "Extramarital secret?"

He shook his head. "No! In Carthage, a mistress is often held in higher esteem than a wife. I — I've never respected nor wanted a woman more than you."

How did ancient women tolerate such misogyny? I held up my forefinger. "Am I to understand that you want me to give up hope of marrying and having children. All so you can deign me with your presence whenever you tire of Aurelia?"

"You make me sound awful. I only want to keep you in my life, and I'm trying to find a way to accomplish this." He sighed. "Please, understand, honor and duty to my family are foremost. Unfortunately, a union with Aurelia is what's required of me." He gently grasped my shoulders. "Look me in the eyes and tell me there's nothing between us. If you can, I won't broach the subject again."

I shrugged his hands off my shoulders. "I care for you as my friend. Please understand my dilemma. We're from two different worlds and our journeys aren't meant to converge. Like you, I have a duty to *my* family. Once I'm reunited with my father, I must ensure he receives the medical treatment he so desperately needs. This can only happen in my homeland."

Adones eyes narrowed. "This is it for us? Once this mission has ended, we'll bid each other farewell, never to speak again?"

"You ask a question for which you already know the answer." Still, his use of the word 'never' hung in my ears. Like it or not, this was my one chance to warn him about his death. Misogynist or not, he deserved to live so I added, "There's something I must tell you, and though I may sound mad, I need you to believe me."

He crossed his arms over his chest. "I'm listening."

I mopped my hands over my face. "After marching over the Alps, your uncle's army will meet the Romans on their soil in Cannae and the battle will be bloody." I swallowed hard. "Unfortunately, you will become one of the casualties taken by death."

His mouth gaped open. "How could you possibly know such a—"

"Amara," Sophie called.

Adones backed away without averting his gaze from me. "This conversation is not over."

I nodded.

"Where were you?" Greg asked, eyeing us.

"By the skiff. Um, we were just coming to get you to help us search for water."

"Is our supply that low?" Sophie licked her dry lips.

"Yeah, like a few sips between us and dehydration low," I said.

Greg scanned the beach. "Where's Moqerhe and Tanno?"

"They're looking on one part of the island. We're supposed to check the other side and meet up around noon."

Sophie pointed at my robes. "Unless you've got a sundial tucked under there, how are we supposed to know when that is?"

"Midday is usually when the sun's directly overhead." Greg raked a hand through his sweaty hair. "Just when I had put my eagle scout days behind me, they pull me back in."

I rolled my eyes.

"What? You don't believe me??" he said. "If we had to, I could make gun powder. All I need is a little NaNO3 from my piss. For the sulfur and sodium nitrate, I'd use some of the charcoal from the fire. It can—"

"That's no good without guns," said Sophie.

With a dismissive wave, I turned to Adones. The lines on his forehead had deepened as he gazed at me like he had a thousand questions. "Um, Greg's experienced at finding water so he'll be a great asset."

Greg stopped debating with Sophie long enough to spit out in ancient Greek, "I can speak for myself."

"We should begin our search," Adones still watched me. "The sooner we find water, the sooner we can return, right, Amara?"

Before I could respond, he headed toward the trees.

"What's up his ass?" Sophie walked beside me as we followed Greg and Adones.

"It could be that I shot him down when he asked me to be his mistress, or that I told him how he was gonna die, I'm not sure."

Her head snapped toward me. "What?"

We stopped talking long enough to traverse thick vegetation broken up by rocky terrain.

At the other side of the brush, she pointed at his back. "How did he take the news about his death?"

"You all interrupted us before I got a feel for his reaction. I didn't get a chance to tell him how I knew. He only learned when and where he'd die."

"I'm sure he'll expect an explanation."

"Yup. Guess I'll cross that bridge when I get to it." I had no idea what I'd say yet.

When our group came to a small ravine, Adones gestured toward a dry wash, thick with brush about a half mile away. "With all the greenery there, perhaps we'll find water."

"I agree," Greg waved Adones on.

We ascended a steep hill. It was slow-going because of all the loose rocks, and Sophie and I fell behind. Greg and Adones, on the other hand, moved like a couple of marathon hikers.

She huffed from the effort of climbing. "Switching gears here. Am I imagining things or is there a connection between you and Moqerhe?"

I blinked. "You're imagining things. I'm not here to find a boyfriend or a husband. Getting you all home and helping Dad is my priority."

She shook her head. "You've always found an excuse not to let anyone in. Keep that wall up, and you'll end up a lonely person."

A stew of emotions ranging from hurt to fear swirled in my chest. "Thanks for the support, friend."

"This is me supporting you." Sophie leaned forward as we came closer to the top of the hill. "I see how Moqerhe looks at you, the want in those golden eyes. If I thought those feelings were one-sided, I'd keep my mouth shut but you forget how well I know you. I see how you react to him too. There's a serious connection there. Not to mention that he's a magical being. If you gave the green light, I know he'd make the long-distance thing work."

My heart stumbled in my chest as last night's shit-show of a conversation with Moqerhe came to mind. If Moqerhe had feelings before, he'd long since gotten over them. I shook my head. "Let's talk about something els—"

When we finally crested the hill, Sophie brought her hands to her hips and caught her breath. Greg pointed at a depression rimmed in thick green bracken about twenty feet below us. Though we couldn't see anything, a gurgling sound echoed against the silence. He and Adones quickly descended the hill.

Sophie smiled from ear-to-ear. "Water."

My dry mouth did a happy dance. "Good, I'm about to fall over from all this hiking."

With slow methodical steps, Sophie inched downhill with me on her trail. The slight angle of the hill bent my ankles in an awkward direction, sending sharp aches up my legs. It didn't matter. My focus was on the babbling stream's fresh, clear water, just waiting for me to lap up buckets and buckets of it.

Adones leapt the last few feet, landed on the ground, and ran toward the dense brush ahead. Greg jumped down next and looked up at us. "Hurry up!"

Sophie squealed with excitement and descended faster.

A crackling noise resounded beside me. I stopped. The bracelet went ice cold and the neon blue stone swirled on my wrist. "Seekers!" I yelled.

Adones reemerged from the brush. Greg and Sophie's eyes widened, and their mouths hung open. Panic surged through me as a glowing dot floated beside me and grew wider by the second. I descended quickly, trying to keep my footing, despite the loose shale.

Adones climbed to the bottom half of the hill several feet below me, extending his hand, "Jump, I'll catch you."

"C'mon," Greg shouted from just behind him.

Adones climbed a little more still reaching for me. "Do it now!"

I took a deep breath and pushed off the hill with both feet. I barely caught air, when rough hands pulled me backward, sending me spiraling into a glowing vortex.

Chapter Twenty-Nine

I plunged into the vortex at dizzying speeds, grasping in the darkness for anything solid, screaming so loud my throat burned. Then, I slammed against the ground with a thud and all the air erupted from my lungs in a single whoof. Miles of tan sand, like Sahara sand, lay ahead. Several palms and a large pond of water were several feet to my left.

Is this an oasis?

Voices echoed above me. When I looked up, two humanoid beings with skin as pale as their robes stared down at me through ember eyes. One of them scrunched his thin nose like he smelled something bad.

Heat blossomed across my cheeks as I realized they could tell I hadn't bathed in several weeks. I quickly got over my embarrassment when the taller being yanked me to my feet and pulled back my sleeve. He sneered at my bracelet. Fear clutched my chest, and I forced myself to breathe as Jasim's words ran through my mind. *"The Seekers will do whatever it takes to have that. Even if it means your life!"*

"Wh-what do you want?" I asked in ancient Greek.

The tall Seeker released me. "Your questions will be answered soon enough, *human*."

I flinched, more surprised by the fact he spoke English than the shove that followed. Then I remembered these beings were from the same dimension as Jasim. If they were half as smart as him, they probably spoke multiple languages.

The creatures wheeled me around. Each of them grabbed one of my arms and escorted me past several palms, opening to a green valley. About a quarter mile in, we passed a wooden wagon parked before a huge rectangular tent, surrounded by blooming cedar trees. Two horses grazed out front as we stopped before the opening.

The shorter Seeker swept the door flap aside and glowered at me, a silent command to enter the tent. I inched inside on shaky legs. The spicy scent of incense burned my nostrils. Two flaming crystal chandeliers floated about eight feet above us, bathing the area in burnt orange light. Paintings of landscapes that reminded me of the Monets I'd seen at the Smithsonian hovered along each side of the tent.

"You've done well," a masculine voice called in English from a far corner of the space.

I couldn't get a good look at him because he was shadowed. Both guards bowed.

Then the owner of the voice emerged from the corner, pencil-thin and dressed in blindingly white robes. He had smooth skin and long gray hair, framing a high forehead and cheekbones.

I rolled my shoulders back, trying to put on a brave face, but inside, I was a ball of nerves. "Wh-why have you taken me?"

"I needed to speak to you in secret." He gave me a once-over with those neon blue eyes. "How did the likes of *you* bring one of the fiercest warriors I've ever known to his knees?"

"I don't understand."

"Moqerhe. I'm referring to Moqerhe," he said flatly. "The djinni I knew, detested your kind. Now that you're here, I truly don't see the appeal. Surely, it's not your boyishly thin body. Your pretty face might turn his head, yet it certainly wouldn't captivate him. No, there must be more to you than meets the eye. A superior intellect. A compassionate soul. Perhaps both?"

He studied me like a puzzle he couldn't figure out. "Otherwise, Moqerhe wouldn't have risked his life to spare yours."

How did he know about that? Clearly, he was trying to bait me and I couldn't allow myself to fall for it. "I don't know who you're talking about."

The head guy pointed his long finger at my wrist. "That stone tells me otherwise."

Sweat ran down my lower back. "Is this why I'm here, so you can cut it off my wrist? Or can I expect the same fate as the Shadu and his master?" The question was a fishing expedition to learn what had happened to them since the market.

My captor's thin lips compressed together. "You believe I killed them?"

"Didn't you?"

"No!" he said flatly. "We merely detained them to get information. They were released days ago. Though, I'm beginning to wonder if I made a mistake. Vicram vehemently denied any association with you. Clearly this isn't the case."

"I *don't* know him."

"How, pray tell, did you know we had him?" asked the short Seeker.

Head guy held up a pale hand. "It's a minor point at best. Currently, I need you to lend me your ear. Can you do that?"

I nodded. It wasn't like I could refuse since he held all the cards.

Head guy's neon blue gaze moved toward the two Seekers beside me, and he clucked his tongue at them, ending with a dismissive wave of his long fingers.

The two Seekers bowed. They blurred in my vision, then flickered between light and shadow, before disappearing in a poof.

I flinched. After all I'd been through, I shouldn't have been surprised. Yet, here I stood, staring at the empty space like I'd seen a ghost.

My captor motioned toward a seating area in the middle of the room. "Please, make yourself comfortable. We have much to discuss."

I walked to several oversized cushions and pillows, casually placed in a cozy seating arrangement before a wooden coffee table. After I sat down, my captor glided toward a narrow table a few feet away, laden with a silver pitcher and tray. He poured a dark red liquid into two silver goblets and handed me one.

Standing within arm's reach, he sipped while regarding me thoughtfully. "Drink, it's not poisoned."

The goblet shook in my grasp. I steadied the stem with both hands and brought it to my mouth. The liquid barely touched my lips. After faking a swallow, I leaned back casually, despite my thumping heart.

He met my gaze. "I mean you no harm."

Apart from sneering and glowering at me, my captor hadn't made an aggressive move, which gave me hope.

He lowered himself onto the cushion across from me. The movement was graceful, like he had practiced it all his life. He smoothed his robes before speaking. "You've been quite elusive, young lady. If not for King Himilco, we may never have found you."

I suddenly understood the reason I saw a sea djinni this morning. The scaly bastard had been spying on us. It also explained how my captor knew Moqerhe had sacrificed his life to save us. Himilco probably blabbed.

I shrugged and said, "Who's King Himilco, and why does he care about me?"

My captor leaned his head back and laughed. The sound boomed against the silence. "Care is too weak a word to describe the king's feelings for you. If the monarchs had their way, you would have died a slow death, since you wear a stone that enslaves their comrade."

"I don't *want* to enslave anyone." I'd said this so many times since I had donned the bracelet, it was tough to keep the frustration out of my voice. "Whatever your friends have told you is not true."

He scoffed. "Friends? They're war criminals. Nothing more. I merely reminded Himilco of how he and his ilk were allowed to live quietly at sea. When his spy saw you on the beach this morning, he disclosed your location. It's that simple."

I sat straighter, praying my voice didn't betray my brave façade. "Clearly, you've gone to a lot of trouble to get me here. What do you want?"

"You're important to a war I'm involved in."

My eyebrows knitted together. "The Punic War?"

"No," my captor said. "The war I'm referencing happened long ago, when a powerful warrior species known as the djinn found the realm of man."

"I'm confused. How does this involve me?"

"It's complicated so perhaps I should provide some background." My captor smoothed his robes before continuing. "You see, Jan-Ib-Jann, the king of the djinn, had become fond of your species and decided to live among you. He even ordered his subjects to work beside the humans in this dimension and to treat them as equals without unduly influencing their progression. However, it was Jan's son, the crown prince and heir, who refused to pay respect to such a subordinate species. He even sought to enslave man. Factions were formed, and a war for control between father and son began. After centuries of fighting alongside man, the king won, and only twenty-four enemies remained.

"Twenty djinnis escaped to the sea. Later, it was discovered that the prince's four generals had formed a coup to usurp him after he ordered all remaining djinn to fight to the death. Always a master strategist, the prince was one step ahead of them. Before they could act, he had them imprisoned in an unknown location. Jan-Ib-Jann eventually captured the prince. As punishment, he stripped his son's powers, then banished him to the Carthage in your dimension, a place devoid of magic."

"That's surprising," I said. "I mean that a father would punish his son so harshly."

My captor gave a tight smile. "A fair king must always put his crown and his subjects before the role of father. He had to show that even his own offspring wasn't above the law."

I nodded. "Makes sense."

"Now, where was I?" My captor paused. "Oh yes, as I was saying, for the first time in his life, the prince was lost, alone, and without his powers. This forced him to integrate with the people of Carthage, and to his surprise, they welcomed him with open arms. With the passage of time, he came to love man. He even bonded with the Barcids and aided them in their war against Rome. Eventually, the people revered the prince as a god."

Recognition sparked in my mind. This was Jasim's story. Although my captor's version was close to the one I already knew, Jasim had lied about the reason he was sent to the Carthage from my dimension. Instead of his portal device malfunctioning, he had gone to war with his father and was sent there as punishment for his coup. This meant he was once prince of the djinn. What else had he withheld?

My captor took another sip from his goblet before continuing. "When the king first banished his son to live as a human, he had secretly hoped this would teach him more compassion toward your species. Despite this progress, the king was most displeased when he learned of his son's interference with Carthage's military, and his position as a false deity. Both events had altered Carthage's natural progression. Hoping to prevent further damage, the king sent his Seekers to return the prince to this dimension.

They searched for many years, and this caused the prince to go into hiding during a pivotal time when Hannibal's father fought the first Punic War, and Carthage lost to Rome."

"Yeah, I remembered reading about that."

"Unfortunately, the prince was determined not to let this happen again, so he met Hannibal in secret during the second Punic War. Although the prince's guidance had assured General Barca's victory in numerous battles against Rome, many men were still lost. This included young Adones. On the day of his funeral rite, one of the prince's guardians killed a Seeker and procured a portal device."

Tension clenched my shoulder muscles as my captor's words sunk in. The Seeker's murder had conveniently been left out of Jasim's explanation, as well. This only confirmed what my Spidey senses had told me when we first met. Jasim was a dangerous and desperate being who would do whatever it took to achieve his goals. Something told me that I was collateral damage. I leaned forward, hanging on each of my captor's words as he continued his story.

"Then the prince bonded to the device and ordered it hidden in Adones' tomb where no one could find it while charging. Just before he could make his escape, the prince was captured. For his role in the murder of the king's Seeker, he was imprisoned. Centuries later, he escaped custody and—"

"Jasim returned to Adones' tomb to use the portal." My hand flew to my mouth. What was wrong with me? How could I have slipped up like that?

My captor's lips thinned. "*Jasim's* the name the prince used in your time. Here, he's known as Ba'al Hammon." He set his goblet down and sat forward. "Now, that we've done away with all pretenses and you've admitted knowing *Jasim,* allow me to introduce myself. I'm Jan-Ib-Jann, king of the djinn."

Chapter Thirty

I blinked, unsurprised by the king's admission. His regal carriage and the anger in his neon blue eyes as he had told his story hinted at his identity.

Jan-Ib-Jann jutted his pointy chin at my bracelet. "Tell me why my son passed that to you. Careful how you answer. As stated previously, I know he still possesses the stones and the generals."

Since I had already given myself up, there was no use lying. I held Jan's gaze and said, "All I know is Jasim asked me to transport the bracelet and Moqerhe to Hannibal Barca's camp in Saguntum. He also promised to use his portal device to return me home."

"Clearly Jasim used the forbidden spell from my book of incantations, otherwise, Moqerhe wouldn't be human." Jan shook his head. "I can't imagine how Moqerhe is responding to his new form."

"Not well," I admitted. "He hates being human and he'd probably kill Jasim if given a chance."

"Moqerhe's fate is well deserved." Jan's voice dripped with vitriol. "He was once my greatest general and advisor. That is, until he betrayed me for my son."

I clenched my teeth to keep the shock off my face. "He was one of the generals in your story?"

"Yes," Jan said curtly.

I suddenly understood why Moqerhe tried to stay at the market with the Shadu and Vicram. He realized that he'd chosen the wrong side and wanted to make amends.

"For what it's worth, Moqerhe saved my life and helped my friends. We're alive because of him."

Jan's cold gaze swept over me, assessing, pondering. "Doesn't sound like the djinni I know. That's neither here nor there. Can you tell me where my son's holding the generals?"

"No, he blindfolded me, and we descended a bunch of steps beneath a temple or a monument. It's tough to say. We walked for what felt like an hour until we came to an underground chamber, but I don't have a clue where it is."

"I should have known better than to ask." Jan rubbed his long chin. "My son and his guardians have been underground for centuries, and they never remained in the same place for long. He wouldn't risk exposure now."

"With all his means, I'm surprised Jasim needs me at all."

"He has a plan. My son's a master of deception with military skills to rival my own, and I've no doubt that you, my dear, are a dispensable pawn in his game."

Jan's words sliced through me. He had just confirmed my worst fears, and I felt trapped and helpless to change a freaking thing.

"Jasim's allegiance is to Carthage and Hannibal," Jan continued. "And you've just confirmed my suspicions. My son's planning to use Moqerhe to change history and destroy Rome. If this comes to pass, the ripple effects will cause chaos across all dimensions."

I gasped. "Are you saying Jasim's plans could mess with *my* timeline?"

Jan stared at the ceiling for a moment as though considering how to respond. "Let's pretend our worlds are like two interconnected rivers, flowing alongside each other, heading in the same direction. Then a small variation like wind or a fallen tree causes a small ripple in the current of one river, changing the trajectory of a world. Once the ripple settles, the worlds resume their parallel flow, mirroring themselves once more. A ripple occurred in this dimension after I landed with my djinn. Thus, allowing magic to exist here, but not in your realm. Understand?"

"Yeah, I'm following."

Jan raised a finger in the air. "If something catastrophic like a hurricane were to occur, the current could become large enough to spill into the other river, or in this case, a world since they're interconnected. This could potentially change the past, present, and future across dimensions. If Rome fell before its time, the results could be catastrophic."

"I see. Has this ever happened?" I asked, unable to keep the fear for Dad out of my voice.

Jan sipped from his goblet before answering. "Yes, once, long ago, before my kind arrived in this dimension. Rival factions had tried to reverse history in my plane and dethrone me. My army stopped them, but not in time to prevent a horrible war that left my world, and the one parallel to it, in dark ruin. I saved as many of my subjects as I could. Then I destroyed the portal gates to those dimensions. My enemies were forever locked away in an inhospitable plane of their own making. I can't allow this to happen again. Therefore, I need your help stopping my son."

"Me. What can I do?"

Jan leaned forward, regarding me through a narrowed gaze. "I need you to unbind Hannibal's sword and break the blade's connection with the Barcids."

"How?" I asked. "I never saw Hannibal without his sword. Not once. Even if I somehow got to it, the blade is cursed. Anyone outside his bloodline who touches it, dies."

Jan was stock-still for several heartbeats. When he spoke again, his voice held an edge of anger. "I wouldn't say, cursed. My son found a loophole around the sword's spell. One that prevented me from using it to banish him to the nether regions."

"A loophole?" Jasim seemed one step ahead in all things.

"Yes," Jan said. "Before my son stole the weapon, no other djinni apart from me could wield it. However, this didn't apply to humans, so my son overrode the spell and bound the sword to the Barcids' DNA."

"Are you saying Hannibal can send people to the nether regions?"

Jan pulled up the sleeve of his robe, revealing a tattoo of a gate with an arrow across it on his lower forearm. "No, I wear that spell, which is now useless without my sword. Thanks to my son, no one outside the Barcid bloodline can touch it without dying. I've sent my Seekers to try to disarm the weapon but the sigils on the blade warned the bearer of their presence, and lives were lost. Attempts to turn some of the Barcids to my side also proved futile. They were too loyal to Hannibal to deceive him."

"And you want to send me?" I pressed my finger against my chest, hard. "That's a death sentence."

"No, it's not," Jan said with a shake of his head.

"How can you be sure? I'm not a descendant."

Jan grinned. "Aren't you?"

"What are you saying?" It was a rhetorical question. The implication was obvious and not possible.

"When you and your brother passed through the portal with my son, we read your DNA and it just so happened to be a match for the Barcid line," Jan said.

"Wait, I thought you didn't know we were here. Jasim said my aura was invisible to you since I wasn't from this time."

"True, we couldn't see your aura. However, when my guards noticed you and your brother's special DNA, we suspected that my son had brought beings from another dimension through the gate. Later, King Himilco confirmed this, and I also learned of the young girl who had accompanied you as well."

I shook my head, questioning how this was possible. "Thousands of years have passed. The bloodlines are probably so convoluted that my family ties to the Barcids are barely traceable."

Jan shrugged. "A tie is a tie, regardless of how small. Unlike your brother, you have a connection to Hannibal. When combined with that stone on your wrist, you're the only person who can help me." He flicked his hand to the right and a silver baton about the size of a diploma holder appeared in his hand. "You only need to touch the blade with this to break the DNA connection. Then the sigils will call to me, and I'll sweep in and send my son to the nether regions." Jan paused a moment before continuing. "Make no mistake, this adds more risk to your journey."

Obviously. "Look, even if I agree to help, which I haven't, how am I supposed to get close enough to Hannibal to pull this off? He's a general with excellent fighting skills. He'd cut me in half before I came within a foot of his sword."

Jan rose from his seat, glided to the table in a sea of white, and rang a small silver bell. Two humanoid silhouettes faded in and out of my vision and took shape in front of Jan. They were the Seekers who captured me earlier. Except now, a tall, thin boy with dreadlocks and wide brown eyes stood between Jan's minions as they bowed. Based on the kid's thin shoulders and stick legs, he'd missed a lot of meals.

Jan snapped his fingers, literally snapped them, and a large cage with flaming bars appeared above us. It drifted downward and the door opened when it touched the ground.

I leapt from my cushion. The goblet fell from my grasp. Wine spilled on the floor. "Tanno," I yelled.

Bear shot out of the cage toward the boy. The Seekers stepped back, allowing Bear to embrace him.

The shock on my face must have been obvious because Jan said in English, "That's Inkatu, the Numidian's brother. I wanted to wait till after we had spoken before bringing them in."

"How did you find him?" I asked.

Jan shrugged. "It was quite serendipitous, and frankly, I've been questioning the significance of the human belief in fate. After all, what are the odds that you, a descendant of Hannibal, happened to come through the portal at a time when you were needed most? Then my Seekers stumbled upon one of my son's guards returning from Rome with this boy."

I gestured toward Bear and the boy, who were now hugging and speaking in whispered tones. "What tipped you off that the Inkatu was important?"

"It took some persuading," Jan said in the silken voice of a master torturer. "And the guard finally talked. As it turns out, *Ba'al* dispatched him to rescue the boy from slavers in exchange for the Numidian's loyalty."

Despite my mounting unease as Jan's words confirmed what he was capable of, I still let my mouth override my better judgment as I blurted, "Seems like Inkatu has traded one captor for another so you can use him as leverage."

Jan clicked his tongue. "He's nothing of this sort. I knew you'd need help distracting Hannibal to procure his sword. Reuniting them could sway the Numidian to our cause."

Jan didn't give me a chance to respond. He turned toward Bear and spoke in what I assumed was Numidian.

Shoving Inkatu behind him, Bear wheeled around, glowering at Jan with his broad chest puffed out. A lengthy exchange followed. Bear's expression transitioned between wide-eyed shock, to utter disbelief. By the time his gaze drifted to me, I had taken a play from Sophie's book and nearly bitten my nails to the quick.

"You're from the future?" Bear asked.

"Yes," I said, forcing myself to hold his gaze.

"Greg and Sophie?"

I nodded.

"This explains much," Bear observed.

Jan chimed in, speaking in ancient Greek this time. "Apologies for interrupting this reunion. I need to know if we have a bargain and whether you both will aid me in my son's capture."

My shallow breaths were the only sounds cutting the silence as I considered who I should trust. I had become a pawn in an imperial war between father and son. There had always been something about Jasim that screamed shady guy, and Jan only confirmed this. Yet, when I looked into the king's eyes, my gut told me he was the more honorable of the two. It seemed the enemy of my enemy had just become my friend.

This knowledge didn't ease my mind. Agreeing to help Jan came at a great price. If his plan worked and history progressed as it did in my time, Rome would win the war, and Carthage would fall. Best case, Elissa, Melania, Pallab, and countless others I cared about might become Roman slaves or worse. How could I make such a choice and live with myself?

Refuse Jan, and Jasim's plan to alter history in this version of Carthage could affect all the worlds, including my own. What did this mean for Dad, Greg, Sophie, and I? It was possible that we may never be born. No matter what I chose, there was a sacrifice.

"This is impossible!" I muttered under my breath.

"No, it is *necessary,*" Jan's lips pinched together at the corners. "Heavy is the burden of the deaths you choose, but you must make a decision."

Bear stepped up to Jan. "I'll help Amara distract Hannibal on one condition. You must promise to deliver Inkatu to my homeland in Maghrib, where he'll be safe."

Following a few measured beats, Jan said, "On my honor, I'll do as you ask."

The king turned his attention to me, watching, waiting.

I fidgeted under the king's scrutiny. Like it or not, I only had one choice. Carthage had already fallen once in the history of my world, and life went on. I couldn't risk the destruction of my timeline as well. This meant acting fast if I hoped to stop Jasim.

"Yes, I'll do my best to unbind Hannibal's sword." The words were bitter on my tongue.

Not only had I betrayed the man who'd taken me in, but this decision probably sentenced his family to slavery or maybe death. I was also risking Greg and Sophie's lives without so much as consulting them. If Hannibal caught us, we'd all be impaled. I just hoped they'd forgive me, that *I* could forgive me.

Jan handed me the baton. "You've both chosen wisely."

Smooth and cold to the touch, I shoved the baton into a small pocket within my dirty robes.

"Tell no one of our conversation here today," Jan said in a cold and calculated voice. "My son won't risk his plan to chance. He'll meet your party at Saguntum. Once you unbind the sword and my son is captured, I'll return you and your party to their time."

I cleared my throat. "If, for some reason, I don't make it, will you promise to send them home?"

Surprise flickered across Jan's features. "That's a brave position for one so young, but yes, you have my word as king."

"What about Moqerhe?"

There was a swishing sound behind us. When I looked over my shoulder, a third Seeker in white robes had appeared. He took a knee before Jan, clucking his tongue.

The king's thin lips pulled into a frown as his gaze raked over me. "Seems Moqerhe has found our position sooner than expected. He and your friends are attempting a rescue."

My stomach flipped. "Can't you release me before they arrive?"

"Too late." Jan pointed overhead toward a human size bird cage. "I need to seal you and Tanno in there. It must look like we haven't questioned you yet. We'll feign a good fight until you're rescued."

Bear stepped back. "Wait, Inkatu, I need to bid him—"

"There's no time," Jan said. "We'll take the boy home now."

Inkatu called out and reached for Bear. The Seeker grabbed his arm. When Bear clenched his jaw and turned away, the Seeker shimmered between smoke and matter for several seconds. Then the duo disappeared into thin air.

Jan waved his hand to the right, and a lightheaded feeling washed over me. My vision blurred, and my body tingled. I closed my eyes and breathed deeply. When I opened them again, I was in the cage, standing beside Bear. Our prison bars flickered and ignited into blue flames, and the glowing gate in front of us slammed shut with a loud clang.

Chapter Thirty-One

My prison bars hummed against the silence as I scanned the empty cage. The ceiling was at least twenty feet high, and the circular floors, vacant of furniture, were hard and white. Clearly a bathroom break was out of the question.

Bear crossed his arms over his broad chest. "Why did you keep the truth from me?"

I considered lying, and immediately dismissed the thought. Bear deserved a straight answer, so I confessed everything. I began with the disc that had transported me to this dimension and ended with how Moqerhe had hypnotized Bear on the beach.

"You allowed the djinni to violate my mind?" Bear's voice was laced with thunder.

"Yes, for the mission." I resisted the urge to look away from his angry stare. "You were upset and frightened."

"And now your secrets have put us in peril."

I threw my arms up. "What's happened, has happened. Are you having a change of heart?"

Bear rubbed his forehead. "No. Given what's at stake for both our homelands, I will remain by your side until the general's sword is disarmed."

The bracelet warmed against my wrist and the stone swirled blood red.

Bear's eyes widened.

I ran to the front of my cage and looked out, searching for some sign of Moqerhe. What I saw nearly choked me. Beyond the silence of my cage, smoke billowed into the air while the front of the tent burned down, leaving an opening large enough to see outside. Daylight held on by the skin of its teeth. Through all the gray, I spotted Greg with torch in hand, taking cover behind the wagon I had seen earlier. They must have set the tent on fire, which was stupid since we were inside.

Blue laser projectiles shot from the side of the tent and flew toward the trees. Adones peeked around a wide trunk and returned fire with his arrows. Amidst the chaos, Greg emerged from behind the wagon and ran toward Adones' tree.

"Move faster!" I yelled.

Bear watched with his mouth agape.

The wagon exploded in a mushroom of fire and black smoke. The shockwave shook my cage. Bear and I fell onto the floor. We slid sideways with his full weight against my back as I braced for impact. A breath whooshed from my lungs when we stopped mere inches from the glowing prison bars. Once the cage steadied, I crawled to the front and peered outside. Amidst the smoke and fire, Greg stood hunched over, clutching his stomach with hands covered in crimson blood. I screamed high and loud as my brother collapsed.

"Amara!" Bear yelled.

My hands burned and I realized I was holding the flaming prison bars.

He yanked me away from them. "What is wrong with you?"

Tears ran down my face. I only had one hope of saving Greg. Ignoring the stabbing pain in my swollen palms, I looked down at the stone. It now swirled blood red, bidding me to command it and I did just that. "With permission granted to me by Jan-Ib-Jann, the first of your kind, the leader who bestowed this stone upon man, I command thee, Moqerhe, to do my bidding. Rescue me and—"

Our prison bars burned out and withered to ash. Thick fronds of smoke entered the cage and ripped at my lungs. Bear coughed. I coughed, hardly able to breathe. Someone touched the back of my shoulder. I recoiled and wheeled around.

"It's okay," Moqerhe stared down at me through blood-red eyes. He now stood about seven feet tall with his crown of horns.

"You ... save Gre—"

Bear doubled over gagging.

Moqerhe patted his back. "Don't be alarmed, my friend. It's me, Moqerhe. I'll return for you."

I coughed. "No, take Tan—"

Moqerhe swept me into his arms, leapt off the cage and glided downward on translucent, bat-like wings. Flames hissed around us. I couldn't see through all the smoke. My lungs ached from coughing.

Moqerhe's arms tightened around me. "We're nearly there," he whispered soothingly in my ear. His words sent a current of calm through me. When we landed on the ground outside, fresh air filled my lungs. A gentle breeze cooled my skin.

"I'll return momentarily," Moqerhe flew into the burning tent.

Pain surged up my palms. I gritted my teeth and ran between the trees, stopping behind each one as I hastened toward the battle zone to help my brother and my friends. Through the haze of smoke, I spotted Adones and Sophie bent over Greg's motionless and bloody body. The laser pulses had stopped. For now. Something swished near the trees behind me. I wheeled around and found Bear leaning against the trunk coughing up a lung.

Moqerhe moved to me. Still in his djinn form, he gently took my swollen hands into his and examined them. "You're hurt."

I yanked at my hand. "Help Greg."

Moqerhe tightened his grip on my wrists, closed his eyes and muttered under his breath. My body shuddered as a tingly sensation rippled across my palms, followed by a sparkle of golden light. Seconds later, the throbbing and aching sensation stopped, and my palms were pink and healthy again.

A loud roar echoed above us. I glanced upward as the Shadu flew through the smoke; golden wings spread wide with Vicram mounted on its back.

My jaw went slack. I thought Jan had sent them away.

The blue laser pulses resumed. The Shadu weaved between them and swooped down on my wounded brother. The animal grabbed him with sharp talons and lifted him into the air. Sophie and Adones took cover behind the brush.

I stared into Moqerhe's ember eyes. His skin was deathly pale. Clearly, he still hadn't healed from his near-death experience. Using his powers to rescue Bear and me must have weakened him more. Despite this, Moqerhe grabbed my shoulders and said,

"Command me to take our group to Saguntum," his voice was a thread. "They won't last much longer if you don't."

The stone in my bracelet still swirled red. Once again, Moqerhe had put everything on the line to help our team, and I feared the consequences. If I summoned his magic in his weakened state, could he handle it?

I brought his clawed hand to my lips and kissed it. Couldn't help myself. Warmth wrapped around my heart like a blanket as I spoke. "I-I'm sorry about the other night. I don't think I could handle it if anything happened to you."

He arched a brow. "So, you do care?" It was a rhetorical question because he added. "I will live. Now do as I ask and summon my powers."

This time, I obeyed him. Looking down at the stone, I commanded Moqerhe to teleport us to Saguntum before all was lost.

His goat mouth curled into a slight smirk, and he flicked his hands to the left.

A crushing sensation stole my breath. It was as if a giant boa constrictor had coiled itself around me and squeezed. Darkness danced before my eyes. Just as I was about to pass out, my invisible captor released me. Moqerhe and I now stood before a forest of trees. Less than a foot away, the rest of our crew were beside Greg's unconscious body.

I glanced at Moqerhe. "Is this Saguntum?"

"We're close," he said breathless. "Though it was the strangest thing. While transporting you all, my energy dwindled to nothing. We shouldn't have made it this far."

"Amara, he won't wake up," Sophie shook Greg's bloody torso, sobbing. "C'mon, please wake up."

I dropped to my knees beside my brother. When Bear lifted Greg's tunic, I gasped at the golf ball-sized puncture wound. I counted backward by five, summoning all my strength as I jumped into action. "We should elevate his legs. To keep the blood in his upper body."

Adones removed his cloak, rolled it into a big ball and placed it beneath Greg's feet.

I thought back to the ABCs of first aid that I had learned in school. First, I checked the airway. Greg's breathing was shallow and rapid. There was no sign of obstruction, and I heard no gurgling, which meant I could concentrate on stopping the bleeding. I considered what I could use to replace sterile gauze. Only one thing came to mind. I gestured toward Bear.

"Hand me your dagger."

He quickly complied then I hastily cut a four-inch strip off the cleanest portion of my robe. It wasn't ideal but I needed to make-do with what I had. I folded the material into a rectangle and pushed hard against the wound. Greg's unconscious body shook.

"I can help," Moqerhe said in English.

I'd been so caught up with Greg, I forgot we had access to a magical being with healing powers.

"Do whatever you have to," Sophie said.

The Shadu roared. Vicram petted the top of the animal's golden mane and stepped forward. "My Shadu fears the djinni is too weak to invoke his powers."

Sophie shot me a questioning look. "What did he say."

"It matters not," Moqerhe said in English. He retracted his bat-like wings and stepped toward me, stiffly, deliberately. "Our friend needs help, and I intend to give it." He wobbled and leaned against a tree for support.

"Keep compression on this wound," I said to Bear.

He took over, and I scrambled to Moqerhe's side. Clearly the rescue had drained him. He stiffly turned his head and met my eyes, wincing. The pain on his face was hard to take.

"Greg's still losing way too much blood," Sophie shouted.

I wrapped my arm around the lowest part of Moqerhe's waist careful not to touch his wings. "Do you have the strength?"

"Time to save the day *again,*" he said with a frail smile.

"That's the humble djinni I know."

"It's part of my charm."

When we made it to Greg, Moqerhe rested his palm over the gushing wound. A white light pulsated from his hand then retracted. Beads of sweat ran down Moqerhe's temples. He closed his eyes and set his jaw in deep concentration. Again, the white light pulsated for just a second. Moqerhe sucked in a wet, raspy breath and toppled onto his side. Within seconds, millions of white dots appeared and sparkled around the djinni like diamonds, encasing him in a glowing nimbus.

"Moqerhe!" I inched my hand toward the sparkles needing confirmation that he was alive.

Just as I was about to touch him, Adones yanked me to my feet. "Are you mad?" He stared at me through angry green eyes.

"You're trifling with forces you don't understand. That is likely a protective barrier to help him heal."

"And what do you know of such forces?" I asked accusingly. He seemed a little too knowledgeable and calm about the whole Moqerhe is a djinni thing.

"Stop arguing!" Sophie yelled. "We need to help Greg."

I winced at her crimson-stained hands, at my hands, wet and sticky with my brother's blood. Everything had slowed to a dreamlike state as I took in his ghost-white face.

Bear's voice cut through my haze. "If we don't cauterize this wound, the boy will surely die."

"Do what you must." This had to work. Just had to.

While Sophie and I maintained pressure on the wound, Bear and Adones collected twigs from the tree line and started a fire. Bear then placed the dagger blade on the flames until it glowed.

"Amara, is that safe?" Sophie asked.

I shrugged. "It's our best chance of saving him."

"The boy will likely startle when I use this so we must restrain him." Bear's voice was grim.

Sophie and I each grabbed a leg, while Adones and Vicram took the shoulders. Bear then brought the red-hot blade to Greg's wound. A hissing sound followed and the skin sizzled. The barbecued scent of scorched blood and human flesh filled the air. Greg's eyes snapped open. He let out a chilling scream and thrashed about. It took every bit of strength I had to restrain his leg. When Bear removed the blade, the wound was charred, and the bleeding had stopped. Greg's shoulders slumped, and Adones caught his head before it hit the ground.

Sophie moved Greg's sweat-slick hair away from his face. "You're gonna be okay."

I swallowed the golf ball-sized lump in my throat. If my brother died because he rescued me, I would never get over it. No, I shook my head, realizing my pity-party could wait until later. I needed to be present for them.

Vicram frowned. "We've done all we can. What comes next will be decided by the gods."

Bear's eyes watered as he stood and scanned the lush vegetation around us. "We'll collect more wood. Meanwhile, burn these bandages. We don't want the scent of blood attracting predators."

Without another word, he and Adones commenced gathering twigs.

Greg's eyes fluttered open. "What happened?"

Sophie brought the water bag to his lips. "Drink."

As he sipped, I said, "You were shot in the stomach during my rescue, and we cauterized the wound." I pushed down the mounting tsunami of guilt within me.

"I remember. What did you think about the explosions?" He coughed. "Told you I could make gunpowder."

I grinned. "Let me get this straight. You were shot by a Seeker's bullet, had the wound cauterized with a scalding hot blade, and the only thing you can ask is what I thought about your gunpowder?"

His chuckle was followed by a pained grimace. He rigidly turned his head to the left and glanced at Moqerhe, resting in his glowing nimbus. "What happened to him?"

"He used magic to rescue us. It took a lot out of him," Sophie said.

I patted my brother's hand. "Adones thinks those sparkly things are a protective healing barrier."

His gaze moved to the Shadu and Vicram. "Where did they come from?"

I shrugged. "Not sure. He kind of appeared from nowhere and saved your ass." Once Greg was settled, I planned to find out why.

"Where are we?" Greg asked.

"Somewhere in the mountains. I had commanded Moqerhe to take us to Saguntum so I'd say we're close. We'll scout things tomorrow."

He rested a cold hand on mine. "Love you, Sis."

My eyes stung and I closed them a few beats until the feeling subsided. I wanted to tell Greg how I felt but I hadn't uttered those words since I was ten. Mom's death and the hurt and pain of waiting for Dad's calls that never came still felt raw. I'd pushed so many people away. Because of this, I had missed the one chance to forgive, to return my father's love. I surveyed my brother's bloody tunic, swallowing hard. It was time to let go.

"I-I love you too."

Greg and Sophie exchanged surprised glances. "Wow!" He gave a breath of a laugh and coughed. "You must really be afraid if you're saying that."

"Don't get used to it." My voice was a thin rasp.

He grinned and turned his attention to Sophie. "I need to tell you something."

"What is it?" She gazed deep into his eyes.

The intimacy between them made me feel like an intruder.

"I-I love you," Greg whispered. "I need you to know in case, you know."

"Enough of that *in case* crap. We're going home, and we're gonna be together," Sophie said.

He squeezed her hand. "I plan on holding this when we're eighty."

She bent down and kissed Greg's forehead. "Get some rest. We can talk more tomorrow." He relaxed his head on her lap and closed his eyes. She stroked his hair, regarding me with serious concern.

I nodded and turned away, strangling my sob. I didn't have it in me to watch my brother's decline and Sophie's worry for one more second. Instead, I headed to Vicram. He sat against the trunk of a tree next to the Shadu. The yellow-eyed creature stared at the forest, ever vigilant with its massive wings retracted.

"I have a question."

Vicram straightened. "Yes, I've been waiting to speak to you."

I inclined my head. "What about?"

He leaned forward conspiratorially. "I've been serving the king since that day at the market."

I balled my hands into fists. "Serving? Did he make you a slave?"

"Never!" he gestured toward the Shadu. "We've chosen this path for personal reasons. Regarding your brother, the fire fight needed to appear realistic so as not to draw suspicion. Unfortunately, the king made a grave miscalculation. He thought your djinni would save the boy. When he saw the creature's weakened state, he summoned me to help. Then he aided the djinni's teleportation here."

"Help, you call this help? My brother is gravely injured and Moqerhe's unconscious."

"This is most unfortunate." Vicram stood up. "The king's done what he can, for now."

I didn't realize I was pressing my nails into my palms until a stabbing pain shot through my hand. "That's unacceptable. My brother requires medical aid."

The Shadu rose, expanded its wings, and watched me with a glint of sadness in its eyes. Vicram climbed onto its back. "Jan-Ib-Jann says you must keep your end of the bargain, or all is lost."

Before I could respond, the Shadu leapt off its muscular haunches and flew toward the darkening sky. With all that had happened, unbinding Hannibal's sword was at the bottom of my list. Without antibiotics and surgeons to work on Greg, magic was my only hope of saving him. I didn't want to think about what would happen if Moqerhe remained unconscious.

Chapter Thirty-Two

When I awoke the morning after the battle with Jan, Sophie was propped against a tree trunk with Greg's head on her lap. I approached them, gently lifted the cloth off his forehead, and placed my hand against his skin. He was burning up. In high school CPR class, I had learned that wound infection, if left untreated, usually presented within twenty-four hours. Greg's fever was a telltale sign he was in the danger zone. Though I hated to even consider this, internal bleeding could have also been causing his symptoms.

A quick glance around the camp revealed that Adones and Bear were gone. Hopefully in search of water to cool my brother's fever. Since darkness was giving way to the first hints of daylight, and the fire still burned, they couldn't have been gone long. Moqerhe was still unconscious but the sparkles that surrounded him last night had disappeared. He had also returned to human form, which gave me hope.

I rushed to his side and shook him, gently at first, then harder. When I didn't receive a response, I checked his breathing, feeling my shoulders relax when his chest rose and fell.

"C'mon, wake up." I gently slapped both his cheeks.

Moqerhe's color had returned, and his cracked lips were healed. His black hair was swept away from his face, like it had been combed that way. Long lashes fanned over high cheekbones. He really was beautiful.

"Any luck?" Sophie called out.

Heat bloomed up my neck as I rose and faced her. How long had she watched me stare at Moqerhe? "N-no, unfortunately. He's still out."

"Well, maybe he'll wake soon," Greg said in a thin voice. His face was so pale.

I strained to smile. "How are you feeling?"

Twigs snapped in the forest. When I looked over my shoulder, Bear and Adones emerged on horseback. Two men rode behind them. One was a giant with a chest twice as broad as mine and skin that gave a worn leather purse a run for its money. The giant's mouth was barely visible through a forest of black facial hair. The other guy was thinner and older, around late thirties, with long braids that hung below his shoulders.

Adones' face was unreadable.

"Who are they?" I asked.

"My uncle's scouts. We came across them during our search for water." His eyes slid to Moqerhe then back to me. "He's human once more. That's promising."

"Indeed," Bear said. "The djinni brought us closer to Hannibal's camp than we thought."

Adones pointed toward a wooden travois attached to the back of Long Braid's horse. "We should load the wounded. My uncle has a healer waiting."

"What's the distance to the fortress from here?" I asked.

Bear's horse took a couple of steps forward and he tightened the reins. "We should be there before the general's men breakfast."

I nodded. Although moving Greg could open his wound, the reward of getting medical attention outweighed the risk. At the very least, he'd have a warm bed and access to clean water.

"Amara, what's the plan?" Sophie regarded me with serious concern.

"These are Hannibal's men, come to escort us to Saguntum."

Sophie squeezed Greg's arm. "Missions nearly complete. Home's right around the corner."

If Jan and I can stop Jasim.

Greg entwined his fingers with Sophie's. "Things—" He inhaled deeply. "Are looking up."

Panic rose within me as I watched my brother labor to breathe, heard the thread of a voice. I cleared the emotion from my throat. "First, we need to get you to the healer."

When I turned to Adones for help, Bear had already stepped up. He knelt beside Greg and rewet his cloth with water from a leather skin. Sophie moved aside as Bear poured the contents into my brother's hair. He responded with an achy moan.

Sophie frowned.

I shot them a thin smile. "He's gonna be okay."

Bear wiped down Greg's face and upper torso before lifting the makeshift bandage. The cauterized wound was inflamed with yellowed scabbing around the edges, and his stomach was blue and bruised.

Bear stood up. "We must move now."

The riders dismounted and strapped Greg and Moqerhe in separate travois. Then we all headed out. Hannibal's men led the way, maintaining their horses at a slow pace with Greg and Moqerhe hitched behind them.

Sophie rode with Bear, and I was with Adones, but he didn't say much. Greg moaned every time the travois hit a bump, leaving a palpable air of dread among us. Bear never stopped frowning. Sophie kept her eyes closed and her head buried in his back. I could relate. My heart broke a little more each time my brother cried out.

Adones cleared his throat. "Once your brother's health improves, I would like to continue the discussion we had on the beach, about my demise in battle."

"Of – of course." Hopefully, this would give me some time to come up with a plausible excuse. I could tell him I saw it in a dream.

Greg cried out again and I winced.

Soon, we emerged from the forest and traveled up a winding dirt road that led to a walled fortress at the top of a hill. A clanging sound of metal-on-metal echoed from a multitude of tents in an adjacent valley. As we drew closer, men stood among mounds of javelins and rows of hanging armor, pounding out dents. The scent of cooked meat, maybe a stew, wafted from an area where women with veiled faces stood over an open fire. They stirred large black pots suspended by tripods.

Several yards past the tents, mammoths, mounted by bearded men in wheat-colored tunics, dragged small boulders to catapults. A crew of at least twenty men scrambled to load the weapon. The quick release of a lever sent a boulder about a quarter mile into the air. It hit a hundred foot tree that shattered it into a thousand pieces.

"Looks like the men are training hard," I observed.

Adones nodded. "Indeed. Now that Ba'al's weapon has arrived, my uncle can fight the Romans on their soil."

My chest dipped as the word 'weapon' hung in my ears. How did he know Ba'al's plans? Had he been a spy for the god this whole time? Betrayal seared me like a red-hot knife. If I hadn't been so busy flirting, I wouldn't have missed the obvious and fallen for his act. I was such an idiot.

I sat quietly in the saddle, simmering in my cauldron of distrust as we ascended the hill. If nothing else, Adones' words also confirmed Jan's suspicions. Ba'al planned to use Moqerhe's powers as a weapon against Rome. If this happened, the ripple effects across dimensions would be devastating. Worse, I'd been so preoccupied with Greg's wound, I failed to formulate a plan with Bear to disarm Hannibal's sword.

When we stopped before the gates, archers on toothed battlements granted us entrance into an arena-sized courtyard bubbling with people. Everyone in our party dismounted and handed off the horses to two guys about my age in tan tunics and plumed helmets. Camels chewed cud in the middle of the square. Off in the far corner, a group of men smelted silver pots and vases. Gaseous, oxidized metallic fumes mingled with sour straw and pungent animal scents.

Captain Aharim approached us, grimacing like he'd eaten something foul.

I looked Aharim straight in his squinty brown eyes and said, "Thank you for agreeing to tend to our wounded." Hopefully, he took the hint and would help Greg.

"We've prepared quarters for your brother," the captain said flatly.

The soldiers unhitched my brother and the djinni. "What are your plans for Moqerhe?" I asked.

"You needn't concern yourself with him," he snapped.

Why would he say that? Surely, they'd have to remove my bracelet soon. I looked to Adones for support. He just stared past me with his jaw clenched. Bear shot me a concerned gaze from behind Adones. Judging by the slew of soldiers and workers here, we wouldn't get a chance to talk alone.

"Sophie!" Greg wheezed as the barbarians carried him away.

She caught up and grabbed Greg's hand while I trailed them. Inside, the soldiers carried his travois down a long hall and stopped before an elderly woman with white hair. Her brow scrunched together when she rested her wrinkled hand on his face. Then she spoke to the soldiers in Punic and gestured toward a door. When they carried Greg's travois inside, she blocked our way.

I glowered at her. "Let us pass!"

She regarded me through chocolate brown eyes, creased from too many years in the sun. "I must first examine the boy."

The woman's accent was so thick I barely understood her words. "He's my brother, please let me—"

"You'll only distract him, distract me from my work."

"She's not letting us in. Why isn't she letting us in?" Sophie said in a strained voice.

I pushed past the old woman, but only made it a few steps when the giant soldier blocked my way. "Let us in!"

The man shoved me into the hall with such force, my teeth clacked together. The healer slammed the door and a latch clicked from the other side.

Sophie banged her fists on the door. "Don't do this," echoed down the silent hallway.

Momentarily jarred, it took a second to get it together. Sorrow crushed me. My brother's fate was in the hands of a stranger with limited knowledge about health care and I couldn't help.

I gripped Sophie by the shoulders. "Don't make this any harder on him."

She crumbled to the floor, sobbing. "I — I just want to be with Greg. I love him."

"I know, I do too." My face was wet with tears as I knelt and pulled her into my arms.

We cried, paced, and repeated for what felt like several hours. When the old woman emerged from the room, my feet ached, and my eyes were puffy. The two soldiers who carried Greg earlier headed down the corridor.

"Has he improved?" I asked the old woman.

Her lips pinched together. "I gave the boy tea from the willow bark to lower his fever. We washed and treated his wound. I used all my skills to save him." She shook her head. "It made no difference. The boy has internal injuries beyond my skills. He isn't long for this world."

My body shook and I leaned against the wall for support.

Sophie gripped my arm, hard. "Amara?"

"Compose yourself and bid him farewell," the old woman said before hobbling away.

"What did she say? Tell me!" Sophie said.

"Greg's…" I couldn't bring myself to speak the words.

Disbelief then fear flickered across her face. "No," she stormed into my brother's room.

It felt like a mountain of rocks had been dumped on my chest as I followed her. An oil lamp burned on the night table beside the long bed where Greg lay. Sophie's face was white with shock as she brought a shaky hand to his forehead and swept an errant hair back.

His eyes fluttered open. The skin beneath them had darkened to a bluish black, and he looked a lot older than twenty-three. "You took your time."

"Sorry, we had to wait till the healer finished," Sophie said with a thin smile.

Unable to look at Greg without breaking down, I focused on how the candlelight danced on the wall above his bed, how the room was shadowed in gloom. I counted every flicker of the flame. One, two, three.

"You okay, Sis?"

Greg's thread of a voice pulled me from my despair. "I'm fine." Unsure what else to do, I grabbed a woolen blanket off the foot of his bed and tucked it around him. "You comfortable?"

"Yeah, just glad you're here."

I strangled a sob. "Where else would I be?"

A faint smile touched Greg's lips as he dragged his dull green gaze to Sophie. "Wish we had more time."

"Hey, it's not over, you hear me?" Her voice cracked.

I checked my bracelet, praying to whatever magic ruled the universe. *Please save my brother, please, please, please.* A solid stone stared back. My heart ripped into a million pieces as I realized there would be no swirling red stone, bidding me to summon the djinni's powers. There would be no magical cure for my brother.

Disappointment glistened in Greg's eyes when he glanced at my bracelet. "No Moqerhe?"

"Not yet." With a deep breath, I bent forward and wrapped my arms around my brother. "I'm so sorry."

He buried his face in my shoulder, shaking, breathing heavily. How would I make it through life without him? Tears burned the back of my eyelids, begging for release. This was supposed to be about him, comforting him. When he said, "I love you, I need you to finish this," the sobs obliterated my dam of control and flooded down my face like a raging river.

We held each other, finding comfort that only existed between family. Sophie must have moved away from the bedside and fetched water from the adjacent table, because when I looked up, she was holding out a wooden cup.

"Thank you." I lifted Greg's damp head and brought the cup to his cracked lips.

He took a sip, coughed, and spit it out. "Promise me something." The fever had drained all his strength.

I swallowed to moisten my dry mouth. "Anything."

His gaze lingered on Sophie a moment before returning to me. He spoke Greek. "Do whatever it takes to get back home, to get *her* home. Take care of Dad and Yia Yia. They'll need your strength."

If I didn't disarm Hannibal's sword and stop Jasim, home as we knew it may no longer exist. I resisted the urge to do what I always did, to pull away, to run until my legs could carry me no further. I had to dig deep to stay planted before my brother.

"Promise me," he said.

I gave a tense smile and said in Greek, "I'll do everything in my power to make it happen."

Greg's pale mouth twitched upward as he turned his attention to Sophie. "Don't cry. I can't take it if you cry." He raised a trembling hand to her cheek and dried her tears.

She laid her head on his chest, sobbing so hard her shoulders shook.

He fell back and closed his eyes. His breaths were rasps. "I just need to rest a minute."

My chest was so tight I could hardly breathe as I took his hand into mine. The warmth of it served as a reminder of the brother who had walked me to school each day – who wiped my tears when Dad forgot to call – and kicked ass when I was bullied. He had been my heart, my best friend for so long. How was I supposed to go on without him?

The answer came too soon when a rasping breath pushed from Greg's lungs and his hand went slack.

My heart stopped. The room blurred in my vision. "No, no, no. Don't leave me. You can't leave me," I screamed.

But he had left me. My beautiful older brother just stared at me through dull and vacant eyes. Eyes that would never see me married, or watch my children grow. Eyes that would never see this world again.

Chapter Thirty-Three

I stared at Greg's pale face unable to cry or even move. Sophie's head was still buried in his chest as she wailed.

Voices resounded from somewhere down the hall and the door squeaked open. Bear approached Sophie and rested his hand on her shoulder. She twisted away from his grasp and shrieked, "Leave me alone!" A banshee mourning her lost love.

Her cries sounded far away. A floaty, light-headed feeling washed over me, and I suddenly felt like an observer watching myself stand in this place of death.

Captain Aharim entered the room, glancing between Sophie, me, and Greg's lifeless body. There was no compassion, no sadness in his gaze. He spoke to Bear in Punic, and he approached Sophie.

"Get away from me!" she spat.

Bear's eyes softened. "I'm sorry, little one." He then yanked her off my brother and threw her over his shoulder.

Sophie's sobs erupted through the room. Her fists pounded his back, and she kicked at Bear. It did no good. He just carried her toward the door as I watched in stunned disbelief.

"The general's waiting for you," said the captain.

His words pulled me from my stupor. "No, I can't leave my—"

Aharim unsheathed his sword. "Move!"

The steadiness in the captain's gaze and his set jaw told me he wouldn't ask twice. I shuffled toward the door, knowing I'd go insane if I looked back at my brother and said goodbye. My promise to get Sophie home was the only thing that kept me moving.

As we proceeded down a long hallway behind Sophie and Bear, I barely noticed Aharim's fingers squeezing my arm, or my shuffling feet moving me forward. I was a zombie, numb and indifferent to space and time.

When we stopped before a set of tall double doors, the captain pulled them open and pushed me inside. Sunlight filtered through the barred windows, brightening a large room with high, gilded ceilings. At the front of the space, Hannibal and Adones sat in high back wooden chairs watching us with their chins held high.

Bear set Sophie down a few feet from the general and Aharim positioned me next to her. The far-off stare in her eyes spoke to her pain. I pushed down all my grief, threatening to come out as a scream. Instead, I replaced it with anger far hotter than the reddest fire. This was easier to handle.

I glowered at Hannibal. "Why have you brought us her—"

Something flickered in my periphery. About twenty feet away, Moqerhe paced back and forth in a flaming prison, sneering at our captors. I scrambled toward him but didn't get far when Aharim yanked me backward.

"Let me go!" I swung at him with all my strength.

Aharim ducked, laughing haughtily and flung me to the floor. I landed hard beside Sophie's feet. Then Hannibal rose from his seat and spoke in Punic. Sophie helped me stand.

"What's happening?" she asked.

Bear stepped up. "Have mercy. They've lost much this day."

The general, clad in leather armor and a pleated skirt, approached us with Adones by his side.

Aharim snapped to attention.

After ordering the captain at-ease, or whatever term a Punic general would give in that language, Hannibal returned his attention to us. I glanced at the ivory hilt of his sheathed sword. Without a plan, how was I supposed to get to it?

"My condolences for your loss," he said to me.

I nodded, unable to speak without crying.

"Greg was a loyal comrade-in-arms, Uncle." Adones didn't glance my way.

I schooled my expression into careful blankness to avoid reacting to his coldness, his sudden indifference toward me. Could he have somehow found out about my plans with Jan? But there was no way. Bear and I were the only two who knew. Unless he had betrayed me.

Hannibal whispered to Aharim. With a nod, the captain marched to a side door and opened it, granting entry to a masculine figure in a hawk mask. Everyone except Moqerhe, Sophie, and I fell to their knees. The masked figure's Tyrian purple robes rustled against the silence as he glided to us and spoke to Hannibal in Punic. I immediately recognized the voice as Jasim. After everyone rose, Aharim sketched a bow and left the room.

Jasim removed his mask and settled his dark gaze on me. "I'm sorry to hear about your brother," he said in English.

My voice was deadly calm when I spat, "Like you care."

I couldn't say whether it was losing Greg or this untenable situation, but I was done.

Jasim frowned. "You think me insincere?"

My body shook as I spoke. "My brother's dead because you needed a pawn to transport Moqerhe here."

"Collateral damage is an unfortunate result of war." Jasim glanced at the general then jerked his chin toward Sophie.

Hannibal's hand moved so fast, I barely caught him unsheathing his sword. Then everything happened at once. Bear tackled Hannibal to the ground. Adones dove on Bear's back, wrapped his arm around my friend's neck and pulled. When they toppled backward, the general dropped his weapon.

"Now, Amara, now!" Bear yelled while wrestling Adones.

There was no time to think, just act. I yanked the baton from a belt beneath my robes and dove onto the floor. Hannibal and I scrambled toward the sword at the same time. The baton connected with the blade mere seconds before he got to it. Cold sweat beaded across my brow, and my surroundings fell away as the blade blazed bright orange. A burning sensation simmered at first and slowly rose to a scorching heat that consumed me. I groaned and tried to release the baton, but the force maintaining my grip was too powerful.

After what seemed an eternity of unrelenting torture, the beam retracted into the baton and the blade returned to its original silver. My grasp loosened, and the baton rolled from my hand onto the floor. I lay on my back gobbling a lung full of air. As my vision came back into focus, I caught sight of Bear, holding his stomach with blood-covered hands. Sophie was now beside him, stroking his cheek. Adones stood above them. His mouth was curled into a cruel smile as he held a dagger blade, stained crimson from my friend's sacrifice.

I pushed through the lingering pain in my stomach, struggled to my feet and ran to them, sneering at Adones. "How could you do this to Tanno? He was your friend."

Adones' jaw flexed. "He's always been my enemy."

"No, he—"

Bear's grunt drew my attention to him. I loosened his ties and winced at the long slice of gaping skin below his ribs. "You're going to recover." I couldn't lose anyone else.

"If it is the will of the gods."

"It is." Using what little strength I had left, I ripped off a piece of my tunic, folded it into a square and pressed the fabric against his wound. My hands had been washed with so much blood lately, I no longer flinched at the sight of it.

As I stared at my friend's ashen face, it occurred to me that this whole thing seemed too easy. Neither Hannibal nor Adones had made a move against me. Why was Hannibal's sword still on the floor, unclaimed? I glanced up at the general, the crease between my eyes deepening. Adones had joined him and was cleaning his dagger blade with a kerchief. Jasim just watched me with a smug smirk on his face.

"This isn't funny." I gestured toward Bear. "He's bleeding out, you sadistic son of a—"

A high-pitched buzzing noise filled the air.

"Amara, look!" Sophie pointed ahead.

Just a few feet away, a thread of light slowly expanded into a swirling pool of yellow energy that I'd come to know as a portal.

I tensed, awaiting the call that would send Hannibal's soldiers or Jasim's guardians busting through the doors. They would be armed with the spell book, along with the three other djinnis the false god had in his arsenal. But no call for help followed. Surely Jasim wasn't stupid enough to think he could face Jan alone.

The portal or vortex soon reached the size of a doorway. Thousands of black specks emerged and formed a tight circle. Then they diffused into four humanoid figures that shimmered between full bodies and nothingness until they formed three Seekers. Their white robes rippled as they stepped aside and cleared the way for Jan.

The only break from the king's monochromatic appearance were his neon blue eyes and the golden amulet around his neck. Without missing a beat, Jan steepled his fingers together and whispered like he was saying a prayer.

Hannibal gasped as his sword rose from the floor, floated across the room, and landed in Jan's hands. The king passed the weapon off to a Seeker behind him. His thin lips were pursed when he turned to Jasim and clicked his tongue.

Jasim gestured toward me. "Since Amara's the reason we're here, let's do her the courtesy of conversing in English. It's the least we can do after all she's lost."

Jan studied Jasim for a heartbeat. "Very well. It's over!" he said in English.

Jasim threw his head back and laughed. "You believe you have the upper hand."

"Why wouldn't I?" said Jan. "While you've put up a good fight, you're no match for me without your powers."

"Once again, your ego has bested you, Father." Jasim pointed at my bracelet. "My guardians discovered a loophole in the book of spells. One you, the great king Jan-Ib-Jann, overlooked. We tweaked the incantation, so it connected me to the stone on the bracelet even when donned by another." His voice was sunny and full of pride. "Think of it as a supernatural listening device. Every word you exchanged with Amara resounded through my mind."

I handed the bloody bandage to Sophie. She maintained compression on Bear's wound as I stood up. "You knew? Why let Adones fight Tanno when you could have taken the baton and stopped me?"

Jasim glanced at Jan before responding. "That wasn't my plan. I had to put on a good show, in case my dear old dad was watching. Besides, Tanno deserved to die for his betrayal."

His indifference sent chills down my spine. "You don't care about human life at all. Greg's dead because you sent us on this futile journey. For what, to trap your father?"

Still maintaining compression on Bear's wound, Sophie shook her head. "How can you use people like this?"

"I care about human life more than you know," Jasim snapped. "You and your lot were traitors seeking to impede my plans."

"You're done," Jan said between gritted teeth.

"If you insist." Jasim stepped forward with his arms raised overhead. "Consider that sword a gesture of good will, Father."

Jan's brow wrinkled. "Why, after all this time?"

Jasim shrugged. "Why not?"

"What are you plotting?" Jan glanced at Moqerhe's cage. "Let's hear what Moqerhe has to say, shall we?"

I could have sworn excitement flickered across Jasim's face. "Do what you must."

Jan clapped his hands together and spoke in whispered tones once more. Thin rays of blazing blue light appeared above the cage and enveloped the entire surface. Seconds later, the bars withered away. Moqerhe bolted from his prison and charged Jasim.

Jan's Seekers blocked Moqerhe and seized his arms. One of them traced a figure eight in the air, and a cord, sizzling with electricity, appeared around Moqerhe's wrists like supernatural cuffs.

"Don't hurt him," I screamed. "He's not the bad guy."

"Don't be fooled by the prince," Moqerhe yelled. "I overheard everything. His surrender's a diversion, while my brothers sack Rome."

First anger, then alarm flashed across Jan's white face as he turned to his Seekers.

"You're too late, *Father*," Jasim's dark eyes glinted with triumph. "Don't bother to send the Seekers to Rome."

"What. Have. You. Done?" Jan's voice boomed against the silence.

Jasim gave a nonchalant shrug. "I've corrected an injustice toward my people."

"Your people! You claim to be a god. Yet you fail to understand the natural order of the universe. Some things are not to be meddled with."

Jasim shook his head. "That's your opinion."

Jan steepled his long fingers together and whispered. A yellow light materialized and morphed into a man-sized 3-D holographic image. It panned from tree-capped hillsides to an ancient city in the valley below, surrounded by a massive stone wall.

I studied the scene. It wasn't Carthage, the walls weren't big enough. "Am I looking at Rome?"

"Yes, my father's showing you what's happening in the city as we speak."

Blue light flickered across the hologram, and in a matter of seconds, the destruction began. Through a screen of smoke, three djinnis hovered before the arched gates of Rome. Their translucent, bat-like wings flapped against the wind as they surveyed the enemy through eyes like fire. Sentries in plumed helmets stood behind toothed battlements and shot a barrage of arrows at the enemy. The three djinnis thrust their clawed hands outward. Beams of blue light shot from their palms and connected with the arrows flying toward them, sending the weapons to the ground in a rain of ashes.

"What the?" Sophie said.

A dizzying surreal feeling washed over me while one djinni continued deflecting arrows, and the other two circled above the city. The hologram panned over thousands of people scurrying toward the arched gates. Mothers maneuvered through wall-to-wall crowds, clutching their children protectively against their chests. Elderly citizens were trampled underfoot by those trying to escape. My stomach burned as sentries on horseback slashed their blades at mobs of people pulling at their legs, trying to steal their horses.

The three djinnis hovered above the city. Their pale faces were taut, and their red eyes glinted with sorrow as they surveyed the chaos. Like Moqerhe, they were prisoners to the stones that controlled them. The guardians were probably nearby pulling all the strings. I envisioned them smiling as the djinnis conjured a neon blue fireball about the size of a car tire and hurled it toward a temple in the center of Rome.

The ball connected with the domed roof and detonated. I screamed as a superheated blast of blue fire rippled across the city and expanded out toward the surrounding hillsides. The fire compressed around the edges, and a powerful shockwave of destruction followed. Structures built from solid stone, standing a hundred feet high, crumbled into millions of pieces like confetti. The remaining buildings were quickly overtaken by a storm of fire. Crowds of thousands were incinerated where they stood. Shrill screams of agony lingered in their wakes.

By the end of the blast, my jaw hurt from clenching it. Marble temples were nothing more than pieces of charcoal, and the great wall protecting the city lay in ruin. Scorched black earth, that used to be the countryside, now surrounded the devastation. Citizens, whose flesh had been stripped from their bones, lay strewn across the barren wasteland of fire and ash. Through the screen of black smoke, billowing over the Roman city that stood no more, hovered three djinnis, surveying the carnage before them.

Jan brought his hands together in a loud clap. The hologram folded in on itself and disappeared, leaving everyone in stunned silence. His pale face, illuminated by light, filtering through the windows, was filled with hatred as he glowered at his son.

"Those poor people," Sophie said, hoarsely.

Bear who had propped himself against a column, while compressing the cloth against his wound, sat there with his mouth agape.

"Save your laments for a country who deserves it," Jasim snapped. "You know as well as I, nothing of Carthage would remain if Rome continued to flourish. At least I afforded the Roman citizens a quick death."

"How *dare* you. Those were not your lives to take!" Jan's voice boomed through the hall.

"It was my people or theirs," Jasim said flatly. "If the history from Amara's dimension tells us nothing else, this Carthage would have fallen by Roman hands, had the timelines continued to run parallel."

"You're mad!" Moqerhe yelled.

Even Adones and Hannibal were gaping at Jasim.

"Mad enough to outwit you, the greatest general known to djinn. Now, a new world has begun, and you can't stop it. With an African country in power, all the racial issues in the world may never exist. Perhaps, a better religion will arise instead."

"Like Ba'alism? You really think *that's* better?" I said.

Jasim winked at Jan. "Hammonites has a nice ring, don't you think? If the citizens of Carthage continue to adopt my teachings, the inquisition may never happen. Citizens in early Europe won't be murdered over minor distinctions in their faith. North African colonization of the Americas might be more peaceful. Don't you see, allowing Carthage to stand will not only improve the future in this dimension, but in all the worlds."

"You've changed nothing," Jan spat. "I'll ensure your precious Carthage falls to rubble, like it should've in the first place. Then I'll rebuild Rome. History *will* go forward as intended."

Jasim's lips curled into a cold smile. "No, you'll allow Carthage to reign."

"Why would I do that?" Jan said.

"Because I'm surrendering to you."

Jan considered his son's words. "And what of the book of spells, the stones, and the djinnis?"

"Those, I won't give up," Jasim said flatly. "You'd have your precious subjects believe you're bound by honor. I can't trust that. The djinnis and the book are insurance to keep you honest."

"How do I know you won't turn them against me in the future?" Jan asked.

Jasim shook his head, incredulous. "I have too much to lose. You would hunt me to the edge of time, and all I've accomplished today would be reversed. This is why I'm making the ultimate sacrifice and surrendering, so my people can live. My love for them holds no bounds. If Carthage can progress from today on, our accord will remain." He gestured toward the Seeker beside Jan, holding the sword. "I'll gladly rot away in the nether dimensions to make that happen. Just remember, my bargain includes allowing General Barca to become emperor with his nephew as advisor."

"And if I refuse?" asked Jan.

"As you know, my guardians are masters at going underground and they'll reemerge when the time is right. Fail to comply and the carnage you observed today will be nothing compared to what will befall all dimensions. Agree to my terms, and we'll have peace." He glanced at the windows. Sunlight flowed between the bars, casting splinters of rust and orange light across the tiled floors. "You have till sundown to decide."

I looked at Jan. "Tell me you're not considering this. You'd be giving into a terrorist."

"Silence!" Jan's body was rigid as a board when he returned his attention to Jasim. "I've no choice but to accept your offer. However, my only consolation is you'll never see your precious Carthage evolve through time. I doubt you'll be so cavalier once you're ripped to shreds by the monsters in the nether dimensions."

Jasim's face blanched.

Jan took the sword from the Seeker beside him and extended the weapon toward his son. The geometric sigils on the center of the blade glowed red. A beam of light shot from the tip, connected with Jasim, and encircled him in a blue prism.

"No!" When Adones stepped toward his god, Hannibal gripped his nephew's shoulder and spoke in Punic.

Adones' green eyes watered as he reluctantly backed off.

Jasim sneered. "You're still naïve as ever, Father. My arrest makes me a martyr. I, Ba'al Hammon, will forever be revered as the god who sacrificed himself to save his people. There's nothing you can do about it."

"You've won the battle, but I'll win the war." At that, Jan chanted words I didn't understand.

The magical prism encasing Jasim narrowed into a long, transparent tube that lifted him into the air and pulled him toward the blade. Jasim writhed and screeched as his body stretched into a thin line and retracted into the sword. Just before his head disappeared, "I'll live forever," blazed through the room and melted away, like a candle that burned no more.

Chapter Thirty-Four

Bear's shallow rasps dragged my attention away from the blade in Jan's hand. I knelt and relieved Sophie of the compression rag. She leaned back on her knees and rubbed her bloody palms on her robe. Her beautiful face was contorted in pain.

I looked Bear in the eye. "I'm so sorry this happened to you."

The corner of his mouth twitched upward. "Inkatu is safe, and we stopped Ba'al." He coughed. "This is all that matters."

Desperation twisted in my chest. I glared at Jan, now standing just a few feet away. "I've lost one brother today; I won't lose another."

Adones and Hannibal stood in the middle of the room. Both were every bit the hardened warriors painted by history. Straight backed with their hands resting on the sharp blades at their sides, they never averted their gazes from Jan.

"We have much business to attend to," Hannibal said.

Screw his negotiations. I glowered at Hannibal. "No, *you* can wait. Tanno needs help."

Adones' grip tightened on the ivory hilt of his sword. "That traitor deserves no mercy."

Hannibal raised his hand in a gesture of silence. "His wound is beyond a healer's abilities. You must accept what is."

The back of my neck cramped, and I rubbed the area. "Never." I looked at Jan once more. "Tanno risked his life to help you. The least you can do is—"

"Enough. I do not intend to let him die," Jan said in an uninflected almost dismissive tone.

He handed off his sword to a Seeker and glided to Bear. The moment the king rested his pale hands over the wounded area, thousands of golden sparkles radiated from Jan's palms. My friend gritted his teeth and stifled a moan as the wound knitted together. Seconds later, the skin had scarred into a pinkish line, and the sparkles receded into Jan's palm.

"The Numidian will be sore, but he is otherwise healthy." The king rose and glided to his Seekers in the middle of the room.

Sophie and I helped Bear sit up. It was amazing how quickly the color had returned to his face.

"Can you stand on your own?" I asked.

"I-I've never felt stronger." Bear found his feet in a matter of seconds.

There was no sign of blood on his baldric. He quickly fastened it and stood protectively in front of Sophie and me. We all watched intently as Jan and Hannibal had a discussion in Punic. The general's face reddened a couple of times, and Adones scoffed once. Conversely, Jan's face remained a mask of calm.

I shot Moqerhe a questioning look from across the way.

With his hands still magically cuffed, Moqerhe's answer hit my mind like pebbles skittering across water. *My king is allowing Hannibal to reign as emperor of Carthage. The Senate will be informed of his victory over Rome, and I'm certain this will include the false god's plans for him. It's unlikely the general will meet with resistance since the city will hail him as a conquering hero.*

After lots of back and forth with Hannibal, Jan and his Seekers fanned outward in a sea of white, leaving a path between them. A leader among men, the great general marched past us with Adones by his side. Both held their chins high, and shoulders squared.

"Adones!" I yelled as he passed. I couldn't say why or even what I expected. Despite the fact he had stabbed Bear, and set us all up, some part of me hoped the guy I cared about was still in there.

He stopped mid-stride, staring with contempt in his emerald eyes.

"I wish you all the bes—"

His mouth contorted into a sneer. "Save your hypocrisy. I invited you into my home, and unwisely wanted to take you as my mistress. The entire time you had plotted to betray Ba'al and my country. I shudder to think of House Barcid's fate had you succeeded."

My chest tightened. "This wasn't an easy deci—"

"Others have lost their heads for far less." Adones' nose flared, and his breaths were shallow as he gestured toward Jan. "Be thankful he granted you clemency. Nothing you say will erase this betrayal, so save your words, as I have no interest in them."

He turned his back to me and nodded at Hannibal. Together, they marched toward the double doors at the front of the room and pushed them open. A bleak heaviness weighed on my heart. Although I knew helping Jan was the right move, Adones' hatred still stung. There was so much left unsaid. I wanted to tell him I'd miss him, I'd miss Elissa, that I appreciated his family's kindness, and I was happy the people in House Barcid were safe. Instead, as he and Hannibal faded into the hallway, I said a silent goodbye to one of the greatest generals of all time and his nephew who used to be my friend.

Once the doors closed behind them, Jan spoke to Bear in what I presumed was his native tongue, since it didn't sound like anything I'd heard before. After a short exchange, one of Jan's Seekers diffused into a puff of smoke and materialized beside Bear.

I glowered at Jan. "What is your Seeker doing?"

Moqerhe chimed in in English. "He will now reunite Tanno with his brother."

"That's a relief." Sophie's eyes were bloodshot and puffy, making her look much older than twenty.

"Can we at least say goodbye?" I asked Jan.

The king gave a regal nod. "Of course."

Sophie and I pulled Bear into a group hug, allowing all the fear, anger, and grief of the day to flow in a lake of tears. After several minutes, Bear stepped back and gave me a final once-over with those brooding brown eyes I'd come to love.

"If I tell you nothing else, Amara, know I'm proud to call you friend."

My heart thudded dully in my chest. I stored the long scar on Bear's cheek and the stoic way his full lips pressed together into my memory and said, "You'll be missed."

"As will you." He turned to Sophie and kissed the crown of her matted hair then looked at me. "Please extend my apologies for taking her against her will earlier. I had no choice if I wanted to get you close enough to the general to disarm his sword."

I translated his words. She leaned in and gave him a hug. His dark eyes shined as he returned the gesture.

After a long stretch of time, his gaze moved between her and I. "Greg was a brave warrior. He deserved a better death."

I nearly choked while repeating his words to her in English.

"He deserved better," she said hoarsely. "It's been great knowing you."

Once I had passed along her message, the Seeker dematerialized into a glowing nimbus that enveloped Bear until they evaporated. A heavy silence followed.

Sophie shot me a *what now* look.

I peered at Jan. "I've done everything you asked. We just want to return to our dimension."

Without Greg, there was no joy in this victory. How would I explain his death to Dad and Yia Yia? The thought made my pulse race. I counted backward by five, while simultaneously breathing in through my nose, then exhaling through my mouth. I needed to hold it together for Sophie.

"We'll get to that in a moment." Jan faced Moqerhe.

The djinni's brow knitted, and his face twisted like he was confused. They must have been communicating telepathically. Several seconds stretched into minutes before Moqerhe took a knee.

Why would he do that?

Jan's long finger traced an inverted number eight through the air and the glowing cuffs over Moqerhe's wrists disappeared. Then Jan removed his amulet and placed it around Moqerhe's neck, gesturing for him to rise.

Moqerhe's face was unreadable as he turned to me. "My anger once blinded me to man's beauty but no more. I have much to atone for." He waved a hand toward Jan. "In his benevolence, my king has allowed me the honor of returning you both home."

The thought of saying goodbye sent a pang of sadness through me.

"Thank you," Sophie whispered with wet cheeks.

"Be forewarned," said Jan. "It's possible the place you call home may be different than when you left."

Sophie's forehead crinkled. "How so?"

Jan shook his head. "I can't answer that. Rome was destroyed and Carthage now stands. We've never experienced anything like this in the history of all universes."

"What about our families, our lives?" Sophie asked in a tremulous voice.

"That depends on how this change to history affected your ancestors," Jan observed. "Moqerhe will return you to the day you were brought here. You may find your world just as you left it, or you could awaken at home, school, or a swamp."

I breathed through the mounting dread in my chest. "And what will happen to the body I'm in now. Won't there be two of me running around, one from this time and one from then?"

"The portal will absorb your body, and your consciousness will transfer to the Amara from your dimension," Jan said. "It's complicated but trust no harm will befall you."

Sophie cleared her throat. "If things have changed in our timeline will Greg be alive?"

Moqerhe shrugged. "If the history from the Carthage in your dimension has changed, that could affect the future there as well."

"Will we remember everything that happened here?" I asked.

Jan nodded. "You should."

"No." Sophie looked up at the king. "Can you erase my memory?"

I gripped her arm. "Have you lost it? You don't even know if that's safe."

She twisted away from me. "It is. We've seen Moqerhe hypnotize a few people. They seemed okay."

"You can't be sure."

Sophie rubbed her hands over her face. "Don't you get it? I can't deal. Too much has happened here. All the trauma when we first arrived, and now Greg's … I can't live with this baggage."

Admittedly, I didn't want to remember those traumas either. Despite all the loss and pain, my experiences in Carthage changed me. Forgetting them meant forgetting my growth.

I wrapped my arms around Sophie. "I wish you hadn't gone through this."

"I did." She pushed away from me and faced Jan. "Please, I want to feel like my old self again."

Jan's voice was softer when he spoke to Sophie. "Normally, I'm reluctant to alter the course of human life. However, this situation is unique. My son's choices have caused you great suffering, so I'll grant your request."

A loud breath whooshed from Sophie's lungs. "Thank you."

Jan approached her, placed his hand beneath her chin and tilted her face upward until she met his gaze.

Sophie's nod told me Jan had communicated telepathically. After a few seconds, her eyes dulled, and she wavered on her feet. Jan slowly lowered her to the floor until she was lying on her back and said aloud, "Sleep, little one. Think only of home, of those you love. When you awaken in your time, you'll have no memory of this place, and you'll feel rested and calm."

"Um, will she be okay?" I asked.

"She will," Jan said.

Moqerhe took my hand. The warmth of his touch sent a slight tingle up my arm. "We need to remove your bracelet." He scrunched my sleeve back, revealing the jewel.

"How? Don't you need the book of incantations?"

"You forget, child, I wrote that book," Jan's eyes glinted with pride. "After I stripped my son of his powers and made him human, he relied on spells to conduct magic. Since I'm the most powerful djinni alive, I need only to move my hand like this." He flicked it to the right.

The stone swirled blood red. My wrist burned hot. A red light beamed out of the jewel and my hand shot into the air without permission. I clenched my teeth as a tingling sensation rippled over my wrist and threads retracted from my skin. The bracelet's golden clasp opened, and it fell to the ground with a clink.

Moqerhe picked up the bracelet and extended it to Jan. "I'm at your mercy."

"Keep it," Jan said. "I rue the day I created those infernal stones. The power they yield is too great a temptation for evil. Hide the bracelet." He glared down at me like I was a peasant and added, "That stone and the girl are your greatest weaknesses. You'll do well to be rid of both."

The reality of his words made my heart sink. After today, I'd never see Moqerhe again. There was more to him than met the eye and I wished we could have explored our friendship.

"It's time," Jan said.

Moqerhe bowed then faced me. "Let's get you home."

Seeing Dad and Yia Yia again should have made me want to break into cartwheels. Instead, dread pooled deep within me. If Jan was right, and Rome's fall somehow changed the timelines, I was about to enter the unknown. Again.

Chapter Thirty-Five

Moqerhe led me across the room. The way his hand enveloped mine was so preoccupying, I almost tripped over Sophie when we stopped before her. She slumbered like she didn't have a care in the world. I glanced up at Moqerhe's chiseled profile, his straight nose, and full lips one last time. Could I really say goodbye to this beautiful being?

His face was an emotionless mask as he spoke. "Prepare yourself. Teleportation can be quite uncomfortable."

After all we'd been through, I would have expected more than a brief warning about time travel. He might have struggled with goodbyes.

Extricating his hand from mine, he pressed the amulet on his chest. A flash of light erupted from the center and surrounded the three of us in a golden orb. The room faded from view. My stomach dove as I fell backward through a dark vortex. Just as I opened my mouth to scream, everything froze.

It took a second to figure out we were floating in a glowing cannister of energy about ten feet wide and ten feet high. The golden orb around us had frozen. Above me, Sophie drifted inside our cocoon, oblivious to her surroundings under a spell of sleep.

"Are you alright?" Moqerhe's voice echoed against the silence.

"I-I think so. Where are we?"

"We're between dimensions." He bobbed beside me like a space cadet in a satellite station. "I need to talk to you, away from the king's ear. We only have a small window before the portal starts again."

"I don't understand."

Moqerhe withdrew the bracelet from a leather pouch on his belt. As he did so, I could have sworn I glimpsed anger then sadness flashing in his eyes. "This is the only thing that can enslave me."

"I'm aware." *Where was he going with this?*

"Good, because you're the only person in the universe I trust with it." He took my hand and pressed the bracelet in my palm.

My heart stopped as I realized the significance of the gesture. "Why me?"

"The jewel will allow you to summon me if the need arises, but for this to pass, you must wear it always."

"Wouldn't that enslave you again?"

He tilted my chin up until I met his beautiful golden gaze. "No, it's different if I give it willingly." He paused. "I've learned so much from your passion for life, the way you fight for your friends. Even your sarcasm showed me the beauty in your species, the beauty in you."

Heat bloomed across my cheeks.

"I told myself these feelings were a product of my human vessel, that a relationship between a mortal and a djinni could never be. I tried pushing you away, into Adones' arms. Yet, when you no longer cast your attentions in his direction, my heart leapt for joy. I was drawn to you, and this confused me, still confuses me." He shook his head. "My human part wishes we had more time together to understand what's growing between us."

Every nerve in my body warned me to run. I'd lost so much already, and maybe that was the point. I needed to embrace each moment because the next one wasn't promised. I'd always regret it if I didn't see where this led. I resisted my fear and looked into his eyes. The pull was undeniable. Despite my doubts, I moved closer and forced myself to say, "I also wish we had more time."

Moqerhe wrapped his arms around me and rested his chin on top of my head. "Now that I've found you, it will be hard to let you go."

My voice was low and hoarse, filled with emotion as I blurted, "May I kiss you?" I immediately kicked myself for being so vulnerable.

His full lips curled into a wide smile. "I believe this body would like that."

Unable to deny the palpable energy between us, the intoxicating warmth of his body, I melted into his embrace. Moqerhe's hands slowly, tentatively moved to my hips, exploring them. His lips grazed mine with feather softness at first and then pressed more urgently. I groaned into his mouth, and he pulled me against him.

It was tough to know how long we kissed. When I finally pulled away, we were breathless.

His mouth curled into a sidelong smirk. "Now, I understand why humans pursue touch."

"Yeah, it's one of the perks of my species," I grinned back.

The orb around us shimmered like it was unfreezing, and his smile faded. He folded my fingers over the bracelet. "I pledged my life to my king, and he's expecting my return soon."

"When will I see you again?"

"I'm but a prisoner to my honor." He was still breathing heavily as he pulled me against him. "My king will require me and all my brothers-in-arms to work tirelessly to undo what the prince has done. First, we must hunt down my captive brothers-in-arms and procure the book of incantations. We'll also have to realign the worlds. I can't say how long this will take."

"Is this goodbye?" My voice was a thin rasp.

He gazed at me through smoldering amber eyes. "No. We'll always share a connection if you wear this bracelet, and I'll visit you as often as possible."

I tightened my hold around him, unable to look away and said, "I'd be honored to wear it."

The orb shimmered again. Moqerhe grabbed my wrist, closed his eyes, and whispered words I didn't understand. Slivers of golden energy burst from the bracelet, floated to my wrist, and wrapped around it.

"Prepare yourself, Amara, this may sting."

The process was just as it had been before, and after we were bound again, I was breathless.

"Are you hurt?" Moqerhe asked.

I brought my hand to my heart to calm it. "No, just a little stunned."

The orb shimmered so hard it shook me to my core. I grabbed Moqerhe's hand. "I'm not ready to say goodbye."

"Never. I'll see you soon, Amara."

This didn't console me. Soon could be tomorrow or a year from now.

"Close your eyes," Moqerhe whispered.

The orb's glowing energy rippled upward. It was only a matter of seconds before we parted. I reluctantly did as he asked. Trembling lips pressed against my cheek. They were so soft and warm that my heart ached as he moved to the next.

"See you soon," he said.

There was another tug at the top of my head. Then the G-force ripped me through time, whirring in my ears like wind blowing through car windows. Seconds later, I landed on something hard and squeaky, and I knew with every bit of my being, Moqerhe was gone.

Chapter Thirty-Six

My eyes snapped open. It took a second for my dazed brain to figure out that I'd landed on a cot in a tent. I had to be back at the dig site. With Tunis so close, why would I be camping when I could have gone to my apartment? Unless I wasn't in Tunis anymore. I scanned my surroundings, finding the unfamiliar in a familiar place.

Empty beer cans overflowed from a garbage pail beside my cot. A gray metal cube about the size of a coffee cup sat on a plastic table in the corner. My cell phone, mounted next to it, flickered on. I kicked my feet over the side of the cot, noting that I was fully clothed in safari pants, green tee, and hiking boots. I stood up and wavered a moment. My head pounded, and my mouth was like sandpaper.

No way those beers made me feel this way. I don't drink. The trip here could have done a number on me.

I rubbed my aching forehead and walked to the table, hoping to pull up Google maps to figure out my location. When I reached for my cell, my hand went straight through it.

A hologram.

Maybe it was voice activated. I inched closer. "On." "Hello?"

Nothing.

Sighing, I picked up the metal cube beside my cell and turned it over. All the sides were smooth except for a small button on the bottom, which I pressed.

The cube shook in my grasp. I dropped it on the table and backed away, unable to believe my eyes as the sides unfolded and flattened into a paper-thin laptop, about ten-by-ten inches. The lid hissed open, displaying a blue screen with Punic lettering across the top that read 0800 on August 3. How could I read this language? Jan had said my essence would be absorbed into the portal. This could have meant that part of the Amara from this dimension remained within me. Needing answers, I stepped toward the tent opening and hesitated when I heard voices drawing closer. Familiar voices.

The flap flipped outward, and a man stepped inside. All the blood drained from my face. "Gr-Greg?"

"The one and only. Were you expecting someone else?" he asked in Punic as Sophie entered.

"Hey, girl, you're late."

Tears burned my eyes. I smiled at her, relieved she wasn't somewhere in Timbuktu and wrapped my arms around Greg. For too many years, I allowed fear to keep me from sharing my feelings, and this had led to an emotional crash and burn. I wouldn't let this second chance get away.

"I love you," came out in a voice, shaken by emotion.

"You okay?" Sophie asked.

I placed a hand on my stomach to steady myself. "Ye-yeah, I'm fine, just had a, er, bad dream, that's all." Punic flowed from my tongue with the same ease as English.

"I bet." Greg winced. "Smells like a brewery in here. How much did you drink last night?"

My gaze gravitated to the empty cans. Despite the irony of this situation, I was happy to hear the judgment in my brother's voice. "For what it's worth, I appreciate that you care, that you're here."

Greg rolled his eyes. "Whatever. Look, you should have been at the dig site thirty minutes ago. You know how extra strict Dad is about being on time."

"Yeah, he's not too happy right now," Sophie said.

With all the emotion from seeing Greg, I'd forgotten that Dad might be here too. I took this opportunity to get some answers. "Er, what's the agenda for today?"

"Same as every day," Greg said. "The Roman Forum won't unearth itself. Dad's words, not mine."

I blinked. "Rome, like the Vatican and Colosseum Rome?"

Sophie cocked her head to the side. "What's a Vatican?"

Think quickly. "Uh, something I dreamed about last night. I'm kind of off today."

Excavating the Roman forum could have only meant one thing. Rome must have fallen in my timeline too. Not that this was all bad if Greg was alive. Still, it was odd that he hadn't mentioned our journey. His death in Jasim's time could have prevented his essence from being absorbed into the portal. I just couldn't say. Since Sophie was acting clueless too, Jan's hypnotism job must have worked.

"C'mon, let's make you presentable." Sophie grabbed my arm and led me to the cot.

She pressed a button on the lower left corner and a drawer slid out from underneath, revealing cargo pants, several tees, bras, and underwear. The other half was filled with toiletries. I glimpsed a bottle of shampoo labeled in Punic and grabbed it, longing for the warmth of a shower after so long without one.

"Uh, uh, you're already late." She snatched the shampoo, set it on the cot and pulled out a hair band and brush. "Here, pull those locks back."

Staring into the drawer, my heart practically leapt from my chest. "A toothbrush!" I grabbed it and a small tube of toothpaste.

Greg's brow knitted together as he watched me.

"Er, gotta get that morning taste out of my mouth." I applied the toothpaste on my toothbrush and went to town. It was all I could do to stifle a moan as the cool mint flavor burst in my mouth. Funny how small things could affect a person's happiness. I grabbed a bottled water from my nightstand, rinsed my mouth with it, and spit it outside the tent.

Sophie handed me the hairband and I quickly pulled my hair into a ponytail. I even smiled at Greg's impatient huffs as he extended a ball cap my way.

"Thanks." I put it on, grabbed my sunglasses off the table and headed outside.

The morning sun hung like a fiery orb against the blue sky as we passed several tents and walked onto a platform overlooking a rectangular plaza. I bit my bottom lip while taking in the scene. As the daughter of an archeologist who loved art and history, Dad had brought Greg and I to Rome the summer of my senior year in high school. Back then, the cobbled paths bustled with tourists as they meandered past ruins of palatial buildings, lined by marble columns. The streets surrounding the ruins had been flanked by towering buildings. There were traffic jams with honking cars, and pedestrians bustled down the sidewalks.

Today, shoveled dirt remained where the Roman Forum should have been. The topmost member of a couple of columned buildings barely showed above the soil. What I knew as Rome in my time now consisted of grass-covered hills extending as far as the eye could see. Egg-shaped dump trucks with solar paneled hoods, square airplane wings, and deep beds filled with rocks, flew, not drove, to and from the excavation site. Workers in safari hats bent over, brushing and troweling spots around the ruins.

"Why?" I cleared my throat. "I mean, I'm surprised the surrounding countryside hasn't been developed."

"That's a good thing," Greg observed. "If the Phoenician government hadn't made this federal land, it would be ruined by yet another city." He paused and added, "And you know how the government feels about keeping the earth green."

"For sure," Sophie said with a nod.

They confirmed my suspicions. Carthage also reigned in this dimension, and from the look of things, they had expanded into Rome and made it a territory. I gestured toward the dig below us. "Carthage sure did a number on this place."

"Yeah," Greg observed. "They burned it down. And it's a shame too. Ancient Roman culture is fascinating."

"Yup," I said, trying to hold it together. Did America even exist in this dimension? I opened my mouth to ask and closed it when a voice called out from behind us in Punic.

"Glad you could join us."

I froze. In those seconds, the breeze, Sophie and Greg, everything except that voice faded from my consciousness. Slowly, I turned on shaky legs, questioning what I had heard, and gulped when I met a set of familiar green eyes.

"Mom?"

She crossed her arms over her chest. "Mind telling me why you're late?"

She was more beautiful than I remembered. Thin and elegant in her black cargo pants and red T-shirt. Aside from the traces of gray in her short auburn hair and the lines around her eyes and mouth, she didn't look a day over forty.

I yanked her into a tight embrace. "I love you so much."

"Love you too." She gently pushed me back enough to bring her hands to my cheeks. "You feeling okay?"

"She's fine, Mila. Probably out late with the other interns, *again*."

Unable to hold back a smile, I wheeled toward the voice. "Dad!"

I must have been so caught up in emotion, I didn't notice his approach. Without the dark circles beneath his eyes and the intense lines across his forehead, he looked ten years younger.

"You're buff," I stared at his muscular biceps.

He and Mom exchanged confused glances.

"Thanks," he said.

Greg brought his hand to his mouth and fake coughed while saying, "Kiss-up."

Sophie elbowed him. "Stop."

After a long beat, I forced myself to back away from my parents. *My parents* who were both alive and staring at me like I had lost it. I adjusted my ball cap and gave the best excuse for my behavior that my overloaded brain could muster, "Er, I didn't get much sleep."

"You'll learn," Dad said.

I pointed at the logo on his T-shirt. "New Carthage University?"

He smiled. "What, can't a dad be proud? Not many parents can say both their children are attending the most prestigious university in the world."

"Yeah, I guess," I felt more confused by the second.

"What's wrong with you today? You seem off," Dad observed.

Off didn't begin to describe what I felt, but I couldn't tell him this. Instead, I said, "Er, just a bad night."

"Must have been." Dad gave me a once-over.

Then it hit me. I could use this to get answers. "I had the weirdest dream about this place thousands of miles across the sea called the United States. All the countries had come together as one and their schools were among the greatest in the world, and farmlands were plentiful."

"That's pretty specific," Dad observed.

"Sounds like Barcia." Greg smiled.

Mom shook her head. "It never ceases to amaze me how far the Carthaginian explorers were able to sail. Especially with the rudimentary technology they had a thousand years ago."

Her words stayed with me a second. It seemed that America had been discovered by a North African nation instead of by the

Italians and Spaniards. I was also betting that Barcia must have earned its name from an ancestor of the Barcid line.

Mom frowned. "Makes me sad that the three of you will be returning there without us next month."

Sophie nodded. "Time flies. Fall semester is around the corner."

"Then we head to Barcia?" The words just fell out of my mouth, and I tried to reframe them. "I mean—"

"I know what you mean, and yes, I wish we could return to New Carthage with you all. I miss teaching at the university," Dad said. "This job—"

Greg wrapped an arm around Dad's shoulder. "You and Mom worked hard to get here, and you deserve to lead this dig. We'll be fine."

"Speaking of my job, enough of this chitchat," Dad said. "The Phoenician government didn't put Mila and I on this dig to stand around. We have many people to supervise so let's eat and start our day." Dad headed down the stairs toward the dig site, followed by Mom.

I grinned at Greg, feeling freer and happier than I had in years. Yeah, this world was different. The technological advancements like cubes that turned into computers, holographic cell phones, and solar-powered flying vehicles suggested that the North Africans had done a far better job than the founders of my world. Plus, my brother and my parents were alive and well. Sophie and Greg were together and happy. It didn't get much better than this.

He elbowed me. "Oh, God, it's Nguyen, the religious nut."

"I don't know, he made some good points the other night," Sophie said.

Greg jutted his chin toward the stone steps ahead. "You're crazy, c'mon, and don't make eye contact."

"Why?" I asked.

"Hello, Amara," Nguyen flashed a set of straight white teeth.

"Hi." Sophie smiled at him as Greg pulled her down the steps with him.

It would have been nice if they had waited for me instead of disappearing. Now, I was standing eye-to-eye with Nguyen. He surveyed me beneath a headful of straight black hair and thin eyebrows.

I reminded myself to kick their asses when I got to the dig site. "Er, guess I should follow—"

He handed me a flyer. "Hope you'll join us at the temple next week. We've chartered a bus to take us there."

I glanced at the flyer, immediately honing in on Martyr Day written in bold black letters. "What's this?"

"Remember, I told you about it the other night at the bonfire," he said.

Since most bonfires included alcohol, I felt it was safe to say, "Refresh my memory. The beers were flowing."

Nodding, he responded with a high-pitched laugh that was contagious enough to make me smile.

"Yes, yes, a lot of beer." He pointed at the flyers in his hand. "Like I told you before, Martyr Day happens every ten years, and everyone in the world will be watching the ceremony."

"Er, right. How do you think it will go this year?" Not the best way to glean information, but the word *martyr* set off my Spidey senses.

He shrugged. "Not sure. This is the first time I've participated in the ceremony. You see, easterners don't worship your god, but New Carthage University's religion class showed me the way. The Phoenician countries are so advanced, and the people are free to worship as they like. Despite this, they all chose the same god and now I'm part of the culture."

Greg was right about the whole religious nut thing and yet my curiosity got the best of me. "How does Martyr Day play into your new beliefs?"

He leaned closer. "I volunteered for the lottery. To honor Ba'al Hammon's sacrifice for his people."

Every muscle in my body stiffened. "Did you say, Ba'al Hammon?"

"Yes." He was smiling so wide I saw his molars.

I closed my eyes and exhaled slowly, trying to hold it together. "Jan-Ib-Jann's son?"

He nodded. "His son sacrificed himself to save Carthage, to save us who believe in him. You can be saved too, Amara."

My stomach burned. I wanted to slap that smile off his face, to tell him what a dumbass he was. "No—"

"It's such an honor to give my life in Ba'al's name. Though it's unlikely I'll be chosen. Only one person from each country will be selected from hundreds of thousands of volunteers."

It was all I could do to stand, so I gripped the edge of the stair rail to steady myself. Jasim had been true to his word. Humankind remembered him as their savior. This meant everyone prayed to a poser. Worse, people were sacrificing themselves in his name.

Nguyen placed a hand on my arm. "What are you thinking?"

"I don't know." I swallowed the bitter bile crawling up the back of my throat. "Um, can I have a few minutes? I don't feel so well."

"Okay, hope you'll join us at the temple."

I turned my back to him, peering at the dirt-covered ruins that used to be ancient Rome. How could I stop this? Warning Nguyen and the rest of the world about Jasim wasn't an option. After all, I couldn't disclose that I had traveled through time and knew the truth without coming off like a fruit loop.

The bracelet on my wrist reminded me that I could summon Moqerhe. It wasn't like he could use compulsion on the whole world to make them stop the sacrifices. Guess I could take some consolation in knowing things wouldn't always be this way. When Jan and Moqerhe caught Jasim's guardians and took custody of the book of incantations, they would return the dimensions to their original state.

This also meant that I'd be forced to live in a dimension where my mother was dead, and my father struggled with alcoholism and cancer. After having a normal family again, could I go back to the way things were? My conscience said yes. A world where people sacrificed themselves in the name of a false god wasn't right. I had watched my brother die, swapped one man's life to save Greg at the games. Not to mention all the suffering he and Sophie had gone through before then, all so Ba'al could rewrite history. This journey had left such a stain on my soul, nothing would ever scrub it clean. No, I couldn't let Jasim win.

So, I would wait for the king and Moqerhe to right the false god's wrongs. Until then, I'd make the most of this short gift of family and friends given to me in this dimension. For one thing I'd learned, tomorrow could change on a dime, and only time could tell what the future held.

THE END

YOUNG ADULT FICTION

Lodestone Books is a new imprint, which off ers a broad spectrum of subjects in YA/NA literature. Compelling reading, the Teen/Young/New Adult reader is sure to find something edgy, enticing and innovative. From dystopian societies, through a whole range of fantasy, horror, science fiction and paranormal fiction, all the way to the other end of the sphere, historical drama, steam-punk adventure, and everything in between (including crime, coming of age and contemporary romance). Whatever your preference you will discover it here. If you have enjoyed this book, why not tell other readers by posting a review on your preferred book site. Recent bestsellers from Lodestone Books are:

AlphaNumeric

Nicolas Forzy

When dyslexic teenager Stu accidentally transports himself into a world populated by living numbers and letters, his arrival triggers a prophecy that pulls two rival communities into war.

Paperback: 978-1-78279-506-3 ebook: 978-1-78279-505-6

Time Sphere

A timepathway book

M.C. Morison

When a teenage priestess in Ancient Egypt connects with a school-boy on a visit to the British Museum, they each come under threat as they search for Time's Key.

Paperback: 978-1-78279-330-4 ebook: 978-1-78279-329-8

Bird Without Wings

FAEBLES

Cally Pepper

Sixteen-year-old Scarlett has had more than her fair share of problems, but nothing prepares her for the day she discovers she's growing wings...

Paperback: 978-1-78099-902-9 ebook: 978-1-78099-901-2

Briar Blackwood's Grimmest of Fairytales

Timothy Roderick

After discovering she is the fabled Sleeping Beauty, a brooding goth-girl races against time to undo her deadly fate.

Paperback: 978-1-78279-922-1 ebook: 978-1-78279-923-8

Escape from the Past

The Duke's Wrath

Annette Oppenlander

Trying out an experimental computer game, a fifteen-year-old boy unwittingly time-travels to medieval Germany where he must not only survive but figure out a way home.

Paperback: 978-1-84694-973-9 ebook: 978-1-78535-002-3

Holding On and Letting Go

K.A. Coleman

When her little brother died, Emerson's life came crashing down around her. Now she's back home and her friends want to help, but can Emerson fight to re-enter the world she abandoned?

Paperback: 978-1-78279-577-3 ebook: 978-1-78279-576-6

Midnight Meanders

Annika Jensen

As William journeys through his own mind, revelations are made, relationships are broken and restored, and a faith that once seemed extinct is renewed.

Paperback: 978-1-78279-412-7 ebook: 978-1-78279-411-0

Reggie & Me

The First Book in the Dani Moore Trilogy

Marie Yates

The first book in the Dani Moore Trilogy, *Reggie & Me* explores a teenager's search for normalcy in the aftermath of rape.

Paperback: 978-1-78279-723-4 ebook: 978-1-78279-722-7

Unconditional

Kelly Lawrence

She's in love with a boy from the wrong side of town...

Paperback: 978-1-78279-394-6 ebook: 978-1-78279-393-9

Readers of ebooks can buy or view any of these bestsellers by clicking on the live link in the title. Most titles are published in paperback and as an ebook. Paperbacks are available in traditional bookshops. Both print and ebook formats are available online.

Find more titles and sign up to our readers' newsletter at www.collectiveinkbooks.com/children-and- young-adult.